The Derishz Ruby

MEIR ANOLICK

Dedicated to Esther, my wonderful sister,
without whom this book would never have
been written

CONTENTS

CHAPTER 1
A Stranger Arrives

Carolyn loved the feeling of the wind blowing through her hair. She was soaring high in the sky on dragonback, her golden hair streaming freely behind her as the earth passed by far below. Her friend Robin was flying alongside on her own dragon, her brown hair tied in a neat ponytail that trailed behind her. The two of them soared through the clouds without a care in the world.

She looked down at the rapidly passing landscape. There were miles and miles of green fields, giving way far ahead to rolling, forested hills, and beyond those the jagged peaks of a distant mountain range. Nothing could be more relaxing than sitting back in her comfortable saddle and taking in all the sights.

This was how Carolyn liked to spend her free time, far above ground with the sun on her face and the wind in her hair. Just her and her dragon—what was his name again? Dargoth, or something like that. No wait, it was Daragon. No, that's not creative enough, maybe Garadon? And what color was he again? Purple, probably. No wait, it must've been red, red was Carolyn's favorite color. That didn't sound right, though... Orange! That's what it was, an orange dragon named...

RIIIIIIING

The sudden peal of the school bell snapped Carolyn out of her reverie. She was not flying on dragonback, as she often wished she could, rather she was sitting in class next to the window, her cheek resting on her hand as she imagined being far away from class and Mrs. Oak, who was reminding the class about the upcoming math quiz next week. Carolyn quickly grabbed her pen to write down the homework assignment.

"So make sure you study well," Mrs. Oak concluded as half the class was already streaming out the door. As she said this, she stared squarely at Carolyn, her eyes narrowed and her lips pursed. Carolyn did her best to ignore it and keep writing, then got everything in her backpack so she could get out the door as quickly as possible.

Mrs. Oak was well aware of Carolyn's constant daydreaming in her class, and had already given her several warnings about it and called her parents twice. She couldn't get her in trouble any worse than that since, while Carolyn might not have been a straight-A student, she was doing well enough in all of her classes. So she just ignored the inconvenience of having to talk to her parents when it came up, and kept up her daydreaming, which was considerably more interesting than class.

As soon as she was out the door Carolyn saw Robin, her best friend, waiting for her.

"What were you doing today?" she asked with a smile as the two started down the hall.

"Riding a dragon," Carolyn answered casually. Robin found Carolyn's daydreaming pretty interesting, too.

"Cool, did it eat anyone?" Robin asked excitedly.

"No," Carolyn sighed. "It was supposed to be relaxing."

"I think people getting eaten by dragons is pretty relaxing."

"Well, maybe if they were eating Mrs. Oak," Carolyn agreed.

"Or Mrs. Hill," Robin added, "Or Mr. Wilson."

"Robin, haven't I already told you," a voice came from behind them, its tone humorless, "plotting to get teachers killed will not get you out of homework."

The two girls turned to see Rachel, Carolyn's other closest friend, coming up behind them. "Oh well, was worth a try," Robin said with a shrug.

The three friends made their way into the library quietly, finding an empty table at the far end of the room. Carolyn slumped down and slowly pulled out her books. Rachel, the most studious of the trio, took it upon herself to ensure her friends were at least able to pass their classes and move on to high school. They had been meeting together after school for years at this point, with Rachel helping Carolyn and Robin—especially Robin—complete their homework and making sure they understood the material.

Carolyn kept up with her homework—mostly—even without Rachel's help, but she did benefit from the extra tutoring. Robin, on the other hand, seemed to be undecided between trying to fail all her classes to set a record, or trying to be the best to prove to her teachers she wasn't actually a lost cause. The result was that she did very little on her own, but she got most of her homework done with Rachel's help and was keeping up a passing grade, if barely.

"Or maybe Mr. Creek," Robin continued thoughtfully as she pulled out her math workbook, with a look that made Carolyn think she might actually be considering it.

"That's enough of that," Rachel said sternly, "Let's try and do something constructive instead."

Robin shrugged, as though unconcerned, which broadened Carolyn's smile. Nothing put her in a better mood than Robin's wry sense of humor, especially when Rachel's generally humorless attitude was there to provide such a stark contrast. Of late, she'd been needing a lot of such cheering up, it seemed.

"We have a lot of work to do if you hope to pass the math quiz next week," Rachel said with a tone of voice that said all jokes were done. She was entering her no-nonsense, study mode, and that meant any further attempts at humor would be met with a cold stare of death. When she was like that, it was sometimes hard to distinguish her from an actual teacher, but it worked well for getting them all to focus and get some studying done.

Rachel was a very good tutor, much better than their teachers. Even in no-nonsense mode, she often showed her odd sense of humor in their lessons, which made them more enjoyable than class and the material easier to absorb. Eventually, though, Robin could only handle so much of studying before she lost interest completely.

"I'm done," she proclaimed about an hour later, throwing down her pencil.

Rachel glared at her for a moment, her mouth twisting in a grimace of disapproval, though more because Robin was speaking louder than was appropriate in the library than because of her declaration.

"I don't think I could take any more today, either," Carolyn admitted, putting down her pencil too. She leaned back in her chair and breathed a sigh of relief.

"We'll just have to hope Robin's dragon can get to the school before next week," Rachel deadpanned, pushing her hair out of her face. Rachel's sense of humor was interesting; even when she told a joke, it was often hard to tell if she was actually joking or not. After spending a few years with her, Carolyn was usually good at telling the difference... usually.

"I'll let him know he's needed then," Robin replied, packing her books back into her bag. She glanced at her watch and frowned; an uncommon occurrence for Robin. "Oh, we lost track of time, we have to get going Carolyn, we're late for gymnastics."

"What!" Carolyn snapped back to attention quickly; she had been on the verge of starting another daydream.

"Sorry I kept you so long, I wasn't paying attention," Rachel admitted. She helped Carolyn gather up her things and waved them off, "See you tomorrow."

Carolyn waved as they hurried out of the library and headed for the gym. While Rachel was having fun studying in her off hours—something Carolyn would never understand—Carolyn and Robin took gymnastics. Mrs. Hill was very strict and made sure to scold anyone who showed up as much as three seconds late, claiming that tardiness caused the whole class to suffer distraction and reduced their ability to focus. Really, her reprimands caused more distraction than the latecomers did, but Carolyn had never been so brash as to point that out. Now Carolyn and Robin were coming in three minutes late and knew they wouldn't escape some reprimand.

Since gymnastics was voluntary, it wasn't like Mrs. Hill could actually punish them, but she could make them regret it. Luckily for Carolyn, she usually was let off pretty easily since, unlike in math, she was really good at gymnastics. As for Robin, while she was equally as skilled as Carolyn, her sense of humor gave her the reputation of a troublemaker among the school staff, and that's how she was treated.

The pair split off in the locker room. After taking off her vest and folding it messily inside her locker, Carolyn glanced over at Robin, making sure that she couldn't see, and slipped off her necklace, placing it carefully in the fold of her vest.

It's not that Carolyn tried to hide her necklace specifically from Robin, it was that she tried to hide it from everyone. This was a very special necklace, a family heirloom of sorts. Carolyn got it from her grandmother a couple years ago when she turned twelve. She remembered being awed by it the first time she saw it. Made of pure gold, the pendant was in the shape of an eight-pointed star, and in the center was a ruby larger than any Carolyn had ever seen, let alone held. It was about twice the diameter of a quarter and three times as thick; she had measured it before.

"This necklace is very special," her grandmother had warned her, "I got it from my grandmother Naritha when I turned twelve, and you will pass it on to your granddaughter someday. You must be very careful to take good care of it, and never let anyone know about it, not even your parents."

Carolyn had no problem keeping a secret or two from her parents, so she was willing to meet that demand. Having to keep it from her friends was hard, but she knew that as soon as one person saw it, news of it would spread quickly. Obviously the reason for keeping it secret was to prevent thieves from mugging her, considering how expensive it looked. At first she thought it would be easier to just leave it hidden in the bottom of her closet, despite being instructed to keep it with her, but she found it too beautiful to be stuffed away, hidden from the light of day. Instead, she wore it at all times, tucked under her shirt. She liked to think of it as her lucky necklace. But there were times she couldn't leave it on, and gymnastics was one of those times. So she left it in the folds of her clothes in her locker while she was away and hoped it would still be there when she returned.

When Carolyn and Robin entered the gym, they found the class arranged on the floor doing stretches. Mrs. Hill glared at them as they tried to nonchalantly add themselves to the back of the group and pretend they had been there all along. The ploy didn't work any better than it ever did.

"Ms. Jones and Ms. Jacobson," Mrs. Hill started slowly, eyeing Carolyn and Robin respectively, "seem to have decided to finally grace us with their presence." She paused for a moment, and Carolyn stood there awkwardly, not sure if she should still just sit and start stretching or if she should respond somehow, but Mrs. Hill continued. "If you're so confident that you don't need to join us with stretching, why don't you come sit at the front so everyone can see what experts you are."

Carolyn felt her cheeks grow warm, but moved forward without complaint. Robin walked beside her, no smile on her face, but still displaying an air of importance like this was some kind of honor. Carolyn couldn't understand how she could brush off embarrassment so easily. *How is she always so confident?* she wondered. The two of them seated themselves at the front of their class and joined in the stretches without another word.

The rest of the class went as usual. Despite the obnoxious attitude of their instructor, gymnastics was Carolyn's favorite activity. She was in good shape and was one of the most talented girls in the class, and she spent a lot of time imagining herself jumping over dragons or cartwheeling away from danger. Her favorite skill by far was somersaults, and she was good at them, too. Robin was also an expert, except that she always tried crazy stunts in the air, sometimes resulting in a sloppy landing and almost always resulting in Mrs. Hill rebuking her for showing off.

"Thank you for your expert demonstration, Ms. Jacobson," their instructor said dryly after one such attempt. "You may step off the mat now." Robin just shrugged it off with her usual smile. Carolyn envied her ability to ignore insults so easily.

"Class is over, girls," Mrs. Hill announced. "Time for stretches."

"So, what did you learn in school today, Carolyn?" Carolyn's mom inevitably asked her during dinner that night.

"We learned how to ride dragons and shoot fireballs from our eyes," Carolyn responded, not even looking up from her meal.

"Carolyn, please just answer the question," her father told her, the hint of a smile on his lips.

"We learned stuff about events leading up to the Civil War," Carolyn conceded. "which I suppose isn't too boring, if there weren't so many numbers to remember."

"Oh, history isn't all bad," her dad replied, "You know, they say that those who don't learn the mistakes of the past are doomed to repeat them."

"Oh, good, so now I know not to start any civil wars," Carolyn responded cheerily.

"Nevermind..." her father sighed. "What about you,

Jessica?"

"Hmm?" was the only response Carolyn's older sister gave, her gaze locked on her phone as her fingers typed quickly. Carolyn wondered if Jessica even realized she was at the dinner table.

"Try asking William," Carolyn suggested, jabbing a thumb at her younger brother, "maybe he did something useful today."

"Carolyn, don't be rude," her father sighed.

"I'm more useful than you!" William responded angrily.

"Oh, yeah, when was the last time you helped set up for dinner?" Carolyn retorted, "Never, right?"

"Only because I'm too special to do work," her brother humphed and crossed his arms.

"Right," Carolyn scoffed and rolled her eyes. "Well, I'm done." She stood up abruptly, cleared her plate and headed upstairs.

Carolyn went to her room to finish up her homework, but after half an hour this devolved into doodling funny shapes on scrap paper. Giving it up as a lost cause, she pulled her chair over to her open window, crossed her arms on the windowsill and rested her chin on them to stare up at the night sky. It was hard to see the stars because of all the streetlamps, but there were some visible. She loved to sit there and think about how big the universe was, and wonder if there really was any life out there.

Most of all what Carolyn wanted... well, she wasn't really sure what she wanted. She always felt like she was missing something, something that she couldn't quite put her finger on; like a hole inside that needed to be filled. Perhaps that's why she'd been daydreaming so much more lately, as if attempting to find something exciting in life that could break the monotony of it all. She was spending more time daydreaming than with her friends, and she was pretty sure they were starting to notice. Even her birthday, just a couple weeks earlier, had not been enough to lift her from her odd stupor.

"If only I knew what I was missing," she whispered to the sky.

Carolyn was running down the hall of her school trying to escape Mrs. Oak, who was busy trying to hand her back some homework. She went through the door at the end of the hall, and found herself sitting on a large, orange dragon. They were flying in the night, the sky filled with stars and no moon to be seen. Below them was a castle on a hill, lit up by torches all around, and inside Carolyn could somehow hear sounds of fighting despite the distance. Her dragon craned his neck around to look at her.

"I wouldn't get involved in their fight," the dragon said in a voice that sounded oddly like Robin, but much deeper, "but maybe you should."

Somewhere in front of her, a blue light appeared, but Carolyn couldn't quite figure out where it was coming from. Then there was a loud crashing sound...

Carolyn jerked awake, slamming the top of her head on the top of the window frame.

"OW!" she shouted, pulling her head back inside the room and rubbing at the top where she had banged it. *I'll probably have a bruise there,* she thought with a grimace.

Carolyn picked up her phone to check the time. It was just after midnight. *I have to get to bed,* she thought, and made to pull herself out of the chair when she heard a loud scraping sound outside, like metal being dragged on concrete.

Carolyn peeked back out the window. By the light of the streetlamp she saw what appeared to be a mass of metal on the street, just next to the sidewalk. Then the pile moved. It was a person wearing a suit of armor, she realized, who was pulling himself up into a sitting position. A chill ran down Carolyn's spine as she saw the sword lying on the ground beside him. The figure sat for a moment on the street with his legs sticking out and his arms behind him so he could lean back. His eyes were open, staring at her house, but he did not seem to be taking anything in.

His suit of armor was different than anything Carolyn had seen before. The breastplate appeared to be made of multiple overlapping pieces instead of a single curved one, probably allowing more mobility, and the underarms were covered in chain mail and no plate at all. His helmet consisted of a thick metal band around the top of the head with chain mail over the top and falling around the sides, covering most of his head and neck. There was also a strange band of crimson around the waist.

With horror, Carolyn realized the crimson was blood, and there was actually a gash in the armor right over the stomach. She glanced at where he had been lying and saw a pool of blood staining the concrete. His face betrayed the intense pain he was in. Carolyn wanted to help him somehow—she couldn't just leave someone bleeding to death outside! But before she could do anything, the strange knight reached his left hand into small pouch hanging from his belt and pulled out a glass vial filled with some sort of liquid. The knight pulled the stopper with one hand, grimaced, and drained the vial in one gulp. Soon after the expression of pain receded from his face, replaced by one of relief. With a small grunt, he lifted himself to his feet, stretched, and ran a gauntleted hand across his stomach. Though blood still stained his armor, it appeared that whatever injury he had sustained was gone.

Carolyn pulled herself back inside the window again as the knight began walking across her front lawn, the clink of metal and the muffled thump of heavy boots on grass getting steadily closer. *What is going on?* she wondered, her heart pounding in her ears. *I must be dreaming. This is all a really lucid dream... then why am I so scared?* After a moment's hesitation, Carolyn chanced a look out the window again and found the knight standing right under her window. Their eyes met, and Carolyn froze, her thoughts on the sword in his hand.

"Greetings, lady," the knight spoke. His voice was

polite, but he had a rushed, urgent tone, "I am Sir Sarin of Herin. Is this the home of the Great Sage Naritha?"

Carolyn looked at him dumbly, blinking a couple times. "What?" she answered finally.

"The Great Sage Naritha," he repeated quickly. "She lived long ago, but I must find her descendant, it's urgent."

"I don't know of any great sages living around here..." Carolyn answered slowly, looking at the stranger as though he had three heads. Though the name Naritha sounded familiar. *Where have I heard it before?*

"You don't know where she lives?" he asked, seeming genuinely distraught, "Do you know anyone who might? It's very important."

"Why should I even help you?" Carolyn replied, feeling lost, "I don't know who you are or what you want. You just showed up with a sword; for all I know you want to kill the person!"

"I'm not here to kill anyone!" Sarin answered, "I just need to find the Great Sage's descendant and bring them back with me to Herin. The kingdom is in danger and we need help now!"

"Well, I can't help you, sorry," she shrugged.

"Uch," Sarin grumbled. Either he was genuine, or he was a really good actor. The look in his eyes and the tone of his voice seemed to indicate that he was, in fact, in a rush to save a dying kingdom. However, there were no kingdoms anywhere near Carolyn's house. She'd checked before.

Sarin removed his helmet and ran a gauntleted hand through his hair. Without the metal framing his face, Carolyn could see for the first time that Sarin was much younger than she thought, probably not much older than herself.

"How old are you?" she asked in surprise.

"Fifteen," he answered off-handedly, not even looking back up at her. He was scuffing the ground a bit with his foot, a frown plastered on his face. "How old are you?" he added.

"You don't ask a girl how old she is," Carolyn responded in surprise, attempting to sound indignant.

"Why?" Sarin asked, looking up at her, "You asked how old I am."

Carolyn didn't have an answer to that. He looked at her with genuine curiosity, clearly not understanding any need for her to hide her age. She didn't really have one, she was just told that you don't ask a girl their age and accepted that, but she didn't know why. Seeing her hesitation, Sarin shrugged and went back to kicking at the ground.

"Fourteen," Carolyn answered finally, "Since a couple weeks ago." Sarin looked back at up at her for a minute.

"Oh, happy birthday, I guess," he said slowly, then looked away again. After another moment of silence, he looked back up, "Are you sure you don't know anyone named Naritha?"

"Well," Carolyn admitted slowly, "the name does sound familiar." Sarin perked up immediately.

"Really? Do you remember when you heard it? Maybe that will help me find her."

"I don't..." Carolyn began, lost in thought. It was not so long ago she heard the name, in passing, but it was someone important...

"She has an amulet," Sarin went on. "A powerful, magical artifact. That's why we came—or, I mean, I'm the only that came through the portal, but the rest of the knights are still fighting." His voice trailed off as he glanced back toward the street, his hand moving instinctively to the rent in his armor.

"A magic amulet?" Carolyn wondered, feeling her heart beat faster at the thought. What if it was true? She'd love to see real magic. "What did it look like?"

"What?" Sarin said, turning back toward her, stirring from his thoughts, "Oh, the Ruby, right. It's—"

"Ruby?" Carolyn interrupted, feeling a chill run through her. *It couldn't be.*

"Yes, The Derishz Ruby," Sarin explained. "I've never seen it. Well, of course I haven't, Naritha had it here, and was supposed to pass it on to her descendants. It was considered too powerful to fall into the wrong hands, so the Great Sage Naritha placed an enchantment on the Ruby which bound it to her bloodline. It can only be used by her or her descencants. Then she fled to another dimension as an added precaution, one where no one would know what it was and it could remain hidden."

"Naritha," Carolyn was only half listening, delving into her own memories, "I think I remember... she was—"

"Yes?" Sarin cut in expectantly, "You remember who she is?"

Carolyn gripped the necklace hidden under her shirt. "This Ruby, what did it look like?" she asked.

"I was told it's a pendant shaped like an eight-pointed star, made of gold, and on the front is a large ruby. And it's on a gold chain. Have you seen it?" Sarin asked quickly, a hopeful glint in his eyes.

Carolyn paused, feeling the edges of the pendant through her shirt. Could this be an elaborate plan to steal the necklace? That seemed a bit far-fetched, though, when it would have been much easier to mug her. Besides, she had kept her necklace a secret from everyone, even her parents; no one could possibly no about it. Her grandmother had sworn her to secrecy, just like...*OH!*

Carolyn pulled the necklace out from under her shirt and held it out for Sarin to see. "Is this it?" she asked with trepidation.

Sarin's eyes went wide. "By Adenil's sword!" he whispered, enthralled by the sight of the necklace, "The Derishz Ruby!"

"My grandmother gave it to me when I turned twelve," Carolyn explained, "She said that was the age when a girl turns into a young lady, and I could be trusted with it. She also said that she got it when she was twelve from her grandmother, Naritha."

"Then it's you," Sarin pulled his eyes from the Ruby to look up at Carolyn with a sudden sense of awe in his eyes, "You are Naritha's descendant, and the Ruby is bound to you."

"So what does that mean?" Carolyn asked, tucking the necklace back under her shirt. "You said you wanted this to help you win your battle, or something, but only I can use it?"

"Yes, yes," Sarin nodded, "You have to come back with me! With the Ruby, we'll be able to rout Ferdri and his army from Herin Castle and retake the kingdom!" Carolyn didn't understand half of his sentence.

"So you want me to go with you," Carolyn said slowly, "but I still don't know if I can trust you. I'm not in the habit of trusting boys in armor who come bothering me in the middle of the night."

"But... But..." Sarin stuttered, his shoulders slumping, "You have to! We don't stand a chance without the Ruby! Is there anything I can say that would convince you to come with me?" Sarin asked desperately. Carolyn just shrugged. Sarin drooped a bit again, but quickly looked back up at Carolyn with a sly look in his eyes, "All right then, I'll go back without you."

"You're just gonna leave?" Carolyn asked in surprise, "After all that?"

"Yup," Sarin said casually, turning and walking away, "I'll let the King and Queen know that Naritha's descendant doesn't care about Herin anymore. I'll tell them you'd rather see the kingdom brought to ruin then to budge from your comfortable bed."

"Hey!" Carolyn shouted, getting angry, "That's not fair! I never said that, I just... I just don't know how I can trust you."

Sarin shrugged without turning around, stopping at the edge of the street, "That's your problem. Now let me return to meet certain doom in a hopeless battle."

Carolyn leaned back and crossed her arms. *Go on!* urged

a small voice inside her. *More likely than not he's telling the truth. Besides, isn't this just the kind of opportunity you've been waiting for? Something to break the monotony? Some excitement and adventure?*

Carolyn jumped out of her chair, pulled on her shoes, and snuck out into the hall. Fortunately, her conversation, and even her shout, hadn't woken anyone in the house. She tiptoed quietly down the stairs, slipped out the front door and locked it behind her, gripping her necklace the whole way.

There was Sarin, still standing on the sidewalk facing the street. He seemed not to have moved, as though he were waiting for her. Carolyn walked cautiously up beside him, wary of the sword on his hip. Standing next to him, she saw he was holding a flat blue stone about the size of his hand, cut with smooth sides into a perfect circle. She also noticed he was only a couple inches taller than she was. Sarin turned to face her, his helmet back on his head, a mischievous smile on his face.

"So you decided you'd come along after all?" he asked, his gaze triumphant.

"Sure," Carolyn said casually, though she could feel herself trembling, "It's not every day a stranger comes along and asks you to use your lucky necklace to save a kingdom."

Sarin's smile widened. He lifted the blue disc in his hand and held it up in front of him, holding it flat as though it were pressed up against a wall. Then it started to glow.

Carolyn gasped as she watched it change. At first it was a faint glimmer, but rapidly it started to shine brightly, reminding Carolyn of the blue light that she had seen in her dream right before waking up. The disc expanded rapidly, growing until it was large enough for them to walk through, a shining circle of blue. There were faint shapes moving within, but they were too vague to make out.

"Are you ready?" Sarin asked, gesturing toward the

circle.

"I don't think so," Carolyn answered in wonderment, "but I'll follow you through."

"Actually, you need to go first," Sarin explained, "Since I'm the one who opened the portal, it'll close when I walk through.

"I just walk into it?" Carolyn asked, starting to reach a hand forward to touch it. It seemed too solid.

"No, you just—" Sarin began, but Carolyn didn't hear the rest of what he said. As the tips of her fingers touched the shimmering portal, her whole body yanked forward into the light.

CHAPTER 2
Through the Portal

Carolyn's body was lurching forward at breakneck speeds through a tunnel of blue light. All around her she could see small circles, like windows of sorts, showing scenes of other places, probably other worlds like Herin. Most of them went by too quickly to make out, but here and there she caught brief glimpses: the middle of a forest, the sunlight peeking through the tops of trees; the inside of a chamber; the middle of a cornfield. Carolyn couldn't help but stare in wonder at all the worlds out there. Were any like hers, or were they all drastically different?

Coming up ahead of her was another such window, but this one was much more distinct. It showed a room beautifully decorated with scarlet and gold trimmings. Before she knew it she was already being hurled into it.

Carolyn's feet slammed to the floor so hard that her knees buckled and she toppled forward on to all fours, ears ringing, vision swimming. She also felt a funny tingling all over, and her necklace was unusually warm against her chest. She heard another thud as Sarin landed beside her.

"Sorry! Here, let me help you. You'll be okay in a

minute," he assured her, lifting her to her feet. She gripped his arm and blinked until her vision cleared and the ringing stopped, though the tingly feeling remained.

She was standing in the room she had seen a moment ago. It looked large enough to fit half her house in it, with a high ceiling and large, double doors to the left and right. On the wall directly in front of her was a beautiful tapestry depicting a white horse reared in front of a gold-and-blue shield, with a scarlet background and gold trimming on the sides. The carpet, however, was heavily trampled, torn up in some places, and very dirty, while the doors on the left side of the room were splintered and one of them was hanging on its hinges, obviously having been forced open. The whole room was poorly lit by a couple of torches on either side of the double doors.

I'm in another dimension! Breathing its air! Carolyn marveled.

"We're too late!" Sarin exclaimed beside her, "They've already left!"

"Who've left?" Carolyn asked, turning around. It was then she saw a shimmering blue circle similar to the one she just stepped through, rapidly shrinking and fading into a cylindrical bronze device behind them. Beyond the device was a shadowy alcove and in the fading light of the portal she could just see something moving closer. "Sarin..." she said in a soft voice, grabbing at his shoulder.

Sarin turned immediately, drawing his sword. She was impressed to see a boy his age wielding a weapon, and with well-trained reflexes. *Isn't he too young for this?* she thought, but had no time to consider the question, though, as three figures stepped out from the shadows.

They looked like soldiers, but instead of full armor, they had only scuffed chain link breastplates with thick leather covering their arms and legs. The two in front looked more like ruffians than soldiers, and they brandished their swords with all the excitement of a hungry dog who just cornered his prey. The third one looked more put together, with an expression that showed, of all things, boredom. The sword he raised was no less deadly, and one side of it looked serrated.

"Yes, they've already left," the third man said casually, looking at Sarin like a nuisance to be rid of. "I'm going to take you to Ferdri now."

"Not on my life," Sarin proclaimed bravely, holding his sword at the ready. Carolyn felt a chill run up her spine. Did she come here just to die immediately? Even if Sarin was skilled, there were three grown men in front of them, and she highly doubted he could take them all on his own, and she would only be a liability with her lack of combat experience.

Worse, the odd tingling sensation she'd been feeling since she arrived was getting stronger, like there were thousands of bugs crawling all over her. Sarin was talking again but she barely heard it, her whole focus absorbed by the awful tingling. *GET OFF OF ME*, she found herself shouting in her mind Or possibly out loud, she wasn't quite sure.

What she was sure of, however, was that the tingling immediately stopped, and changed. The warmth from her necklace flared white-hot for a moment as the tingling coalesced into a warping sensation in the pit of her stomach, and then burst outward. And as it did so, something actually *did* burst out of her, pushing out in all directions: fire, shooting outward toward the edges of the room. Carolyn froze, nonplussed, and started when Sarin grabbed her hand and pulled her forward, *toward* the ruffians. They didn't seem to be in any position to stop them, as their leather armor had caught on fire and they were desperately trying to roll on the ground to put it out. As Sarin pulled her, she realized that his gauntlet was quite warm, and there were small burn marks on his cheeks Other than that, he appeared all right, thankfully.

Sarin quickly pulled Carolyn over to the wall behind the portal device, yanked a small object from his belt pouch, and held it up against the wall. The wall slid aside, revealing a dark room. While the ruffians were beginning to recover and shout, Sarin pulled Carolyn through, held up the object behind them, and the hidden door slid shut again.

All was dark around them before light slowly started to fill the room. Carolyn looked around for a source, but there was none, there was simply light. The room was small, with a ladder at the opposite end and nothing else of interest.

"What," Carolyn began, finding her voice, "just happened?"

"I was hoping you could tell me," Sarin said through gritted teeth.

"Are you all right?" she asked, concerned.

"Well, a wizard just tried to cook me alive in my armor, but otherwise I'm all right," Sarin answered with a shrug.

"Oh no," Carolyn gasped, "I'm sorry, who—oh wait, you mean me."

Sarin stared at her.

"You didn't know you could do that?" he asked, smiling incredulously.

"I don't even know what I did," Carolyn answered simply.

"You used magic."

"How?"

"Beats me," Sarin shrugged, "I hardly know the first thing about it. If we can get out of here, though, I'm sure Treton could answer your questions for you."

"Okay, great," Carolyn nodded, "I'll just stay confused then. Can you at least tell me where we are? And why people are trying to capture us? I think you may have missed some parts in your story."

"Oh," Sarin answered, "sorry. I was in a hurry. The short version is, a usurper invaded the kingdom and took the throne. His forces control Herin castle now." He gestured vaguely around him, indicating that that's where they were. "And now we have to get out of here. This is part of a secret system of passages only known to the Herin royalty, and can only be opened with the talisman I have. We were told about them and given the talisman as part of our mission." Sarin started walking over toward the ladder, seeming to study the floor carefully.

"Great, now how do we get out?" Carolyn asked. Before she finished speaking, Sarin found the spot he was looking for. He held out the talisman again and a section of the floor slid open, revealing a ladder leading into a dark hole.

"This way. I'll go first." Without another word, Sarin started to climb down. Carolyn watched as he sank in the darkness, and then the room he had descended into lit up in the same way the one above had. Carolyn immediately started to climb down, grateful she had leggings on under her skirt. Once she had climbed down, she saw they were in a narrow hallway that extended in both directions as far as she could see, lit down the entire length by the unnatural light. Sarin used the talisman on the trapdoor above them and it slid closed, the only indication of its existence being the ladder that led to it.

"Will this get us out of the castle?" Carolyn asked as she followed Sarin down the tunnel.

"Yes, but there are other exits," he explained, "I'm going to check some of them on the way and see if the rest of the knights are still in the castle. I'd rather ride Midnight back to Cansition than have to walk the whole way."

"Midnight?"

"My horse," Sarin answered absently as they came up to another ladder, "A black mare. I'd hate to lose her." He started climbing, using his talisman on another hidden trapdoor. As before, the room was dark until the unnatural light gradually began to fill it. Sarin pulled himself up and vanished from sight.

Left suddenly alone, Carolyn felt a wave of anxiety threaten to overtake her. She had taken a chance that Sarin's story was true and there might be adventure to be had, but it hadn't occurred to her just how quickly that adventure would turn dangerous. Of course, every good adventure had danger, but she was hoping she would at least have gained an understanding of what was going on, and have had some means of defending herself, before she became involved in it. Then again, she could, apparently, use magic.

"Come up, quickly!" Sarin said urgently, his head appearing at the top of the ladder, "The other knights are still here, trying to fight their way out. Ferdri's men are holding them back, but won't last long. If we hurry, we can join them and ride out together. Come on."

Carolyn started climbing up the ladder as fast as she could with shaking hands. Sarin made sure to close the trapdoor once Carolyn was up before he opened the exit door from the nondescript chamber.

The hidden door slid silently open, but even if it had made noise, it would have been drowned out by the sudden cacophony that assaulted them: loud shouting, metal clanging, and horses neighing from just around the corner.

"You go out first," Sarin told Carolyn urgently, "I'll close the door behind us. Stay against the wall!"

Carolyn did as she was told, feeling shaky as she pressed herself against the wall. Sarin was quick to move in front of her and guide the way, closer to the shouting. Carolyn had a chance to look around a bit, trying to get some bearing on her situation, and realized how spacious the room was, with a massive chandelier hanging from the ceiling far above. All around the walls were decorated with the same scarlet-and-gold style as the portal room, with various pictures, tapestries, and statues. Like the last room, it showed signs of recent battle, like the trampled carpet that stretched off down the middle of the room and through the doorway behind them.

They moved quickly from the hidden doorway and toward the sounds of fighting. The wall beside them was the side of a grand staircase dominating the chamber, sloping down toward grandiose double doors, open wide. The bottom three stairs wrapped around the edge of the staircase ahead of them and here Sarin crouched down, motioning for Carolyn to do the same.

This was Carolyn's first sight of battle, raging on the other side of the staircase. Mounted knights were fighting viciously against a swarm of foot soldiers. The foot soldiers kept the knights at bay with merciless stabs of their spears, but didn't look like they'd hold for long. The closest ones were on the opposite end of the stair Sarin and Carolyn were hiding behind. Behind the ranks of soldiers was one mounted knight, shouting orders at the soldiers arrayed before him. His armor was punctured and soaked in blood, but he showed no intention to retreat.

"Do you think you can use magic again?" Sarin shouted over the raucous din of combat.

"I still don't know how I did it the first time," she yelled back, shrugging.

"Ok, so stay here until I come back for you," he answered. He was off before Carolyn could respond, creeping onto the wide stair and stalking along, as best as he could in heavy armor, toward the enemy soldiers on the other end.

Carolyn suddenly felt very vulnerable and wished fervently for the tingly feeling to come back. As much as she had hated it, that was what seemed to allow her to use magic. To her delight—and shock—she *did* feel something. It wasn't the same tingly sensation she had felt initially, but the odd feeling of *something* building up inside her, the same warping sensation she'd had right before she used magic before. She still wasn't sure how exactly to use it, and it seemed like a risky prospect to start experimenting with it at that moment, so she tried to take her mind off of it and focus on Sarin instead. As if in response, the feeling within her subsided.

Sarin reached the soldier on the other end of the stair. While his target was not engaged in combat, he was focused on the battle raging in front of him. The enemy commander near the door, however, seemed to have noticed the movement. He started shouting and pointing in Sarin's direction, but too late. Sarin tackled the soldier in front of him, pulling him down to the ground. Carolyn expected some kind of domino effect where that soldier would knock over the one on the stair below him, then he would knock over the next, resulting in a comical defeat. To her disappointment, this didn't happen. The next soldier was hit in the back by his falling companion and bumped forward into the next one, but both remained on their feet. That did get their attention, however, and turned quickly toward Sarin.

Sarin pulled himself to his feet and drew his sword, lashing out at his opponents. They were caught completely by surprise to find themselves apparently flanked, and confusion started to overtake the other soldiers on the stairs as they tried to figure out where the new attack was coming from. A few of the knights of Herin closest to the stairs, noticing the distraction, pressed their efforts on the foot of the stairs. With the confusion Sarin had successfully sown, one of them broke through the ranks and led his horse to leap onto the stairs beside Sarin, with two more quickly following.

It seemed the knights were very much outnumbered, which was the only reason the soldiers on the ground had kept them at bay for so long, but now that some were taking the stairs, they had gained an advantage. The enemy commander started shouting at his troops to fall back, to better block the entrance. Without a tight defense, though, the knights were striking back hard. They rushed the retreating troops, stabbing with spears and trampling with horses. It seemed evident that the battle would soon be won.

Distracted by the scene in front of her, Carolyn almost didn't notice the noise from behind her. It was faint, nearly drowned out by the din of combat, but there was definitely someone shouting. Carolyn turned in time to see the same three soldiers they had met in the portal room now rushing up the hallway behind her. Sarin said to wait for him, but Carolyn didn't have time to wait. She sprang to her feet and started running toward the knights on the stairs.

Most of them had moved off toward the main entrance below, but there was one on the lower half of the stairs that saw Carolyn coming. He immediately turned to face her, spear at the ready, a deadly look in his eyes. Carolyn froze, eyes locked with the knight, seeing his fierce determination and readiness to kill. The tip of his spear moved closer and Carolyn tensed further. *I've only been here a few minutes, and this is the second time someone's trying to kill me. I knew I shouldn't have come!*

Then another knight began riding up the stairs, and he shouted something at the knight facing Carolyn down. It was Sarin, now mounted on a black, armored horse. The other knight turned and stood guard while Sarin reached Carolyn and held out a hand to help her up. She gratefully took it and swung into the saddle behind him, still shaking.

"Hold on tight!" Sarin shouted, not giving Carolyn a chance to react before he turned his horse, drove it down the stairs, and headed for the main gate. Carolyn frantically threw her arms around him and held on for dear life as they charged. With the enemy ranks broken, the knights had decimated most of the remaining troops. Some of them stood bravely in the doorway, but they were quickly trampled. Many were fleeing. Carolyn couldn't see the commander anymore. Most surprisingly, some of the soldiers appeared to be frozen in blocks of ice, while others were surrounded by bits of rock, as though boulders had been dropped on them.

As they rode toward the open door, they passed by a couple knights who were dressed in robes instead of heavy armor. These knights had no spears or swords, but instead carried staves with jewels set at their heads. Carolyn got a brief glimpse of one with a ruby in their staff. They waved it and a large spear of ice shot out of it toward an enemy soldier.

Magic!

Before she could get a better look at what was going on,

she and Sarin were out the door, traveling down a covered path between two large courtyards. They built up speed as they charged down the path and soon found themselves bursting out the large opened double doors at the other end, over a heavy wooden drawbridge, and onto a cobbled path. In the light of torches sparsely placed along the path, Carolyn could see they were headed down a slope toward a towering perimeter wall. Over the wall, Carolyn could make out the silhouettes of houses, like a city. The gate was guarded by a few soldiers, and they bravely stood up to the oncoming rush of knights, but to no avail. They were brushed aside, stabbed, or trampled, and the path was clear.

The knights continued to drive their horses at breakneck pace, their hooves clacking loudly against the cobblestones of the street. Once they passed through the gate, they came out onto a wide boulevard, lined with tall torches like streetlamps. This continued in a straight line to an imposing wall in the distance. Carolyn expected them to go for that, but after traveling straight for a bit the knights suddenly turned down a side road. As they turned, Carolyn saw more knights coming up behind them, and realized that she and Sarin were almost exactly in the center of the troop. *Are they escorting me?* she wondered briefly.

Up ahead, the street darkened, and Carolyn saw, or rather didn't see, that all the torches had been extinguished. The sound of hooves on stone also lessened at the same time. She looked down to see that straw had been strewn thickly across this part of the road. Horses aren't very good for sneaking, but with the lights out and straw to dampen the sound of their passage, they could be a little better at it. This was obviously a well-planned operation. It wasn't long before Carolyn found herself completely engulfed in darkness, the only light being the twinkle of stars far above them.

With nothing more to look at, and no more sense of imminent danger, Carolyn was finally able to take stock of her situation. She had followed a stranger through a magic portal because the thought of adventure enticed her, but where had it gotten her? She had already faced death twice, and now she was being hurried off *away* from the device that brought her here in the first place.

Then there was the magic. How did she do it? Had she always been able to do that, or was it just because she was in a world of magic? Experimentally, she tried to summon forth the feeling of magic as she had before, and she could feel it again, but she wasn't certain how to use it and released it. There was definitely some kind of power she could use, and she wasn't sure if she should be excited or scared.

She still wasn't even sure what they were doing. Other than the fact that the kingdom was in danger, Sarin hadn't explained anything, and having to fight their way out of a palace hadn't provided much explanation either. Things were getting more confusing, and she still couldn't be certain she had even chosen the right side. Maybe these knights were bandits and were kidnapping her for ransom, or worse. She shuddered at the thought, but pushed it away. Sarin didn't seem like a bad person and Carolyn trusted her instincts on that.

Most of all, she was tired. She had only gotten a couple hours of sleep before being whisked away. *Wherever we go, hopefully there will be a bed,* she thought to herself. *Bouncing on a galloping horse is not a very comfortable place to get some rest.*

Eventually Carolyn heard the sound of water running and felt like they might be going over a bridge. After that they got onto a dirt path and the noise subsided a lot, but still they didn't slow. Carolyn had never ridden a horse and began to wonder how long they could push them this way. Finally, the troop started to slow, and Carolyn could hear the faint creaking of branches in a light breeze, the rustling of leaves, and the snap of twigs underfoot. It seemed they had entered a forest.

"Almost there now," Sarin whispered to her. "You can stop trying to crush my ribs now."

Carolyn pulled her arms off of Sarin, her cheeks growing

warm. She settled herself as best she could behind the knight, keeping herself steady with years of practice at balancing.

"Where are we going?" Carolyn whispered back, feeling that there was still a need for caution.

"Cansition," Sarin replied, "It's a secret hideout. We can talk more when we get there. We need to stay quiet for now, just in case."

Carolyn nodded, which was a useless gesture, of course, but she did it anyway. The troop crept along through the dense forest, with only the sounds of an owl hooting overhead, the rustling of thick underbrush from the passage of the horses, and the howls of a wolf somewhere in the distance to accompany them. Carolyn occasionally heard a whisper from one of the other knights, but otherwise silence was maintained.

They were moving much slower now, unable to rush among the trees. Not far ahead, Carolyn could hear the sounds of some knights moving off to the left or right, as though the path split and they couldn't agree on which direction to take. Soon they reached the point where the split was happening and Sarin spoke up in a loud whisper, "It's Sarin." Before she could ask why he thought she forgot who she was riding with, Carolyn heard a reply.

"You have her with you?" the voice replied in kind. It was almost right next to them, but in the darkness of the night Carolyn couldn't see a thing.

"Yes," Sarin responded, continuing forward slowly. Carolyn knew he must be referring to her, but it was strange. She wasn't used to having people treat her with such importance.

"Take the straight path," the voice ordered.

Sarin continued his horse forward, but then veered to the left suddenly. He continued in that direction for a bit before veering right. Soon they started moving a little faster as the sound of underbrush lessened and the brief glimpses of stars became more frequent. Finally, they came out to an area with a large, open patch of sky: a clearing in the forest. Carolyn could still hardly see anything, but in the starlight she could make out silhouettes of looming trees all around, looking dark and ominous in the night. Sarin seemed to be heading right for a very large one at the edge of the clearing.

"Are we walking into a tree?" Carolyn whispered, not sure if she was allowed to talk yet.

"Kind of," Sarin answered quietly, with a hint of amusement in his voice. Without another word, he marched straight into the dark silhouette.

Much to her surprise, the horse did *not* bump its head and snort in anger. Instead it continued forward into the dark shape. Once through, Carolyn found they were surrounded by odd, shimmering, blue walls which resembled the shape of a tree. The small amount of light generated by the walls illuminated a dirt slope on the ground immediately in front of them, leading down into the ground.

Heading down the slope, Carolyn soon started to see the flickering light of a fire burning as the scent of smoke reached her. The walls and ceiling of the tunnel were supported with strong wooden columns and crossbeams that lined the whole slope. At first she thought they would be descending for miles until the slanted ceiling gave way, revealing an open chamber before them.

It was large, about the size of the room with the portal, with a couple torches burning on the wall at the far end. There they illuminated a solid, wooden gate that blocked their path. Sarin approached confidently. A small peephole slid open in the door

"Halt!" a voice shouted. "Who goes there?"

"Open up, Rick," Sarin shouted back casually, pulling back on the reins. "It's Sarin."

"Oh, you're back. How fortunate," the guard replied in a tone that told Carolyn he wasn't expecting survivors from the night's mission. "Hey, open up the gates!"

The loud scraping of wood and metal assaulted them as one of the double doors of the gate swung outward. The other side was about as gloomy as the chamber they were in—all dirt walls and ceiling-though with better lighting. Sarin started forward as soon as there was enough space.

Inside was a somewhat larger but still relatively boring chamber. Immediately ahead of them was another large, wooden gate, though the wall surrounding it was made of stone and the gate looked more ornate than sturdy. To the right was another short gate, probably no more than four feet tall, with the wall above that was mostly open, revealing a stables on the other side. To the left was a series of four smaller doors in another stone wall.

"Where are the others, Sir?" said a guard as he walked up, the same one that had spoken to them through the door. Other guards began to close the gate behind them.

"They'll be along soon," Sarin answered, climbing off his horse, "Weren't you told we'd split up on the way back?"

"Oh right, right," the guard nodded, "I'll keep'n eye out, then."

A man from a corner by the main gate hurried over. He wore a fine red silk shirt with gold trimmings and the symbol of Herin was proudly displayed on the left breast. He glanced at Carolyn as he came but kept his focus mainly on Sarin. Carolyn turned her head and noticed that everyone else in the room—a number of guards lining the walls and congregated by the door—were staring at her openly. She glared at a group of them until they looked away.

"Welcome back, Sir Sarin," the man said formally, offering a polite bow of the head, and adding something in a whisper that Carolyn couldn't make out. Sarin nodded in response.

"Milady," the man said, turning to Carolyn and offering a deep bow. "It is my great honor to welcome you to Cansition Palace. I am Rissin, Steward of Herin Castle."

"Hi," Carolyn replied awkwardly. "I'm Carolyn."

"Lady Carolyn, might you permit me to escort you to the meeting room? The King and Queen wished to meet with you personally the moment you arrived." With that, he extended a hand to help Carolyn off the horse.

Carolyn took it and climbed down, following Rissin toward the large double doors on the other end of the room. The doors began to slide open on their own as they stepped forward, revealing a remarkable sight: a palace, right there underground. While not as tall as the castle they had just fled, it was still impressive, with the same scarlet-and-gold themed carpeting and tapestries and portraits lining the walls. Directly ahead of them was a large staircase, neither as tall nor as grand as the one in the main palace, but striking nonetheless. The whole room was illuminated by the same source-less light that had lit up the secret passageways in the castle.

Rissin led Carolyn to the left, walking up a hallway alongside the staircase, into a narrow passage with doors along either side of the hall. They stopped at the first door on the right side.

"I will go in first and introduce you," the steward said with a slight bow of respect to Carolyn. He gave a short knock on the door, waited a moment for a muffled voice to call back an answer, and opened it up. He stepped just inside, blocking Carolyn's view of the door, and started a formal announcement.

"Your majesties," he began, sounding quite pompous, "may I present to you the heir of the Great Sage Naritha, Lady Carolyn." With that, he stepped aside and bowed toward the door.

Carolyn stood dumbstruck in front of the open door as the King rose from his seat at her announcement. She had never met a King or Queen before, nor had she ever imagined herself important enough to be introduced to any with such flair, and yet there they were, and there she was.

They were every bit as impressive as Carolyn could have imagined. The King was tall, with short dirty blonde hair and a neatly cropped beard and mustache. He wore a splendid outfit of scarlet and gold, with a cape that reached his knees. A gold emblem with the symbol of Herin adorned the left breast of his doublet, cascading, gold-threads underneath it, and a gem-studded, gold crown on his head. Most arresting, however, were his eyes. They were brown, but when Carolyn looked at them, she saw strength and determination, but also a kindness that permeated his very being.

Seated beside him was the Queen. She had long, dark brown hair that hung in loose waves past her shoulders, with a braid running over the top of her head just under her own crown, which was equal in splendor to the King's. She wore an emerald green dress with a pale yellow sash wrapped around the waist. Centered on the bodice of the dress was a triangle of light yellow fabric embroidered with abstract patterns, which was also used on the cuffs off the dress. On her right middle finger was a ring of gold set with a large ruby, and from her neck hung a long necklace that bore the symbol of Herin. Her eyes were dark brown, and they looked at Carolyn with incredible perception and understanding, showing both strength of will and her concern for others.

In comparison, Carolyn felt really plain. Her hair was a mess from the frantic run on horseback, and her blue eyes lacked the depth of character and strength exuded by the royalty before her. She was wearing a plain red shirt under an open denim vest and a stretchy grey skirt with black leggings underneath. She found it comfortable, but just now she felt herself to be quite unimpressive. *No wonder all those guards were staring at me*, she thought. Finally, after what felt like hours—but was hardly ten seconds—Carolyn realized she was staring at a King and Queen while they waited for her to enter the room.

"Come in, please," said the Queen gently, sensing Carolyn's discomfort. Giving herself a shake, Carolyn forced herself to walk into the room. Once she did, the steward closed the door behind her. For a moment, nothing else happened. Carolyn noticed out of the corner of her eye that Rissin was shifting uncomfortably and clearing his throat, as though trying to hint at something. *What am I supposed to be doing?* she wondered, *I wish Rissin would just tell me. Oh, maybe I'm supposed to bow?*

"Welcome to Cansition Palace, Lady Carolyn," the King said as though nothing had happened, "It is an honor to meet you, though I wish our meeting could have occurred under more pleasant circumstances. Please sit." He indicated the chair beside him.

Feeling awkward and not sure what to say, she walked over to the chair indicated. They were in a long room with a large table in the center, ringed by many chairs, with two throne-like chairs at the head. The Queen sat in one of these, which was gilded, with jewels set into the headboard. The King moved over to take an equally elaborate chair beside her.

"Rissin, you may leave us now," the Queen said as the King took his seat. The steward bowed and left the room. Once he was gone, the King spoke again.

"I presume that you were rushed here with no time for a formal briefing, so let's start with the basics. I am King Ketra, 23rd King of Herin."

"And I am Queen Rorina," the Queen added.

"You are the heir of Naritha, correct?" the King asked.

"Yes," Carolyn said finally, finding her voice. The King and Queen spoke with such calm and patience. She wasn't accustomed to authority figures speaking so pleasantly or treating her with such respect.

"And you have the Derishz Ruby?"

"Yes," Carolyn nodded, then pulled her necklace out from under her shirt. The King and Queen's eyes went wide with awe, much as Sarin's had. The queen quickly recovered her composure, while the King's expression turned somber.

"These are dark times for us to have to call for such an artifact," the King sighed, "dark times indeed."

"Why?" Carolyn asked, hiding the Ruby once again. "What exactly does it do?"

"You mean you don't know?" the King said with

surprise.

"Not a clue," Carolyn answered, shrugging, "I didn't even know it was anything more than a necklace until Sarin showed up."

"Sarin..." the King started questioningly.

"One of the knights, dear," the Queen reminded him.

"Ah, yes," the King nodded, "Brave fellow that one. So you had no idea about the Ruby's power? Or how to use it?"

"From what little Sarin told me," Carolyn said, "Naritha went out of her way to *hide* its power. I don't think she would have bothered telling anyone what it was."

"Good point," the King said with a nod, "It belonged to—"

"A powerful mage," the Queen interrupted suddenly; the King looked shocked for a moment but didn't say anything, shooting her a quick, questioning glance. "He was attempting to use the Ruby's power to destroy any nation that stood in his way," she continued. "Finally, an army was formed, combining the might of the strongest nations of the time, including Herin, to march on the mage's lair. Ultimately he was defeated, though at great cost. Most thought the Ruby was lost, but Naritha captured it for the sake of hiding it away where no one could use it again—"

"Through the portal device," Carolyn finished, nodding thoughtfully, then blushed when she realized she had interrupted a Queen. "Sorry," she added quickly.

"This is a private audience, and you are clearly not familiar with our customs, so think nothing of it," the Queen smiled knowingly, "but do try to refrain from interrupting me in public."

"The intention was for the Ruby to remain there indefinitely," the King went on before Carolyn's blush could deepen, "but the knowledge of its existence has remained a royal secret, known to none outside the royal family, in case a situation arose where it's power was needed."

Carolyn nearly opened her mouth to say something, but stopped herself and nodded instead.

"Which brings us back to today," the King continued. "Some ten years ago, there was a royal advisor named Ferdri. He was intelligent, but overly ambitious. For years the kingdom has prohibited the capture of unicorns in our land, since—"

"Unicorns?" Carolyn said abruptly, unable to restrain herself this time, "You have unicorns here?"

"Yes, it's on the royal emblem," the King answered, tapping the emblem on his shirt, "You don't have unicorns where you live?"

Carolyn examined the emblem closely and saw the horn on top of the horse's head. "No", she answered simply, marveling at it.

"Strange," the King shrugged, "They're not uncommon here in forests and open plains, and come in various colors. But here in Herin it's different. Since the time the land was settled and Herin was established, there have been unicorns living in this forest, where Cansition is hidden. Most unicorns are not very different from wild horses, just a bit more aggressive and nearly impossible to tame. But the Herin unicorns exhibit a greater intellect, even near-human sentience; they are all white, possess strong magic, and are more reclusive, only ever being spotted as individuals.

"Needless to say, that has made them a topic of some fascination, especially amongst scholars and mages. All attempts at capturing them for study, however, led to an extremely violent reaction from the Herin unicorns, even worse than with other unicorns, and with their magic they were able to resist the attempts of even the best wizards to restrain them. After multiple capture attempts ended up with someone dead, and sometimes even the unicorn killed, King Menith, the 13th King of Herin, banned all attempts to study the unicorns."

Carolyn nodded her head absently, trying to pay attention to the deluge of information while also fighting her mounting exhaustion. There was a lot to take in, and she hadn't had enough sleep to take it all in with.

"Then came Ferdri, a royal advisor to my father, King Terangrad of Herin. Ferdri was insistent that we study the Herin unicorns and unlock their secrets finally. He formulated a plan, convincing a number of royal advisors and some leading wizards that it would work, and presented the idea to my father. He rejected the idea out of hand. Ferdri was undaunted and tried presenting it again. After due consideration and consulting with Archmage Treton and some other leading wizards, my father determined the plan to be too risky and still forbade it.

"Ferdri continued to persist, presenting the idea again on a number of occasions to try and win my father over, but it only increased my father's frustration. Finally, Ferdri was forbidden to speak of the topic again, and we thought that would be the end of it.

"Then there came attacks on our western border. They were nothing major, at least at first, but they diverted my father's attention. Then tragedy struck: while surveying the border, my father's honor guard was assaulted and overtaken, and he was slain." The King sighed heavily, his eyes downcast.

"In the midst of the mourning and turbulence as I rose to the throne, Ferdri convinced a number of trappers and wizards that he had received royal approval for his plan and attempted to capture a unicorn. Only two members of the expedition survived, a trapper by the name of Kelin and Ferdri himself. Kelin was quick to admit to what happened and told us that not only did the unicorns react violently, but they seemed to be ready for them, with a large number appearing at once and ambushing them.

"The trapper was let off with a warning since he was deceived, but Ferdri was a different story. The normal punishment for attempting to capture a unicorn is a year-long imprisonment, but this was the case of a royal advisor who had been explicitly warned not to involve himself with the unicorns. His actions bordered on treason and I could well have had him executed, but I couldn't find it in me to deliver a death sentence within the first month of my reign. Instead I sentenced him to banishment. He was stripped of his title and possessions and sent north to our neighboring kingdom of Zafon with minimum funds to give him a fresh start on life. We are allies with Zafon and they promised to keep an eye on him and let us know if he was making any attempts to cause trouble. Within a year he ran afoul of some... colorful folk, and he fled east into the mountains. The terrain there is harsh and is home to some scattered barbarian tribes. We expected that to be the end of him."

The King paused for a moment, his still eyes downcast. The Queen placed a hand on his arm, giving him a warm smile.

"That changed about five months ago," the Queen continued, "when reports started to come in of attacks on our northeastern border. It is not uncommon for the barbarians to come down from the mountains and raid our towns, and we do what we can do prevent this, but these attacks were different. There were perpetrated by trained soldiers, and no one was ever harmed except for the border guards. Food and supplies were stolen, that was it. Then the attacks began occurring further into our territory, and we couldn't find where they were coming from. At the same time, the various wandering mercenary bands that roam throughout Herin vanished and reappeared in the raiding parties, helping to steal food and the like. All of them were being hired out, and evidence pointed toward them all having the same employer.

"Obviously we did not sit idly by while all this occurred. Our armies were mobilized, knights were arranged, and the wizards readied. Our forces did what they could to defend, yet our inability to find the source of the invading forces made this difficult. There were also reports of some kind of super-soldier among their ranks. He had distinctive armor and was somehow able to slay anyone who tried to fight him, soldier, knight, or wizard. Even the elite assassin squads we sent after him ended up dead."

"And that was what worried us most," said the King, taking up the story again. "We feared this unknown enemy had a hidden source of magic for which we had no recourse.

"A month ago, the invading army showed itself not far from the capital, and in greater numbers than we had anticipated. That was when we discovered it was Ferdri leading them. We assumed he wanted revenge against me but meant no harm to the people, based on how his forces seemed to go out of their way not to hurt anyone who didn't threaten them. That was when I made the decision to hide here, in Cansition. And I still worry I made the wrong decision, just as I worry that I erred in sending for the Derishz Ruby."

Both the King and Queen were silent for a moment, considering the significance of what seemed a forbidden topic. Carolyn idly fingered the necklace beneath her shirt.

"What exactly does it do?" she said finally, breaking the silence. The King looked at her gravely.

"I think that discussion is best left for the morning," he said, "It is late, and we all need our rest. Tomorrow will be a big day." With that, the King stood and went to the door, pulling it open. "Rissin, please show Lady Carolyn to her room," he called into the hallway.

The King moved aside and the steward came back in, bowed to the King and Queen, and then, surprisingly, to Carolyn. "Please come with me, milady," he said to her, gesturing for the door.

Exhausted by the exciting events of the night, Carolyn stood eagerly. As she was about to walk out the door, however, she couldn't help but feel she was going to miss some other important social cue, so she turned and gave a quick attempt at a curtsy. Not waiting to see if what she did was right, wrong, or taboo, she turned around again and left the room. Rissin followed after her and closed the door behind them.

"Don't fret, milady," he said softly, not in a kind voice as much as in a well-trained, respectful tone. "We will find someone to properly tutor you in the ways of our etiquette."

Carolyn blushed, but said nothing. *I guess it's inevitable that I stand out around here.* She followed Rissin up the hall, through an open doorway into another hall on the left. This hallway was shorter and had a few doors along each side with large double doors at the end. He brought her to the second door on the right and produced a key from his belt to unlock it.

Unlike the rest of the palace, this room was dark inside, not lit by the source-less light that illuminated every other room Carolyn had been in. Rissin entered before her and turned on a small lamp, filling the room with a warm white light and revealing a lavish bedroom. Within a gold-painted frame was a large bed covered in soft blankets and huge, fluffy pillows. Beside the bed was a small table, carved with intricate patterns of flowers on its sides and legs, atop which sat the lamp, which had a small dial at its base. On the back wall on either side of the bed were large black rectangles that looked like windows—not that there would be windows underground—framed by thick crimson curtains. On the right side of the room was a writing desk of fine wood with a chair of the same make, fully equipped with paper, stoppered bottles of ink, and a quill. On the left side of the room was a large wooden changing screen, a full-length mirror, and a wardrobe, also of decorated wood. Beside the wardrobe were a pair of doors, one of which was stood ajar to reveal a bathroom. All of it together looked very... royal.

"If there's anything you lack, just let me know," Rissin said. "Accommodations here are not what they are in Norostar Palace, but I will send a maid to wait on you shortly."

"Why?" Carolyn asked before she could stop herself, overwhelmed at the treatment she was receiving, "Why am I being treated so well? Am I really that important?"

Rissin looked taken aback. "I'm sorry if I step out of line in asking this, Milady," he said carefully, "but did the Great Sage Naritha not leave you with any indication of your heritage?"

"My heritage?" Carolyn was even more confused now.

"The Great Sage was daughter of King Terasin, then King of Herin. You are of royal descent."

CHAPTER 3
The Derishz Ruby

Carolyn had had such a strange dream the night before. There was something about a magic portal, fighting through a horde of soldiers, and finding a secret palace hidden under a forest. It had been such a spectacular and strangely detailed dream. To top it all off, right at the end she was told by someone that she was actually a princess.

She slowly opened her eyes, blinking in the light. It took her a moment to take in her surroundings, but it was immediately obvious that she was *not* in her room. Sitting upright and looking around she saw that it was her room in the palace, the one Rissin had led her to the night before. It wasn't a dream after all; Carolyn had traveled to another dimension, Carolyn had met a King and Queen, and Carolyn was royalty.

The soft silk and cotton of the bed was very comfortable, coaxing her to stay and snuggle up, but after a full night's rest she felt full of energy. As she looked around—blinking a few times to make sure this lavish bedroom wouldn't disappear and change into her bedroom back home—she noticed a small table had been erected right beside her bed.

On it was a tray holding warm bread, jelly, fish, slices of meat, salad, breadsticks, some manner of dip, wine, and what looked like fruit juice. It was much more lavish than most meals Carolyn had, especially for breakfast, and never had she been so privileged to have it brought to her.

Before she partook of it, Carolyn made use of the bathroom connected to her bedroom. The bathroom came fully equipped with a bathtub, towels, and various containers of shampoo, soap, and perfume. Though she felt like she could use a bath, with no clean clothes to change into it seemed like a futile endeavor, so she put it off. *I'll ask for some clean clothes later,* she told herself, *I can ask for that if I'm a princess, right?* Unfortunately, there was nothing resembling a toothbrush in the bathroom, giving her concern for the state of her teeth, so she made do with rinsing vigorously with water. Returning to the bedroom, she was surprised to find someone standing there.

Carolyn jumped in surprise before realizing it was just Merilda, the maid Rissin had sent to "wait on her" the night before. There was a second side door in the bedroom a few feet from the bathroom door that led to maid's quarters, so she was always available in case Carolyn needed anything. Not that Carolyn *wanted* someone to wait on her, nor was she sure what exactly she would want a maid to do for her that she wouldn't rather do herself.

"I'm sorry for frightening you, milady," Merilda said with a deep bow, "I heard the bathroom door and I came to see if you needed anything." She remained in a bowed posture, trembling slightly. She was older than Carolyn, but not by much, and she seemed so easily intimidated by anyone of importance. The way she spoke and acted around Carolyn and the steward, it almost seemed she was afraid of being eaten alive.

"It's all right," Carolyn said quickly, trying to sound casual and reassuring at the same time, "I just forgot you were here. And stop bowing, please. Stand up straight."

"Of course, milady," she said, straightening up quickly,

eyes wide, "Is there anything I could assist you with?"

Carolyn looked at her for a moment in thought, then finally said, "Yes, I need you to smile." Merilda's eyes went even wider.

"Smile, milady?" she said slowly, "I don't understand."

"Yeah, smile," Carolyn repeated, "relax a bit, loosen up, you know. You're too tense, you need to just chill."

At first, the maid looked more concerned, but finally her posture began to relax and her lips did curl into the faintest hint of a smile. "I'll do my best, milady," she answered.

"Great. For now, I don't need anything else, at least not until I've had my breakfast." Carolyn went to sit on her bed to partake of the delicious feast that had been brought to her.

"Beg pardon, milady," Merilda said hesitantly, "but this is lunch."

"Lunch?" she turned on Merilda questioningly right before taking a bite of a breadstick. "What time is it?"

"About a quarter past noon, milady," she answered. "The lunch was brought only a few moments ago. I think you were awoken by the servant leaving."

"Huh, I must've been tired," Carolyn responded slowly, then shrugged. "Lunch it is then. Are you hungry?"

"Milady, I can't eat with you," Merilda's eyes went wide again; Carolyn briefly wondered if she would faint from being treated with such casual respect, "I have my own meal in my room," she added quickly.

"Oh, ok," Carolyn nodded, and dug into her meal with an appetite. Merilda stood around for a couple minutes in silence before Carolyn thought to dismiss her. The maid graciously returned to her own little bedroom and shut the door. As she ate, Carolyn looked around the room again, trying to digest her situation as much as her food. *It's all real,* she thought, coming to terms with that fact.

The room was filled with light now, but not the same source-less light as in most other rooms. The large, black sections on the wall were, in fact, windows, but when

Carolyn looked at them she could see nothing on the other side, just a white shine that filled the room with what looked like real sunlight.

Magic.

Next to her was the bedside table with the lamp. The lamp had a wide, round base that narrowed to a skinny stand, then widened into a sphere the size of a baseball at the top. The top half of the sphere would glow when it was turned on. She picked it up and turned the dial on and off, watching it glow and fade. It had no cord connecting it to the wall and she could find no battery cover on it.

Magic.

She remembered their flight from the castle. As they were running, there were men in robes waving staves at the enemy soldiers. One of them was launching icicles that appeared out of thin air. And then there was the shimmering blue portal that brought her here in the first place.

Magic.

There was magic everywhere, Carolyn was surrounded by it. She also seemed to have some herself and had used it, unwittingly, in their escape. Could she do it again? The strange, tingly feeling she got when she first arrived was still there, but it felt different now, more like a slight warmth focused inside her chest, waiting to be drawn upon. She tried to focus it, and immediately the warmth began spreading, filling her whole torso, her arms, her legs, and her head. She could feel it as easily as she could one of her limbs, ready to be used like a third hand.

But how do I use it? she wondered. It didn't seem like a very good idea to experiment here, seeing as how her last use resulted in things catching on fire, but it was very hard to resist the urge to try. Just a day ago she'd had no inkling such a power existed, and now, suddenly, she could call on it so easily. What had changed?

She finished her meal while lost in thought about these matters. There was still plenty of tempting, delicious food left on the tray, but she felt too stuffed for another bite.

Now that she had a full stomach, it was time to figure out what she was doing here. Carolyn went over to knock on Merilda's door and the maid opened it almost immediately.

"Yes, milady?" Merilda asked.

"Am I supposed to be doing something now?" Carolyn asked.

"Your presence was requested as soon as you were awake and feeling able by His and Her Royal Majesty," Merilda started, "but they are probably still at lunch now and will not be seeing anyone for a little bit."

"Ok," Carolyn answered slowly, considering what else she might be able to do. It seemed there was nothing for her to do in this room, and she had little desire to sit around doing nothing. Other than the King and Queen, the only person here she knew was Sarin. "Where do the knights sleep? I mean like their barracks, not their beds."

"By the main hall. Would you like me to take you there?" Merilda asked in confusion. It seemed this was not a request she was accustomed to.

"Yes, please," she answered, moving aside and gesturing toward the door.

"Of course milady," Merilda answered. Carolyn caught a glimpse of the meal laid out for Merilda inside the small room as the door closed. It was much more modest than what Carolyn had been offered, and there was very little left. She felt embarrassed to have been given such a large portion when someone else was being given so little.

"Oh, did you want to finish eating first?" Carolyn hesitated as Merilda started toward the door to the hall. Merilda seemed unable to hide her surprise as her eyes went wide once again.

"It's all right, I was finished," she answered quickly. She moved swiftly for the door, as though eager to get moving, and Carolyn followed her without another word. Merilda led them back into the main hallway and turned toward the entry hall. They came back out into the spacious room with the grand staircase beside them.

"Where do the stairs lead?" Carolyn wondered aloud.

"To the throne room, milady," Merilda answered.

"Is that where I'll meet the King and Queen?"

"I don't think so. They haven't been using it much since we got here, spending most of their time planning and consulting with their advisors. Here are the knights' barracks." Merilda stopped before a small door along the front wall to the right of the main door. It was relatively plain compared to the grandeur of the rest of their surroundings. Carolyn moved forward to open the door.

As the door swung open, Carolyn was briefly very concerned that she was walking into what was basically the men's locker room. A disturbing image of half-dressed men eyeing her suspiciously flashed through her mind, but it was quickly dispelled once the door was open. The room they were looking in on was some kind of recreation room, with various small tables set up and a shelf by the side of the room stacked with small boards, playing pieces, and cards. In one corner there were also a couple of easels set up next to jars of paint.

There weren't many men in the room, but a few were sitting at a table at the far end of the room, wearing plain white shirts and decorated crimson-and-gold pants. There were a couple others standing not far from the door who looked to be conversing when one of them noticed the door open. A brief look of surprise flashed on the knight's face before turning to walk over to Carolyn, but not as surprised as Carolyn supposed she looked.

The knight moving toward her was wearing a full uniform. It was a finely tailored, crimson uniform with actual gold buttons. It was trimmed with gold-colored fabric in strips along the sleeves, pant legs, and adorning the shoulders. There were also a few shiny pins decorating the front of the shirt, probably indicating some manner of importance, and some conical-shaped bars on the sleeves, most likely denoting rank. The knight looked as crisp and proper as did the uniform, but neither of those facts were what caught Carolyn's attention. What she noticed immediately was that the knight approaching her was a woman. She had tanned skin, light brown hair that reached her shoulders, and dark brown eyes. Something about her face seemed familiar, though Carolyn couldn't imagine where she might've seen her before.

"Lady Carolyn," the knight said with a deep bow, her body firm in stance but smooth in movements. She straightened herself with equal grace as she continued, "I wish to apologize for frightening you last night when I moved to attack you. I didn't realize who you were and thought you to be an enemy. Please forgive my error." Her tone was clear, her words precise, and her posture practiced, yet it all seemed so sincere.

"That was you?" Carolyn blurted out, remembering the second of her near-death experiences the night before. This was the same knight that looked ready to charge her on the stairs last night, the one with the look of a warrior, ready to kill without hesitation. She saw such determination and courage in those eyes last night, and now she was seeing in those same eyes sorrow and kindness. It was hard to believe that both faces belonged to the same person. Carolyn was at a complete loss of words.

"I see that my presence has upset you even more," the knight went on after a moment, her eyes now downcast, "I pray that you'll forgive me for being so forward with you. If I may excuse myself, I'll try to avoid offending you in the future." With that she bowed again and stepped back before turning and walking away. The knight she had been talking to, also a woman, exited the room through a door to the right. Carolyn continued to stand there for a moment. *A female knight? I thought only men were knights.*

"Are you all right, milady?" came a voice from behind her. Carolyn turned to see Merilda was still standing there behind her and had witnessed the brief interaction.

"Yes, I'm fine," she said casually, turning to face her. Her gaze went past the maid, however, and noticed a small group of knights on their way over, one of whom looked familiar. "Oh, there's Sarin," she said as she stepped back into the hallway to greet him.

The four knights approaching all wore their own sleek, crimson uniforms, though none had the rank or number of pins that the female knight did. One of the knights looked about the same age as Sarin while the other two were at least a couple years older. They were conversing among themselves much as high school boys did, and for a moment it was hard to remember that these were trained fighters who had just been in a fierce battle the night before. When they noticed Carolyn and her maid standing in their path, they stopped talking immediately.

In unison, they all bowed, with some declaring "Milady", and others saying "Lady Carolyn" by way of polite recognition of her presence. They then proceeded to walk past her toward the door with much more formality. Most of them avoided looking at her, but Sarin was eyeing her questioningly.

"Sarin," Carolyn said as the group moved past. All the knights stopped in anticipation, while Sarin was having a hard time fighting back a smirk. "Can I talk to you for a bit?"

"Of course, Lady Carolyn," Sarin said with a bow. He then seemed to wait for something that didn't happen, so instead he waved casually to the other knights as they closed the door behind them.

"Can I drop the formality now?" Sarin asked with a huge grin on his face, glancing briefly at Merilda. She seemed shocked at his bluntness, but Carolyn appreciated it.

"Yes, please!" Carolyn answered desperately. "Everyone keeps bowing to me and calling me by titles, it's driving me crazy!"

"I wouldn't know what that's like," Sarin shrugged. "The only title I get is 'Sir'. I don't think Sir Sarin has a nice ring to it."

"It's not bad," Carolyn nodded, "at least you deserve your title. At least, I think you do? I know I haven't done anything to deserve being a princess."

"I spent a long time training to become a knight," Sarin confirmed, "I think I've earned it. I think most princesses don't do anything to deserve the title—with all due respect—but they usually don't complain."

"Well, I didn't exactly grow up like a princess. I grew up as an unimportant girl in an unimportant family in an unimportant town. I don't know what to do with all this formality."

"I get that. My family lives in Norostar, the capital city, so I always had royalty nearby. Lieutenant Polyer could probably relate to your problem, she grew up on a farm. She's told me she had a rough time getting used to all the formalities when she became a knight."

"She?" Carolyn asked, "Are there a lot of female knights? Like, is that normal?"

"Um..." Sarin gave Carolyn an odd look, "I don't...why wouldn't it be normal? I don't know how many knights are female, I never paid attention."

There was an awkward silence for a moment as Carolyn tried to figure out how to explain that this was abnormal while Sarin was looking at her like she asked if the sky is blue. Eventually Sarin broke the silence again. "So what did you want to talk about?"

"Nothing really," Carolyn shrugged, "I just feel so lost here. Everything is so different from what I'm used to. I don't know how to handle it all."

"Well, you can come talk to me anytime," Sarin nodded knowingly, "but next time we should find somewhere more secluded to talk. I could get in trouble if I were seen speaking with you so openly."

"Oh, I'm sorry!" Carolyn said quickly, "I didn't mean to get you in trouble. But wait, did you know I was a princess already? Like when you came to get me?"

"Yeah, we all did," Sarin said casually, "but I'm guessing you didn't. Your grandmother didn't tell you anything about where Naritha was from, I guess."

"Nope, nothing at all," Carolyn shook her head. "Anyway, I think I have to meet the King and Queen now, and I don't want you to get in trouble, so I'll see you later."

"Of course, milady," Sarin said formally with a bow and a smirk. He didn't move to enter the barracks until Carolyn had turned to walk away.

"So, where are we going to meet them?" Carolyn asked Merilda, who had been hanging around nearby during her conversation with Sarin and now moved quickly to join her with a thoughtful look on her face. "Is something bothering you?" Carolyn added.

"I..." Merilda started uncertainly, "I'm sorry for...I didn't mean to listen, but...you really didn't know you were a princess? This is all so foreign to you?"

"Really," Carolyn confirmed, "I'm used to helping other people out, not having everything done for me. Honestly, if I actually knew my way around this place and customs and stuff, I would take care of it all myself. Not that I don't appreciate your help, of course," she added quickly.

"I understand, milady," Merilda walked on in silence, guiding Carolyn down the hall to a small door on the right and knocking on it. A voice from inside permitted them entry and Merilda opened the door.

Inside was a small study. The King sat at a desk with a map laid out before him and a number of full bookshelves behind him. The room was lit with the same source-less magical light as the rest of the palace. Merilda bowed as she entered the room.

"Your majesty," she said without standing up, "Lady Carolyn has come to see you."

"Thank you, Merilda," the King said, glancing up from the map, "Please summon Treton immediately." Merilda dipped her head and backed out of the room.

"Please come in, Lady Carolyn," said the King, turning his attention to her. "Take a seat." He studied Carolyn as she closed the door and took a chair across from him.

"How are you feeling?" the King asked, his expression

soft.

"I'm all right, I guess," Carolyn replied, shrugging. "As all right as someone can be when they are met by a stranger in the middle of the night, told their necklace is a magical instrument of destruction, brought to another dimension, nearly die, and are told they're a princess."

"That's quite an ordeal you've been through," the King said with a sigh. "I'm sorry to have dumped this all on you. We are also going through rough times."

"Right," Carolyn blushed. "Sorry, I didn't mean to sound selfish or anything, it's just..." She trailed off, feeling guilty.

"I understand that our worlds are very different from each other," the King said, "I debriefed Sir Sarin personally and he gave me an account of what he saw. I didn't realize you weren't even aware of your heritage, or how different things would be here for you. I will try my best to be more accommodating of your needs and help you adjust to our way of life."

"Thank you," Carolyn said softly, still blushing. The King clearly cared very much to help, but Carolyn sensed that his care extended to all of his subjects, not just her.

"For now, we have other matters to take care of," the King continued, his tone business-like. "I never quite wrapped up your briefing on the current situation last night. To sum things up, we came here to hide out and plan while letting Ferdri take the castle. Based on his actions and those of his army, he seemed to intend no harm to the people, he only wanted the castle, presumably so he could pursue his selfish goals with the unicorns. After making numerous attempts at trying to isolate and kill his super-soldier, though, we started to get desperate, and came up with the radical, possibly very foolish, plan to retrieve the Derishz Ruby."

A knock at the door cut the King off and he called for the new arrival to enter. Merilda had returned, this time with an elderly man in tow. Though his carefully tended white beard and mostly bald head spoke his age, he stood tall, swathed in a long, dark yellow robe, a staff in his hand. The staff was very ornate, with a thick head that had the likeness of a unicorn carved into it, and an opal held securely in place at the top.

"Your majesty," Merilda said with a bow. "Archmage Treton has come."

"Thank you, Merilda," the King said with a nod of his head. "You are dismissed now."

Merilda again backed out of the room and Treton walked in. He gave a deep bow before closing the door and taking a seat beside Carolyn.

"Treton, this is Lady Carolyn..." the King paused momentarily, then turned to Carolyn, "My apologies, Carolyn, but I was never informed of your full name."

"Jones," Carolyn answered simply, feeling like such a plain name was out of place among royalty. "Carolyn Jones."

"Thank you. Treton, this is Lady Carolyn Jones," the King concluded as though nothing had happened out of the ordinary, "Carolyn, this is Archmage Treton Zavider, Head of Herin Wizardry and one of my advisors."

"A pleasure to make your acquaintance," Treton bowed his head to her.

"Nice to meet you, too," Carolyn replied.

"Now, as we were coming to," the King started, "Carolyn is here to use the Derishz Ruby to help us rout our enemies from the castle, primarily this 'super solider' of Ferdri's. The first question we have to ask is: how do we use it?"

"Beats me," Carolyn shrugged.

"I understand your experience with magic is limited, Lady Carolyn," Treton began. His voice was deep and rich, seeming too strong and confident for a man of such advanced age. "But you did manage to use it last night, from what I hear. Have you been able to draw upon it again since then?"

"Well, I've tried, and I felt like I could use it again, but I was scared I would burn something in my room, so I decided against it."

"I appreciate that," the King said with a slight smile.

"Good," Treton nodded. "You draw upon it by concentrating on the power inside you, right? Can you do that now? Don't use it! Just focus on it."

"Okay," Carolyn answered slowly. She concentrated on the now familiar feeling of magic inside of her. It responded immediately, filling her with a strength she didn't know she had. She held onto it and wouldn't release it like last time, keeping her focus on it instead. "Okay."

"Excellent," Treton nodded again. "Now can you try and move it around inside yourself?"

Not quite certain what she was doing, Carolyn tried willing the magic within her to move and felt that it *did* respond to her. When she focused on it, the magic seemed to fill her whole body, but she could shift the focal point around. It had been in her chest, but she could easily shift it to her shoulder, her leg, or even her hand. "It's working," Carolyn said, half surprised, half excited.

"Very good," Treton kept nodding. "Now hold out your hand and focus the magic there."

Holding out her palm, Carolyn again focused her magic into it. She could feel it thrumming inside her, willing to burst forth with but a thought. Yet to the casual observer, there was no indication of this power; her hand still looked like an ordinary, unspectacular hand.

"Now slowly release a small amount of it in your hand."

Carefully, she did so, willing the magic out, causing small flames to burst into life in her palm. Carolyn gasped, but didn't recoil or stop the release of magic; the fire didn't hurt her at all, though she could feel the heat from it. "Is it supposed to do that?" she wondered aloud.

"Not usually, no," Treton replied, "but we'll worry about that later. For now, retract the magic, and then try to push it out again, slowly and carefully, but this time into the Derishz Ruby." As he said this, Carolyn noticed the opal on his staff was glowing slightly and his brow furrowed.

Carolyn pulled the magic back in. Though the amount of

magic she released was brief, she could feel somehow that the power inside her was diminished. It was as if she had a vast reservoir of magic hidden in her body that was now missing a few drops. The difference was slight but noticeable. Ignoring it for now, she pulled out her necklace—drawing looks of wonderment and awe from both the King and archmage—and concentrated on moving the magic's focal point from her hand and into the Ruby.

The effect was instantaneous. She suddenly felt a massive reserve of power, so great she felt like it was choking her. It was like she was an ant that had been floating in space and had now crashed into a planet and couldn't figure out what to make of it or where to start. There was such immense power, so overwhelming!

But there was more. A strong desire emanated from this fount of power: a desire for destruction. Carolyn could see through it like a lens, one that tinted everything in red. She saw the King and Treton, and the power wanted to destroy them both; she could see the room around her, and the power wanted to annihilate it. Her vision expanded rapidly, soon encompassing the rest of the underground palace, all the people in it, all the belongings, and it wanted to destroy it all. There was hatred, hatred for all people, hatred for everything man-made. Her vision expanded further as the burning desire pressed against her, searching for more victims to be unleashed upon. She could see all of the forest around them, the river to the north, the capital city beyond that, full of more people that needed to be killed. It continued to probe, finding the castle they had escaped but the night before, filled with more potential victims—and something else. There was someone in the castle that it didn't want to destroy, someone the power felt connected to. Someone it wanted to reach, but couldn't.

Despite its overwhelming desire to act, Carolyn sensed that the power couldn't do anything of its own volition; it needed someone else's will to direct it. Eerily, she could tell that the power recognized this limitation as well. The more the vision expanded, finding more and more people it wished to see dead, it pressed itself harder and harder on Carolyn, trying to make its desires her own so that she would direct it and unleash it. Carolyn would not use this power to destroy so wantonly, she couldn't, but the strength of its insistence was so strong, it wanted to be released so badly...

"CAROLYN!" Treton yelled. With a gasp, Carolyn felt herself pulled back into reality. She immediately retracted her magic and broke the connection with the Ruby, dropping it like a hot potato. It hung innocently from her neck, belying its intense power. The opal on Treton's staff was now glowing brightly.

"Are you all right?" Treton asked, his voice trembling a bit; not just from fear, Carolyn realized, but also from great effort. She looked at him, reeling, remembering that burning desire to see him slain and shuddering at the thought.

"No," she answered firmly, "No, I'm not. What is this thing?!?"

The King and Treton shared a significant look that told Carolyn there was something she was not privy to, though neither seemed ready to admit it yet.

"What happened?" Treton asked, his expression grave.

"It wants to kill everyone and destroy everything. Death and destruction, that's all it wants."

"Then why doesn't it?" Treton asked, his brow creased with worry.

"I knew this was a bad idea," the King declared, leaning back in his chair and placing a hand over his eyes, "This is just another mistake I've made in handling this whole affair. I never should have sent for the Ruby."

Carolyn looked at him in surprise for a moment. In her brief meeting with him, the King exuded an air of confidence, yet he was showing serious doubts about his decisions. Carolyn had never seen that from an adult before. Was it a sign of weakness, or was it a positive trait?

"It can't," Carolyn explained, turning back to Treton, "I

don't entirely understand it. It seems to have desire, but no will of its own to carry out those desires. It tried to get me to do it instead."

"Was it speaking to you?" Treton sounded worried. The King took his hand from his eyes to look at Carolyn as well, also showing great concern.

"No, it was just... a feeling. I can't really explain it better than that." She shrugged in a gesture of helplessness.

"But you didn't listen," the King pointed out, sitting up straight again, "You resisted it?"

"She was slipping," Treton said somberly. "I was channeling a spell that would strengthen your resolve, Lady Carolyn," he explained. "I started trying to rouse you when I felt a power too strong for me to resist."

"So I guess that means I can't use it, right?" Carolyn felt deflated, realizing now that it was no great feat of her own mental strength that allowed her to resist the terrible desire, but rather Treton's magic. "If even *you* can't resist it for long, then how can *I* ever use it?"

The question hung in the air, answered only with silence. Carolyn was reflecting on her brash decision to abandon her home and family to embark on an adventure to help with something that, it now appeared, she couldn't even do. The King looked like he was contemplating alternate plans for how to kill Ferdri's super-soldier. Treton, on the other hand, was staring intently at Carolyn, still looking determined to get the Ruby to work.

"No," Treton finally stated firmly, "No, you can use it. You need to strengthen your mental capabilities in order to give you better ability to resist the Ruby's desires. And you need to have a better understanding of how to use magic so you can find the correct way to utilize its strength. I think if I can teach you how to properly control your magic, it should give you the strength of will you need to utilize the Derishz Ruby."

I'm going to learn magic? Carolyn said to herself. She meant to say it out loud, but she was so shocked by the suggestion that she seemed to have lost her voice.

"You really think it can be done?" the King asked, looking uncertainly at the archmage. "You say that even with your magic she couldn't resist."

"No, but she was close, I think. She has a strong will of her own, she was just ill-prepared to face the power in the Ruby."

"She can do it with proper training then?"

"I can't say for certain," Treton sighed, "since we have very little experience with the artifact. It would seem to be our best option, however."

Carolyn watched the exchange between the two older men eagerly. She was going to learn magic? Was that even possible? *Will I be able to shoot fireballs and fly?* she wondered. Excitement bubbled up inside her, threatening to burst out.

"How long will it take to train her to that point?" asked the King.

"Quite some time, I should think," Treton answered, "Even if I devoted all my time to her training, it would be months before we made any real progress."

All at once Carolyn deflated. Months? Just to make some progress? He sounded like he wanted to say years but was trying to sound optimistic. *How long am I going to be here?* She thought this would be a fun adventure. Come out, do something neat with her necklace, then get back home before excuses to her parents for vanishing had to get too complicated. How could she stay away for so long? *They're probably already worried about me...*

"All right, then," the King nodded finally, "Train her. Make it your primary task. Assign most of the managerial aspects of your position to one of your lieutenants in the meantime. At the same time, I will keep looking for other options."

"Of course, your majesty," Treton nodded.

"You are dismissed. Please keep me up-to-date with her progress." Treton rose to leave, bowing appropriately as he did so, while the King turned back to Carolyn, "If there's anything you need, feel free to ask Rissin for assistance, or come speak with me or the Queen. We will be happy to help you."

The door shut behind the archmage as he left, but Carolyn paid no heed. "How long am I going to be here?" she asked, failing to articulate well. The King gave her a quizzical look.

"I'm afraid I don't... you mean to say, you thought you were being asked to come for only a short time?"

"Yeah," Carolyn answered in a "no, duh" tone of voice, immediately regretting it when she remembered to whom she was speaking, "I mean, I didn't realize how long I'd be out, I guess, so I just assumed it would be quick."

"I see," the King leaned back in his chair, his expression lined with worry, "I understand that Sarin didn't have time to properly brief you on the situation. I doubt you could have known what you were getting into, but it's a bit late now. The portal device is the only way for you to get home and it's still in the castle, controlled by Ferdri. We couldn't get you back home now if we wanted to."

"So I'm stuck here?" Carolyn said, dismayed, "For months? Maybe even a year? But my parents will be worried about me! And I have school! I can't just be gone for months!" Her tone rose as she spoke, on the verge of hysterics.

"You didn't tell your parents you were leaving?" the King answered in surprise.

"Of course not," Carolyn scoffed, "they never would've let me go if I'd asked them. Besides, they were sleeping."

"Why wouldn't they have let you go? You're not so young, it couldn't have hurt to try," the King replied. "It doesn't make a difference now," he went on before Carolyn could respond. "You're here and there's nothing we can do about it. We will do everything in our power to take back the castle at the first possible opportunity and send you home. In the meantime, learn magic with Treton. If you do well in your lessons, you can help us rout Ferdri much faster than we could without you."

Carolyn felt the need to protest more, but saw there was no point in it. "All right," she sighed resignedly, accepting her fate. If she was going to be stuck in an alternate dimension embroiled in someone else's dispute, she might as well learn some magic from it, right?

"You are dismissed now," the King said kindly, "but as I said, don't hesitate to ask for anything you might need."

"All right, thank you." Carolyn mumbled, rising from her chair. As she reached her hand for the door she paused for a moment and turned around. "Do I have to bow to you when I leave?"

The King smiled at the question. "Only when there are others present," he answered, "but you should back out of the room when you leave."

Carolyn did so, closing the door after her. She was alone in the hall now. Tretor must've gone back to his room, wherever it was, and Merilda was nowhere to be seen. With nowhere else to go, Carolyn headed back for her own room, lost in thought. How was she going to explain her absence to her parents? How was she going to explain it to the school? Then again, if she came back with magic, maybe they would be more easily convinced. *That's a long time to go without seeing any friends or family, though,* she told herself, *and a long time for them to be worried sick about me.*

Opening the door to her room, Carolyn's thought process was disturbed by the discovery of strangers in her room. Merilda was there, of course, but there was also a middle-aged woman in a cobalt blue dress with many layers of skirts, whose graying brown hair was held in a neat bun with a couple thin braids wrapped around its circumference. Her pointed face looked weathered but kind. Next to her was a female knight who looked to be in her late teens, with short blonde hair and an expression of being out of place.

"Hi?" Carolyn offered by way of greeting. Merilda immediately walked up to her with a bow.

"Apologies, milady," she said quickly, "They only just

arrived and I let them in. I was going to come and inform you immediately."

"Ok," Carolyn answered, slightly unnerved. "Who are you?" she asked the older woman bluntly.

"I am Trelina of Cassens, milady," the older woman said with a deep bow. "I was honored when I received a request from the King himself to make a dress for a princess."

"You're making me a dress?" Carolyn wondered.

"You weren't informed?" Trelina furrowed her brow.

"Things have been happening very quickly since last night," Carolyn said in a tone she hoped was reassuring and not panicked. "Someone probably just forgot."

"Oh! All right, then," said Trelina briskly. "I brought with me a few dresses that you could try on. The Queen herself—I could hardly believe it, but it was the Queen herself!—wrote me a letter with an estimation of your height and a brief description of your complexion, hair color, eye color, and the like. Based on that I tried to pick out dresses that would suit you well. I'd be happy to make you a dress from scratch as well, as suits a princess, but since I don't think I'll be allowed to leave until you have something suitable to wear, I thought I might offer you an existing dress first that we can have fit to you."

"That works for me," Carolyn shrugged, noticing the dresses laid out on the bed. There was also a large sack on the floor beside the bed containing bolts of cloth of various colors and probably other supplies. The four dresses laid out on the bed were all very beautiful, much nicer than anything Carolyn had ever owned. One was an emerald green, one a dark purple, one ruby red, and the last was sapphire blue. Red was her favorite color, but she didn't like the style of the bodice, so she skipped over that one, and she wasn't a big fan of green. Both the purple one and blue one looked beautiful and comfortable, so it was hard to choose between them. The former was relatively simple, which she liked. The bodice was made of two pieces, the top layer a royal purple jacket that was sewn together right in middle of the chest, which then widened as it went down to show the second, lighter purple layer underneath. The skirt was straight, also a royal purple, and ended with a ruffled hem. It had long sleeves, which Carolyn hated, but they were wide sleeves that flared at the end, so they looked comfortable enough.

"I'll take the purple one," she said, pointing at it.

"Excellent choice," Trelina clasped her hands together before coming over to carefully lift the dress, "Please change and then we'll see what adjustments need to be made."

Carolyn wasn't used to changing with other people in the room, but that's what the changing screen was for, which was already standing ready in the corner. She took the dress and slipped behind the screen, making sure she was fully covered by it before undressing. It was actually a relief to take off the dirty clothes she'd been wearing since the previous morning. She did wish she had brought a spare change of underwear with her though. *Nothing to do about it now*, she sighed, *unless I can buy some here.*

The dress felt very soft and comfortable as she pulled it over her head. Taking a moment to try and straighten out the skirt, she saw that it actually fit surprisingly well. There were ribbons in the back for closing it up that she would need help with, but once it was on properly as best she could manage, she came out.

"Lovely," Trelina said as she saw her, with an odd look in her eye. Carolyn suspected she had felt some disdain for her other-worldly outfit. "Come and stand up here, please." Trelina gestured toward a footstool on the floor by the bed. Carolyn went over and stood on it, feeling like a trophy set up for display, as Trelina pulled out a measuring tape and the knight went to tie up the ribbons in the back. Soon the two of them were working together to examine various parts of the dress, seeing where it was loose and where it was tight, making notations, and talking between themselves. Carolyn didn't know the first thing about dressmaking, so she tuned it out. *But what is the knight doing here?* she wondered.

"How fortunate," Trelina sounded pleased as she finished her examination. "It actually fits you quite nicely. We have a couple small alterations to make, but it shouldn't take us more than a few hours, if we work together."

"Okay," Carolyn shrugged, "You can work here."

"I will go and find some more chairs so everyone can sit comfortably," Merilda offered.

"Yes, please do," Carolyn agreed.

"Wonderful," Trelina replied as Merilda headed out, "Madam Deeris, untie the ribbons so her ladyship can remove the dress."

"Of course," the knight called Deeris answered crisply, moving to help Carolyn. Once the ribbons were open, Carolyn went behind the screen again to change back into her dirty, other-world clothes. She joined the others just as Merilda returned with another servant, both carrying two finely crafted wooden chairs. The other servant was quick to leave after setting down his burden, shutting the door behind him.

Carolyn's initial guess was that the knight was there as a bodyguard—even though she didn't seem to be carrying a weapon—but seeing her sit down and help with the sewing seemed to discredit that conclusion. Why was a knight sent here to do sewing work? Why does a knight even know how to sew? Carolyn sat in silence and watched for a few minutes, mulling over these questions.

"I don't mean to sound rude," Carolyn asked Deeris, her curiosity finally getting the better of her, "but what are you doing here?" Deeris looked up from her work in surprise.

"I'm... sewing," she answered slowly, as though this weren't obvious. She shifted uncomfortably under Carolyn's attention.

"Right, I see that," Carolyn replied quickly, "but you're a knight. Why is a knight coming and sewing me a dress?"

"Oh, well we didn't want to bring any more civilians here than we had to, so I was asked to come help instead."

"Bring civilians?" Carolyn was missing some information here. "You mean Trelina? She was brought here?"

"Yes, milady," Deeris nodded, "This morning a pair of knights rode out to Cassens to bring her here and have an outfit made for you."

"Ok, but I still don't get why you're sewing."

"It's my hobby," she answered simply, as though this was a complete explanation.

"Your hobby?"

"Oh!" Deeris exclaimed. "I suppose you don't know about the laws of the Knight's Order." She lowered her sewing in her lap. "The order of Herin knights was established by Adenil in the formative years of the kingdom. One of the laws he established for all Herin knights was that they must have some manner of hobby not connected to their duties as a knight. He taught that if a knight does nothing but learn how to fight, they end up becoming a killing machine with no real meaning to their life. By having a hobby of some sort, something to spend your energies on that does *not* involve trying to harm others, it helps the knight to maintain a sense of humanity. That way they won't be overly eager to fight and kill and they won't give in to bloodlust or lose their sense of morality in the heat of battle."

"Really?" Carolyn asked, dumbfounded.

Deeris nodded.

"And does it work?"

"Mostly," the knight shrugged, returning to her sewing. "No system is perfect; there have been cases of knights who went into a rage in battle and have even killed innocents before, in extreme circumstances. But it's not common here. From what I've heard, knights of other kingdoms are much less... hmm, contained? I guess that's a good way to put it."

"Huh," was all Carolyn could think to answer. As she considered this, she noticed that Trelina was sewing with a sudden haste. She must've been discreetly listening, probably curious what a princess would talk about, and more so why she would be unaware of the knights' customs.

"Do you know what Sarin's hobby is?" Carolyn asked Deeris after a minute of silence.

"Who?" she asked, looking up from her sewing again.

"Sarin. He's one of the knights that came for me last night," Carolyn explained.

"Oh, so he's in Lieutenant Polyer's unit. No, I don't know him."

Carolyn nodded in silence, noting the name was the same one Sarin had mentioned earlier. Was it the same knight who had introduced herself to Carolyn when she'd entered the knights' barracks? The markings on her uniform could easily have been an officer's rank. Carolyn still had a hard time seeing that women were knights equally with the men. Not that the idea bothered her, *per se*, it was just so different from the way things were back home.

Carolyn lay back on her bed and relaxed, lost in thought, as the women in her room continued to work on the dress. The task probably would've benefited greatly from a sewing machine, but clearly those did not exist here.

A few hours later, Carolyn was finally up on the stool, modelling the dress again. She was delighted, and slightly relieved, to hear Trelina go on about how it fit her perfectly and how she now had an outfit suitable for a princess.

Carolyn walked over to the mirror to see herself in the dress for the first time. Her jaw dropped. She was stunning, even she had to admit that. Carolyn had never worn anything so beautiful and elegant in her life. Admittedly, she had never cared to; fancy was nice and all, but she preferred practical and comfortable. But at that moment, seeing herself in the dress, she felt for the first time like a real princess.

CHAPTER 4
Magic Lessons

After the dress was fitted, Trelina packed her supplies and prepared to go, but not before asking Carolyn to choose colors for two more outfits. She had been commissioned to provide a total of three outfits for Carolyn: two dresses and one wizard's robe. With Carolyn's measurements, Trelina could work on the outfits from her shop and bring them for final fitting once they were ready. Carolyn chose red for her robe, which she was actually more excited for than the dress, and blue for her second dress. Trelina left and Deeris returned to the barracks, leaving Carolyn to admire herself a little longer.

She moved around the room experimentally and found it took some getting used to doing simple things in such a fancy dress, but it was not stiff and didn't prove overly difficult. She went to wash her face in the bathroom without too much difficulty, but she didn't expect to be doing cartwheels or backflips any time soon. As she returned to the mirror there was a knock at the door. Merilda moved quickly to answer it.

"Yes?" Merilda asked questioningly as the door opened.

Rissin was standing outside.

"Queen Rorina has requested that Lady Carolyn come to her chambers," the steward replied most officially.

"Of course," Merilda nodded, turning to Carolyn. "Queen Rorina—"

"Yeah, I heard," Carolyn answered, coming over. *What could the Queen want?* Carolyn wondered. *Probably she wants to see my beautiful dress.*

Carolyn followed Rissin out, leaving Merilda behind, and followed him to the large double doors at the end of the hallway. The steward knocked and waited for approval to enter before opening the door and letting Carolyn in, closing the door behind her.

This bedroom was, understandably, a lot more extravagant than her own. The bed was a huge four-poster with large silk curtains, fluffy pillows and an embroidered satin duvet. On either side of the bed were small bedside tables, each with its own lamp. There was also a dresser, wardrobe, changing screen, mirror and writing desk here, but all of them were much fancier, with gold inlaid in all of them. There were also paintings on the walls of what looked like kings and queens of the past. Most prominent in the room, however, was the Queen herself, sitting on the edge of the bed with perfect poise, smiling broadly as Carolyn entered the room. Today she wore a beautiful dress of deep blue, her elegant crown on the table beside her.

"Hello, Carolyn," the Queen said in a soft, warm voice, helping to ease some of Carolyn's tension. "That dress is absolutely gorgeous."

"Oh, thank you," Carolyn said timidly, not having moved from the door. A minute ago it looked extravagant to her, but that was before she saw this room. Now she felt like a simple peasant playing dress up.

"Come in, please," the Queen beckoned, standing up. "No need to stand by the door. Come and give me a turn so I can see the dress better."

Carolyn moved forward awkwardly and gave a small

twirl. *I guess the Queen really* did *want to see my dress*, Carolyn thought as she turned.

"Excellent," the Queen nodded approvingly. "Now you just need some jewelry and makeup to complete the outfit." Queen Rorina walked over to her dresser and began opening some of the many drawers, pulling out a few choice pieces and setting them down on the desk. Then she began to take out small glass bottles and other containers, evidently holding makeup. Carolyn blushed deeply, uncomfortable with the thought of wearing the Queen's jewelry. Despite everything that had happened so far—and it had all happened so quickly—she still felt like a simple commoner who had no place among royalty. But refusing an offer from the Queen was impossible.

"Please," Carolyn started meekly after an extended silence. "No... You don't have to give me anything." The Queen turned to face Carolyn, her expression soft as usual.

"We are kinsmen, Carolyn," she said simply, "Do you not share among your own family?"

"Yeah, ok," she conceded with a sigh, still feeling awkward, "but no makeup, please; I'm not a fan of it."

"A fan?" The Queen looked confused.

"I don't like it," Carolyn explained. Apparently, even such a simple phrase was foreign here.

"Ah, all right," Queen Rorina nodded, returning the makeup to the drawer. Then she beckoned Carolyn over to look at the jewelry she had selected.

The Queen had laid out an impressive selection of jewelry. There was both gold and silver, simple and ornate, gemstones of various shapes, sizes, and colors. Most of the gems were amethysts, or something else purple, but there were also some blues, greens, and reds.

Carolyn picked each piece up delicately, like it might break if she weren't careful, as she examined it. The craftmanship was superb, far beyond anything she had seen before. Well, anything other than the Derishz Ruby. After trying a few things on and looking at herself in the mirror, she determined the silver looked better with her dress than the gold, and focused on those. After process of elimination, finally she made her selection.

The necklace she chose was long, with a round, turquoise pendant in it and smaller stones set into diamond shapes around it. She found a bracelet that wrapped around the stone set in it with the shape of a bird's head and wings on either side. She also took two rings, one for each hand, each with a simple setting. One of them had some kind of figure carved into the stone, but she didn't know what it meant. She skipped taking any earrings, though; Carolyn had never gotten her ears pierced.

Carolyn admired herself in the Queen's mirror, thinking that she really did look like a princess now. Just twenty-four hours ago she was sitting at home, feeling like a nobody, and now here she was in the presence of royalty and dressed as one as well. How had her life changed so drastically in such a short time? Even stranger, why was she not more excited by it? Most girls she knew dreamed of being princesses, yet Carolyn was living the dream and wasn't enjoying it. She left like an imposter placed in someone else's shoes that were too big for her to fill.

She noticed the Queen looking at her in the mirror and saw the look on her face. It was a look Carolyn recognized, the kind a parent gets when they're about to talk about something that they don't want to but know they have to. Carolyn braced herself for what was coming.

"Carolyn," the Queen started softly, "I'm sorry." Carolyn was taken aback. *That's not what I was expecting.*

"Sorry?" she questioned, turning toward the Queen. "What for?"

"We—the Herin royalty, anyway," the Queen began slowly, the usual conviction in her tone absent and her gaze averted, "have always viewed the Derishz Ruby as readily available in our case of need. We just assumed that Naritha would have instructed her heirs to be ready to come to our aid when we needed it, and we had but to ask. Now that you're here, we realized we were wrong."

The Queen's eyes were downcast and her normal composure seemed to be lacking. Carolyn felt like she was witnessing a rare event, the face of the Queen when there was no mask of royalty covering it. She was being perfectly honest, exposing her inner emotions, and Carolyn wasn't sure how to respond.

"We've taken you away from your life and involved you in a war that should have nothing to do with you," she went on, looking up at Carolyn now with a sad expression in her brown eyes. "It was wrong of us to do so, and I'm so sorry for it."

Queen Rorina sat down on the bed, looking away from Carolyn again, her face sorrowful. Carolyn wasn't sure exactly what to do. She had never witnessed one of her betters being so open with her about their feelings, nor did she think she had ever been in a position where she felt she had to comfort someone like this. *What am I supposed to say? What am I supposed to do?*

There were times Carolyn was feeling down and Rachel would try and talk to her to calm her down. On occasion, Robin had been with her when she was upset, and her method was usually just to hug Carolyn until she had calmed down a bit. The latter method usually worked better, but could she act so casually toward a Queen?

After a moment of awkward silence, the Queen closed her eyes and took a deep breath. When she opened her eyes again, she seemed to have recovered her normal composure. She looked back at Carolyn finally, smiling once again.

"I hope we can resolve this situation quickly so we can return you home," she said softly, the warmth returning to her voice, "I know that it must be hard for you here. I've been feeling that our customs are very different from yours."

"Yeah..." Carolyn said quietly, not quite recovered herself.

"We can talk about it, if you'd like," the Queen offered

as she stood up, "while we walk. It's just about time for the evening meal. You can ask me anything about our ways while we walk to the dining hall."

Carolyn nodded dumbly as she followed the Queen out the double doors and into the hall. She saw how the Queen walked slowly, with dignity and an air of command. She was also amazed by how modest she was, both in mode of dress and the way she carried herself, unlike famous female figures Carolyn was accustomed to. Yet she was still one of the most beautiful women Carolyn had ever seen and seemed to deserve all the respect she was given.

"Do you want to ask me about anything?" the Queen asked as Carolyn fell into step with her. Carolyn wasn't accustomed to walking slowly.

"Yeah," Carolyn answered slowly, recalling a comment the King had made earlier that day, "The King had said—what was it again?—he said I'm not that young."

"You're..." the Queen paused, seeming to consider where the confusion lay, "Well, here a person is considered an adult at the age of fifteen."

"Fifteen!?!" Carolyn nearly shouted in surprise. "But that's so young!"

"Why?" the Queen wondered. The question was not made with a challenging tone, but an inquisitive one, inviting Carolyn to provide her reasoning. "The most important development of a person's life happens during their teenage years, so what better time to expect them to have the responsibilities of an adult? Otherwise they may squander opportunities that may never return."

"But," Carolyn began, entering a narrow hallway with the Queen, "yeah, exactly, they're developing, so how can they even know what they want to do? It's such a confusing time. I mean, you were a teenager once, right? Don't you—Oh, sorry..." For a moment Carolyn had forgotten she was speaking with a Queen. Her cheeks started to grow warm.

"Yes, I was," the Queen answered with a smile, "and I remember it being a difficult time. I was rather vain at the time, I admit. I was born to a prestigious family and was accustomed to looking nice. If I hadn't been expected to help with the family business and had responsibilities to occupy my time and thoughts, I might have focused on my beauty for years.

"Wait, you mean you weren't born royalty?" Carolyn asked, surprised.

"No, I was not. I was born to a wealthy family from Welden, a city in Jerenair Province," she explained, "My family is the largest trader of gemstones in Herin. Most of the gems owned by the royal family were purchased from them, which is how I met King Ketra, then the crown prince of Herin."

"Ok, now I'm more confused. I thought royalty only married royalty."

"That would leave them with a very limited pool of possible marriage partners," the Queen noted as they entered a larger hallway facing a pair of large double doors, "though I can see the sense in it. But no, here princes and princesses can marry whomsoever they please, so long as the King and Queen approve of the partner. Usually they do, except when security concerns are an issue."

"Got it," Carolyn nodded. *But it still seems weird to me.*

They reached the double doors and the Queen pushed one of them open, guiding Carolyn inside. They entered into a very large room with big tables throughout. Directly opposite the doors, placed horizontally at the far end of the room, was the main table. Two large chairs, like thrones, were centered , facing the rest of the room. All of the tables in the room were set with plates, goblets, and platters spaced at intervals, but none were as lavish as the dishes on the main table. A few people were already sitting at some of the tables, including the main one, but none were eating yet. Carolyn noticed a number of knights, including Sarin, all sitting at the first table on the right.

As soon as everyone in the room noticed the Queen entering, they stood immediately. Carolyn continued to keep pace with the Queen, not knowing where she was supposed to sit or what else she was meant to be doing. Queen Rorina walked in silence, keeping her gaze fixed straight forward. Carolyn, on the other hand, kept looking around, consciously aware of the fact that she was being seen publicly in her new dress. She couldn't help but feel that everyone saw how ridiculous she looked, like a simple commoner playing dress-up. She tried not to look at anyone, but kept glancing around to see if they were looking at her. Every face in the room was turned toward them, but most of them seemed interested in the Queen only. The only face looking directly at Carolyn was Sarin's. When she noticed him, he smiled and gave a wink. Carolyn smiled back and quickly turned away, her cheeks growing even warmer.

The Queen walked up to the main table with Carolyn still in tow and sat in one of the large thrones, indicating to Carolyn to take the seat next to her. As the royalty sat, finally all others in the room retook their seats. Conversation resumed, but still no one ate.

"I still think fifteen is too young," Carolyn said after a brief silence. "Some people don't even know what they want to do with their lives until they're twenty, sometimes older; so how can you expect them to choose at fifteen? What if they make the wrong choice and they're stuck with it?"

"That's a valid point," the Queen replied. "In my experience, the people who don't know what they want to do until twenty haven't stopped to think about it until nineteen. Not everyone agrees with us on that, though. Some of our neighboring kingdoms say adulthood is not until later, even as late as twenty-five. Others have it as early as the age of twelve. I don't know for certain what's best, but fifteen is the age that works for us here."

"Twelve! That's crazy," was all Carolyn could think to say about that. After further consideration she added, "So wait, Sarin is an adult?"

"The knight? Of course. A squire can't be inducted as a full knight until adulthood."

"So he can get married already?"

"Yes," the Queen nodded, "though it's uncommon for a knight to get married at fifteen. They don't have much time for courting as a squire, and it takes time to meet someone and court them."

"Hmm," Carolyn grunted, then realized that wasn't very ladylike. "I see."

After that they sat in silence for a while. Nobody was eating yet, even the Queen, and Carolyn wasn't about to start eating before her, despite the grumbling of her stomach. Over the next few minutes, more people arrived, some individually and some in groups, moving to the various tables to take their seats. Finally, the doors opened again and this time the King walked in. Like with the Queen, everyone in the room stood and watched him as he walked across the hall. Everyone, that is, except for the Queen. Carolyn wasn't sure what to do, so she made to stand up, but the gentle pressure of the Queen's hand on her arm stopped her.

"Royalty need not stand for royalty," the Queen whispered, "unless you're visiting another's kingdom. Then you stand for your host."

The King came around the table from the opposite side as Carolyn and took the second throne-like seat next to Queen Rorina. Almost as soon as he sat, a servant came running up from a side door with a small tray holding a single roll, and offered it to the King. The King took the roll and bit into it. As he did, the clatter of silverware and dishes suddenly filled the room. Clearly the roll was a signal for the meal to begin. As Carolyn examined the array of breads, salads, and spreads set out on the table, servants started to come from the kitchen with delicious smelling, covered platters. Soon there were a variety of foods available at every table, with the most impressive platters sitting on the royal table. Carolyn spent a few moments staring in wonder at the fantastic display of food available before she finally began to dig in.

The royal table was the smallest of all in the dining hall and not every seat was taken when the meal began. As they ate, more people began to come in and joined the meal immediately. At her table was also Treton, a middle-aged man with a highly decorated knight's uniform, and a few other important looking people Carolyn had not seen before. These were probably the official advisors to the King and Queen. One thing seemed to be missing, but it took her a few minutes to finally realize what it was.

"Queen Rorina," Carolyn tried to say casually, not certain the correct way to get her attention, "Are there... Uh... Am I the only... Am I the heir to the throne?"

Queen Rorina put her fork down and turned to Carolyn with a smile, "Not really," she answered, "We sent our children off to safety when we fled here. We wanted to ensure the royal line survived in case anything happened to us."

"Oh, ok," Carolyn nodded, "So I'm not an heir. I think I'm happier that way."

"Technically, you could inherit the throne," the Queen mused, "though only if great tragedy befell us, and even then there are other, more closely related relatives of the Herin bloodline who would inherit first."

"That's a relief. I don't want the responsibility of taking care of a whole kingdom. It sounds like too much work."

"It certainly is difficult," the Queen nodded, "It's not a position anyone is really prepared for, but so long as a person has the desire to make it work, they rise to the occasion and find a way."

Carolyn spent the rest of the meal just listening. The King and Queen spoke with all of their advisors on various topics, so she was able to get a glimpse of what was going on outside the palace. Apparently there was now a stalemate between Ferdri's forces and Herin's troops. Originally, when Ferdri took over the castle, he also willingly took and held the responsibility of the kingdom as well. Most of the people were not harmed and were hardly even troubled by the change. Residents of the more remote towns probably didn't even know what was happening. Other than the King and Queen and their closest advisors, the governmental structure was left in place and everything continued to run.

So long as the people were safe, the knights were remaining in hiding here in Cansition while the formidable armies were holed up in various fortresses around the kingdom. Many of the fortresses near the capital were under siege by Ferdri's forces, but they had more than enough emergency supplies to keep them going for months. Others on the outskirts of the kingdom were left untouched. They were all ordered to remain and not to engage until a plan could be formed for dealing with the "super soldier" Ferdri had found for himself. So, in the meantime, Ferdri and his troops had free reign of the kingdom.

However, the status quo seemed to be changing. In order to stage the risky invasion of the palace to retrieve Carolyn and the Derishz Ruby, a feint attack had been staged by Herin knights not far from the capital. That meant most of Ferdri's troops in the area had been mobilized and were not available during the attack, hence the relatively minor resistance they met during their escape. But now Ferdri was making troop movements in the area in a way that boded attack, but the random pattern of the movements made it impossible to tell what his target was.

Even more troubling, however, was that no one knew what, if anything, Ferdri was after. It had been assumed that he simply wanted to continue his experiments on unicorns, and yet he had, thus far, made no attempt to even scout out the forest, the very forest where Cansition was hidden. Furthermore, while his troops were mainly not harming civilians, they had been traveling to many large cities in the kingdom searching for anything magical, but then never claimed the magical objects found. Theories abounded as to what he wanted to find, but no one knew for certain. The possibility that it was the Derishz Ruby itself was brought up but immediately dismissed; its continued existence was a closely guarded secret that was known only to the royal family. Ferdri could not have known of it; not even the other advisors knew until the plan was suggested to them by the King.

Carolyn woke up early the next morning and made it on time to breakfast. Merilda helped her into her dress and walked her to the dining hall, where they parted ways. Apparently, there was a smaller dining room next to the main hall where the servants would eat. She was the first royal to arrive, much to her surprise, and stood awkwardly in the doorway for a moment as the few people already seated stood and looked toward her patiently. She did her best to put on a royal expression and walk with purpose, the way the Queen had, but she couldn't help but feel she looked like a fool. Finally taking her seat, she did her best not to look around the room, certain that everyone was still staring at her.

It was only her second morning in Herin and already so much had changed. One day her biggest concern was finishing her math homework, now she was a princess soon to be fighting in a magical war. She was living the kind of life that many teenage girls would dream of—a princess with a personal servant, lavish meals, and fancy dresses. Not only that, but she would soon be learning how to use magic. It frustrated her then that she wasn't enjoying it. She kept feeling that everyone was staring at her, judging her, and knowing she didn't belong. It was like the shame she felt walking in late to gym class, only worse. Here she was *always* the center of attention.

"Lady Carolyn," a voice said beside her, jolting her out of her reflections all of a sudden. She jumped slightly as she looked up to see Treton sitting next to her.

"I'm sorry, I didn't mean to startle you," he apologized.

"No, it's fine," Carolyn answered quickly, "I was just thinking."

"A good habit to be in," Treton nodded, his serious tone

making it hard to tell if he was joking or not. "I wanted to ask that you meet me in my office after breakfast to begin your training."

"Already?" Carolyn brightened up quickly. "Where's your office?"

"Merilda knows, she can direct you to it."

"Great, I can't wait to start," she answered eagerly.

"Your enthusiasm is expected, but please remember to retain your patience as well," Treton smiled knowingly. "There is much to learn."

Carolyn opened her mouth to respond, but Treton quickly stood up as the King and Queen entered the dining hall together. They each walked past the table on opposite sides to take their seats, and then went through the same ceremony with the roll before everyone dug into their food.

Breakfast included many types of cheeses, jam, fish, fruit, and various spreads that Carolyn didn't recognize but looked appetizing enough. She was hardly paying attention to what she ate, though, her mind focused entirely on her upcoming spellcasting lesson. Carolyn had never enjoyed lessons much before; long lectures and lists of names and dates were never able to catch her attention. This was different, though, this was something from out of a fairy tale. She imagined she'd be given a wand—or staff, or something magical like that—and told what magic words to say, and then fireballs would shoot out wherever she wanted. Soon she would be an adept wizard, the best of the best, master of shooting fireballs.

It wasn't long before her mind wandered away from the subterranean dining hall to an intense battlefield, riding bravely into danger. She could see her enemies running in fear while her allies were awed by her mere presence. She started smiling to herself as she leaned back in her comfortable seat, enjoying the praise she received.

Except I hate when I'm the center of attention, Carolyn sighed, shaking herself from her reverie, *not that I'd ever be that great anyway.*

Looking over to Treton, she realized he was no longer present at the table, apparently having left while Carolyn was lost in thought. She stood up hurriedly and walked quickly out of the room, looking at the floor and avoiding what she was certain were the many staring faces of others in the room.

"Hi," Carolyn said hurriedly to Merilda as she entered her room. "Can you take me to Treton's office? I mean, if you're not busy."

"What would I be busy with?" Merilda furrowed her brow in confusion. "My job is to wait on you. I'll lead you there."

Carolyn stepped aside so Merilda could get out the door and followed her into the main hallway. It turned out Treton's office was just a couple door's down from the King's study. A reply came almost as soon as Merilda knocked and the maid opened the door. Carolyn stepped into a small room that looked very similar to the King's study. There was a desk, a few chairs, and a couple of bookcases filled with leather-bound tomes and scrolls. Treton was sitting behind the desk, reading from an old book, when Carolyn came in. His staff was resting against the desk beside him. He put the book down and stood quickly when Carolyn entered.

"Lady Carolyn," he said formally with a bow, "Thank you for being so prompt. Merilda, you may leave us," he added to the maid.

"Do you have to bow to me every time?" Carolyn wondered aloud as the door closed behind her.

"Of course, you are royalty," Treton nodded, still standing, "though if you prefer, we can put formalities aside so long as we are in lessons. I am not accustomed to teaching a royal."

"That's fine with me," Carolyn said as she took a chair by the desk.

"Excellent," Treton sat back down in his chair, looking relieved, "it will make things easier."

"Great, so when do we start?" Carolyn asked eagerly.

"Now," Treton smiled, "Before you can learn to use magic, however, you must understand what magic is. Given the gravity of the situation we find ourselves in and the urgency of completing your lessons, I'll give you the short version, but it's still important to understand before you start trying to use it."

"I used magic yesterday," Carolyn pointed out, "and I didn't have a clue what I was doing."

"True," Treton nodded, "but you also weren't attempting anything difficult. Well, not from a magical perspective at least. Obviously trying to control the Derishz Ruby—but never mind that for now. Our first lesson is to give you a solid foundation of what magic is and how it is used." Carolyn's shoulders slumped a bit. She could tell there was a long lecture coming. Hopefully this one would at least be interesting. She pulled her seat in closer and tried to look attentive.

"The world and everything in it are composed of a basic, physical structure," Treton began. "Though there are stark differences between animal, plant, mineral, and human, all are constructed from the same basic building blocks. In addition to the physical composition of the world, and the physics associated with them, there are other extant forces. The first and most easily recognized is the consciousness, a non-corporeal force in all humans and animals which gives them the ability to think, to feel, to reason. Some refer to this consciousness as the soul or spirit of the person, bestowed upon them by The Divine, while others say the soul is a separate entity.

"In addition to these, there is another force that permeates all of creation. This force is commonly referred to as 'magic'. It exists within everything, even the air, but it is not corporeal and cannot be sensed in the normal way. Inherently, from what we know, it does nothing. It is simply a force which exists and is available for use but doesn't do anything on its own. Think of it like a rock: it can be used to build, to destroy, or simply be sat upon, but only if someone comes and exerts physical force on it. Magic is a force that can be used for a variety of purposes, but only if someone comes along and applies *magical* force to it. Also, like with your physical body, which can tire itself after too much exertion, expending magical force can exhaust you. Think of it like your 'magical stamina'. You have the ability to exert magical forces, but you are expending a reserve within yourself by doing so. With rest, you can replenish this 'magical stamina.'"

Carolyn remembered that feeling when she tried using her magic the day before. It was slight, but she could tell that her small use of magic had somehow drained her reserve. It was a relief to know it wasn't permanent. *How much magic can a person use before they run out? Maybe I'll only be able to use a couple spells before I have to rest*, she worried, *so maybe I won't be any good with magic.* Treton didn't look strong physically, but he was an archmage, so that couldn't be the only factor, if it even was one. She tried to think what it would be like, being an archmage. She imagined herself launching spell after spell and never getting exhausted. Everyone would be amazed by how great she was. Soon she found herself back in the palace where she had first emerged from the portal, except this time she was throwing fireballs at all the enemy soldiers and standing at a safe distance where they couldn't reach her. A smile spread across her face as she handily defeated her foes.

All at once, Carolyn realized she had been day-dreaming again and snapped back to reality. *Why do I do that?* she berated herself. Even now, when it was an interesting topic and she really wanted to learn, she still couldn't manage to focus on it? She tried to quiet her brain's ramblings and focus again on Treton's words.

"...to create different effects." Treton was saying, leaving Carolyn wondering how his sentence had started, "For example, a ruby will allow for elemental magic to be used, while an emerald is used for enchantments. The way wizardry works is by taking a gemstone and placing a small amount of your magic within it, creating a permanent bond between you and the gem, and then casting your spells through the gem. This allows you to create much more powerful spells than you could have done on your own. This is the type of magic I'll be teaching you."

Carolyn tried to make sense of what he was saying, hoping she hadn't missed anything vital. Treton didn't seem to have noticed her lapse and was continuing as though nothing happened.

"There are other types of advanced magic, but most of them are frowned upon or even banned from use for various reasons. For example, druidism involves connecting one's magic with the forces of nature. While it allows the druid to harness the powers of nature to great effect, it also causes them to lose a part of their humanity and act with a more primal, animalistic nature. Needless to say, warlocks who use the power of demons are shunned. Other forms of advanced magic are used on occasion, such as ritual magic. It was actually ritual magic that created the bond tying the Derishz Ruby to your bloodline. That's very complicated, though, and not something you'll be ready to learn for a while. Did you understand all that?"

"Yeah," Carolyn answered with a nod, though really she didn't and hadn't even heard it all. She was too embarrassed to admit that she didn't pay attention the whole time. *What would he think if I can't pay attention to my first lesson?*

"Good," Treton nodded, "I can explain more about the different masteries when you're at the point that you can choose one. For now, I think we'll start on some practical lessons." Treton stood up suddenly, grabbing his staff, and started heading for the door, "Come with me, please."

Her embarrassment at letting her attention drift quickly turned to excitement at the prospect of a practical lesson. Carolyn followed the Archmage down the hall, toward the entry room. He led her to the front wall of the palace, near where the barracks were, but a door closer to the main entrance. Inside she found a large, open room with weapons hanging from the walls and some archery targets along one wall. Suddenly a number of weapons from the nearby wall started flying toward them. Carolyn jumped back in surprise, as they floated obediently in the air beside Treton, following him to the center of the room.

"Since we don't have proper facilities for magic lessons in Cansition," Treton explained, "the General has allowed me to make use of the knights' sparring room. It will be off-limits to the knights so long as we are here, so we don't have to worry about being disturbed."

Treton stood in the center of the room and turned to face her. The weapons that had been hovering beside them, which were a collection of wooden training swords, settled gently to the ground.

"The first and most important thing to learn is how to properly control your magic," Treton began, and Carolyn thought she could sense another lecture coming on, "You started the first part of this exercise yesterday. Focus on your magic now."

Carolyn did so. She focused on the odd feeling resting in the pit of her stomach and it immediately expanded, responding to her will. She felt its strength, waiting for her commands. This part of using magic, at least, she had gotten down pat. "Done," she said confidently.

"Now move it throughout your body, like you did yesterday. Move it down one arm, then the other, then each leg, one at a time."

"Ok," Carolyn concentrated, moving the focal point of her magic around inside her. It was an odd sensation as her shoulder started tingling from the magic passing through it, then her arm, then her hand. It was amazing how easily it responded to her, no different than flexing a finger or blinking an eye. She closed her eyes as she focused, moving it down her other arm, then each of her legs, as instructed.

"Excellent," Treton smiled, "you have wonderful control. Now try and do it faster. Move the magic into one hand, then instantly into the other."

"No problem," Carolyn was starting to feel confident. This magic thing wasn't proving too difficult so far. Standing with her arms at her sides, she moved the magic into her left hand, then tried pulling it as hard as she could into her other hand.

Before she was certain what had happened, a stream of fire came out of her left hand and slammed into her side. The stream split, passing across her stomach and around her back, before crashing into her right hand and vanishing. "Ah!" she shouted in surprise and pain at the heat of it. She pulled up her right hand to look at it; it seemed to have a lot of minor burns on it and it was throbbing. She didn't even want to think what had happened to her dress.

"Usually, that doesn't happen with *fire*," Treton said as he moved closer to inspect Carolyn's hand. He placed his hand under hers as the opal on his staff began to glow. The burn marks and the pain vanished as quickly as they had appeared. He then waved his hand again in the direction of her dress. Carolyn looked down quickly enough to see singe marks vanishing from it.

"That's useful," she noted, "So why did it happen with fire for me?"

"It seems you have an affinity for fire. It's an uncommon occurrence, to have an affinity. I can explain what that means more at a later time. For now it will simply pose an additional challenge for you in your training."

"What's that mean?"

"Take this exercise. Most students are quick to be able to move the magic around within them and grow overconfident, so we give them this simple exercise to remind them how difficult magic is. Usually they blast themselves with a little bit of magic, learn their lesson, and move on."

"But I nearly set myself on fire," Carolyn said with a hint of anger.

"That's an exaggeration," Treton stated flatly, "And I'm

a restoration wizard in any case, so there's little concern of serious injury."

"That's not very reassuring," Carolyn crossed her arms.

"I can live with that," Treton responded with the first hint of humor Carolyn had yet seen in him, "In any case, you will have to exert extra concentration to keep your release of magic as pure magic rather than fire."

"How?" she demanded.

"With practice. Try it now. Hold out your hand and slowly release magic from it and try to turn it into pure magic." Carolyn sighed, frustrated at the lack of explanation.

"All right." She held out her hand and focused her magic into it. Like the last time, she slowly released the magic into her palm and it came out as small flames. She focused on it, trying to still the flames, or change them, or something. She wasn't really sure *how* she was supposed to change or *what* exactly she was changing about it. Frustration welled up. She'd had no inkling that magic existed just a couple days ago and was now expected to understand its complexities. It made it difficult to concentrate on the task at hand, instead she was thinking up excuses for why she couldn't. Slowly she discarded those thoughts, conscious of Treton's watchful eye, and just concentrated on the magic coming from her hand.

Staring at her palm, watching the small flames flicker and lick the air, she felt herself connecting on a deeper level with the magic within. Up until now, the feeling of magic was like a large *something* inside her with a focal point she could move around. Now she could sense that it was made up of many tiny pieces, just like the body was made up of tiny cells, but each piece had different sides to it, and each side had a different effect. It was like having a thousand dice and each one had the same number face up. She focused now on the side that was showing, trying to turn it so a different side was showing.

It was a strange sensation; it felt like the side was weighted, like it was the default, but as she forced her will on it, she felt it start to give way, obeying her commands. She didn't know which side she wanted to turn it to, but one side seemed to natural slide into place as it turned. When Carolyn opened her eyes again, the flames had vanished. Instead a faint, red light was emanating from her hand.

"Excellent," Treton was smiling broadly, "The process to change the form of magic from an affinitive element to pure magic is difficult to explain until you've experienced it, and I've never experienced it myself as I've no such affinity. This was something you had to learn yourself and you performed admirably."

"Great," Carolyn found herself smiling too. She still wasn't certain what she did, but she felt accomplished for having done it with no real instructions to guide her.

"With pure magic, now we can really get to work. Start moving it away from yourself, slowly and carefully. Then try moving it around a bit in the air."

With a nod, Carolyn turned her attention back to her hand, now glowing red. Just like she moved it around within her, she felt she could move the magic away from her. Slowly she pushed it upward, the light expanding into a short tower of red emanating from her palm. She moved her hand a bit experimentally and found that the magic remained connected to it precisely, moving with her and always pointing away from her palm when she turned it. Next she tried moving it out in other directions, first directly away from her, then to the side. With Carolyn and her instructor bathed in red light from her glowing power, she found her confidence with it beginning to grow. It obeyed her perfectly, never deviating from her intentions in moving it. She tried drawing loops in the air, creating a figure eight, moving faster and faster. She watched as an intricate web of magic formed in the air all around her, surrounding her, with a faint warmth emanating off of it and giving her the feeling of power.

As it moved further, though, she could feel her reserves steadily depleting. As Treton explained, magic was not an unlimited resource, and this was a good test of how much she could utilize before she ran dry. There was still a lot in her, even with all the red glow that now surrounded her, but this was only simple moving about. Once she got to *real* spells she was sure it would run out a lot faster. As she considered these things, she began doodling in the air with red light, starting to form the shape of a dragon. Or at least, she thought it looked like a dragon, but her drawing skills left something to be desired.

"I think that's enough, now," Treton said finally, causing Carolyn to jump slightly. She was so focused on her magic she had nearly forgotten he was there. "Now retract it."

"Oh, like the plug on a vacuum cleaner?" Carolyn asked.

"A what on a what?" Treton's brow furrowed in confusion.

"Never mind. You mean to pull it all back in through my hand, right?"

"You can," he answered with a shrug, "but it can enter your body from anywhere, just like it can leave from anywhere. Go ahead and try."

Looking around at her random squiggles of magic, still obediently hovering in the air as she had commanded them, Carolyn began slowly moving it all inward. She could feel the warmth emanating off of it as it reconnected, like a warm blanket providing comfort on a cold night, absorbing into her flesh like a sponge. Soon the last vestiges of it had returned and she felt her reserves renewed.

"Very good," Treton nodded approvingly, "As you noticed, you maintained a connection with your magic the whole time. The next step is to detach it from yourself. Try it with a small amount at first: release a bit of magic, detach it, and then try to move it."

Carolyn gave a brief nod and held out her hand again. She released a small amount of magic, then attempted to convince it to detach itself. Figuring out how was an ordeal. The magic wanted to cling to her, refusing to let go. Moving her magical energy about was something as natural as moving her arm, but that meant she was treating it as an arm, and convincing her hand to fall off wouldn't work. Once she realized this, it was a simple matter to change her thought process and treat it more like a wad of clay.

It took a minute of focus, but it was easy enough to pull the clay apart, leaving a small bit of magic hovering in the air above her hand. She attempted to move it now that it was separated, but found that she couldn't feel it anymore, at least not in the same way. She could still feel the warmth of the magic and some kind of connection, but it wouldn't budge when she told it to, like a finger that had been cut off.

"I can't move it," she finally admitted after a couple minutes of trying, "It's as stubborn as I am."

Treton smiled. "That's right, you can't. Once magic has been disconnected from its source, it can no longer be controlled."

"So in order to cast a spell, I always have to keep my magic connected?"

"On the contrary, the only way to cast a spell is by disconnecting it. Once you have broken your connection with your magic, it will follow whatever 'instructions' you gave it before disconnecting it. In this case, you gave it no instructions, so it merely stays in place. A spell is when you provide your magic a set of instructions and then disconnect the magic required for that spell."

"Oh, so I send my magic on special missions. Got it."

"I suppose so," Treton answered, bemused. "Your manner of speech is very...foreign to me."

"So what am I supposed to do with this," she said with a wave of her hand to indicate the floating light.

"That's the next essential step. Even once you've disconnected the magic from yourself, you still maintain an unseen connection to it. This allows a wizard to abolish any magic created by them at a whim. Merely think it away and it'll vanish."

Though her rogue, magical light refused to obey her other commands, Carolyn found that it responded immediately when she attempted to wish it away. The small bit of magic vanished, leaving no trace behind.

"This is an important lesson," Treton continued, "Many spells are persistent and will last until abolished. Especially when you find yourself in a battle, you must know how to remove your spells on a whim as the need arises."

"Great, so now can I learn some actual spells?"

"Patience, Carolyn; nothing worthwhile comes without effort. But now you will learn the most basic spells: Pulling and Pushing." One of the training swords at Treton's feet floated up and into his hand. "Pushing is the easiest spell to perform and the most straightforward. When you push something with your hands, you exert physical force in one direction away from yourself. It's the same thing with a push spell: exert magical force in one direction away from yourself. The harder you want to push, the more force you exert. Try pushing on this wooden sword."

"How hard should I push?" Carolyn wondered.

"As hard as you like."

Carolyn took the challenge with enthusiasm. She focused her magic into her hand, held it out to face the wooden sword, then shot out a huge amount of magic toward it. She well expected the sword to go flying out of the older wizard's hand, but to her surprise it merely wobbled wildly but remained held steadily in place.

"Why didn't it work?" Carolyn wondered aloud.

"For a couple reasons," Treton started, sounding like a lecture was coming, "For one thing, you're just a beginner, so your magic is still weak. When you used it for the first time in the palace, you probably expended all or at least most of your magic at once, so it appeared to be strong, but now when you're using small amounts, you can see that it's not. Secondly, you're not being careful with your magic, you're simply shoving it out wildly. You hit the sword for sure, but much of your magic simply went around it as it wasn't focused on the sword itself. I should also point out that you never disconnected your magic, so it wasn't actually a spell," he added.

"Ok," Carolyn answered, feeling chided. She took a breath as she readied herself to try again. Gathering her magic for another attempt, Carolyn focused this time on the wooden sword and again shot out her magic, remembering to disconnect it as it went. This time the wooden sword noticeably thrust itself backward in the archmage's hand. Though he kept a firm hold on it, Treton was now smiling.

"Much better," he said, "try again, harder this time."

Carolyn continued to practice pushing on the sword. Each time she tried, her focus was a little better and her push was a little stronger. As she got better, Treton shifted his position so that if the staff went flying out of his hand it would not then smash him in the face. After what seemed like an hour of trying, the sword finally went flying out of the archmage's hand, hitting the ground with a loud clatter. After that, Treton set up the rest of the wooden swords on the ground around Carolyn and had her practice pushing outward in all directions, shoving all the swords at once. By that time, she was running low on magic, so she couldn't make many attempts before having to call it quits for the day. Treton assured her he was very pleased with the progress she had made.

CHAPTER 5
Life in Cansition

During the next week, Carolyn continued to improve in the basics of magic. She had mastered Pushes—anything around her, a specific object amongst a group, even Pushing a specific set of objects among a group. Next came the Pulling, which was a little harder, but once she understood the concept, she took to it rather quickly. The more she practiced, the more naturally the magic came to her, and the more of it she seemed to have available. By the end of her first week, she was already able to call on her magic at a whim. Treton kept saying that she was advancing faster than average for a beginner, but she was pretty sure he was only trying to compliment her because she was royalty.

Just as exciting, by the end of her first week, a delivery arrived at the palace for her. Trelina and her apprentices had been working hard to fulfill their royal commission. A robe came, almost perfectly fitted for Carolyn. It was maroon with ruby red highlights and suited her perfectly. There was a patch on the left side of the breast that prominently displayed the Herin coat of arms. It needed some minor fitting work, but Deeris was able to take care of that for her.

The next day, Carolyn proudly wore her new wizard's robe and never looked back. She got the impression that some of the nobles were unhappy with her dressing as a "common wizard" rather than as a princess, as befit her station, but she didn't care. Queen Rorina made one comment about it, but made it evident that the choice was Carolyn's in the end and they would respect that choice. Carolyn appreciated that; dresses were never much her style.

Carolyn's life also started to develop a regular pattern. She would go to breakfast in the morning, head to magic lessons after that, then rest up before lunch. Her afternoon was free, so she spent the time looking over maps of the kingdom to get an idea of where she was. Carolyn always loved looking at maps and had soon memorized the names of all major cities near the capital. She also tried learning a little more of Herin's history—but quickly became bored with that—and customs—and quickly became overwhelmed with that. When she wasn't trying to study anything, she would often go to the knights' rec room and spend time just chatting with Sarin and his friend Elis.

Unlike Sarin, who was energetic at best and boisterous at worst, Elis was much more reserved. He was not without a sense of humor, but spoke in much quieter tones and had benefitted from a fuller education. The difference was partially in their upbringing, Carolyn surmised. Sarin had been the son of a poor shoemaker and had never been patient or gentle enough to learn his father's craft. Apparently, it was a great honor to a family to have their child join the knightly order—and there was a stipend in it for the family as well—so when Sarin announced his desire to join his parents were happy that he had found his calling.

Elis, on the other hand, came from a wealthy family that ran a security business, hiring out guards to institutions, merchants and noblemen all over the kingdom, as well as providing insurance. He'd had little interest in the family business, however, seeking to find a more fulfilling life for himself. His parents were less thrilled about him joining the knights, but supported him nonetheless. Both Sarin and Ellis had grown up in the capital city of Norostar and had been friends from a young age. When they were old enough, they had signed up to join the knights together.

The two knights would talk about life in Herin, which to Carolyn sounded amazing, and she would tell them about her world, which to them sounded bizarre.

"You'd never ridden a horse before you came here?" Sarin asked her one such afternoon. He and Elis had been teaching Carolyn a card game with confusing rules while they chatted. "What, you walk everywhere?"

"No, we have cars," Carolyn answered like this was obvious.

"What's a car?" Elis wondered.

"It's a machine we use to drive around," Carolyn explained simply, not accustomed to describing a vehicle.

"Oh, another machine," Elis nodded; she'd tried explaining them before, "How does it work?"

"Honestly, I don't really know," she shrugged, "It has something to do with creating an explosion from fuel—or something like that."

"It explodes?!" Sarin was wide-eyed. "Is it safe to get in those things?"

"Well, yeah, of course."

"Even though it explodes."

"It only explodes inside, like in the engine," Carolyn tried explaining, "in the machine part."

"I'd take a horse over an exploding machine any day," Elis chuckled.

"But it's really fast, much faster than a horse."

As Sarin opened his mouth to respond, a shout from behind cut off all conversation.

"Sarin! Elis!" the voice shouted. It was Lieutenant Polyer, the same female knight Carolyn had met when she first walked into the barracks. She also happened to be the officer that headed Sarin and Elis' unit. She had a fierce look on her face that told Carolyn the two knights were in trouble. They stood quickly and turned around to face her, standing at attention. The officer gave them a glare like she was trying to melt them as punishment.

"You're late for roll! We began six minutes ago! Explain yourselves!" She spoke in harsh tones, but without yelling or losing her temper.

"We lost track of time," Elis admitted, "It was careless and inexcusable, madam."

"It won't happen again, madam." Sarin added quickly.

"It wasn't their fault," Carolyn spoke up, coming to stand next to her friends; she hated to see them berated like that, "It was my fault, I was distracting them. Please don't be upset at them for it."

The lieutenant turned her gaze on Carolyn, her expression softening as well as her tone. "I appreciate that you're trying to help your friends, milady, but they have their duties and must be held responsible for them. It's no fault of yours if they're slack in them."

Carolyn couldn't think of anything else to say. She glanced at Sarin with a feeling of helplessness. Though he kept his focus on his commanding officer, Sarin gave her a quick sideways glance that seemed to say "it's ok". Carolyn looked back at the lieutenant and saw she was still looking at her. Being a royal meant any interaction with her could not be dismissed out of hand. The thought of using that as a means to help somehow occurred briefly to Carolyn, but she couldn't think of how and figured it would just get them in more trouble. Finally, she nodded to indicate she had nothing more to say.

Lieutenant Polyer turned back to her chastened knights and immediately her expression hardened. "Get going. We'll discuss repercussions for your carelessness after roll."

"Yes, madam!" the two knights said in unison, giving a quick salute. For all their normal gusto and bravado, the two turned tail like frightened dogs and hurried off to the knights' equipment room. They both gave Carolyn a bow as they walked past and a quick "Milady", but nothing more.

After they left, Carolyn realized the officer was still there, and she seemed to be waiting for Carolyn to notice her.

"May I speak frankly for a moment, milady?" she said politely. It was the kind of question that seemed to say a lecture was coming, but even with permission to speak openly, would she dare to give such a lecture to a royal? Carolyn decided to give a chance, though.

"Sure," she tried to say casually, though feeling tense.

"I understand that you find yourself in difficult circumstances," Polyer started, speaking in soft, reassuring tones, "that before we brought you here, you were a commoner with no notion of royal duties."

"That's right," Carolyn nodded.

"I can't say I really know how that feels, but I think I have an idea. I started off as a commoner, and now I'm a knight with the need to speak properly, care for duties, and worry about things much bigger than myself."

"Yeah, it's kind of a bore, honestly."

"Sometimes," Polyer smiled, "but it's important to hold yourself to your duties once they come, even if you never asked for them. If you'd like, I can come by sometime and we can talk about how you're feeling."

She's... offering to help me? Carolyn wondered, trying to see through her intentions. She didn't have any real connection to Polyer; an offer of support seemed to come out of nowhere. It took a moment of awkward silence for Carolyn to consider how to answer her. "Sure, I think I'd like that," she said finally.

"By your leave then, milady," the lieutenant bowed low, smiling at the young princess, before following her knights into the equipment room.

Carolyn headed back to her room, confused. Polyer was very difficult for her to read: one minute she looked like a raging demon rebuking her charges, the next she was smiling sweetly like a kindly matron. Then there was her combat face, that steely-eyed determination Carolyn saw staring her down in the palace, the look of death. She couldn't shake that image from her mind; it always came to her when she was speaking with Polyer. She couldn't understand what she was: kind or cruel? Sweet or violent? Maybe some mix of all of them? And now this offer to give advice?

Not that she didn't appreciate it. If there was anything Carolyn needed most, it was someone to confide in. *What I wouldn't give to have Robin here!* she told herself. Sarin and Elis were great friends and she loved spending time with them, but she could never meet with them outside of the rec room. Apparently, it was not appropriate for young knights to have a private audience with a princess in her bedchamber, so they could only ever meet in public. Most of the other knights seemed to be intimidated by her royal status, so few of the others ever spoke to her. Some of them were slowly warming up to the idea in the past couple days, but they still spoke reservedly, clearly conscious of her status.

Polyer was the exception to all that. She had approached Carolyn willingly that first day in the rec room and has since not been scared to initiate conversation with her. Mostly they exchanged pleasantries, but she could always tell that she made a genuine effort to speak in a familiar way. Thinking back on it, Carolyn realized that she had always been concerned with her well-being. *Maybe she sees in me what she herself had to go through?*

Arriving back at her room, Carolyn flopped down onto the bed, laying on her back with her hands behind her head, and just let her mind wander. She spent the rest of the afternoon lying there, thinking, wondering again what kind of situation she'd gotten herself into, and how and when she would get back out. She never knew an adventure came with so many boring parts—or responsibilities—or that the exciting parts were so frightening.

The next morning, while taking her magic lesson with Treton, all these thoughts were still running through her mind, leaving her distracted.

"It seems like you're not even trying now," Treton

sighed, "You need to focus, Carolyn."

Treton had dropped all pretenses of formality during their lessons, speaking with her freely like he would any other student. Carolyn appreciated this more than he could know, but it also meant criticism came more easily and sometimes sounded harsher than he meant it.

They were practicing the crush spell, which was as exciting as it sounded. It involved concentrating a large amount of magic around a single point, then compressing it inward suddenly. It was essentially like wrapping a magic fist around your target and squeezing as tightly as possible. The strength of the spell varied according the effort you put into it, like with most spells. At its weakest, you could apply light pressure and make someone feel like a million pins are tickling their finger, but at its strongest it could crush a human skull. Carolyn was practicing on an inflated leather ball, not much smaller than a basketball. The leather ball was too tough for a beginner to burst, but she should have been able to squeeze it enough that the stopper would pop out and deflate it. She was nowhere near that point.

"Yeah, you're right," Carolyn shrugged. *No point in arguing about it,* she thought.

"Is something bothering you?" Treton asked. He sounded genuinely concerned, but Carolyn didn't feel like he was someone she could unburden herself to.

"No..." she lied, "Maybe. I just have a lot on my mind right now."

"I understand," Treton nodded knowingly, "I..."

"No, you really don't," Carolyn said bluntly with a shake of her head, "I don't mean to be rude or anything, but I don't think you've ever been plucked out of your home, sent to another dimension, and left to fight for your survival in a weird, underground castle."

"Uh, well no," Treton stammered, taken aback by the outburst, "I suppose I haven't." He seemed at a loss for words as he eyed his young student with surprise.

"Well, I have," Carolyn continued, unable to stop herself

now that the dam had burst, "and I can tell you that it's pretty life-shattering. Everything here is so different to me, nothing seems to make sense, and people are treating me as way more important than I deserve." She kept telling her mouth to stop and control itself, but it didn't seem to want to listen. All of Carolyn's concerns from the past few weeks came pouring out like a fountain and washed over Treton, who was the one unfortunate enough to be around when it came gushing out.

"Now I find myself training to use magic, which I'll probably never be good at, and am expected to use an evil apocalypse necklace of doom, which I probably can't control, to somehow save the day! In the meantime, my parents are probably at home worried sick about me. They might even think I'm dead by now, and I can't even call them or send them a text to let them know I'm okay. Not to mention all the schoolwork I'm missing. My life as I know it is pretty much a wreck at this point and I don't know if I'll ever be able to recover! It's all a bit much to handle."

Once she had unburdened herself, Carolyn suddenly felt exposed. She wished she hadn't said anything, that she could take it all back somehow, but it was too late. She wasn't one to be so open about her fears and concerns; having laid them all out to someone she barely knew was uncomfortable, to say the least. The archmage had regained his composure during her tirade, and was looking at her gravely.

"You're right, Carolyn," he said with a nod, talking in a soft, comforting voice, "It's a lot for us to have put on you and we're truly sorry, you must believe that."

"No, you don't have to be sorry," Carolyn said quickly. "I'm sorry I got so upset like that."

"It's all right, you've done nothing wrong," the older wizard responded. There was a brief, uncomfortable moment of silence between them before he spoke up again, "Do you mind if I ask you something?"

"Sure?" Carolyn was uncertain, but felt too guilty to say

no.

"Do you have any older siblings?" Treton asked.

"Oh," she blinked a couple times. *Wasn't expecting that.* "Yeah, an older sister, Jessica."

"I see," Treton nodded knowingly, "And do you know why it is that your grandmother entrusted the Derishz Ruby to you and not to her?"

"I—" Carolyn paused. She had never considered the question before. When she was first given the necklace, not knowing anything was significant about it other than the fact that it was clearly very expensive, she assumed Jessica had received a similar necklace on her twelfth birthday as well. Jessica never mentioned it, but neither had Carolyn, so she figured they were both keeping it a secret like they were instructed to do. Now that Carolyn knew it was a unique artifact, the question suddenly seemed very obvious. *Why didn't Grandmother give it to Jessica?*

"No," she admitted, "I don't."

"Hmm," the archmage nodded again, "And tell me, if Jessica had been the one Sarin met when he went through the portal and had asked her to come along, would she have agreed?"

"No way," Carolyn shook her head emphatically. "She's not into adventure and excitement like I am, she's more into makeup and spending time at the mall."

"I see." Treton turned away from Carolyn so she could only see his profile, but he had a thoughtful look on his face. Something seemed to make sense to him, but Carolyn couldn't guess what it was; she was still busy pondering the question he had put to her. "I think we should conclude our lesson for today, Carolyn. Take the rest of the day to relax."

"Thanks," she said slowly. Without another word, she turned and walked out of the practice room. Once on her own in the large entry hall, she leaned against the wall for a good, long while. What about all her complaints caused Treton to ask about her sister? And why was it important whether or not she would have come with Sarin? But most importantly, why was Carolyn the one given the Ruby?

All these thoughts and more ran through her head as she struggled to make sense. Absent-mindedly she started walking while thinking it all through and found herself headed for the knights' rec room. She stopped for a moment with her hand on the handle, wondering what she was planning on doing in there. She took a moment to collect herself before opening the door and walking in.

A lot of knights were in the rec room at this time, all engaged in various activities. She caught a glimpse of Elis with a few other knights at the far end of the room, lounging around and chatting. He saw her and made to get up to come over, but Carolyn looked away and continued to scan the room. In the meantime, all the knights nearest her were standing at attention, wary of the presence of a royal. Finally, not finding whom she was searching for, she turned to the nearest knight.

"Where's Lieutenant Polyer?" she asked directly.

One of the female knights standing nearby quickly stepped forward, bowing to Carolyn as she did so, and responded for her companion. "Lieutenant Polyer is in the knights' quarters, milady. Would you like me to go and summon her for you?"

"Yes, please," Carolyn responded with a quick nod. She waited while the knight rushed to enter the women's quarters, standing impatiently amongst a group of anxious knights. They were all accustomed to seeing her at this point, but usually she was hanging out casually and not making demands. Her current demeanor seemed to have caught many of them off-guard. Presently Polyer came out the door followed by the knight that had gone to fetch her. In her usual manner, she approached Carolyn with crisp etiquette and bowed formally.

"You wish to speak with me, Lady Carolyn?" she questioned. Her tone sounded curious, though her eyes showed she understood Carolyn was here to make good on her offer.

"Yes," Carolyn nodded, "Are you available now, or would you prefer after lunch?"

"I am available whenever milady wishes to speak with me," she responded formally, "though seeing as the midday meal will commence in under an hour, I would think that after would be a better time for us both."

"All right, I'll see you then," Carolyn nodded again. She abruptly turned around and left, heading back to her room.

After lunch, Carolyn paced her room, waiting for Polyer to arrive. Merilda waited with her, watching her mistress anxiously, too timid to try and talk. As Carolyn tried figuring out what she was even going to say, and starting to think this was a terrible idea, there was a firm knock at the door. Carolyn almost went over and answered it herself, but Merilda was there first and cracked it open enough to see who it was. She then turned to announce Polyer's presence.

"Let her in," Carolyn said quickly, "then you can wait in your room." She was afraid she may have sounded curt, but she was too preoccupied to think about that now. Polyer came in, with the normal bow and "Milady" while Merilda closed the door and retired to her room. When she was gone, Carolyn offered the desk chair to Polyer while sitting on the bed herself.

"Thank you, milady," Polyer sat down properly while Carolyn started thinking about how their entire conversation would be littered with "milady's" and how it would drive her crazy. Silence descended. Polyer seemed to be waiting for Carolyn to say something, but she was too nervous to speak.

"May I speak freely in our meeting, milady?" Polyer asked finally.

"Yes!" Carolyn nearly shouted, "Yes, please!"

"Of course," Polyer smiled, and as she did, she seemed to relax in the chair, even slumping a bit, "You're not the only one who gets tired of formality. I've been surrounded by it for seven years."

"I don't know how anyone does it. It drives me nuts. Why can't people just call me Carolyn? I'm not a lady!"

"Well, you are a lady," Polyer shrugged, "but I can call you Carolyn if you prefer, at least in private."

"You have no idea how much I'd appreciate that," Carolyn answered with a smile.

"I think I do. That's why I'm here, after all," the knight smiled in return, "My own first name is rarely used. It's Isana, by the way."

"Isana," Carolyn repeated, "that's a nice name."

"Thank you, I've always thought so."

"So, Isana," Carolyn started, "How did you come to be a knight?"

"That's quite a story, actually," Isana sighed, a glimmer of sorrow flashing in her eyes, "Are you sure you want to hear it all?"

"Not if it upsets you, no," Carolyn said quickly.

"No, it's all right," Isana smiled again, though the look in her eyes was still there, "I was born a farmer in the northern village of Ransefried, at the foot of the mountains. It's a nice, quiet village. Lots cf open pasture for animals, plenty of space for crops. The cnly problem is the bandits."

"Bandits?" frowned Carolyn, "That doesn't sound good."

"It's rilly not," Isana added with a shake of her head. As Isana spoke, Carolyn noticed her proper tone slipping instead into accented speech. All of her e's turned into ih's and her i's seemed to turn into uh's. This must've been her natural way of speaking, something she normally kept hidden from the world. "They live in the mountains, trubs of barbarians with primitive, warrior socuetis. They usually live us alone, but on occasion, raiding partis of bandits come down and attack us and other nirby villages."

She told Carolyn—who struggled to understand the accent at times—how the bandits had wiped out the local fortress one day in a surprise attack, and then took over the village. A band of mercenaries, Razik's Ruffians, came along and accepted the job to drive out the bandits, which they did with surprising efficiency.

"We were very apprihensive at first," Isana explained, "they were not a veri large band, maybe thirti altogether, but they had a certain... confidence about them that strengthened our resolve. It turns out, that confidence was justifud. One of them was a powerful enchantress by the name of Jiselda. They were all talented futters, really, but it was Jiselda that tipped the scales. I didn't know anithing of magic at the time, but her spells were able to throw the barbarians into disarray and she single-handedly carved through mani of them herself. There were over a hundred of them, but Jiselda and her alluz won the fut."

"And just like that, the village was saved," Carolyn smiled, always glad for a happy ending.

"Not exactli," Isana sighed.

She went on to explain how the mercenaries demanded payment, despite the village having lost so much. They took almost everything of value that was left in Ransefried, leaving the villagers to wonder how they would survive the winter.

While they made preparations, Isana secretly left the village to head south for the capital. As a bull-headed fifteen-year-old, she had every intention of telling the King off for not sending aid when they needed it. Upon arriving at Norostar, however, she found out the King had just been killed in battle and she arrived on the day of his funeral. She learned only then about the fighting on the western border that was occupying so many of their troops and was the real reason there were none to send up to Ransefried.

After spending a few days in the capital, she attempted to see the new King, with no success, until she happened upon his carriage in the street. To her surprise, King Ketra heard her cries to see him and invited her to speak with him, listening sympathetically to her plight. He then pledged to send troops and supplies within a few days and they would take Isana back home with them. By the time she was ready to leave, she realized that wasn't what she wanted to do anymore.

"So you joined the knights then," Carolyn nodded.

"Uh did. It took *a lot* of getting used to. Caring for animals and crops usually meant kipping to a strict schedule, but as a nut it was even more so. I had to learn to speak proper—" Isana switched suddenly back to her unaccented speech, "—and I was reprimanded more than once for acting out of line. Eventually I trained as an officer, and I got to where I am now."

Isana sat quietly after finishing her story. There was an air of relief about her. Carolyn surmised she had not shared the whole story before, at least not since she'd told the King, and it was therapeutic for her to get it all off her chest for a change.

"It's not easy," Isana said sagely. "I was accustomed to responsibility from growing up on a farm, but as a knight people have certain expectations of you, and I kept doubting my ability to live up to them."

That's exactly how I feel, Carolyn thought, nodding. "And how do you feel now?" she asked.

"The same way, honestly. Sometimes being responsible means always worrying that you're doing a good enough job. The few times I felt overconfidence in my abilities were exactly the times I made the worst mistakes."

"That sounds too stressful," Carolyn sighed. "No fun at all."

"Sometimes the things that are worth doing are not very fun," Isana said with a shrug, "but they can be the most rewarding."

Carolyn lay back on her bed. She didn't feel like she could live up to the expectations of Treton or the King and Queen, but maybe that wasn't a bad thing? So long as she felt she had room to improve, she would keep working to improve, after all. The problem was the feeling of hopelessness and wanting to give up. How was she supposed to get over that?

"Did you ever feel it was hopeless?" Carolyn voiced her concerns, "You never wanted to just give up?"

"Sometimes," Isana admitted, "That's when it's good to have a hobby. You need to find something else to spend your energy on that you find refreshing or relaxing, when you get the chance. It can really help to renew your strength."

Carolyn nodded absently. "That makes sense," she said slowly, "I could practice my gymnastics, I suppose. I wonder if there's a balance beam around here?"

"Oh, are you an acrobat?" Isana sounded surprised.

"Kind of, I guess. I've been learning gymnastics for a few years now and I'm pretty good at it. That would help put my mind at ease, I think."

"That sounds like a great idea. If there's anything you need, I can try and help you with it."

"I'd like that," Carolyn smiled. For the first time since she arrived, she felt genuinely happy.

The next afternoon, after lunch, Carolyn was called in for an emergency meeting. While she had not been to any previous meetings held in the palace, she was required to come to this one as a member of the royal court. She showed up in the same room where she had first met the King and Queen, taking a seat next to her majesty by the end of the table.

All members of the royal council were present, who Carolyn had been introduced to or informed of at some point. There was, of course, Treton, the Head of Wizardry of Herin, and General Drakson, head of Herin's military. Though she hadn't gotten a good look at him at the time, General Drakson had led the mission to bring her through the portal device. There were also the chief ministers of various governmental offices, including the High Priest, Head of Construction, Official Treasurer, and other titles that sounded important. Carolyn couldn't remember most of their names, but she was pretty sure she wouldn't be quizzed on them. In addition, there were four other ministers who were advisors to the royal court. Once everyone was seated, King Ketra opened up the proceedings.

"Now that every is here," he started formally, "we can begin. As you all know, following our raid on Herin Castle, Ferdri has been moving his forces quite rapidly, seemingly in search of our location, but it seems that was not the case. As you all know, Ferdri has been searching for magical artifacts around the country, yet he never made a move against Dor Palace and the Magicron until now. He has had troops in the vicinity of the palace for some time—which is why we've been unable to move the Magicron or its guardian—but now they're moving into offensive positioning. It seems they're planning not just an inspection, as they have in other areas, but a large-scale attack meant to capture and hold the palace."

The King paused while his words sunk in. Many of the advisors looked thoughtful, others worried, and a couple surprised. Not much of what she heard made any sense to Carolyn, but evidently this Dor Palace and the Magicron, whatever that was, were pretty important.

"How many forces are moving against us?" one of the advisors asked, looking more toward the general than the King.

"A sizeable force," General Drakson responded, "It was difficult for us to determine which of them were actually headed in that direction, since their movements have been so erratic, but it seems to be a force of roughly three thousand."

"And our fortress in the region?" another advisor added.

"Two thousand strong, with defender's advantage," replied the General. "It may be enough to hold them off, but chances are not great."

"It should be noted that there are no wizards in that region at this time," Tretor put in, "If a single enemy wizard shows up, then the battle would easily go in their favor."

"Send some over there immediately," the King ordered, then turned back to the general, "How long do we have until the attack begins?"

"A couple days at best. It gives us little time to react."

King Ketra began rubbing his chin as he considered this information. Then he turned to Treton again, "Who can you get there in only two days?"

"I believe Sevina can get there in time, that would already make a huge difference. Tristina and Berin should be able to arrive quickly, as long as I can get a message to them."

"Excellent. What of the super-soldier? His participation will make all the difference." The King turned to the General again. The whole room seemed to hold its breath.

"Our contacts In Norostar tell us he has remained behind," another advisor answered, this one the Minister of Intelligence, "It seems he has not left Ferdri's side since they took the castle."

"Excellent, then there's hope," the King's whole figure seemed to relax, a reaction shared by most others in the room, "What other troops are in the area who can reach the fortress quickly?"

"None," the General gave a terse shake of the head, "The closest fortresses would not be able to send out any sizeable forces without first contending with enemy troops in the area. We can do that if you feel the time has come for all-out war, otherwise they need to remain where they are."

"What of the knights here? We're not that far from Dor; can they arrive quietly?"

The General took a moment to consider this before responding. "Yes, I believe they would be able to." Then he paused briefly before adding, "With all due respect, Your Highness, we need the knights here in case Cansition is discovered and attacked. We have no other means of defending ourselves."

"I'm aware of that," the King nodded, his tone grave, "but I won't squander our resources for my sake. Send out two of the companies, leave the third one here. It may not be much, but it should help boost morale, which I fear is too low at the moment."

"Of course, Your Highness," the General gave a brief bow of his head, but his expression looked less deferential. Carolyn surmised he wanted to refuse but wouldn't dare to disagree with his King. She hoped that Sarin's company would be the one chosen to stay behind. If he and Elis left, she'd have almost nobody to talk to. And if they left, there was the chance—*No*, Carolyn scolded herself as a chill ran down her spine. *I can't think of that. They would come back fine.*

"With so many of Ferdri's forces moving, are there any areas left vulnerable that we could attack?" one of the other ministers spoke up, looking between General Drakson and the Minister of Intelligence. "I don't think we can keep being reactionary, especially if we know the super-soldier is staying put in Norostar for now."

"Possibly," the Intelligence Minister nodded, looking thoughtful, "Many of the troops are moving out of Jerenair, and we have a significant force stationed by Trinsgard. If we coordinate properly, we could take out the enemy forces left in the city and reinforce it to prepare for a counterattack."

"That would force him to move his forces south out of Fenthrol province to reinforce Jerenair province," the General seemed to agree. "We don't have many forces there, but enough that we could prevent any armies from easily leaving the area."

"And what do we do when Ferdri chooses to mobilize his super-soldier?" the King sounded skeptical.

"Even he cannot win the war on his own," another advisor spoke up. "I've been analyzing the reports and noticed some trends in his behavior which might show him not to be as unstoppable as we have thought. While he never seems to be injured in combat, anytime he has suffered a number of blows, he quickly retreats. It also appears that his preferred tactic is to flanks our troops, taking out many of them by surprise before there's a chance to react. He is indeed quite strong, but I postulate he's not invincible and has been manipulating the battlefield in such a way to make him seem stronger than he is."

"What are you trying to say, Ozmen?" the King asked.

"If we can coordinate this attack properly, we can probably take out much of Ferdri's forces and throw many of the others into disarray," Advisor Ozmen continued. "At that point, even if the super-soldier showed up, I don't think he would be a concern any longer."

There was stunned silence at the table. Carolyn, for her part, was suddenly feeling like a bad solution to a problem that didn't exist. She felt like shrinking back in her chair, already uncomfortable and out of place in the room full of aristocrats, now no longer relevant or worthy of being privy to this secret meeting.

"All right, we'll do it," the King said finally, with a tone of conviction in his voice that Carolyn hadn't heard before, "Dasren, how well can you track the super-soldier's movements? How quickly would you know if he left Norostar?"

"Immediately," the Intelligence Minister responded, "Our spies have been watching him closely and have been given orders to return any information they have to me by the quickest means possible."

After that, the King and his ministers, mainly the General, continued to discuss details of their attack plan for at least another half-hour while Carolyn sat around wondering why she had been invited to this meeting in the first place. At some point she noticed the Queen looking at her, giving her a warm smile. She smiled back, but turned away quickly, not wanting to attract anyone's attention.

Will they keep training me now that I'm useless? she wondered, *Probably not, they'll probably just stick with the experienced mages and leave me behind.* Maybe they would just leave her to sit in her room to fester until the castle was retaken and they could send her home? But what if they still wanted her to use the Derishz Ruby? Ever since her brief encounter with the dark power within, the thought of actually having to use the Ruby haunted her.

Unfortunately, Carolyn soon discovered that Sarin's company was one of the two to leave. Carolyn found out from the Queen during breakfast that Sarin's company would be leaving shortly after the meal ended. That would mean Elis and Isana would be leaving as well. Carolyn was already feeling lonely.

After finishing her meal quickly—easy enough after losing her appetite on hearing the news—she rushed down to the barracks.

I have to say goodbye to them. I don't know when I'll see them again, or…or if I'll see them again.

Once she got there, she reasoned, she'd pull them aside privately so she could say goodbye properly. She was worried about getting too emotional and really didn't want a room full of knights to see her crying. She'd also have to find Isana and wish her luck. Now that she felt something growing between them, it would be too much to lose it already.

She reached the door to the equipment room and immediately pushed it open. To her surprise, she found all the knights lined up with their equipment, being inspected by General Drakson. He was about three-quarters up the line when Carolyn quite unceremoniously burst through the door. All heads in the room turned to her.

This wasn't what she had planned. She hadn't imagined she would be running into them in front of two whole companies of knights and the General. *Now what?* she asked herself as her cheeks grew warm and panic began to rise.

Carolyn quickly straightened her posture, trying to remember to act princess-like, and stepped forward boldly. She tried to think of Isana—which was easy since hers was one of the heads turned to Carolyn now—and how she had taken on the role of a knight when she didn't feel worthy. Carolyn walked with a slow, careful gait that she hoped was fitting for a princess. As she did, the General walked quickly over to her.

"Princess Carolyn," he said with a deep bow. "Is there anything I can help you with? We're in the middle of the final inspection before our departure, which, as you know, is quite urgent."

"Yes, I'm aware," Carolyn replied, trying to sound as important as she could, "I've come to inspect the troops before they head out. A... royal inspection."

The edge of General Drakson's mouth quivered and, like in the meeting yesterday, it seemed he wanted to retort, but didn't dare to disagree with a royal. Instead he carefully hid the faint hint of a glare and stepped aside, indicating with his hand for Carolyn to proceed. *There are some benefits to being a royal.*

"As you wish, milady," he said with a bow of the head.

Continuing with her careful, lady-like step, Carolyn walked down the line of prepared knights. She had seen many of them before, some she had even spoken too, but she didn't know most of their names. As she passed each knight, giving their equipment a cursory glance, each one's posture straightened. She noticed the looks in their eyes— there was worry on so many of their faces. *Aren't they supposed to be brave? Aren't they trained warriors? How could they be afraid?*

Continuing carefully along the lines, she finally reached Sarin's squad, and here she slowed her pace. As she reached the young knight, Elis at his side, she halted briefly. Sarin kept his stare locked forward, like all the others, but Carolyn could see the concern on his face as well. When she stopped, however, he seemed to relax ever so slightly, and Carolyn could swear she saw the faint hint of a smile on his lips. She regarded him carefully.

"Are you feeling ready?" she asked, trying to sound authoritative, though her voice had a noticeable quiver.

"Yes, milady," was the careful response, his tone betraying no emotion.

Carolyn leaned in ever so slightly and whispered just loud enough for her two friends to hear, "Be careful out there."

She continued walking, her pace a little more hurried. Carolyn paid little heed to the rest of the knights, except Isana to whom she gave a slight nod, before reaching the end of the last row. Returning to the door—where the General was waiting impatiently—she considered giving some words of encouragement before leaving. However, looking over the room of trained knights one last time, words failed her and she simply left.

Back out in the hallway, Carolyn leaned against the wall, slowly lowering herself onto the floor and breathing heavily. She couldn't believe what she had just done, putting herself at the center of attention like that. She hated when so many people were looking at her. That awkward feeling only got worse the more people that were around to see her. She wasn't cut out for this kind of parading around in public and she didn't think she ever would be. *At least I got to see Sarin and Elis,* she tried to encourage herself, *so it was worth it.*

Her mind wandered back to the question Treton had asked her just a couple days before. *Why did Grandmother choose me over Jessica?* Carolyn was not fit for all this princessy stuff; Jessica would be much better at that. She loved having all the attention and being glamorous. Carolyn was neither of those, she was just... Carolyn. *Maybe Grandmother made a mistake,* she realized, *it shouldn't have been me.* The answer seemed unsatisfying, though.

Finally composing herself, Carolyn got up from her slump and returned to her room, where she waited for her magic lesson of the day to begin, knowing that the next few afternoons were going to be very lonely.

The next few days, Carolyn occupied her afternoons by looking over some detailed maps of the kingdom, with Merilda's help. For some reason, all the characters were written in a strange script she couldn't read, so Merilda read them off for her. The problem of reading had been bothering her for some time, but she always ended up forgetting about it by the time she got to her lesson with

Treton. Finally, one morning, she brought it up.

"Good morning, Carolyn," Treton greeted her with a smile.

"There's something I've been meaning to ask you," Carolyn responded bluntly.

"Oh, of course," the archmage seemed taken aback. "What's the matter?"

"How come everyone around here speaks English?" she asked.

Treton's brow furrowed and he opened his mouth to respond, but closed it again as he seemed to consider how to respond. "Why wouldn't we speak English?" he asked finally.

"Well, because that's the language from my world," Carolyn half-asked, half-stated, uncertain why her question was so bizarre.

Treton seemed ready to respond when realization overtook his expression. Carolyn half expected him to facepalm. "Of course!" he said at last, "It's the magic of the portal device."

"Huh?"

"The portal device is a powerful and strange artifact," Treton explained, "It was discovered at some point that anyone who travels through it has a lasting enchantment placed on them: so long as they are in a dimension not their own, they hear all speech in their own language, and everyone else hears the person's speech in their own language."

"Really? Does it even translate accents? And how come I can't read your text still?"

"I guess it's only spoken language, not written," Treton shrugged, "It even translates the name of your language to the name of my language, so when you said English I heard it as English, which is not what you said."

Carolyn rubbed at her forehead in confusion, "Doesn't that seem a bit too convenient?" she wondered aloud.

"Not if you hang a lantern on it," the archmage

responded.

"Hang a... What?"

"It's a phrase. It means..." Treton started, then gave his head a shake, "Never mind, let's start the lesson for today. Do you know of the four elements?"

Shaking out of her confusion, Carolyn focused on the question put to her, "You mean like, fire, water, earth, and wind?"

"Exactly, very good," the archmage said with a smile, "These are the four basic components of creation. Most wizards are unable to manipulate these forces, unless they take their mastery in it, which requires a ruby. However, there are exceptions to this."

"My affinity," Carolyn realized, thinking back to the wave of fire that came off of her when she first used magic.

"That's right, your affinity," Treton replied, "Each element corresponds to some aspect of a person's being. Some people, even ones that are not magically inclined, find they have a natural ability to control one of these elements, to a certain extent. This ability—this affinity, as we call it— shows that this aspect of their being is stronger than average.

"Earth corresponds to the physical strength of a person. Some people are born with above average natural strength and constitution, and such people might have an affinity for earth. Water corresponds to the mental acuity of a person. Some people who are naturally more receptive to receiving and utilizing information might have an affinity for water. Air—or as you referred to it, wind—corresponds to the spirit, the soul of a person. Some people have a natural inclination to sense the spiritual realm and the impact our actions have on it and that it has on us, and such people might have an affinity for air.

"And lastly is fire, the rarest of them all. Fire is the passion, the emotion, that makes a person who they are. It is the driving force that brings people to strive for greater heights, to love and laugh, or to hate and fear. It brings us to our greatest accomplishments or our deepest regrets, all depending on how we use it. Those with an affinity for fire have the ability, albeit not always a recognized ability, to pursue even a distant goal until it is reached, to inspire others to renewed strength; it is the ability to continue on, even when all hope seems lost."

Treton ended his speech, watching Carolyn intently while she digested this information. His grand descriptions sounded wondrous, but hardly seemed to match her at all. Pursue distant goals? Carolyn felt like her ideas always failed. Inspire others? Others hardly seemed to notice her, how was she supposed to inspire them? How could this be her? *Why did Grandmother choose me?* The question came unbidden to her mind again, the words seeming to mock her.

"In our first lesson, I encouraged you to dismiss the fire, using magic in its purest form," Treton went on when he saw no response forthcoming, "Now I want you to try and use it. You should find that you can control the fire as easily as you do pure magic. Please try it now."

Carolyn continued staring into space for a minute, only half hearing his words, as she mulled over what he had said. It was starting to bother her, though she wasn't sure why. The worry that everyone was mistaken about her, thinking she was someone she wasn't, was only growing stronger. Finally snapping out of it, she realized she had been asked to do something.

"Oops," she said with a slight shake of her head. Focusing on her magic, she tried to summon it forth. Ever since that first lesson, it had becoming natural for her to focus on it and force it into the pure form of magic that Treton referred to. This time she simply released it, exerting no control over its form. Just like the first couple times she used magic, it came out as fire.

She could feel the heat of the fire emanating from her open hand, but it didn't burn her. On the contrary, it seemed to comfort her. She stared at the fire for a moment, remembering the first time she had summoned it and how confused she was, but this time she actually knew what she was doing. Her mind rapidly reviewed all the lessons in magic she had had since then and a smile crept across her face.

With ease she launched a stream of fire from her hand shooting up a few feet before arcing back down and swirling, surrounding herself in a spiral of flame. From there it spread out further, weaving through the air, drawing figure eights, crossing in front of and behind Treton, filling the room with brilliant heat and bright, burning flames. Carolyn began to write letters with it, using the bit of cursive she knew to spell out her name, then made a large lattice-work that covered much of the ceiling while unweaving the fire around Treton. Finally, she pulled all of it together again into a point, forming into a huge ball of flame above her head. For a brief moment she basked in the warmth of the glow. Feeling the heat on her face, she thought again about the words of Treton and considered that they might be true. She felt greater control over her fire than she had over the pure form of magic; using it seemed to come naturally to her. This is what it meant to have an affinity.

"Now for some spells," she muttered to herself, the smile spreading. She looked around at the stone floor and ceiling around her, confident she would not have to worry about damage to them. *Fwoom!* A smaller ball of flame shot off from the large one, impacting the ground the a few feet away from her, the flames bursting and dissipating against the stone. *Fwoom!* Three more shot off, these in a spread behind her and to the sides, each impacting the exact spot she intended. *Fwoosh!* A gout of flame shot out, striking the ceiling, sparks drifted to the ground. Gathering up all the rest of the fire hovering over her, Carolyn flattened it and stood it on the ground behind her, forming a wall about eight feet high and ten feet across, then launched it away from her heading for the opposite wall. With a quick wave of her hand, the wall of flames vanished just before impacting the wall where the wooden door would've caught on fire. Carolyn gave an audible sigh, a smile still on her face.

"Excellent!" Treton's face was beaming as Carolyn turned to face him, "Wonderful! I've seen elemental wizards many a time before, but a wizard with an affinity for an element is always a much more impressive feat. There's a certain... art form to the way they control their element with such natural ease and grace." The old wizard was more animated than usual. Carolyn couldn't help but blush at the praise.

"It was nothing," she mumbled.

"It was certainly something," he countered, "You should continue to practice these abilities. They will help you improve your control over magic in general, and it will also help in battle. Fire is a powerful weapon, as I'm sure you know."

Carolyn gave a nod. The thought of going into battle sent a shiver up her spine. The idle comment caused her mind to wander to her friends who were out in one right now. *I hope they're all right.*

"Now we have more important matters to get to," Treton reached into his robe and pulled out a small, silk pouch with a drawstring closing it tight, "As I mentioned at the start of our lessons, every wizard must choose a mastery. This decision comes early on in the training, and most magic you learn will be part of your mastery. Depending on the mastery you choose, you will receive a gem to place your magic in, which will allow you to utilize the magic of your mastery. Once you've completed your lessons, you will receive a staff such as mine to place your gem into. The staff is the sign of a master wizard. Now, here are the options you have available."

Treton opened the small pouch and began to pull out a ruby, it's multi-faceted face spreading red light on his hand. Before he could say another word, however, the door to her left, the one that led to the entrance of the palace, suddenly slammed open. Treton and Carolyn turned in unison to see a knight stumble in, his armor scratched and smudged with dirt, his helmet badly dented, his hand clutching at his head. As they watched in shock, the knight fell to his knees.

Together the two wizards ran over, calling out to him, but the knight was unresponsive. He merely lay himself down, curling up into a ball, and began to whimper audibly. As they reached him, another knight stumbled in, exhibiting similar behavior, while two of the other three doors opened and knights started to walk in that way.

Carolyn hesitantly knelt and looked into the face of the fallen knight. What she saw in his eyes was pure terror. Something had frightened this knight senseless, to the point where he wouldn't even respond to their desperate questions. As the knight pulled away from them, another one walked into the room, this one with knees shaking but standing his ground. When the knight removed their helmet, Carolyn immediately recognized Isana.

"Lieutenant!" Treton said in surprise, looking up at her, "What happened?"

Carolyn saw the same fear in Isana's eyes that she saw in the knight curled up on the floor, but there was something else as well. Anger. Fury. Hatred. Carolyn had gotten a glimpse of this look from the lieutenant once before, when she first met her and thought she was looking at death itself, but this time it was so much more intense, so much so that the wild fear that seemed to be gripping all the knights seemed to have been suppressed in its wake. Breathing deeply, trying to steady her voice while she stared off into the distance, Isana finally looked down at Treton and said in a quivering voice, "Jiselda".

CHAPTER 6
Disaster at Dor

Carolyn had heard of speaking with such disgust that it was described as being spat, yet she never understood what that sounded like until now. It felt like Isana was trying to get a nasty flavor off her tongue and crush it under her foot. Carolyn was so taken aback by her friend's rage that it took her a minute to remember that she had heard that name for the first time just a few days ago from Isana herself. Jiselda. The enchantress from the mercenary group, so powerful she nearly defeated the invading bandits on her own. *Oh no.*

"The enchantress?" Treton asked desperately; apparently he had heard of her already, "A fear spell?" He reached his hand down to touch the knight on the ground, the other hand clutching his opal-topped staff, the gem glowing faintly. Carolyn watched as a brief shimmer appeared in the air around the knight and the archmage's hand began to glow. All at once the knight's shuddering stopped. He began to uncurl himself from the ground, the fear gone from his eyes, replaced now with shame. Treton stood and placed his hand on Isana's shoulder, repeating the action while the officer stared off into space, still quivering with that combination of fear and rage. When the spell had faded, Carolyn could see the fear had vanished from the lieutenant's eyes, and all that was left behind was pure, unbridled rage.

Without warning, Isana lifted her helmet and threw it against the ground with all of her might. It hit the ground with an earsplitting *CLANG* of metal against stone as Isana began to growl with anger. "That treacherous dog!" she shouted, clenching her fists and leaving Carolyn to wonder if the magic of the portal device would translate swear words. Isana turned to the wall and began to punch it with gauntleted hands, the rhythmic clanging sound reverberating throughout the room. Some of the other knights were aroused from their stupor to stare in shock at the rage of their officer, others seemed only to curl up and whimper louder. With a brief scan of the room, Carolyn realized there were very few knights here, maybe thirty at best. *There had been so many when they left. Where are Sarin and Elis? Did they come back?*

"Lieutenant," Treton spoke in soft tones to Isana once she had stopped punching the wall, instead just leaning against it and breathing heavily, "You must speak with the King at once to make your report. I will treat your soldiers."

Isana glanced up at the archmage, rage still burning in her eyes. Remembering her place, she seemed to take control of herself, closing her mouth into a tight line, straightening up, and giving a terse nod. She immediately began to walk toward the door leading into the palace proper. Carolyn watched her walking away, not sure whether to accompany her or try and help Treton, until the archmage noticed Carolyn still standing there.

"Go with her, Carolyn," he commanded, his tone firm. Carolyn didn't ask twice before rushing off to follow Isana. The knight did not acknowledge her presence and said nothing, so she followed in silence as they headed for the meeting chamber. On the way, Rissin came running down the hall, stopping abruptly when he saw them.

"Lieutenant," he began to say, "wha-"

"Get the King, *now*", she cut him off, speaking with such force that Rissin looked as frightened as the knights had a moment ago. He turned around and rushed back the way he had come.

They reached the meeting room and Isana simply opened the door and walked in, not waiting on ceremony. It was empty, so she sat herself down in one of the seats, still wearing scuffed armor, her scabbard catching on the fancy arms of the chair. The knight crossed her arms and looked down, stone-faced, while Carolyn went and awkwardly sat down across from her. She felt like saying something, but had no idea what.

After a couple minutes of awkward silence while Carolyn worried over the fate of her friends, there was a sudden bustle at the door. The King and Queen entered, followed by a few of their advisors. Carolyn stood in respect—Rissin had taught her to do that—until the King and Queen took their seats. Without waiting for anyone else to sit, King Ketra immediately turned to Isana.

"What happened?" he demanded, not unkindly.

"Jiselda," Isana said again, lifting her gaze to meet the King's. She had not stood up when he entered, remaining in the same downcast pose. "It was a trap; they were ready for us."

A gasp was heard throughout the room, and all eyes locked on Isana as she spoke.

"As we approached Dor, we were attacked suddenly," Isana went on. "They seemed to come out of nowhere, must've magicked themselves away or something. We formed up to defend ourselves and sounded the horn to call out the defenders in Dor, but no one came. We did our best to maneuver ourselves to get around them and make it to the palace so they couldn't surround us, but then more of their forces appeared, coming from the palace itself. We took out many of them and attempted to find a more advantageous position, but then she showed up."

Here Isana paused momentarily, taking a few deep breaths, seemingly working very hard to prevent another outburst like she had when she first arrived. "I don't know what she did, but everyone near her suddenly panicked. Brave knights started screaming in terror and fleeing in all directions. She ran straight toward our ranks, and everywhere she went, knights broke down and gave in to fear. I felt the effects of it when she reached me, but my...my anger against her gave me the presence of mind to remain in control."

Isana paused again, steadying her breathing, her whole body trembling; she seemed to be having a very hard time keeping it together. The King took this opportunity to ask, "How many of you returned?"

"I don't know," Isana shook her head, "I was able to keep control of myself, but not entirely; the fear was muddling my thoughts. I knew we were losing and had to flee, so I rallied whatever knights I could and started heading back at hard gallop. I wasn't in right enough mind to think about counting, or what was the best strategy, I just knew I had to run."

"That's what a fear spell does," Treton said as he entered the room and turned to the King with a bow. "Your majesty," he added as he moved to take a seat at the table. "I have seen to the knights and restored them; they are back in their right minds again, but still shaken from the endeavor. The fear spell causes the victim to be afraid of anything and everything, whether imagined, expected, or actual. The lieutenant should be commended to have a strong enough will to have resisted as much as she did, especially against such a powerful wizard."

"How many knights have returned, Treton?" the Queen asked, concern lining her face.

"I counted forty-two, your highness," Treton responded with a sigh, "out of the two hundred that left. General Drakson is not with them." Then he turned to Isana and added, "What of our wizards, did none arrive? Was Sevira there?"

"I didn't see any," the knight shook her head. "I vaguely recall some lightning shooting around as we left, but I was already under the effects of fear at that time and didn't know who was shooting at whom."

"This is grave news, indeed," the King said, slumping back in his chair. The Queen rested a hand on his arm, trying to give him confidence, though she evidently had little herself.

To inspire others to renewed strength; it is the ability to continue on, even when all hope seems lost.

The words were Treton's, spoken to Carolyn but a scant half hour ago, though it felt much longer than that. They echoed through her head now, unbidden, as though calling to her. She felt so small and meek, surrounded by grand and powerful people who were at a loss for what to do, and her all the more so. Yet those words echoed, urging her to speak, to open her mouth even though she didn't know what words to say.

"So what can we do now?" she asked simply, feeling the words tumble out. All eyes turned to her and all she wanted to do was to shrink into her seat and take back the words.

"We need to return immediately," the Queen said, looking around the table, "We were planning attacks around the nation. The time to retake Herin is now. If word spreads of this defeat, it will crush morale and our hopes with it. We must strike again, decisively, or the war will be lost now."

Everyone at the table took heart at the Queen's words. Where before there had been expressions of defeat, Carolyn saw thoughtful looks as they came up with solutions to the problem.

"Yes, we must send someone strong enough to defeat Jiselda," Treton agreed, and his eyes looked thoughtful, "Once she's out of the picture, we can rally the troops and take back Dor. One of my most powerful wizards, Garinald, just returned yesterday. He is exhausted from his trip, but he is probably at the level of Jiselda. I myself can go as well, since we need to send everything we have."

"No," one of the advisors said, "No, not you. If it's true this was an ambush, then we must consider the possibility that the knights were followed. If that's the case, the King and Queen will have to be evacuated, and they'll need you to stay by their side."

"I'm not keen on ordering an evacuation now," the King responded, "but you make a fair point. Treton, is there anyone else you could send?"

"Tristina and Berin should still be on their way there," Treton rubbed his chin as he spoke, "Hopefully they avoided the ambush but remained close enough to help. There's no one else here—" He paused for a moment and his eyes looked suddenly to Carolyn. She felt a wave a fear grip her as she read the expression in that quick glance. "I have two students who are very powerful. While neither has completed their mastery, I believe they would prove potent contenders for Jiselda. I can send them as well."

"Excellent," the King nodded, "I trust your judgment as always, Treton, thought I can't say I'm not concerned about sending apprentices against such a powerful opponent. Who do you have in mind?"

"Jacim, for one,' the archmage responded; Carolyn relaxed a bit. She didn't recognize the name and had seen no other apprentices in the palace. Treton must have some students nearby that he could call on quickly, "He's close to finishing his mastery in enchantment. I could send him along."

"I've heard of him, a fine student, I believe," the King seemed pleased, "Could you get him here quickly? Where is he?"

"He's back in Norostar, hiding in my laboratory. I can have Garinald meet with him and rendezvous with the knights on the way."

"Good, good," the King nodded, "And the second one?"

Treton looked the King in the eyes and stated calmly, "Lady Carolyn."

A chill ran down Carolyn's spine as she heard her name. Panic quickly took over her thoughts, not unlike the knights she had witnessed collapsing on the floor. *Not me, not me!* her mind shouted, as though doing so would will her words into reality. She had hardly started training, how could she do anything to such a powerful wizard? Voices started murmuring, and she felt the many pairs of eyes that turned to consider her now. Isana, having shaken off her anger, looked at Carolyn with concern and wonder.

"Are you certain, Treton?" the King sounded skeptical, "I do trust your judgment, but Lady Carolyn has hardly begun her training. Is she really ready to face a master of such caliber?"

"On her own, no, she is not," Treton admitted, which seemed to make others even more concerned. "But she has advanced quickly and is already about to begin learning her mastery. I believe Garinald, Jacim, and whatever other mages we can recruit can defeat Jiselda on their own, but Carolyn needs to gain experience in the field. She needs a chance to practice her powers in battle if we expect her to exert control over the Ruby."

Many people at the table started speaking out at once. Some of them expressed a lack of confidence in Carolyn's abilities. Others seemed skeptical about the importance of the Derishz Ruby anymore. All of them seemed to agree that it was a bad idea. The King listened to the opinions patiently, giving each due consideration. Isana continued to look to Carolyn with concern in her eyes. Carolyn, for her part, was trying to disappear, wondering if there was a way to move on to the next scene so she could get out of that meeting room already, but every time she opened her eyes she was still there. *Sending me out to battle? So soon? What is Treton thinking?*

Lost in her thoughts, Carolyn didn't hear the question posed to her, so she was surprised when the room quieted, a sense of anticipation in the air. She looked up to see everyone looking at her—looks of concern, skepticism, wonder, curiosity—and from Treton, confidence.

"Well, Lady Carolyn?" the King asked, not unkindly but with a note of impatience.

"I'm sorry, what?" she asked, feeling her cheeks grow warmer.

"Treton cannot order you to go, you must make that decision yourself," the King repeated, "Will you go to Dor?"

She stared back at him dumbly. Carolyn hated making decisions. She really hated making important decisions. She had never done it before, but now that she was making a decision of life and death, she found that she absolutely loathed it. She wished to get out of it, to run back home, to go back in time and say no to Sarin and remain in bed. But instead, those words repeated themselves in her mind: *the ability to continue on.*

"I'll do it," she said with a confidence she didn't feel. Many faces looked shocked, others afraid, and yet others awed. She wasn't positive she meant to say them, but that was what came out.

"Lieutenant Polyer," the King said, turning to the knight, "Get your troops fed and rested, then leave before evening. Ride through the night if you have to, but get back to Dor as swiftly as possible. See to it that Lady Carolyn has a steed to ride. Treton," the King turned to the archmage, "arrange with the lieutenant where to meet with Garinald and Jacim and prepare Lady Carolyn to leave."

"Of course, your highness," Treton nodded.

With that, the King abruptly stood, the Queen following suit, and the two of them left the room. As they did, other started to get up and rush off. Isana swiftly moved to the door, shooting Carolyn a brief glance she couldn't quite decipher. Carolyn continued to sit. Did she really agree to go and fight a powerful wizard? The one that sent a whole troop of knights fearing for their lives? What kind of chance did she have against that? *Why didn't I say no?*

"Carolyn," a voice to her right spoke up. She jumped and turned to see Treton standing there. "I know this seems sudden, but there is much to prepare. Please come with me."

Carolyn nodded dumbly, rising without a word to follow the archmage. He led her through the hallways to a bedroom door and knocked on it. The door opened, revealing an older man, clean shaven, with a head of shaggy grey hair, wearing a gray and white robe. He looked at Treton with a tired expression.

"Garinald," Treton began, "I know you've just returned, but we have a situation. After you've rested up a bit, I need you to go to Norostar and pick up Jacim, then take him to Dor. I can give you more details before you leave."

"All right," Garinald nodded, his gruff voice betraying no emotion. Carolyn expected him to say more, like complain or ask questions, but he merely stood there. Treton seemed to expect this.

"I will speak with you after you've had some rest," Treton said with a nod. He then turned away with Carolyn as Garinald shut the door behind them.

"Garinald can be curt, but he's a good man," Treton said by way of explanation as he walked off down the hall, Carolyn keeping pace with him.

"Treton," Carolyn finally found her voice, "What is... I mean, what are you... Why are you sending me?" she stammered.

"As I said, I think it's important for you to have some experience in the field," he answered calmly, turning a corner, "With Garinald and Jacim there—and hopefully the other mages I called for previously—Jiselda is not likely to pay you much heed. Do what you can, practice your abilities, and stay safe."

"What about her fear spell? Can't she just do that to us?" Carolyn fought to keep from sounding like a stubborn child who didn't want to go clean their room.

"I'm going to see Cirithem now about some potions. He can provide an antidote to the fear spell, should it occur again." Treton came to a halt outside of Carolyn's room.

"What if it doesn't work?" Carolyn retorted. "The last

mission failed, how do you know this one will succeed?"

"Because this time we know what we're up against and can plan accordingly," was the response, his tone confident, "I also believe you're more capable than you realize."

Carolyn was less certain. She looked back at the archmage's grave expression. "I'm scared."

"So am I, Carolyn," he agreed with a grim smile, "That's why now is the time to be brave."

Treton left Carolyn in her room, adjuring her to rest and even sleep if she could until she was called for. She lay down on the bed for a bit, head swimming, uncertain how she would ever find sleep.

She was so focused on the battle ahead that she realized she never found out if Sarin and Elis had made it back or not. In all the rush, she had been temporarily distracted from this, but now she felt fear grip her heart. Were they among the knights that returned? What if they weren't? Could they be... dead? With trembling hands, she pushed herself out of bed and headed off to the barracks.

When she entered the barracks just a few minutes later, she was dismayed by the sight. While just a few days ago she had been in this room, looking over the rows of proud knights, now she found just a scant handful sitting meekly by their equipment lockers, packing up from their mission. The air of the room was despondent at best, with many of the knights either visibly shaken or looking forlorn. A few of the knights who had stayed behind—among them Carolyn recognized Deeris—were helping their companions take care of their gear. Carolyn did a quick scan of the room, looking over the section for Isana's unit and fearing the worst, when she finally saw a familiar face. Sarin sat alone, unmoving, his face downcast.

Carolyn rushed over, ignoring the looks she got from some of the other knights, and sat down next to her friend. He didn't notice her at first, but when she placed a hand on his shoulder he jumped and looked up at her. The faintest hint of a smile flickered on his face and was gone. "Hey,

Carolyn."

"Are you still under the effects of the fear spell?" Carolyn asked bluntly. Pep talks would likely be of little help if he were still suffering the magical influence of Jiselda.

"No," he shook his head, glancing away, "Archmage Treton cured us all of that, we're fi... better now."

"Coulda fooled me," Carolyn said humorlessly. Sarin only grunted in response.

"I heard what happened," she went on, trying to keep him talking, to find some way of bringing him back, "It sounded terrible."

"You have no idea, Carolyn," Sarin looked up again, now locking eyes with her, "It was a single person. One wizard sent an *entire* force of knights running. How can we ever face someone as strong as that?"

Carolyn could see in his face now what was affecting all of the soldiers. It wasn't some lasting effect of the spell, it was depression. The brave, powerful knights had been broken and were now gripped by despondency, their strength and hope completely drained.

"They have Elis," Sarin went on, his face turned down again, "I don't know what happened to him."

Carolyn gasped. She realized Elis wasn't in his usual place but had hoped that he was still around somewhere. Everything really had fallen apart.

The ability to continue on, even when all hope seems lost.

The words repeated themselves in Carolyn's mind again, refusing to be silenced. Ever since they were spoken a couple hours ago, nothing had been able to get them out of her head. Somehow they seemed to resonate in a way she didn't understand. On a whim, she held up a hand between herself and Sarin; small flames began to flicker across her palm as she focused on her magic. Sarin looked at her hand in confusion, then surprise as the fire grew. Slowly she pulled the fire together into a small ball, hovering in the air in front of her palm, no larger than a marble. Carefully, not really understanding what she was doing or why, she reached her hand forward toward Sarin. He recoiled at first, as if to evade, but he looked briefly at Carolyn's eyes and saw something that made him stay, mesmerized by the ball of flame. Her hand reached his chest, pressing against the solid steel of his breastplate, pressing the ball of flame into and through it.

Carolyn wasn't sure exactly what had happened, but her tiny marble of fire passed straight through, leaving no mark on the armor, and was absorbed into Sarin's chest. A strange, distant look came over his eyes, then he blinked and was back, but with a different expression. It was Sarin again, his humor and confidence finally showing through, shoving back the misery and despair.

"The ability to continue on..." Carolyn mumbled to herself, watching the transformation in her friend as he sat up straighter, as though filled with renewed vigor.

"What did you..." Sarin began with a whisper before trailing off, looking to his friend in surprise.

"We're going to beat Jiselda," Carolyn said, trying to exude confidence she didn't feel. "I'm going to be coming back with you."

"You're coming..." Sarin repeated dumbly as he sought to recover his voice, "You're coming?" He added with more excitement. Finally, for the first time since he returned, Sarin smiled. "We can do it then, together. Together we'll get Elis back." Now his tone was strong, confident, and bursting with energy. The change in demeanor was drastic.

"Lady Carolyn," a voice came from nearby. Carolyn glanced around and saw Isana walking up to her, bowing low. "May I speak with you, please?" she added.

"Certainly," Carolyn stood, giving Sarin a friendly pat on the shoulder and hoping it was encouraging and not awkward, and walked off to speak with the lieutenant.

"Carolyn," Isana said in a whisper when they were far enough away from the gathered knights for anyone to hear her drop formality, "like Treton, I've no authority to give you orders, but I would appreciate it if you left now. We need time to rest and recover our strength before we ride out again. I think that you should try and get some rest as well; we will be riding through the night."

"Right, sorry," Carolyn answered, chastened. "I just had to see if Sarin and Elis were..." She trailed off, remembering that Elis was *not* ok.

"I understand, but worrying about Elis right now will not help him," Isana whispered, though not unkindly. "Try and get some rest for now. Someone will come and fetch you when we need to get ready to leave."

"All right," Carolyn nodded. She turned to go, then hesitated a moment before adding, "You take good care of your knights."

Isana looked taken aback at the sudden compliment. "Thank you," she whispered.

Carolyn turned and left without another word. Soon she found herself back in her room where she lay down, trying to calm her nerves before the imminent ride to battle.

"Lady Carolyn," a voice whispered from somewhere nearby. "Lady Carolyn, the archmage is here."

Carolyn's eyes slowly blinked open as she returned to consciousness, taking in her surroundings. She had spent what felt like hours lying in bed, worrying over her predicament. She hadn't imagined she would actually fall asleep, but it seems she did eventually. How long had she slept? She was probably better for it, since she wouldn't be sleeping at night.

She pulled herself up in bed to see Merilda standing over her, patiently trying to rouse her. "Thank you," Carolyn said with a yawn. "Let him know I'll be right with him."

After taking a few minutes to wake up and refresh herself, she opened the door to see Treton, who was waiting patiently.

"Greetings, milady," Treton said with a polite bow, "I pray you slept well."

"I guess, all things considered." Carolyn shrugged,

stepping out of the room. "I assume we're going now."

"Yes, please walk with me." The archmage started to lead her down the hall. Carolyn paused long enough to turn back to Merilda and say, "Thank you, Merilda, for everything. I... I'll see you when I get back." She almost said, *I hope I'll see you again*, but she caught herself. *Best not to think that way*, she told herself. *I need to stay positive... somehow.*

"First things first, you need your equipment," Treton said, leading Carolyn through the halls to the other side of the palace, where the dining hall was. "I have an apprentice staff to give you; it's good to have as a last defense, just in case. I'm also providing you with a healing potion, an anti-fear potion, and a few days' worth of field rations. That's all you should need."

"Healing potion?" Carolyn repeated. "Like the one Sarin drank?"

"Oh, so you know of them already?"

"Yeah, Sarin showed me one once. It looked like gasoline," Carolyn grimaced.

"I don't know what that is, but I gather from your tone it's not something you generally consume," the archmage reasoned.

"Not at all."

"Well, it may not look so appetizing," Treton admitted, leading her toward the back of the palace, "but it's extremely potent. It can seal up even lethal wounds if taken in time, and with only a small dosage. They are extremely difficult to produce, unfortunately, but definitely worthwhile."

"Is the anti-fear potion any better?" Carolyn wondered as Treton opened a door to reveal a small storeroom, lit with the usual source-less light.

"Yes, considerably. It has a nice, rich blue color and a smooth, sweet flavor. It goes down like a good whiskey."

"I wouldn't know how that goes down," Carolyn answered as Treton handed her a small pouch. She looked inside and saw two small vials in there: one contained a liquid identical to the one she had seen Sarin drinking—a sludgy-looking, brownish swirl—and another one with a royal blue liquid that looked much more palatable. He then handed her a small bag, inside of which were four, sealed packages—presumably the field rations—and a full waterskin. This bag had a loose handle that she slung over her shoulder before tying the pouch to her waist. Lastly, Treton handed her a staff.

It was not an ornate one like Treton's. It was a simple staff, long enough to be used as a walking stick by someone taller than her, and with a knotted head. At first it looked like it had been a simple branch pulled off a tree, but on closer inspection she could see it was actually carved and had a nice finish. There was no gem in it.

"This is an apprentice's staff," Treton explained. "There's no gem in it as you have not selected a mastery yet. There are two main reasons a wizard uses a staff. The most obvious one is to house the gem with which their spells are cast, but it can also be wielded as a means of protection. Sometimes magic is not enough. It is a finite resource that can run out, or its use can be prevented through other spells, nullification magic, or sometimes it can fail us. In such cases, it is vital that a wizard not be without any means of protection. Most wizards will have spent time learning to fight with just a staff, but I've skipped that part of your training in favor of advancing quickly. You should not need it at all, but just in case, be prepared to use it. Even without training, it's not difficult to know how to swing one."

Carolyn nodded, examining the staff. It felt quite sturdy and was roughly the weight of a wooden baseball bat. The thought of whacking someone with it made her feel a bit squeamish, though. She always loved the idea of action and battle, but that was fantasy. This was real. This was happening.

"Come with me," Treton said, leading Carolyn out of the storeroom, "You're being given a horse to ride with the knights. You're going to be riding out in two hours, heading east through the forest. You've looked at some maps, yes?"

"Yeah, but wait," she hurried to keep pace with him as he started toward the main entrance of the palace. "I've never ridden a horse before."

"You've never ridden a horse?" Treton stopped and turned toward her. "How do people travel where you're from? Do you walk everywhere on foot?"

"Never mind that," Carolyn dismissed the question with a wave of her hand. "I still don't know how to ride."

Treton stopped to think for a moment before answering. "The knights' horses are well-trained. So long as you know the right way to sit in the saddle and hold the reins, you should be fine. Come, I'll give you what instruction I can." With that he started off again, continuing his explanation of the travel route. "As I was saying, the forest stretches east before hitting the ridge. You'll ride as far east as you can, then turn north and exit the forest where the ridge slopes down. There's a river east of there; you'll cross to get into the Dragontooth Crags. There's plenty of space for a force of knights to hide out there and make camp. You'll stop and rest there for a bit, then continue north to Dor.

"The ride north from there is mostly open, so you'll be exposed. You'll have to be as quick as possible. Remember that your only concern is to fight Jiselda; leave the enemy soldiers for the knights to deal with. You don't want to waste your magic on them."

"I don't see what good my magic can do anyway," Carolyn grumbled as they reached the stables. The smell of horses assaulted her as the door swung open.

"Don't forget about your affinity, Carolyn," Treton reminded her. "The ability to use an element despite being an apprentice is a very powerful ability. In time, you could learn even the most powerful fire spells that elemental wizards have at their disposal. Even without training—so long as you maintain your calm and focus—you can accomplish great things with it, beyond what other wizards at your level would be able to do."

They walked down the line of stalls and arrived at one

housing a white and brown horse that was on the smaller side. It looked at Carolyn with big, black eyes when she reached out to stroke it. She was amazed at first, this being the first time she had been so close to a horse, before remembering she had actually ridden into the palace on one. She was a bit too preoccupied at the time to feel wonder at the experience.

"This is Mirandi," Treton said, placing a hand on the horse's neck. "She'll be your steed for this ride. She's a fine horse and well-trained, you should do fine. Come, I'll show you how to get the saddle on and how to mount her."

Treton spent the next half-hour instructing Carolyn on how to get the saddle and bridle on, how to check that all the straps were tight enough, how to take them back off, and how to properly mount. The technique for mounting wasn't so difficult, and Treton was impressed by how quickly and easily she grasped it. Carolyn cut off his excessive praise by reminding him she was a gymnast, so pulling herself up and down was pretty easy.

He then led her out of the stall a little bit, just to march the horse back and forth in the little space there was. Carolyn was not accustomed to a vehicle that bounced around so much, but her balance was good, and she had little fear of falling off. Once the horse started doing a bit of a trot, though, she started gripping the reins tighter than she probably needed. By the time they were done, she felt confident enough that at least she wouldn't fall off the horse, even if she couldn't control her very well.

"That will have to do for now," Treton said finally, leading Mirandi back to her stall. By this time, there were several knights in the stable, tending to their own horses. "Just remember to hold on and you should be fine. She is trained to remain with the group, so you shouldn't need to control her much anyway."

"What will you be doing while we're off fighting in Dor?" Carolyn asked as they took the saddle off.

"I will be helping to secure the perimeter of the palace,"

Treton explained, leading Carolyn out of the stables. "The King is not ready to order an evacuation yet, though he has made some preparations just in case. Instead he wants to increase our scouts throughout the area and try to determine if we've been found out before making any definitive decision."

"I wish you were coming with us," Carolyn grumbled.

"I do, too," the archmage sighed, "but I must obey the King's orders."

The two of them walked to the dining hall. It was eerily quiet, almost completely empty except for a couple servants. They were preparing a single seat at the main table, with a couple dishes with covers and a bottle of wine. They seemed to have been waiting for her.

"Since you missed lunch, you'll need to have a bit to eat now," Treton told her, "Eat quickly, though, you need to be leaving soon. I have other business to attend to. When you finish eating, go to the barracks and stay with the knights until it's time to leave."

Carolyn gave a brief nod of acknowledgment as Treton left. It was a simple meal, not like the lavish feasts that had been prepared up until now. Carolyn didn't have much of an appetite, though, and ate little. She tried focusing on the meal—which might be her last meal—but her mind kept drifting to what lay before her. Her imagination was running away with scenarios of how it could end, and few of them ended well. Despite the grand success she usually imagined for herself, her fears were only leaving a bad taste in her mouth.

When she finished, she made her way to the barracks and hesitated before entering. It had been a few hours—how many she wasn't certain of—since she was in there last, and initially it looked the same when she walked in. The mood in the room was still pretty depressing, but now the knights had a bit more vigor from their rest and were putting their armor back on rather than taking it off. There were also considerably more knights in here than last time. She immediately sought out Sarin to sit with him.

"Hey, Carolyn," he said as she sat down. "Get any sleep?"

The young knight sounded a bit melancholy. Despite his enthusiasm after Carolyn had last seen him, it seemed the weight of their current mission was weighing heavily on his shoulders. He was still doing much better than when he'd first arrived and even smiled when Carolyn sat. "A bit," she admitted. "Waiting is pretty boring."

Sarin nodded idly, checking his equipment while strapping on his armor. "I hear two other mages are coming with us. That should put us in a much better position this time." Isana walked by as they talked, checking on all her knights, acknowledging Carolyn with a nod but otherwise not interrupting them.

"Yeah, a master and an apprentice," Carolyn nodded, "I don't know either of them, but Treton says they're strong." *Of course, he also said* I'm *strong,* Carolyn told herself, a fact she was not so confident about.

"If Treton trusts them, that's good enough for me," Sarin gave a brief smile. "I wish he were coming, too, but I guess it's too much to ask that he leave the royal family behind. So were you given a horse—oh wait, you don't know how to ride, do you?"

"Treton showed me some basics," Carolyn answered. "I'm no expert, but he said I can probably avoid falling off."

That earned a chuckle from Sarin. She felt oddly at ease hearing such a mirthful sound, in spite of everything. She hated seeing him so depressed. "You'll do all right," Sarin reassured her. "Just hold on tight and keep him heading in the right direction."

"Her," Carolyn corrected him.

"Hmm? Oh, a mare. Who'd they give you?"

"I'm terrible with names," Carolyn shook her head. "Something with an 'm'. Miranda? Something like that."

"Mirandi," Sarin finished with a nod. "She's a good horse; you'll do fine." At this point, Sarin's armor was completely buckled on, a knight in shining—or at least, recently polished—armor. He seemed so adult standing there, fully armored, sword strapped to his hip. *How can he be so confident?*

"How long is the ride there?" Carolyn asked, unable to take her mind off the task at hand.

"It depends how hard we ride," Sarin's expression darkened; Carolyn regretted breaking his good humor. "If we ride through the night, we can cover most of the distance by dawn. After that it's just a couple more hours to arrive. That's when it gets hard."

The two of them were quiet for a bit. Carolyn kept wanting to voice her concerns but was too scared to say them out loud. Sarin had a thoughtful look on his face, lined with concern, and was uncharacteristically quiet. Finally, when Carolyn thought to say something, Isana came up the line.

"Time to ride, knights!" she shouted with authority, looking her troops up and down as she marched down the line. Officers of the other battalion were similarly rallying their men. "Everyone to the stables and form up in the entry hall!" Isana was also in her armor, reminding Carolyn of when she first saw her, a terror of strength and determination.

"Come on," Sarin gestured for Carolyn to follow him. They walked out the barracks through a door that led into the training room, then through there to the outer door. Carolyn found herself in the stark, barely lit entry cavern of the palace, between the fortified outer wall and the grand double doors that led to the palace proper. They walked straight across to the open stable doors on the other side. There Sarin went with Carolyn to find Mirandi and get her ready to go. Together they saddled her and got the bridle in place.

"Lead her out now and wait for the rest of the knights to form up," he told her. "If you can find Lieutenant Polyer, ask her where you should be in the formation. Officially, none of the knights have authority over you, but the officers in charge of the mission do have a right to give you orders."

"All right," Carolyn nodded, leading her horse. "See you outside."

All of the other knights she walked past were taking a while getting their horses ready. In addition to the saddles and bridles, all of the knights' horses also had armor to put on—barding, she had heard it called. She was the first one out of the stables other than the officers.

Carolyn stood around awkwardly, holding her horse's reins, while the officers nearby conversed quietly. Though no eyes were on her, she still felt exposed, vulnerable. The thought of being in a battle, swords swinging and arrows flying, with nothing to protect her from a deadly strike was certainly not helping. She couldn't help but wish she had armor to put on, even if it did restrict her ability to move. More than anything, she just wanted to avoid attention, curl up in a corner somewhere, and be left alone.

When the officers finally broke their conference, a number of the knights had already gathered behind them, starting to form ranks. Isana noticed Carolyn standing around and walked over to her, her face showing concern.

"Lady Carolyn," she said formally, with a bow, "You'll be riding in my battalion, up in the lead with me. Let me help you." She took hold of the reins, which Carolyn gratefully relinquished, and led her over to where her own horse stood waiting. With all its armor on, it looked like a powerful steed.

"How are you feeling?" Isana asked quietly after glancing about to see no one was in earshot.

"I'm fine," Carolyn answered automatically, but then she corrected herself. "I'm not fine. I feel so out of place. I've never been in a battle before. At least, not one where I'm fighting and not just running," she added, remembering the first time she met Isana.

"Everyone has to start somewhere," Isana said encouragingly, "and I think you're stronger than you realize. The most important thing is not to panic; keep a cool head."

"Sure, shouldn't be a problem," Carolyn answered sarcastically.

Isana gave a slight smirk before turning and starting off, "I need to get my troops together. Wait here until we're ready to go." She walked off to arrange the lines of knights that were slowly forming behind them.

Carolyn watched with fascination, seeing how each knight seemed to instinctively know his place in the marching formation, gathering into neat rows. The entry chamber was now bustling with activity as more knights were coming out of the stables, leading their horses. They'd be ready to leave soon.

It was hard not to think about the coming battle. Carolyn didn't know if it was better to try and forget about it, or focus on it to prepare herself mentally. Instead she bounced back and forth, worrying constantly about everything that could go horribly wrong. On occasion she wondered where Garinald and the other apprentice Treton was sending were, but her own presence was the point that still bothered her the most.

She thought back to the night she first entered the palace, the night she agreed to go with Sarin through the portal. *Why did I ever do that?* she sighed. *I could've saved myself so much trouble.* Ultimately though, the only reason the choice had presented itself to her in the first place was because she had been chosen as the bearer of the Derishz Ruby, and that brought her back to the question that had been nagging at her for the last few days, the one to which she still didn't have a good answer to: *why did grandmother pick me?*

It wasn't long before the large double doors leading to the palace proper slowly opened. There Carolyn saw the King and Queen coming out, accompanied by their various advisors. They spoke briefly with Rissin, who in turn spoke with some of the officers, while they waited for things to settle. Finally, all the troops were in formation, their horses standing beside them at the ready, and Isana returned to stand beside Carolyn.

"Just follow my lead right now, all right?" she said to Carolyn, taking her spot beside her horse.

"What do you—?" Carolyn started to ask, but was interrupted when Isana turned back to face the palace and stood at attention. Getting the hint, Carolyn turned as well.

King Ketra stood just beyond the line of soldiers, Queen Rorina at his side. He regarded the knights for what seemed a long time before speaking up. "This is no simple task I send you on now," the King began, his voice echoing throughout the chamber, "but I have the utmost confidence in your abilities. You are the pride of Herin's military forces; the bravest, the swiftest, the strongest. You will bring glory to Herin and we will lay low all of our enemies!"

The knights gave two cheers in unison in response, pumping their fists in the air. Isana didn't, however, so neither did Carolyn. *I guess the officers don't need the morale boost as much? That's probably why they had the officers at the back of this reception instead of the front.*

After the King finished speaking, one of the officers— the highest ranking, from what Carolyn could tell—started shouting orders.

"About face!" As one, the knights turned about, including the officers, and grabbed the reins for their horses, Carolyn moving quickly to do the same. At the same time, the huge, double doors leading outside started to swing outward.

"Mount up!" came the next order almost immediately. Carolyn easily pulled herself onto Mirandi's back, steadying herself in the saddle. All around her was the scraping of metal as the heavily armored knights climbed onto equally as armored horses. The doors in front of them continued to swing open, revealing the dirt slope leading up and into the forest on the other side.

"Prepare to ride!" came the next order. Carolyn wondered what that meant and looked around, seeing the knights hold the reins ready and bend forward over their horses, ready to start charging.

"Adenil watch over you," came the King's voice from behind, booming throughout the chamber.

"For the King!" the officer shouted.

There was a chorus of slapping leather as reins were whipped from every knight in unison, urging their horses onward. Carolyn tried to mimic the motion and Mirandi, well-trained as she was, got the message despite Carolyn's hesitance. Together the horses galloped out the main doors, up the dirt slope, and emerged into the forest beyond.

CHAPTER 7

The Assault

For the first time in weeks, real sunlight shone on Carolyn. Though the sun was already low on the horizon and mostly hidden behind the wall of trees, the fleeting rays that poked out between the branches brought her warmth and comfort. The fake sunlight of her room was impressive, but nothing compared to the fresh air of the true outdoors.

As soon as they burst forth into the light, the troop turned right, heading east, with the descending sun to their backs. Carolyn did her best to steer her mount, though the mare seemed to just follow the others on her own.

They soon made their way out of the clearing and into the dense forest ahead, forcing them to slow their pace. There was no path through the forest, but they were doing an impressive job of keeping up a fast pace while weaving between the trees and trampling thick underbrush along the way. The smell of fresh leaves assaulted Carolyn's nose, accompanied by the chirping of birds overhead, and the occasional glimpse of creatures leaping among the branches.

The sights and sounds of the forest were so tranquil and made for a welcome distraction. Carolyn's mind was still hung up on the knowledge of what was coming at the end of this journey. *What am I going to do there?* she wondered. She had never fought anyone before, not really at least. There had been times in the past when she'd lost her temper and yelled at—sometimes even hit—her siblings, but never had she been in a real fight with anyone else. All she could think to do was to use her fire affinity to throw some fireballs. That's what you did with magic, after all, you throw fireballs. Other than that, the best she could hope to do was try and Push some soldiers over.

As the sun set behind them, the sky darkened until they were engulfed in near pitch blackness, and still they rode one, the light of the moon above granting them just enough vision to keep from hitting any trees. They continued to ride east and north through the night with brief breaks for rest, the hooting of owls and other strange sounds accompanying them while they traveled.

After a few hours, Carolyn found that riding on horseback had lost its initial charm and was now naught but an uncomfortable necessity. Despite constantly readjusting her seating, nothing Carolyn did could quite make it bearable and she found herself hoping their journey would soon come to an end. Ironically, she started thinking more of the battle ahead to distract herself from the discomfort of the ride. She began to muse about more creative ways of using fire, something a little more clever than a fireball, at least. *I could make a wall,* she thought, *a wall of flames that I can hide behind so Jiselda can't find me.* Many ideas she came up with involved finding a way to hide from the fight, but none of them seemed very plausible.

Eventually, the troop slowed down again and came to a halt. Carolyn had lost track of time while they were riding. It was still night and there was no sign of daybreak yet. Had it been four hours? Five? For all she knew, dawn was just an hour away. She was glad for the rest, though. She leaned her head against Mirandi's fluffy mane and closed her eyes, trying to relax. While she did, there was an insistent *hoot* from above her. She tried to tune it out, but somehow it seemed to be calling to her. She looked up into the trees, trying to find the source.

Sitting on a low branch was an enormous brown owl, unlike any owl she had ever seen. It was looking to the left, and as it did another owl landed next to it. The two of them seemed to look down at the knights, as if trying to determine who they were, before suddenly flying down from the branch toward the ground.

Before Carolyn could wonder about the strange behavior of animals in this world, there was a bright purple flash. The owls were gone; in the faint moonlight she could now see two people, one the stoic wizard she had seen briefly in Cansition—Garinald—and the other a younger boy, probably just a few years older than Carolyn, standing by his side. Garinald held a sturdy looking staff with a faint, purple-ish gem reflecting the moonlight—an amethyst, most likely. The boy wore simpler robes, not unlike Carolyn's, and had a shorter, plainer looking staff with an emerald set in the head. This must be Jacim, the other apprentice Treton had sent for.

"Ah, Garinald! You've arrived." One of the officers rode up to the wizard to speak with him; this one seemed to have the highest rank and was head of the expedition, but Carolyn hadn't caught his name yet, "Did anyone follow you here? Did you have any problems? I want a full report!"

"Nothing went wrong," Garinald answered tersely. The officer seemed to wait a moment as though expecting more elaboration, but none was forthcoming.

"Right, " he nodded, frowning. "We're resting here for a bit. Be ready to ride out with us. Stay with Lady Carolyn."

Garinald gave a quick nod of acknowledgment but didn't speak a word. He abruptly turned away from the officer and headed straight for Carolyn, Jacim in tow.

"How did you do that?" Carolyn couldn't stop herself from asking, a bit louder than she had intended, when Garinald was close enough. He stared at her blankly for moment.

"Do what?" he asked gruffly.

"Turn into an owl?" Carolyn offered, off-put by his attitude. She hadn't been spoken to like that since she got to Herin.

"I'm a Morpher," he responded with a wave of his hand, as though that explained everything. He turned away and faced north, standing silently. Jacim stood behind him trying to look nonchalant, but now that he was closer Carolyn could see that his brow was creased and his expression downcast. *At least I'm not the only one worried,* she thought grimly.

The two of them stood around in silence for the next few minutes while the officers checked on the ranks. Garinald was not a very talkative person and Jacim seemed a bit reserved, so both were content to let the time pass in silence. Carolyn wanted to ask questions or at least have someone to speak to, but this didn't seem like the moment to find conversation, so she just lay forward against Mirandi's mane and tried to get comfortable.

Pretty soon the call went out again to start marching. It had not escaped Carolyn that Garinald and Jacim arrived without horses—owls riding horses probably would've looked a little funny—and she wasn't sure if she should be offering one or both of them space on Mirandi. Once the call came to start moving, however, Garinald lifted his staff and there was another bright purple flash. Garinald was gone again, and in his place was a beautiful, chestnut stallion. Jacim casually climbed on board, as if he was expecting this, and rode bareback on him as they started off again.

Not long after setting out, they broke through the northern edge of the forest, coming out onto open plains. They immediately veered to the right, heading eastward again, on a steady, downward slope. It seemed like Carolyn should be able to see quite a distance in this direction, but the best she could make out was a river some miles ahead of them reflecting a bit of moonlight. This was the river they needed to cross on the way to Dor. Carolyn was not good at keeping time without a watch, but it felt like about an hour until they finally reached the river. Here they slowed as the entire troop was trying to ford through a relatively narrow point of the river that was shallow enough to cross. Being in the lead with the officers, Carolyn was across quickly and had to wait on the other side until everyone was across and back in formation before they moved on again.

Soon the fields gave way to dusty, rock-strewn terrain, and large, jagged shapes rose above them all around. In the darkness they looked like giant spearheads protruding from the ground; in the light they probably didn't look much better. Carolyn remembered seeing this area on the map: The Dragontooth Crags. The entire area was filled with these stone structures jutting up in various directions like giant, sharpened teeth. Despite the ominous look, the area was safe to travel in and the crags provided plenty of cover to set up camp. As they started to slow, coming to a location pre-selected for their rest, Carolyn could just make out the sky to the east starting to grow lighter.

The soldiers reached the location, then each officer guided their troops to different areas, keeping each unit distinct but close. Everyone seemed relieved for a rest after many of hours of nearly non-stop riding. They were not going to sleep here, but take an hour to rest and make sure the horses were in good shape for the final run. Carolyn kept with Isana and her forces, dismounting Mirandi and leading her to remain with their horses before looking for Sarin. Garinald and Jacim seemed to wander close nearby, either not certain where to go or trying to stay with Carolyn.

Carolyn found Sarin soon enough, his voice carrying its distinctive, jovial tone, and sat down beside him. Along with all the other knights, Sarin was eating some of his field rations. Carolyn dug hers out of her bag, too, wondering what there was to eat. Turns out field rations consisted of dried meat and bread; it felt hard as a rock and wasn't particularly appetizing. but it's what she had. With a shrug she bit in, noticing with a glance that Garinald and Jacim were eating the same.

"How was the ride?" Sarin asked as Carolyn attempted to bite into her bread; the crust was hard, but inside it was surprisingly soft and sweet.

"Boring," Carolyn shrugged, "I thought marching to battle would be more exciting."

"Not really," Sarin shook his head, "the real excitement starts when we get there."

"Hmm, yeah, excitement."

"Don't worry," Sarin said solemnly, placing a gauntleted hand on Carolyn's shoulder. "that just makes it harder. Try and relax a bit."

"Hard to relax when it feels like I'm marching to my death," Carolyn answered bluntly. Sarin turned away from her, looking to the ground. *I shouldn't have said that*, Carolyn chided herself, *he's only just gotten over the last battle himself.* "Well, if I'm going to die, I might was well die smiling, right?" she added, trying to sound more cheerful.

"That's the spirit," Sarin said with a chuckle, his spirits lifting, "and with a full stomach." He took another big bite of his bread. "Don' fo-get t' drik, too," he said with a full mouth, taking a swig from his water skin.

They continued to chat while they ate, doing their best to distract themselves before the coming battle. After she had finished her meal, she noticed Garinald walking over to her, Jacim trailing behind. She turned up to look at him quizzically.

"Come with me, Lady Carolyn," he said, "we need to discuss the battle." Without waiting for an answer, he turned and headed off, away from the knights.

With a shrug and a brief farewell to Sarin, Carolyn got up and followed them. By now the sky was a dull grey, the darkness slowly creeping away to the west, but the sun hadn't quite broken the horizon yet. Exhaustion hit Carolyn;

she had never pulled an all-nighter before, and it was a strange feeling, like yesterday had never quite ended.

Garinald and Jacim were standing beside one of the large stone outcroppings a bit away from the other knights, far enough to be separate without being out of earshot. Garinald waited for her to arrive, his face in what seemed a permanent scowl as he watched her approach. He didn't seem like the most pleasant person to deal with, but she'd dealt with grumpy teachers in the past and this would—hopefully—be no different. Jacim was watching her with a critical expression. Carolyn couldn't help but think back to her gymnastics class, being stared down by Mrs. Hill and the other students as she walked to the front, now so long ago. Their eyes seemed to pierce her, revealing her to be unworthy of all the responsibility and trust that she held. Panic struck and all Carolyn wanted to do was run away and hide, but there wasn't anywhere she could go—no one to hide behind, no way to pretend illness and just go home. This she had to deal with.

"Lady Carolyn," Garinald spoke up once she approached, "This is Jacim." He gestured to the younger wizard, who bowed quickly. "Remember our purpose in this battle is to deal with Jiselda. Don't waste time fighting soldiers." Garinald spoke brusquely. Carolyn was torn between appreciating his treating her as a person rather than a royal, and bristling at his rudeness.

"We're going to ride in the middle of the troop for the final approach," he continued, oblivious to Carolyn's slight frown. "When we get close, I will turn us all into eagles and we'll stay in the sky while we search for Jiselda. When we find her, I will engage her directly. Jacim," he turned again to the other apprentice, "you will remain by my side and guard me. Attack only when you have an opening. Your main purpose is to prevent Jiselda from exploiting any openings. Lady Carolyn," he turned back to her, "keep your distance from Jiselda. Do what you can to help from a distance, otherwise just observe. If something goes wrong, come in and help. Any questions?"

Neither Carolyn nor Jacim answered at first. The information had been presented so rapidly that it took longer to process than it took Garinald to give it over.

"We're going to be birds?" Carolyn finally asked, her face brightening at the prospect. She had always wanted to fly, though this wasn't quite how she had envisioned it happening.

"Yes, milady," Garinald answered, "Eagles."

"Sounds like a fine strategy," Jacim nodded, looking to the older wizard.

"Of course," Garinald agreed, a note of annoyance in his response. "When the troop forms up, find me." With that he walked away abruptly, leaving Jacim and Carolyn together. Carolyn was amazed by how he balanced between always referring to her by the proper titles while still treating her as inferior. It was hard to tell, but she got the impression this was just how Garinald treated everyone.

"So, have you been in a fight before?" Carolyn asked Jacim, trying not to sound awkward.

"Of course not, Lady Carolyn," he answered quickly, giving her a bow, "I'm only an apprentice." He didn't quite look her in the eyes, as though intimidated by her. Or by her title.

"How do you feel about it?" she continued, her curiosity piqued by his overly respectful behavior.

"This is what I've been trained for," he answered resolutely, though not in a rude tone. He was still avoiding eye contact, but Carolyn caught a glimpse of something in his expression, like he wanted to add something, but caught himself and shut his mouth.

"Yeah I know, I'm a newbie," Carolyn sighed. "It's not like I wanted to come, it was Treton's idea. If you want to complain that someone with so little training was brought along, complain to him."

Jacim's expression went wide-eyed, a sight that made Carolyn worry for a brief moment that whatever Herin equivalent of the word "newbie" he heard was some kind of dirty word, but just for a moment. He tried to recompose himself, bowing again. "Of course I don't mean to imply such a thing, milady!" he answered, a faint tone of panic to his voice, "I'm confident in Archmage Treton's assessment of your abilities. I would never speak of royalty like that!"

Jacim's constant bowing and reverent attitude was getting irritating and Carolyn didn't see the conversation going anywhere. "Whatever," she said with a wave of her hand as she turned and walked away. Such a dismissive action might be viewed as more severe than she meant it to, but Carolyn didn't care at that point. *Garinald may be brusque, but at least he's honest,* she shook her head, *I can't stand all this being* fake.

The knights were starting to regroup when Carolyn returned to them and she went to find where she had tied Mirandi up. As she walked, she chanced a glance over her shoulder to see Jacim had not moved, rather he continued to stand there, watching her, his expression an odd mix of disapproval and concern. The moment he saw Carolyn look at him, he turned away and hurried off in a random direction. He was an odd one.

It wasn't long before the troop was formed up and ready to move out again. Carolyn held Mirandi by the reins and stood beside Garinald at the center of the troop. Though other thoughts had invaded her mind during the brief respite, concern for the upcoming battle was now all she could think about. *This is it,* she told herself, *no more stopping before the battle. I might never see...* A chill ran down her spine as she banished such thoughts from her mind, but still she couldn't ignore it.

Releasing the reins and fully conscious the order to mount could come any second, Carolyn wove her way between the waiting knights. Though she heard a few grunts of surprise or annoyance, none dared to stop her, of course. She came up to Sarin from behind, very close to the head of the troop, and placed a hand on his shoulder. He turned to face her, surprise quickly turning to concern as he saw who it was.

"Sarin," Carolyn started before he could say anything, "Take care of yourself out there." Though she tried to sound confident, she was certain the waver in her voice was obvious, as well as the worry in her eyes.

"You, too," Sarin replied with a nod, his tone grave, with no hint of humor to color it. They kept their eyes locked for a brief moment, both sharing the same unspoken thought, *I hope I see you again.* With that, Carolyn moved quickly back to her mount, hoping she would make it before the call to march sounded.

Garinald said nothing as Carolyn returned to Mirandi, though there seemed a hint of annoyance in his eyes when she chanced a glance at him. She considered attempting to speak to him, to appease him, or perhaps build a better connection, but felt it wouldn't get her anywhere. Luckily, she had little time to consider. Almost as soon as she had Mirandi's reins in her hand, the officers called out the orders to mount, and the troop started off once more.

The sun broke over the horizon almost as soon as they set off, bathing Carolyn in its warmth as a fresh wave of anxiety overtook her. There was so much uncertainty ahead of her, for her, for Sarin, and for Elis, for whom it might already be too late. *I can't think that way,* she berated herself, *I have to cling to hope, however faint.*

The pounding of the horses' hooves on the rocky ground among the crags echoed all around, surrounding them in a cacophony of hoofbeats. Within the hour, they made their way out of the Dragontooth Crags and onto open plains. Far ahead of them, still some miles off but looming on the distant horizon, Carolyn could make out the peak of a tall building: Dor Palace. When she saw that, a jolt of fear burst through her chest. *This is really happening,* she realized.

They continued to ride on for some time, the sun slowly rising to their right as they rode north across the fields, Dor looming larger and larger as more of it came into view. It was an ornate palace buttressed by a forest along the east side. There were three turrets rising out of it, each with a peaked roof and sporting a blue pennant. An outer wall surrounded a courtyard before the actual palace, with two large Herin banners adorning it. It wasn't long before they reached the southern reaches of the forest, riding hard north with the trees to their right.

There was no sign of enemy troops yet, but that might not be a good sign. Even if they were all holed up in the palace and none were out on the field, they would still have a difficult fight ahead of them. Carolyn could feel fear growing in the pit of her stomach as they approached, expecting arrows to come flying at them at any minute. She had long daydreamed about adventure and combat, but in her dreams she was always an invincible warrior winning honor and glory with ease. This was not a dream. This was real. This was happening.

The palace was getting closer and closer and still there was no sign of the enemy. The knights started to slow their pace, keeping on high alert, spears gripped tightly and ready to strike. Carolyn heard the officers shouting some orders, but all she could make out above the ruckus was to keep an eye out. As she started to look around, there was a sudden tap on her shoulder and she nearly jumped out of her saddle in surprise.

"Lady Carolyn!" Jacim was practically shouting above the noise, "I didn't mean to frighten you, but you didn't hear me calling your name."

"It's fine, just a little wound up right now," she answered, trying to act brave, "What is it?"

"I need to sit behind you for a moment while Garinald transforms," he explained, looking embarrassed, "so that we don't have to stop and break out of the group."

"Oh," Carolyn said, surprised, "Sure, hop on."

Which he did. With surprising speed, precision, and a small green flash from his staff, Jacim leapt perfectly off of Garinald's back and landed behind Carolyn, awkwardly wrapping his arms loosely around her waist to hold on. Almost as soon as he was off, Garinald returned to his human form with another purple flash, looking somewhat ridiculous running among a troop of mounted knights and attempting to keep pace with them. Before the knight behind him could overtake and trample him, there was a second purple flash. This flash was different, though, as it encompassed Carolyn's entire field of vision.

After the flash faded, everything changed. Suddenly, everything looked so *clear*. She could see Mirandi's mane flowing with the wind and could distinguish the individual hairs. Looking to her left she could see the knight beside her and could see every dent and scratch in his armor. Up ahead of her, Dor Palace appeared in perfect detail as though she were standing right next to it. She could see everything in a way she never had before.

She also realized she could no longer feel Jacim's arms holding onto her. She looked down and, sure enough, his hands were gone, but so was Carolyn. In her place was a large, powerful eagle with a zig-zag pattern of stripes of brown, white, and black across the breast. Her feet were two huge talons with long claws holding fast to the saddle on Mirandi's back. She examined her arms and discovered both to be powerful wings with the same pattern of colors. Behind her she felt a *whoosh* of air and saw a similar looking bird launch itself into flight behind her. Instinctively, Carolyn spread out her wings, jumped into the air, and lowered them again in a powerful downstroke.

Carolyn went shooting up into the sky, beating her wings to gain altitude. Above her she could see eagles like her, Jacim and Garinald. Without entirely understanding how she knew, she flapped her wings in perfect, natural movements to catch up to them.

It was a very strange feeling, but so incredible. Thoughts of whether or not she was still herself or, more importantly, if she would still have her clothes on when she turned back into herself, were drowned out by the sheer thrill of being able to fly. High up in the air she looked down at the knights, watching them ride in perfect formation, one armor-less, rider-less horse in the center of them all, still keeping pace with the rest. All around her she could see for miles in a level of detail she never thought possible. And she was flying! That was a fact she just couldn't get over. Carolyn had always wanted to fly. She remembered her daydreams of sitting on a dragon's back, high up in the sky, but the real thing was more incredible than she could ever have imagined.

The fear of impending battle temporarily fled from her, but presently she tried to concentrate on the task at hand. Garinald had made this transformation so they could quickly spot Jiselda and get to her without interference. Carolyn scanned the open plains around Dor, but there were no troops to be seen. She could now see the guards standing on the ramparts, none of whom wore Herin's colors, and knew immediately that meant the palace had been taken, as they had feared. Even if they engaged troops in the field, they'd still need to take the palace. That would be difficult in its own right.

Looking back to the ground, there were no enemies to be seen, but her sharp eyes picked up on a shimmer, like the waves of heat from hot pavement. It was covering a patch on the ground just ahead of the knights. Carolyn couldn't see anything else there, but she had a gut feeling that something was wrong. She immediately called for Garinald.

"Screeeee!" she shouted, surprised by the sound that came out of her mouth. *Apparently, I can't talk,* she realized. That would be problematic for communication. She watched with fear as the knights rapidly approached the shimmer. Having nothing else to do, Carolyn winged her way over there and started to fly circles around that spot while continuing to screech.

Below her, the knights heard the screeching and moved into a defensive position. They slowed rapidly as they came to a standstill, shifting their formation into a line with spears pointed in all directions, as they looked around for any sign of the enemy. Nothing happened at first and the shimmer didn't change. It was possible Carolyn was just confused, still getting used to her eagle vision, and that there was nothing there. Then the shimmer vanished.

In its place was a troop of soldiers, at least three hundred strong, standing clustered together. All of them had spears or swords and shields at the ready, standing in a defensive formation but ready to charge. Even from her height, Carolyn could make out their faces, seeing the thrill of combat in their eyes, the conviction in their faces, and the fear etched in every line of their expressions.

At the center of them all was a woman. She wore a scarlet robe with green trimmings. Her long, light brown hair fell around her shoulders. Held above her head was a simple staff with a large, shining emerald on the head. On her face was a look of grim determination. She looked both beautiful and deadly, a harbinger of death, an angel of destruction. It was immediately clear to Carolyn who this was: Jiselda.

CHAPTER 8
The Enchantress

With battle cries on either side, the knights and soldiers charged each other. There were probably more than twice as many soldiers, but the knights had the advantage of horses and, hopefully, better training. Jiselda, however, was not looking to be idle for long. She lowered her staff as the emerald's shine faded and moved forward confidently. Garinald started to dive, Jacim right beside him, and Carolyn followed suit, trying to stay close.

Garinald was heading straight for Jiselda. She didn't notice him at first, but she glanced up just in time and ducked out of the way with inhuman speed, her emerald flashing as she moved. Jacim followed, also attempting to strike her, but this time she was ready and easily dodged the swipe. Carolyn found she was too scared of this woman to attack her just yet, so she pulled out of her dive in time to follow Garinald and Jacim as they regained altitude for another pass. They gained a bit of height, angling back toward the forest as they did, before diving again.

It was clear Jiselda knew this trio of eagles was her enemy and she showed no fear in facing them. She started pushing through the soldiers away from the knights, closer to where the avian foes were headed. Garinald came at her again, but this time she swung her staff just as he reached her, connecting with his side. He gave a screech and wobbled but remained airborne, attempting to gain height again, continuing to lead her away. Whether she was dumb or brave, Jiselda seemed content to be led away from the midst of her forces, getting close to the edge of the formation.

Carolyn had all but forgotten the knights fighting at this point, focused just on this one, powerful wizard. She watched as Garinald began to descend, but this time he did not dive for her. Instead he landed on the ground far from the edge of the enemy formation. Jacim landed beside him and Carolyn figured she ought to as well, though she moved off to the side a good distance away. Soon they were all standing on the ground as Jiselda moved forward to meet them, her face still the same mask of determination. Her soldiers tried to move with her as a bodyguard, but she shoved them away with a look of annoyance, making it clear she wanted to face this threat alone. Once all three eagles were on the ground, there was another purple flash that took up Carolyn's entire range of vision and she was herself again—fully clothed, thankfully. Garinald and Jacim were also themselves, facing Jiselda as she took an offensive stance, holding her staff as though it was a sword, with the head just under her hand like the hilt.

It didn't take long to understand why. A green, sword-shaped glow extruded from the head of her staff. She moved forward with it carefully, not saying a word, watching her opponents with a perceptive eye. She seemed to be ignoring Carolyn for now, though her eyes did flick in her direction once.

Garinald stood calmly, gripping his staff, studying his opponent for a moment. Jacim looked a lot less composed; his brow was furrowed, his stance unsteady. He, too, adjusted the grip on his staff like Jiselda as it lit up with green energy.

Garinald charged, faster than Carolyn expected given his advanced age. The distance between him and his opponent rapidly closed when there was a now familiar flash of purple. In place of the wizard was a tiger, its body covered with black and yellow stripes, powerful muscles rippling as he charged, fangs bared and ready to pounce.

The enchantress was ready for him, not even flinching as this powerful beast leaped at her. She swung her fist forward, faster than Carolyn's eye could follow, and connected with her opponent's snout. There was an audible crack as Garinald was thrown from the air, rolling quickly to his feet. When he turned his growling face back to the enchantress, blood was running from his snout.

These people are insane, Carolyn shook her head in dismay, *How am I supposed to fight someone that can punch a tiger in the face?!*

Jacim charged forward, holding his bladed staff at the ready as he tried to keep up with the tiger, though his face told Carolyn he was just as worried as she was. Garinald stalked forward, circling his opponent carefully, swiping at her when he saw an opening. Jiselda used both her staff and her arm to block the blows, moving with as much strength and speed as her opponent, not even caring when bloody gashes were left on her arm. As Jacim ran up, standing by Garinald's flank and taking up a defensive position, Jiselda switched to offense, stabbing at the tiger with her sword. The tiger ducked and dodged the flurry of blows as staff and fist came flying at him, backing away slowly.

Carolyn watched on from the sidelines, impressed and terrified and certain she was as useless as she expected. She stood undisturbed, ignored by both the enemy soldiers and the enchantress. The idea to run and hide until the end of the battle occurred to her—it seemed nobody would notice her missing—but she steeled herself. She wasn't about to join the fight, but she would *not* flee, not when her friends were still in danger.

As the main battle moved further from the wizards' duel,

Jiselda continued to move forward, swinging again and again, keeping Garinald on the defensive. She landed a few glancing blows but caused little more than minor scratches. Anytime she came close to getting past Garinald's defense, Jacim was there to deflect it with his own staff. Jiselda, unperturbed, shifted her stance. She swung wide to ward off Garinald, jumped backward slightly, and pointed her enchanted staff toward Jacim. There was a bright green flash from the tip of her staff and Carolyn's breath caught as she waited for the spell to take effect.

Nothing happened.

Carolyn watched in confusion as Jiselda re-engaged with Garinald, attacking with more ferocity, blocking his counterattacks. Jacim was still running to keep up with the fight, but he was no longer keeping up with the two masters. Maybe he was already wearing down? But no, he was moving *too* slowly. The two master wizards had moved away, yet he walked at a casual pace to catch up to them. *The spell!* Carolyn realized, *He's been slowed!*

Jacim stopped moving forward—realizing he was only a liability in this state—and began to back away. Jiselda wasn't done with him yet, though, and maneuvered herself closer to him. The difference in speed between them was quite acute now, with Jiselda moving at inhuman speeds and Jacim at the speed of a snail. In almost comical fashion she easily grabbed Jacim's wrist and knocked the staff out of it with her own before turning away and ignoring him completely, confident that he was no longer a threat. His staff clattered to the ground a fair distance away, practically miles for him at his speed.

Carolyn knew it was time for her to get involved, though what she hoped to accomplish was beyond her. The master wizards continued to slash at one another, landing blows, dodging attacks, and never relenting. Taking a deep breath and ignoring the fear clenching her stomach in an iron grip, Carolyn held out her left hand and formed a ball of fire the size of a tennis ball above her open palm. It wasn't much, but it should be enough of a distraction to give Garinald an edge.

While Jiselda had kept Carolyn in her line of sight for a while, she had her back to her now, no longer viewing her as a threat. Carolyn took the opportunity to draw in a deep breath, focus, and launch her attack. Time seemed to slow as Carolyn watched the fireball streak through the air, worried it would sail clear over Jiselda's head, but it struck true, hitting the enchantress squarely in the back.

Jiselda gave a satisfying yelp in response, the first sound Carolyn had heard from her, as her focus was broken for a moment. Garinald immediately seized the opportunity, lifting both his front paws and raking them down Jiselda's chest and stomach. The enchantress stumbled back, half-turning to get Carolyn back into her field of vision, and attempted to regain her stance.

Carolyn allowed herself a brief moment of pride at what she had accomplished. It may not have been much, but she had made herself useful. *Maybe I can keep pelting her,* Carolyn felt empowered by her success, *keep her on the defensive.*

Her hopes were short-lived, however. As Carolyn began to form another fireball, she looked to her target in time to see Jiselda point her staff at Carolyn. There was a brief flash of green.

Wham!

Carolyn fell forward to the ground *hard.* She felt like she was lying under a boulder. She grunted against the weight, struggling to get back up, but couldn't budge. The fire in her hand went out. Experimentally she wiggled her hands and found they could move freely, but her arms, legs, and torso felt like they weighed ten times her normal weight. As she struggled to find a way to get up, the battle between the knights and the soldiers to her left swelled; they were starting to come closer.

Carolyn began to panic. Pinned to the ground as she was, she could easily end up trampled. Up ahead she caught a glimpse of Garinald and Jiselda still fighting, with Jacim having finally rejoined the battle, while Carolyn lay forgotten.

Panic began to set in as the pounding footsteps and clanging steel of the nearby battle drew closer. Carolyn tried to keep her calm as she struggled desperately against the weight holding her down, trying to get back to her feet. She twisted her head enough to look at her back to try and find whatever magical weight had been placed on her, but saw nothing.

"Ghaa!" came a shout from nearby as a felled soldier hit the ground hardly ten feet away.

Seeing little other choice, Carolyn tried crawling away, trying to get some distance between her and the battle, but that seemed futile as well. Trying to move her arms, the sleeves of her robe stubbornly refused to move, budging only slightly with the effort she put in.

Why won't my robe move…OH! Carolyn realized that Jiselda had not placed a weight on top of her; rather she had affected her robe directly, increasing its weight dramatically. Quickly, Carolyn pulled her arms out of the robe's sleeves, grateful that she was wearing a shirt and pants underneath. With her arms free and pressed to her sides, she scootched backward to pull her head out of the robe's hood, then ducked under the clasp at the neck and began sliding forward like a snake to pull herself out.

Just ahead of her, a couple of soldiers noticed her struggling. They broke off from the main group and charged at her, eyes gleaming with a thirst for blood.

Carolyn felt panic rising in her chest again. Reflexively, she conjured up a spout of flame between herself and the soldiers, surprising them long enough to finish crawling out, grab her staff, and leap to her feet. By the time she was standing, the soldiers had gotten over their shock and were charging again, deadly blades ready to swing. All of the temporary triumph that Carolyn had felt when she hit Jiselda vanished as she saw, once again, her death in that blade. It lifted into the air, the soldier's footing shifting, preparing to come down.

But a spark of hope burned inside her, urging her on. Her gymnast reflexes kicked in and she leapt aside, her movements smooth and practiced. The soldier grunted in frustration but adjusted quickly, attempting to attack again. Carolyn was ready this time. She chucked another fireball squarely into her opponent's face.

"Aaaah!" the soldier screamed in agony, stumbling back. His sword clattered to the ground as he clutched at his face with both hands. Carolyn felt sick inside, not wanting to imagine the kind of pain he was in, trying to remind herself she had no choice.

There was little time to consider. The second soldier was nearly upon her, but this one was more wary, watching her closely as he sought an opening to strike. Carolyn danced backward, keeping out of striking range, as she focused her magic again. A column of flame burst out of the ground beneath his feet, nearly engulfing him as he fell backward with a scream of agony.

Content she had handled her attackers, Carolyn turned to see how the wizards' duel behind her was going. Garinald and Jacim were still together, coming at Jiselda from both sides now. As she watched, the enchantress shot her foot out at lightning speed and kicked Jacim in the gut, sending the young enchanter flying away.

Carolyn took a step forward, but stopped as a soft *clang* from behind caught her attention. She turned in time to see a soldier with a burned face approaching angrily, moments away from slicing his sword through her neck. In a panic, Carolyn Pushed him away as hard as she could. The wave of magic connected with the soldier, sending him skidding backward, but he kept his feet, his teeth clenched, his eyes burning with rage.

She needed a moment to focus and launch another spell, but this soldier wasn't going to give her one. He lunged forward, stabbing for her heart, forcing Carolyn to retreat. She readied another fireball, but this time he was ready, blocking it with his shield and pressing forward. With her opponent wary of her magical tricks, her only other weapon was her wooden staff, which felt woefully inadequate.

Something moved behind the soldier. She raised her eyes to see a knight riding in her direction, spear at the ready, aimed for the soldier's neck. Her opponent, seeing his target distracted, struck again, this time landing a glancing blow before Carolyn could get out of the way. Her left armed seared with pain from a long—but thankfully shallow—gash down her arm.

She glanced down at the wound briefly, and in that moment the soldier gave a brief gurgle and was silent. Carolyn looked up again to see the soldier crumple to the ground as the knight raised his bloodied spear triumphantly into the air. A sick feeling rose in her stomach. This was a battle and death was inevitable, but it disgusted her to see it, wishing beyond anything to be anywhere but amidst the chaos and death.

She chanced a look up at the face of her savior, to see who could kill with such ease. For a brief moment before he turned back to the main battle, she caught his eyes. It was a face she knew well, but never in that way. Sarin. He gave her a quick nod and turned to rejoin the fray.

Of course she knew Sarin was a knight, and of course she knew he must've killed before and would do it again, but it was a totally different matter to have witnessed it. Sarin, always so mirthful and quick to joke, was a fierce warrior on the battlefield, taking the lives of his enemies without hesitation. Carolyn trembled, uncertain how to feel about it.

I can't worry about this right now, she shook herself, backing away from the soldiers and turning back to her fellow wizards. *First we need to get out of here alive.* Still, her whole body trembled, unconvinced.

She found Jiselda alone, holding her staff and watching the skies intently. A ways to her left was Jacim, swinging wildly around as some strange, glowing green object buzzed in the air around him. Looking up, Carolyn quickly made out the form of an eagle high above, circling around and waiting for an opportunity to strike. Garinald must've switched tactics because Jiselda seemed no worse for wear from their encounter. Even the wounds she had suffered previously had vanished, her torn outfit revealing nothing but healthy flesh beneath.

Jiselda had her back to Carolyn, forgetting her once again as a non-issue. Carolyn knew she had to do something to help, but also knew that Jiselda could just dismissively ignore her with another simple spell to take her out of the running. Or worse, she would view Carolyn as a real threat and decide to kill her immediately. *Maybe if I attack at the same time as Garinald,* she reasoned, *she won't be able to retaliate against me because she'll be busy with him.*

She moved slowly forward, watching Garinald above. Garinald noticed Carolyn's movements and angled himself in the opposite direction, preparing to dive. Carolyn stepped closer, trembling at the terrifying figure of the enchantress before her. She might've been considered beautiful, but all Carolyn could see in her was death and misery.

Garinald began screeching loudly as he started to dive. Jiselda readied herself, watching the eagle drop like a bullet. Before he could strike there was a flash of green from her staff. Though Garinald's screeching stopped, he continued to dive for the enchantress, holding his form perfectly. Too perfectly.

Jiselda held out her staff, the glowing green point aimed at the eagle. Garinald continued to hold his pose, not deviating even by an inch. Desperately Carolyn conjured up a fireball to launch at Jiselda, but too late. Garinald slammed straight into the emerald sword, piercing deep into his shoulder. Carolyn choked back a scream, covering her mouth as tears formed in the corners of her eyes.

The fireball impacted Jiselda in the back, searing her robe, but any pain she felt she merely bit back, unconcerned. Instead she lowered her staff—with Garinald stuck in a diving pose on the end – and kicked him off like a piece of trash.

Carolyn was not idle as she did. Seizing the precious moment left to her as Jiselda occupied herself with the morpher, she ran forward and closed the short distance between herself and her opponent. Her fire may have been ineffective, but she still had another weapon at her disposal, one that was sure to work. Without hesitation, Carolyn lifted her staff in both hands and brought it down with all her strength on the enchantress' head.

She learned an important lesson at that moment. Treton had once told her that mages are naturally more resilient to the use of magic than non-mages. However, they are just as vulnerable to a whack to the head with a sturdy staff as anyone else. It impacted with a satisfying *crack* against her skull.

"AAAAHHHHH!" Jiselda screamed in pain, falling to her knees and putting a hand on her head. Temporarily dazed, she was at Carolyn's mercy. Whatever healing power she had, it probably took a moment to kick in. This was the going to be the only chance Carolyn had to finish her opponent. She stood over the fallen enchantress, staff at the ready, about to swing again. She remembered Sarin atop his horse, spear in hand, quick to thrust it into the neck of his foe. And hesitated.

I can't do it.

She couldn't bring herself to intentionally take a person's life.

That moment of hesitation was all Jiselda needed. With speed and grace that would put a cheetah to shame, Jiselda rose to her feet and swung an elbow into Carolyn's gut, sending her reeling and gasping for air. Carolyn had no time to react before the next attack came, this time a fist that slammed against her cheek. Her head snapped to the side and the force of the blow sent Carolyn sprawling several feet away, ears ringing and face throbbing. She tried to regain her composure and lift herself to her feet, but the enchantress' focus was still on her, now with annoyance and frustration. The emerald of her staff pointed at Carolyn and began to glow brightly.

With a green flash, the world changed. Jiselda grew and contorted into some kind of hideous monster with a huge, gaping maw. Carolyn tried to scrabble away from her, holding back a scream, but the grass around her started to reach up, growing into long thorny vines trying to hold her down. She shouted in surprised and tried to beat them down, but more and more were growing, attempting to smother her. Above her the sky turned from a clear blue into a deep orange, raining boiling blood that splattered to the ground with a terrifying hiss. A second, blue monster appeared next to the Jiselda monster.

Carolyn was terrified. The world had turned into a horrifying mockery of what it once was. She clutched her legs to her chest, whimpering and breathing heavily. The thought of having stood a chance against Jiselda mocked her now. *What was the point of coming?* she told herself, misery overcoming her as the vines grew over her, *we never had a chance of winning this battle.* Soon the knights would all be killed, even the ones Carolyn had grown close to. The King and Queen would be found and killed. Everyone else hiding in Cansition or opposing Ferdri in some way would be hunted down and killed as well. Even Carolyn herself had no hope, her only fate was death. There was no hope for them to survive.

She gave no resistance to the thorny grass that wrapped itself around her, scratching her all over, the tips of the thorns red from her blood. She allowed the boiling hot blood rain to splash over her, burning her. *Jiselda should just kill me now,* she told herself, tears forming in her eyes. *Just get it over with.*

Even if, somehow, she did survive and make it back home, there would be nothing to go back to. She had missed so much studying time that she would fail her finals and disappoint her parents. They'd probably kick her out of the house. She'd have to live on the streets, forced to search garbage cans to get a meal, trying to stay dry in the rain.

Wait, why am I thinking about school now? Something wasn't right. She was in a nightmarish landscape, a place of terror, death and misery all around, so why the sudden fear of becoming a hobo? Why was her parents' disappointment on her mind?

It's like everything I think of scares me. I'm afraid of everything... I'm... Fear!

The memory of but a day ago returned to her, when she was standing with Treton in Cansition and a troop of knights scared out of their minds stumbled in pathetically, all under the effects of a fear spell. Now that Carolyn was under the effects of the same spell, she could understand what made the knights act with such pitiful cowardice. Hadn't they planned for this? Before she left, Treton had said something about... a potion!

Taking a deep breath to calm herself, Carolyn forced herself to look again at her surroundings. It was still a nightmarish landscape, but she looked down at her arms and legs and realized there were no cuts on them. The thorns were fake, a result of her own exaggerated fears. She tried moving her hand through them and found no resistance; she simply passed through the vines as though they weren't even there. *I need the potion,* she told herself, trying to ignore the still audible sizzling of blood dripping from the sky. *Then all this will be over.* But when she reached down for the pouch tied at her waist, she found nothing.

My robe! She had slipped out of it when it weighed like an elephant and the belt pouch with the potions was tied to it. She turned around, almost too scared of what she would see. The distant battle was a mass of black creatures with innumerable claws and fangs, all screeching hideous battle cries. On the ground where she had fought those soldiers was a bubbling maroon puddle emitting steam—the fear-induced version of her robe.

"It's all in my head," Carolyn told herself, pulling herself upright. Her whole body was shaking as she walked, and despite knowing it was an illusion, she still jumped back with a little yelp whenever blood splattered down from the sky. She pressed on, scared to run toward the frightening, black creatures, but knowing she had no choice. Each step was difficult, fighting against her every impulse to curl up on the ground again and cry. But the more she steadied herself, the more she focused on the robe, the more her mind was able to perceive it as it actually was.

She carefully lifted the robe from the bed of vines it rested on, thankful to discover that the weight spell had faded. Praying the potion bottles hadn't cracked under the weight, she reached in and found them both intact. One vial contained a rich, blue liquid, as Treton had said it would be. With trembling fingers, she pulled the cork free, tossing it aside, and downed the potion. The archmage was right, it had a very sweet flavor, like a melted ice pop; it burned a bit as it went down, warming her inside.

Immediately the world began returning to normal. The orange sky shifted to a clear blue and the blood faded away. The mass of dark creatures returned to the shapes of knights and soldiers. The thorny vines on the ground retracted, nothing more than innocent blades of grass. Carolyn felt a certain clarity as even her normal apprehensions and worries seemed to melt away. She was cured not just of the fear spell, but of *all* her fear.

Carolyn turned back toward the battle of the mages behind her. Garinald was a bear, bloodied and desperate and wrestling with Jiselda, but his movements were sluggish and his blows lacked strength. He avoided the use of his right arm where a deep wound could be seen, the blow struck while in his eagle form. The end was near for him. Carolyn grabbed her robe and pulled it on as she ran back into the fray, no longer afraid of Jiselda, and no longer afraid to fail. She watched as, once again, Jiselda pierced through Garinald with her enchanted staff, this time in the chest.

"No!" Carolyn shouted. There was a purple flash as

Garinald, still pierced through the chest, returned to his human self. Jiselda retracted her staff and left the body to slump to the ground. Carolyn couldn't tell if he was still alive, but she felt strangely unperturbed by the thought that he might die. It didn't disturb her like it should.

Jacim re-entered the fight, leaping over the fallen wizard, and swinging a sword at the enchantress. His staff was nowhere to be seen, but a sword reclaimed from a fallen soldier would be effective enough. He tried engaging her, but without his staff he might as well have been moving in slow-motion. With her super-human abilities, she quickly forced him back; in mere seconds it was over, the sword sent flying out of his hand. She stabbed him in the gut and Jacim fell to the ground, unmoving.

Carolyn had closed most of the distance, ready to fight, but thought better of it. Rushing in blindly had done Jacim no good and it would only do her worse. She needed to take stock of her situation and devise a plan.

Jiselda stood there, Jacim laying on the ground next to her, Garinald a few feet behind her, as she looked about and saw Carolyn. She no longer looked at Carolyn as a nuisance to be disposed of and ignored. Fire was in her eyes as she studied her last opponent, treating her as much as a credible threat as her fallen enemies, her face a mask of fierce determination as she regained her fighting stance.

Carolyn wasn't afraid. That wasn't a statement that could normally be said of her, but now she really looked at Jiselda—at how heavily she was breathing, the many scratches and cuts that she had not been able to heal, her defensive stance. Jiselda was not invincible and she knew it. If ever there was a time to beat her, now was it, but how?

Jiselda was still a powerful opponent and could not be taken lightly. She was also incredibly clever and had sharp eyes, watching Carolyn's moves carefully. Carolyn's two allies were bleeding out and had to be helped quickly or it would be too late for one or both of them. *Good thing I'm not afraid,* she thought as a reckless plan formed in her mind.

Otherwise I'd never try this!

Carolyn started with the most unpredictable thing she could: she ran screaming like a madman straight for Jiselda.

"AAAAAHHHHHH!" she shouted, waving her arms about and looking downright insane. The tactic seemed to work; Jiselda's composure faltered; whatever she was expecting, it definitely wasn't this. Carolyn could see how she observed her charging opponent, reassessing the situation, ultimately deciding to stand her ground and keep on the defensive, ready for anything. *Just have to keep her confused for now,* Carolyn told herself.

Once she reckoned she had gotten close enough, Carolyn cast her staff aside and threw herself into a cartwheel, heading straight for Jacim. Despite the aching of her muscles, her training allowed her to execute it perfectly, with only a minor cramp in her side. She landed right by the fallen apprentice and turned quickly to face her opponent, holding up her hands as though for a fist fight.

The enchantress had her staff at the ready and was moving forward to attack. A few small bursts of flame were enough to distract her, giving Carolyn the pause she needed to grab the Jacim's sword. It was heavier than she expected, not to mention she had no clue how to wield it properly, instead holding it like a baseball bat.

A curious look came across Jiselda's face now as she seemed to realize Carolyn had no idea what she was doing. Carolyn stepped forward cautiously with the sword, keeping it at the ready. Jiselda's reaction was swift, swinging her glowing staff to keep Carolyn at bay, yet still remaining cautious. Her opponent's unpredictable behavior was working to disturb her.

Carolyn tried moving in from the right, giving the sword a test swing, but Jiselda was quick to parry and riposte. Carolyn pulled back rapidly, barely avoiding the tip of the magical sword, and moved further to the right. She was toeing a dangerous line—at any moment Jiselda could realize Carolyn was hopeless to protect herself and activate her superhuman attributes to take her out. So long as she remained concerned about Carolyn's intentions, she would remain defensive, but not for long.

After a couple more test lunges, maneuvering herself slowly to the right, Carolyn felt she was finally in position. She stepped back, risking a quick glance behind her so she would look distracted. Jiselda took the bait, instantly leaping forward, ready to finish this fight. Carolyn swung the sword forward, attempting to parry the blow, while moving her focus to her staff that was lying on the ground directly behind Jiselda.

Jiselda's staff hit the sword, throwing off Carolyn's grip on the hilt and exposing her to the follow-up strike that would leave her fallen alongside Jacim. But the follow-up never came. Before she could, the simple apprentice's staff, laying forgotten on the ground, had obeyed Carolyn's commands and came flying into the air to slam straight into the small of Jiselda's back with all the force Carolyn could muster.

"Ahh!" Jiselda screamed, throwing her attack wide and providing a very brief window of opportunity for Carolyn to strike. Swinging the sword around like a baseball bat, Carolyn again gripped the handle with both hands, the point of the blade digging itself deep into Jiselda's stomach, cutting a horrific gash clean across.

Jiselda's eyes shot wide open and she fell to her knees, screaming in pain as blood poured out of her new wound like a river. Carolyn lifted the sword up again, ready to strike once more, but this time aiming for the neck.

But she couldn't. Once again she found her opponent at her mercy, yet she couldn't bring herself to do it. She chided herself for being weak. *This is what a hero does, right?* She told herself, *they stop the bad guys from hurting people anymore.* But just because she wasn't willing to kill Jiselda outright didn't mean she couldn't incapacitate her. Focusing on her staff, Carolyn Pulled once more, this time smacking it into the back of Jiselda's head. The enchantress's eyes rolled back and she fell forward with a thud on the blood-soaked grass, unmoving.

There was no time for her to exult or consider what she had just done, Garinald and Jacim still needed her. She rushed over to Garinald's limp body while pulling her healing potion out of her pouch. As she moved, the cramp in her side started to bother her, but she ignored it. The older wizard was lying in a puddle of his own blood.

Treton had said that healing potions could save someone even in a dire situation; so long as Garinald was still breathing, then, the potion could still save him. She might've stopped to check for a pulse but even those couple seconds seemed too long when he could possibly be slipping away. Pulling the cork from the bottle she pulled the wizard's mouth open and poured the disgusting liquid down his throat. Only then did she stop and check for a pulse, finding it to be very faint, but definitely present. As she watched, the scratches, gashes and two deep stab wounds in his torso slowly began stitching back together on their own.

Carolyn breathed a sigh of satisfaction, but still couldn't take any time to rejoice. Seeing Garinald's own belt pouch and unsure if Jacim had one, she fished out the older wizard's own healing potion and ran back to where Jacim was lying. She chanced a quick glance as she ran past Jiselda's body, seeing how she shuddered with rapid breaths as she desperately clung to life. It was only a matter of time before the enchantress' life slipped away and Carolyn wasn't sure whether or not to feel happy about that.

She put it from her mind and rushed to Jacim's side, her cramp starting to hurt more. Luckily his wound wasn't as deadly, but still lethal if left untreated. She once more popped the cork from a vial, opened the young wizard's mouth, and shoved the grotesque liquid in. She could already tell that Jacim was still alive, but she waited by him for a moment anyway. His stomach wound began to close up as well as other cuts and scratches all over his body.

Jacim's eyes blinked open. He looked up at her in confusion at first, then panic.

"Lady Carolyn!" he shouted, sitting up suddenly, something he instantly regretted, as the potion wasn't finished with its work. He fell back again, groaning. "What happened? Where's Jiselda?"

"Over there," Carolyn pointed at her body casually, lying in a pool of its own blood. "I took care of her after you got knocked out." She meant to say it as a simple matter-of-fact statement, but the casual way she was speaking probably came across as arrogance—and, perhaps, a confidence she had never actually felt. Jacim looked at her in awe.

"Milady!" he said reverently, bowing his head slightly, "I'm sorry to have ever doubted your ability before. I admit I was... Milady! You're injured!

"I'm what?" she answered in surprise. She looked down at herself and, sure enough, where she thought she had merely had a cramp was actually a small but deep cut. Jiselda must've slashed her as she was cartwheeling past when she thought she was out of range. Now that she saw it there and with the adrenaline wearing off, the gash hurt *a lot*. Not to mention all the blood.

"I'm bleeding..." she said, her voice distant. She'd suffered her shared of bumps and bruises growing up, but never had she seen so much blood coming from her like this. Was she going to...?

"Your healing potion," Jacim said urgently, pulling Carolyn back to reality, "You need to take your healing potion, quickly!"

"I can't!" Carolyn cried shrilly. "I gave it to Garinald!"

"Then take mine," he said, fishing around in his own belt pouch. He pulled out another vial of the healing potion, thrusting it toward Carolyn. She tentatively gripped her hand around it. Though the pain was immense and the bleeding clearly ongoing, the potion's sludgy, dark brown swirl was very off-putting.

"Quick, milady, please!" Jacim urged her, his expression

pleading. Carolyn didn't think her wound was fatal, but it was bad enough that it frightened Jacim.

Steeling herself, she pulled off the cork. There was a hint of a sweet scent to the liquid, but that didn't make up for the grotesque appearance. Grimacing, Carolyn held her nose, closed her eyes, and took a drink.

Carolyn didn't know if it was day or night, but that's probably because her eyes were closed. What she did know was that the liquid she just poured down her throat was by far the most detestable thing she had ever swallowed, and she'd taken antibiotics before. Though mildly sweet, the potion was thick and slimy and slid down her throat as one large gulp. Though she had never had the displeasure of swallowing a slug before, Carolyn was fairly confident she now knew what it would feel like.

When it was finally over, she opened her eyes again and looked down at her wound. It felt really itchy as the flesh began to seal itself together, not even leaving a scar or a mark. It was completely healed. She felt a rush of energy as her body replicated all of the blood it had lost.

"Well," she said finally, "I guess that was worth it after all."

"Yes," Jacim agreed as he pulled himself to his feet, "Let's check on Garinald."

The two of them silently passed the now still body of Jiselda. Carolyn did her best not to look at her or give any thought to what she had done. The older wizard was just starting to lift himself into a sitting position. The healing potion had healed his fatal wounds, but it still hadn't healed him completely. The grizzled wizard looked at them with his normal, passive grumpiness, then past them to Jiselda's body and back again.

"Good work," he nodded curtly, "she was a strong opponent."

"Thank you, Master Garinald," Jacim, ever formal, said with a bow, "but I cannot take credit for it. Lady Carolyn is the one that struck the killing blow."

For the first time, Garinald showed a hint of emotion, his eyebrows raising ever so slightly in surprise at this bit of news. Carolyn, on the other hand, was uncomfortable with the term "killing blow."

"Very good, Milady," Garinald gave another nod, this one more deferentially. "You're certain she's dead, correct?"

"Well..." Carolyn started slowly.

Garinald didn't wait for further explanation, he immediately pulled himself to his feet and walked over. He kneeled by the body for a good minute, feeling for a pulse, before turning his back on it. He said nothing, which Carolyn was grateful for, and the three wizards turned their attention to the palace and the rest of the battle. While there were many fatalities on both sides, the knights seemed to have the upper hand. The remaining enemy troops were retreating back to the palace while the knights chased them down.

"I have little magic remaining after that fight," Garinald said, "but I have enough to get us to the castle. I will fly in and distract the guards while you two make sure to keep the main gate open so our knights can get inside."

"I'm sorry, Master," Jacim said quickly with a downcast expression, "but I'm afraid I'll be of no help. Jiselda tossed my staff away during the fight and I have to find it if I'm to be of any help."

"We'll have an easier time of spotting it from the air," Garinald responded, 'I'll morph us, then we'll find it together. But we must be quick."

Without waiting for confirmation, there was a purple flash and once again Carolyn found herself transformed into a powerful eagle with vision far beyond what she could normally hope to see. The three of them launched into the air, a sense of urgency between them. Before they had gotten too high, Jacim broke off and dove toward the battlefield, coming back up with his staff clutched in his talons. With the young enchanter armed again, the three of them flew toward the palace.

Up on the ramparts were a couple archers and there were a few more in arrow slits along the walls, all of which were focused on shooting at the knights. A couple of them noticed the eagles coming and loosed a few arrows toward them, but none of them hit their mark.

They made it above the wall and dove for the other side into a large courtyard. There were a number of soldiers gathered there, many of whom were just coming back in through the main gate. Garinald pulled out of his dive and spun around, heading back to the front wall from the outside, Carolyn and Jacim following close behind.

Together they flew through the open window of a guardhouse about ten feet up just beside the gate. There were some shouts from below as the eagles closed in, but no one reacted in time. Garinald slammed the full weight of his eagle form into the one soldier on duty, sending him screaming to the floor, while Carolyn and Jacim attempted to find places to land. Once Garinald was satisfied that he had properly ravaged the soldier's exposed face, causing Carolyn to turn away in disgust, another purple flash signaled their return to human form.

"The gate is still open. We must keep it so," Garinald said quickly. He turned and left the two apprentices to hold the guardroom, turning into a bear the moment he was out of the cramped space. Cries of surprise and fear rose up from the courtyard as the angry grizzly collided with soldiers trying to ascend the stairs to the gatehouse, falling backward into their companions. Carolyn tentatively looked out the window and, finding no arrow had been loosed at her, shot a couple fireballs into the retreating soldiers. Jacim came up beside her, the emerald on his staff glowing slightly; Carolyn felt an odd sensation like she was stronger and faster than she had been before.

"I am honored to fight beside you, Lady Carolyn," he said softly. She turned to him, taken aback by the first, genuine expression of respect she had heard from him. He looked at her briefly, his earnest statement backed by the look in his eyes, before turning to focus on the soldiers outside. There was another green flash as a number of soldiers lost their footing and slipped, as though the ground had suddenly been covered in oil. Carolyn smirked, casually launching more fireballs into the crowd.

It wasn't long before the knights came charging through the open gate, and together with the magical support, retook the courtyard. The battle of Dor Palace had been won.

CHAPTER 9

A Knight's Oath

The next few hours were a blur. Carolyn, Jacim, and Garinald escorted the knights through the palace, routing out the remainder of the enemy troops hidden within and retaking it for Herin. In the end it was not as well manned as they had thought, a fact which concerned them, but they were grateful for the relative ease in finishing up the battle.

Carolyn accompanied a group of knights into the dungeons and were relieved to find many of the knights from the original battalion still alive, though a little worse for wear, crammed into the cells. There were shouts of joy and enthusiasm on both sides as the doors were unlocked and companions were reunited. Carolyn nearly shouted with joy when she discovered Elis, still alive, among the prisoners. There was also a very elderly man who was escorted out, looking like the imprisonment had taken quite a toll on him. Many of the knights who were freed—including Elis—were eager to equip whatever weapons could be found quickly and rejoin the fight to reclaim the palace.

Once all of the enemy soldiers had been killed, driven

off, or imprisoned, Duke Thordic—the Lord of Dor Palace, lately freed from his own dungeon—quickly took charge of operations. Most of the knights, along with Garinald, were left in charge of defense, while others were assigned to clean the kitchens—left a wreck by the enemy soldiers—and take an inventory of supplies to ensure there was food to sustain the forces now present in the palace.

The barracks were also set up for the knights as well as for the surviving palace guards found in the dungeons. By the end of the day, everyone involved was exhausted and hungry. A large but simple meal was prepared, which everyone ate in exhaustion but good spirits, before turning in for the night.

There was, however, one loose end: Jiselda. As the palace was being secured and bodies of fallen knights taken in, some knights were sent to retrieve Jiselda's body, only to find it gone. When he heard, Garinald immediately set out to investigate, but had not returned by nightfall. Rumors were circulating that some of the surviving soldiers took her body when they fled, though for what purpose, no one could fathom. The possibility that she was still alive was brought up—a thought that sent chills down Carolyn's spine—but Garinald had confirmed himself that she was dead, so Carolyn dismissed that suggestion as impossible. She couldn't bear to think of having to fight her again.

The next morning, Carolyn woke feeling gross. She hadn't had a chance to bathe after the battle, and didn't have a change of clothes, so she'd slept in her dirty and sweaty outfit. When she got to bed the previous night she was too exhausted to care. This morning, however, all she wanted was to feel clean.

Still half asleep and yawning, Carolyn stumbled toward a side door of her room, assuming it would be a bathroom, and was distracted by the clear, endless blue sky outside her window. It had been so long since she'd woken up to see actual sunlight, not just a magical image. She paused to enjoy the warmth of new morning's light.

With no maid in sight Carolyn was happy to draw a bath for herself, leaving her clothes to soak in a separate tub. It was such a relief to scrub off the sweat and grime of the previous day, and the terror of her memories.

The effects of the anti-fear potion faded not long after entering the palace the previous day. Once it did, it had felt like her fears and worries came back all at once, threatening to overwhelm her. She nearly collapsed against a wall. Luckily Jacim was there and offered his support. She took a few deep breaths to steady herself, but her worries had been with her ever since.

It frightened her, in retrospect, to think of how fearless she had been in facing Jiselda with such confidence. Other than some fire tricks and her skill in gymnastics, there was no reason she should ever have won a battle with someone as strong as Jiselda. Yet she did. In that moment when it mattered most, when she had no fears to inhibit her, she accomplished something she would have never thought possible.

That's what really frightened her, the realization that she was capable of more than she realized, yet her potential was held back by her constant worry. By all rights she should have lost that battle and died, yet she came out the victor. She was torn between wanting to recapture that feeling of confidence and retreating into her fears and hiding in the comfort of their familiarity.

One more thing bothered from the battle yesterday— the fact that her magic had not been enough to fight off the soldiers that attacked her. *It's probably because I'm inexperienced,* she told herself, *but what if it happens again?* She wanted a backup option, one that was more potent than her simple, wooden staff. She couldn't rely on Sarin riding out of nowhere to save her, she needed to be able to protect herself.

When she finished bathing, Carolyn redressed in her soaking wet—but clean—clothes. She squeezed them out as best she could. Finding a hairbrush in the bathroom, she managed to get her hair back in order before heading down to the dining hall.

The palace was a bustle of activity. The servants, back to work after spending the previous day recovering, had taken charge of the cleanup of the palace. The enemy soldiers had left many of the hallways a mess and seemed to have been breaking things for fun. Despite having had control of the palace for a mere two days, they managed to make the place into quite the pigsty.

There were many knights and palace guards eating in the dining room when Carolyn arrived. The previous night they had not stood on ceremony and everyone ate upon entering. It seemed this morning was the same, as Duke Thordic had yet to arrive. Still, they had enough presence of mind to notice Carolyn walk in and stand for her. If any of them noticed she was walking through the dining hall in dripping wet clothes, none had the audacity to make such an indication. She took her seat at the head of the center table and everyone returned to their meal.

It wasn't long before the Lord of Dor himself also showed up. As he entered, he looked rather perturbed that the meal had started without him. He stood for a moment at the entrance, waiting for his presence to be noticed and for everyone to stand for him.

He was young, probably in his thirties, tall with strong features, a well-trimmed auburn beard, curly hair, and green eyes. He walked with purpose and importance, like he owned the place. Which was fair, since he did, but something about his strut looked more like a display of power than simply confidence to Carolyn. She had sat beside the Duke the previous night, but had been too exhausted and distracted to listen to him when he tried to engage her. All she had gathered was that he was not married and that something about his demeanor disturbed her.

He gave her a wide smile as he took the seat beside her

at the head of the table.

"Good morning to you, my lady," he said formally. "I pray you found your accommodations agreeable?" He was watching her intently, still with that smile.

"Yeah, it was fine," she shrugged, shifting in her seat. She looked away from him and returned to her meal.

"Excellent," he sounded pleased with himself, "Your comfort is my first priority, of course."

"Shouldn't protecting the palace be your first priority?" Carolyn glanced at him briefly as she asked.

"Fear not, Lady Carolyn," his smile seemed to grow wider, "the General and his knights are more than capable of handling such matters. That leaves me to care for the important matters, such as yourself."

Carolyn looked away again, returning to her meal, and remained silent. She could feel her cheeks growing red, but she wasn't sure why she should be blushing. After a brief silence between them, Thordic spoke up again.

"After breakfast I will have my tailors prepare a dress for you," he said, his words sounding careful and calculated. "It is not proper for a Lady such as yourself to be dressed in such lowly garments, especially given their state of disrepair."

Carolyn looked down at herself. There were some tears in her robe, though none were too big and her undershirt kept everything underneath properly covered. Still, he had a point, except that the feeling that he had an ulterior motive was quickly growing clear to her.

"I like my robe," she answered simply, not looking back at the Duke.

"As you wish," he conceded, though reluctantly. "Then my tailors shall take your measurements for a new robe. I'll send them to you this morning."

"Sure, sounds great," Carolyn answered with as sarcastic a tone as she could. She could feel the Duke's eyes on her, and it disturbed her. *Why won't he stop staring at me?* Carolyn tried returning to her meal, but found she had lost her appetite. After taking a few more nibbles of bread, she got up with a sigh.

"Is everything all right, Lady Carolyn?" Duke Thordic asked, a tone of concern in his voice. Or was that disappointment?

"Yeah," Carolyn waved a hand dismissively, not caring how rude it was, and walked off. She needed to get away from the Lord of Dor and get some fresh air. She generally had a good sense about people, and Thordic gave her the creeps. As much as she was glad to be out of Cansition, she wished it could have been anywhere else but *here*. As she entered the hallway, she heard footsteps behind her and turned suddenly.

"Everything all right?" Sarin asked as he and Elis approached. Unlike Thordic, the concern Sarin expressed was genuine. Elis' expression, on the other hand, was odd. His eyes were downcast and his countenance was intense. *He's probably still recovering from imprisonment,* she reasoned.

"Yeah," Carolyn lied, "just needed some space."

"Now that you have some space," Sarin asked, starting to smile, "would you care for some company?"

"Yes. In fact, I have a... maybe strange request," Carolyn replied, her worries from the previous day's battle coming to mind. "I was wondering if you might teach me to use a sword?" She looked between the two knights hopefully.

"A sword?" Sarin blinked in confusion, "But... you're a wizard."

"Why do you want to learn to use a sword?" Elis asked, a little more sensibly, though his voice was almost a monotone.

"Well, I don't think this will be the last time I'll be in a fight," she explained, "and I can't always expect Sarin to save me. I need to be ready."

Elis nodded, his expression grave. "Most nobles are taught swordsmanship anyway," he said, "Seems like a fair request."

"So, you'll teach me?" Carolyn asked hopefully.

"Carolyn, learning to use a sword takes *years*," Sarin pointed out, "and a *lot* of practice."

"But I can teach you the basics," Elis put in. "You know where the barracks are, right? Meet us outside them in a half-hour."

"Sure," Carolyn smiled, immediately perking up. "See you then."

Impatient as she was, that half-hour felt longer than it was, but soon enough she found herself greeting her two friends once again outside the barracks. The knights led her to the empty training room. The first thing Elis did when they entered was hand Carolyn a piece of parchment, holding an inkwell and a quill in his other hand.

"What's this?" Carolyn asked, taking the parchment from him. The words on the page were all a jumble to her.

"It's a waiver," Elis explained. "It's standard that the teacher of royalty request the waiver be signed, forgiving the teacher of any injury sustained during training."

"Is that really necessary?" Carolyn looked up at him. "I won't hold it against you if you hurt me."

"Without it, I would be liable to the death penalty for injuring a royal," Elis answered darkly.

"Oh." Without another word, Carolyn took the quill, dipped it in the inkwell, and signed the parchment.

"Thank you." Elis breathed a sigh of relief. He took the waiver back from her, rolled it up, and handed everything off to Sarin. "Now we can begin."

"I'm just going to watch," Sarin said, moving off to the side, "to make sure Elis isn't making any mistakes, of course."

"Didn't you say yourself I was the better swordsman," Elis looked at him, the faintest flicker of a smile appearing.

"Yeah, but I didn't really *mean* it," Sarin smirked in response.

Elis was not wearing his armor, just the simple, leather padding that he wore underneath. Nor did he have his sword on him. He moved over to the weapons rack at the side of the room and pulled out two wooden training swords, similar to the ones Carolyn had practiced with in Cansition.

"We start with the basics," Elis said, handing her a sword and moving toward the center of the room. "First is your stance. Keep your left foot forward, then move your right foot out a bit, pointed away from you," he demonstrated, standing beside Carolyn so she could easily see what he was doing. "Then bend your knees, but just a bit, not like you're kneeling."

Carolyn did her best to mimic him. It seemed pretty easy to do, though it didn't come as naturally to her as it did for Elis.

"Not quite," Elis said, scrutinizing her position, "move your leg out a bit more. Good, now turn it. Your knees are bent too much, loosen up. Excellent. Next, hold up the sword with both hands."

"Why both?" Carolyn wondered, "I don't expect to be using heavy swords."

"It helps to practice with both hands at first," Elis explained, "to strengthen your wrists and practice control. You'll get to one-handed, don't worry."

Elis then spent the next hour showing Carolyn how to properly hold the sword, how to move in and out of her stance, and take a few practice swings. It was more exhausting than Carolyn expected, considering she was just standing still most of the time. It was hard training her feet to move into position, but her experience with gymnastics gave her good control over her limbs, so she caught on quickly. Elis was satisfied with her progress, so they decided to break and spend another hour later.

Over the next three days, Carolyn remained cooped up in Dor Palace. She was starting to get frustrated with it: after being stuck in Cansition so long, she was looking forward to getting out, and now she was just stuck in another palace.

At least this time she could get some fresh air by going out into the courtyard or onto the parapets, but otherwise she felt trapped.

At least she wasn't completely bored. She had traded magic lessons with Treton in Cansition for sword lessons with Elis. It was much harder for her to learn. While she was in good shape, swordsmanship used a completely different set of muscles than she was used to, and found she was sore half the time from the effort. Still, Elis said she was improving and constantly reminded her it would take years for her to truly master the blade.

The worst part of it all was having to be around the creepy Duke Thordic. She still wasn't sure what it was about him that bothered her, but every time she sat next to him at a meal, she felt like she needed to take a long, hot bath. Fortunately, she had managed to avoid him by hanging out in the barracks or spending time outdoors with the guards, but mealtime was the one time she couldn't avoid him.

"I've sent my tailors to your room almost every day, Lady Carolyn," he was saying to her at breakfast on the fourth day, "but you always seem to be elsewhere. I wonder what could be occupying so much of Her Ladyship's time?"

As usual, Carolyn tried to ignore him, providing monosyllabic responses whenever she could. "Yeah, I wonder," she answered, returning to spreading jam on her bread.

"It's such a shame," Thordic sighed, persistent as ever. "You would look so lovely in a dress made by my personal tailor."

Something about the way he said that sounded wrong to Carolyn. She gave him a sideways glance, and found he was looking at her intently.

"I don't get why you care so much," she said finally, annoyance coloring her tone. "It's not like I'm going to be staying here."

"I'm saddened to hear you say that, Lady Carolyn," he answered in his deep, rich voice. "I would very much enjoy your continued presence here."

That was when it hit her. Carolyn looked up at the older man's dancing eyes and intent stare: he was hitting on her! She was only fourteen, which even by Herin standards was not an adult yet, not to mention the fact that he was more than twice her age. She was equal parts disgusted and shocked and couldn't bear to look at him anymore. She quickly turned away, feeling angry, and found she had no appetite anymore. She stood abruptly and made to walk away.

"Lady Carolyn, whatever is the matter?" Duke Thordic said, grabbing her arm, gently but firmly.

She turned back toward him, for a brief moment feeling trapped and powerless.

No, she reminded herself, *I'm not powerless. I am a princess; I am a wizard; I am important!*

She would not be controlled by this creep nor feel compelled to answer his questions. Without a word she broke his grasp and marched off, head held high and proud.

Once she was out in the hallway, she leaned back against the wall, closed her eyes, and took a deep breath. She could hardly believe what she had just done. Most of her life she had been timid and avoided conflict, yet she had just asserted herself firmly and walked with pride. *Did I, though?* she wondered. In the end, leaving was still avoiding the conflict. If she left because of someone else's actions, was she really showing strength and control? She felt lost and confused, and not for the first time, trying to make sense of what had just happened.

"What happened?" a voice asked her suddenly. Carolyn opened her eyes to see Elis standing there, the same intense stare he'd had for the past three days, but there was a hint of something more. He seemed tense, like he was ready to spring into action, or trying to keep his anger in check.

"Nothing," she lied, not too interested in talking at that moment.

"You don't have to lie to me," Elis said, his gaze piercing

but not unkind, "everyone in the room saw Duke Thordic grab your arm on the way out."

"I just..." she began slowly, feeling awkward, "I can't stand Thordic," she admitted.

"That's no surprise," Elis reassured her, "A number of the soldiers and servants stationed here had few kind words for him, it seems."

"Well, at least I'm not the only one," Carolyn let herself smile and picked herself up, "Can we hang out for a bit?"

"If you wish," Elis gave a little nod, "Would you like to get some fresh air?"

The two of them headed outside to the courtyard. It was looking a lot better since she first dove into it as a bird a few days ago. It had been cleaned up since the battle and stations were again manned by Herin troops. There were soldiers on the wall above and archers along many of the arrow slits. Unfortunately, they had suffered heavy losses when the palace was first taken, so many positions were left empty, but they felt confident they could hold it for now. A messenger had already been sent back to Cansition when the palace was first taken, and the response was to sit tight until reinforcements arrived. Until then, the knights were staying and the general was in charge of arranging palace defenses.

The two of them walked out silently, neither speaking. Carolyn hated walking with someone when no one was speaking, it always felt so awkward to her, but she was feeling too disturbed and didn't much feel like talking. Now she understood why Duke Thordic bothered her so much. Before, seeing him was just a nuisance; now the thought of sitting next to him made her feel dirty.

Carolyn got the sense from Elis that he wanted to say something, but either he didn't know what, or he was working up the courage. He kept looking around at the guards nearby as they wandered about the courtyard, his face betraying an inner conflict. This whole time she thought he was in a mood because of his imprisonment, but she saw something else in his behavior. He was intensely bothered by something, and every time he saw Carolyn looking at him, he looked away quickly. Finally, he opened his mouth to speak just as a shout from the palace gate interrupted him.

"Hey!" Sarin was approaching, smiling wide. "Can I join you two?"

"Sure," Carolyn smiled as the young knight approached. Whatever it was Elis had been about to say, Carolyn didn't get to hear it. He shut his mouth as soon as he saw Sarin, giving his friend a nod in acknowledgment.

"Whatcha two talkin' about?" Sarin asked as he gave Elis a friendly slap on the arm.

"Just getting some fresh air." Carolyn took a deep breath to emphasize.

"Sounds great," Sarin said. "I could use some of that."

"By the way," Elis spoke up suddenly, "we'll have to postpone our sword lesson this afternoon. Sarin and I are heading out on patrol right after lunch."

"Patrol?" Carolyn repeated, perking up. "Where do you go on your patrols anyway?" They had been working regular shifts on patrols since they first occupied the place. Their swordsmanship lessons always had to be scheduled around when Elis and Sarin went out. They usually got to take their patrols together, though Carolyn was never certain where they were going.

"Just along the river," Elis explained, "We go out about five miles to the crossing, make sure no one's coming, look for evidence someone's already come, then we turn back."

"Is there any chance I could come along?" Carolyn asked hopefully. *I need to get out of this palace. One way or another, I need to get away from that guy.*

"You want to come?" Sarin asked in confusion, "Why?"

"For one thing, to get away from the almighty Lord of Dor," Carolyn tried to say it in a mocking tone, but it came out more as disgust. "For another, I've had nothing to do since we got here except for our sword lessons, and I'll go bored out of my mind if I don't find *something* to occupy my time. I am *not* going to just stand around and be doted upon and get fitted for dresses."

"You'll have to talk to the General then," Sarin answered with a smile. "He can't deny you, but he won't like it."

"Great, let's go find him."

A short time later, Carolyn was in the barracks with the General and the few knights brave enough to witness their exchange. General Drakson clearly did not like the idea of sending a royal on routine patrols when he knew he was responsible for her safety, but without direct orders from the King or Queen to contradict, he had to obey Carolyn's wishes. He attempted to persuade her that she was responsible to care for herself now and rest, but she would not have any of it. Finally, he took down the patrol schedule posted on the wall and promised to return with a new one shortly that would include Lady Carolyn. Carolyn left the encounter feeling mighty pleased with herself and surprised for her courage in facing him.

"That was amazing, Carolyn!" Sarin exclaimed when they had finally left the barracks—and were far enough he wasn't worried about the General hearing, "I've never seen him that angry before without someone being punished for it."

"Don't think we're off the hook, yet," Elis warned, "He may not be able to do anything to Carolyn, but he knows we were involved. Just you wait."

"You're ruining the moment, Elis!" Sarin gave him a friendly slap on the arm.

"I'm just glad I won't have to stay in here all day," Carolyn found herself smiling, "I've been stuck in Cansition too long to just bottle up in here instead."

"We'll have to go over some procedures with you," Elis pointed out, "in case something *actually* happens while we're out."

"You're doing it again," Sarin complained, though he was still smiling. "Just be happy!"

"I am happy," Elis' grave expression gave way to a brief smirk, "but I'm also practical."

Carolyn would be leaving for patrol after lunch, but that meant she had to get through another meal with the Duke first. As much as she dreaded the thought, inevitably lunch time came and Carolyn found herself heading back to the seat beside Duke Thordic. This time she had the impending patrol to look forward to, but it didn't remove the sick feeling she got knowing she'd be sitting next to that creep again. She had spent the last couple hours thinking of some ideas for how to get him off her case, so hopefully this meal wouldn't be so bad.

Carolyn found the Duke was already in his seat when she entered. The attending knights and soldiers had returned to proper mealtime decorum and had not touched their food while waiting for Carolyn to arrive. She walked quickly across the room and took her seat beside the Duke.

"I pray all is well with you, Lady Carolyn," the duke began with his incessant, charming smile. "I was thinking I might accompany you after lunch to meet with my chief tailor. That way I can know for certain he will not miss you again."

"I don't think that'll work," Carolyn answered matter-of-factly, "I have to prepare for my patrol after lunch."

"Patrol?" Thordic's eyes widened and, for the first time, his smile faltered. "What do you mean?"

"I'm going on patrol after lunch with a couple knights," Carolyn continued casually, glancing at him sideways while eating. "You know, taking a look around, keeping people here safe."

"This is outrageous!" Duke Thordic exclaimed, sounding absolutely perturbed by the idea; Carolyn, on the other hand, was smiling now. "How could the General have done this, placing you on a patrol! I'll speak to him immediately after the meal, don't worry, you certainly are not required to leave on a 'patrol'."

"Oh, well that's too bad," Carolyn continued, relishing every moment of his indignation, "because I asked to go."

"You..." Duke Thordic seemed at a loss for words, "You what?"

"Yeah," Carolyn nodded, "I didn't want to just sit around, thinking I'm so important, just taking up space and doing nothing helpful. You probably know how that feels, right?"

The mighty Lord of Dor nearly lost his composure at the thinly veiled barb. His expression changed rapidly from indignation, to shock, confusion, anger, and then back to a collected calm. He returned to his meal, no longer smiling, but also not looking at Carolyn anymore.

"I see," was all he had to say on the matter.

Carolyn couldn't help but smile, proud of herself for confronting the creep and not backing down, even though she was feeling nervous the whole time. The rest of the meal passed with silence between them, which suited Carolyn just fine.

A couple times during the meal she glanced around the room to look at Sarin and Elis. Sarin had his back to her and didn't see her, but Carolyn did catch Elis' eye once. He had been smiling, like he just laughed at some joke, clearly at ease with his friends; but for a brief moment he noticed Carolyn's glance and his expression turned grave. Carolyn shivered from the intensity of his glare and looked aware, unnerved.

It was the same, odd expression Elis had been wearing for the past few days, but now she realized that he only wore that face for her. Something was clearly something bothering him, so much that he couldn't fully be at ease. *I hope that doesn't make the patrol really awkward,* she worried. *Maybe I shouldn't have asked to go after all.*

Despite her concerns, Carolyn was still eager to get out of the palace. After lunch, she went first to her room to retrieve her staff, then headed for the stables to get Mirandi saddled and ready to go. When she arrived, Sarin and Elis were already there, tending to their own horses.

"Almost ready to go, Milady?" Sarin asked with a proper bow and only a slight smile. There were stable hands around and he had to keep up appearances in front of them. Elis bowed as well, though he wasn't looking at her, a far-off look still plastered on his face.

"Yup, just need to get Mirandi ready to go," she said as she went to retrieve her saddle, only to discover that the stable hands had already gotten it for her and were already working on fitting it. "Then again, I think I'll let them get her ready. Thank you," she added, directing it at the stable hands.

The stable hands were young, probably about the same age as Carolyn herself. They both stopped briefly in their work and looked at her in surprise, as though confused by what she said. When they saw she was looking at them and smiling, they both blushed and muttered a, "You're welcome, Milady" before returning to work. It seems they weren't thanked very often, if ever.

"We still have a few minutes before we have to leave," Elis said as he finished tightening the straps on Nova's saddle, "We should take the time to review emergency protocols." He spoke in more subdued tones than usual and, while he was looking at Carolyn now, his countenance had not softened from its intensity.

"Sure," Carolyn answered timidly, put off by his expression.

Sarin and Elis covered the basics with Carolyn as they finished saddling their horses. Don't panic was the first item on the list, something Carolyn thought she could manage. After her confrontation with Jiselda, she wasn't sure if anything would faze her anymore.

They led their horses to the main courtyard where they were to await the previous patrol before setting out. Isana was there to see them off, double-checking all their equipment, providing Carolyn with a canteen that could hook onto her saddle, as well as a saddlebag with a few basic supplies. She then asked them a couple questions on the very protocols they were discussing to make sure they all knew them well. Even Carolyn could answer her accurately.

"I'm impressed, Lady Carolyn," Isana gave her a quizzical look. "I didn't realize you had studied any of our tactics."

"Not at all," Carolyn reassured her, "but it's all we've been talking about for the last ten minutes, so it's hard not to know it."

"I see," the lieutenant smiled knowingly. "I'll have to commend you for that, Sir Elis. I doubt it was Sarin's idea."

"Hey," Sarin's shoulders dropped at the insult. He looked like he was about to say more, but a look from his superior officer silenced him.

"We don't expect anything to happen, as this is just a routine patrol," Isana addressed Carolyn again, "but as you are royalty and we can't take chances, we have a squad ready to march for even the smallest of concerns. Garinald should be returning shortly and we'll send him to keep an eye out for you when he does, just in case."

"That's... No, that's too much," Carolyn frowned, uncomfortable with all the fussing. "I just wanted to get out for a bit."

"We're only doing our jobs, Milady," Isana reassured her, "just as we expect you to do yours."

Carolyn wasn't sure whether Isana was saying that, as royalty, Carolyn would be better off staying in the palace and letting the knights to the work, or if she was saying that as a wizard it was good she was helping out and should be sure to take the patrol seriously. Before Carolyn could ponder it for long, though, the previous patrol returned. Sarin, Elis, and Carolyn remained long enough to hear their report that all was well before they started off on their own, heading out the courtyard gates into the fields beyond.

Dor Palace was built right at the split in the Homfeld River, which flowed down from the mountains further north. One branch of it traveled almost due east, the other starting west before turning south. About an hour ride along the west branch of the river was a main road and a bridge that crossed the river. It was wide enough that many troops could easily cross at once, thus enabling a large force to make foothold in the plains south of Dor. This was the main focus point of their patrol, to ensure no one was coming across or even scouting it out.

While there was another crossing further south—the ford that Carolyn had taken with the knights when they'd arrived just a few days earlier—it was not as easy to move foot soldiers through there, which constituted the majority of Ferdri's army. Twice a day an additional patrol was sent to scout out that ford and look through the Dragontooth Crags, just in case, but that was not the main concern.

Sarin explained all of this to Carolyn as they headed south along the river's edge, marveling at the beauty of the sunlight reflecting off the flowing water. Much of the land was open around them, vast plains in almost all directions. On the other side of Homfeld river was the main province of Herin, descriptively called the Capital Province, and there were many villages and cities there. From where they were, they could make out some buildings in the distance, the embodiment of a serene landscape. At least, it would be, if not for the knowledge that it was now occupied by Ferdri's troops.

They continued along at a fair pace and enjoyed the ride, chatting amongst themselves. Elis was still acting odd, though Carolyn had yet to figure out why. He was participating in the conversation, but he wasn't smiling much and would only answer, not initiate conversation. It was worse than it had been the last few days. If Sarin noticed his behavior, he said nothing about it, but he did a great job of filling up the silence himself. Carolyn was starting to realize just how much he enjoyed talking.

Eventually the bridge appeared on the horizon. They put on an extra burst of speed, eager to get to the bridge and finish the first leg of their journey. Once there, they would take about ten minutes to rest, take a look around, and then turn back.

"What's with all the mist?" Carolyn wondered as they approached. It seemed to be growing out of the river.

"The bridge was built just downstream from a small waterfall," Sarin explained. "It's like a nice welcome into this region, or something."

"Although the mist is higher than it should be," Elis noted, peering into it suspiciously, "We should stay on alert."

"You remember everything we went over, right?" Sarin turned Carolyn, the humor gone from his tone.

"Yup," Carolyn nodded, "If we see an enemy, we keep back, observe, and don't give chase. If they engage, we run and throw caltrops to prevent pursuers."

"Good," Sarin looked pleased, "Let's have a look around."

Despite the unusual amount of mist, everything seemed to be in order. Sarin and Elis dismounted at the bridge to examine it for recent tracks, but there were none. Carolyn remained mounted, walking back and forth through the mist on their side of the bridge, just looking around. She didn't see anything out of the ordinary. Not that anything in Herin was ordinary.

"Well, I think we're done here," Sarin said after they had been investigating and looking around for almost twenty minutes, "We'll need to report the weird mist, but otherwise we're good."

"Not yet," Elis spoke up. He had been talking normally while he and Sarin were performing their knightly duties, but now he had that strange, determined look on his face again, and this time he was looking straight at Carolyn.

"Oh, right," Sarin looked a bit annoyed, "Just be quick about it and let's go."

"Quick about what?" Carolyn wondered aloud. Sarin didn't answer but instead looked away, remounting and trotting a bit closer to the bridge. Elis, already mounted again, rode up ride alongside Carolyn and looked her in the eye. She returned the look suspiciously, "What's this about?"

"Carolyn," Elis began, his voice taking a serious tone, "I was sent with my unit to fight a battle. Instead, a single wizard sent me and my fellow knights cowering in fear. It was a pathetic defeat."

"It wasn't your fault," Carolyn countered. "Jiselda was really strong."

"So what?" Elis sounded almost angry. "We've been trained with how to deal with wizards, but we couldn't do anything to her! An entire unit rendered useless by a single person. Isn't that pathetic?"

"Well..." she stammered, but found she had no reply.

"I thought I would die in that dungeon," Elis admitted, casting his eyes downward. "Even after the fear spell wore off, I found I had no hope. I thought all was lost." Now he looked back up, a look of respect and renewed determination in his eyes. "But it wasn't. You showed up, you saved me. And you also killed the very same wizard who'd trounced us."

Suddenly Carolyn thought she knew where this was going, and it made her uncomfortable, even more than the casual mention of her first kill. "Elis, you shouldn't..." she started, finding her voice, but Elis held up a hand to stop her.

"Please, let me finish," he said quietly. "You saved me, Carolyn. As such, I swear, as a Knight of Herin, by the honor of Adenil, to protect you, Lady Carolyn, Princess of Herin, from all harm." As he spoke these words, a strange look came into his eyes, like a brief flash of strength, determination, and courage. For that split second, Elis seemed a different person, like a legend of old, renowned for their might, unparalleled in their bravery and honor. Then the moment passed, and it was just Elis again, locking eyes with Carolyn.

"Oh," Carolyn answered simply, taken aback. *That's not what I was expecting,* she told herself, *and what was that look in his eyes?* "You don't have to..." she started simply.

"It's done," Elis answered abruptly. "I will honor my oath."

"Well, that was fun," Sarin said suddenly, still off by the bridge, "I think it's time to go now."

"Yeah, let's," Carolyn started, breaking eye contact with Elis finally and looking to Sarin; as she did, her eyes went wide, "Sarin, look out!" she shouted.

The mist behind Sarin was coalescing into the shape of many mounted riders. Sarin immediately gave Midnight a quick slap and shot forward before turning around and readying his spear. Elis, too, turned his mount to face the bridge with his spear at the ready.

In that brief moment, the mist formed into eight soldiers, all on horseback, and one older man wearing a robe and holding a staff in his hand. In the blink of an eye the mist vanished and in their place were actual horses and riders, in the flesh. The soldiers were wearing the markings of Ferdri's knights and the wizard had a ruby at the tip of his staff. There was hardly ten feet between them.

"Run!" Sarin shouted as the riders appeared fully. All three of them quickly turned their horses northward and spurred them on. They had not gone two paces before Carolyn felt a sharp, stinging pain in her back and pins and needles all over, as though her whole body had fallen asleep, accompanied by a loud *crack* of thunder, so loud it seemed to be all around her. She shouted, but her tongue was numb and she couldn't form words, so instead she slumped forward in her saddle, her horse no longer moving. She could see that Sarin and Elis had suffered a similar fate, though they were pulling themselves back up, spears at the ready, and turning to fight. Carolyn tried to pull herself up also and turn around.

The eight soldiers were moving their horses into position to encircle them while the wizard sat on his horse, the ruby of his staff still glowing slightly as he kept it trained on Carolyn. Though he didn't speak, Carolyn could tell from his expression that he would not hesitate to strike again. Then one of the soldiers moved forward, this one with special markings on his armor that seemed to indicate his importance. He hefted a weapon in his hand which at first Carolyn took to be a spear, but on closer inspection found it to be a sword, one so massive that no normal human should be able to wield it. His face looked familiar, too, like something she saw briefly, but she couldn't quite place it.

"Wadda we have here?" he began, his voice gruff, "We jus' were gonna find out how Dor is doin', and now I fin' the same girl I saw bein' taken out o' the palace when the stinkin' knights came raidin'."

Carolyn took in a sharp breath, an intense fear growing in the pit of her stomach. She remembered now: this was the commander of the troops in the palace the day she came through the portal, wounded and directing the battle from the back. He knew she came through the portal, and if Ferdri suspected what she carried...

"Well, I guess you'll be comin' with us, then," he continued, motioning to his soldiers. The circle around them tightened, "I suspec' the palace's already been taken, ey?"

"We won't go," Sarin said, glaring at the enemy commander and holding his spear at the ready. His tone was firm, resolute. Beside him, Elis also readied his spear, keeping an eye on the soldiers all around. Carolyn tried to grip her staff tightly, ready to use it or her magic as need be, but she didn't feel anywhere near as confident. Her hands were already sweating, and it was hard to hold onto her staff. Despite her victory—barely—over Jiselda, Carolyn was not confident in her ability to fight, especially not when outnumbered and surrounded. Maybe if there wasn't an enemy wizard she could surprise them with her fire magic, but he seemed ready for anything.

"Eh?" the enemy commander looked amused, "You won' come, ye say? All righ', then we jus' gonna kill you two and take the lady. Tha' all righ' witchu?"

"You will not harm her," Elis spoke strongly, confidently. Did he not see all the soldiers surrounding him? How could he be so certain?

The wizard casually flicked his staff toward Elis as another *crack* of thunder sounded. This time Carolyn saw the bolt of lightning, arching out of the staff and striking Elis in the saddle. In horror Carolyn saw Elis' body lock up the way hers had a moment ago, fearing that this time it would be permanent, but then his body loosened and slumped over, breathing heavily. It didn't stop him from looking back up defiantly, still clutching his spear.

"Tha's enough," the commander waved at his soldiers casually while moving forward with his massive blade, "Ge' rid o' dem."

For a split second, Carolyn felt a rush of fear and excitement as a battle seemed on the verge of breaking out. Time seemed to freeze as everyone prepared to act at once. Both Sarin and Elis raised their spears, looking ready to attack the enemy commander head-on. The commander was holding his sword back, preparing for a wide sweep. All around them soldiers started to move forward, their own spears pointed at the knights. Carolyn tried to focus, to find someone she could pick off with her fire. The ruby on the enemy wizard's staff suddenly began to glow, charging another spell.

Time started to move again, and as the wizard and enemy soldiers moved forward to strike, the air behind Carolyn seemed to ripple and each of their opponents were simultaneously hit with arrows that, rather than impaling them, sent them all flying off their horses a good six feet or more. The arrows all came from behind Carolyn, away from the river.

"GET BACK, ALL OF YOU!" a booming voice shouted, amplified as though speaking through a loudspeaker, "YOU WILL NOT HARM THESE PEOPLE!"

Carolyn turned around in surprise, expecting to see a

troop of archers and instead saw a single person. In one swift motion the figure nocked another arrow in his bow and fired. The arrow seemed to be headed straight for Carolyn, but almost as soon as it left the bowstring it split, forming a total of nine separate arrows, each headed for one of the enemy soldiers who were trying to get up, knocking them even further back. Two tumbled over the bank of the river with a splash.

"GO NOW!" the voice shouted again, and now Carolyn saw that it was the archer speaking, his voice magically enhanced. "NEVER BOTHER THEM AGAIN!"

The archer fired one more time, his arrow splitting again, but this time it was aimed for the horses. The arrows didn't seem to harm them at all, rather they dealt a loud slap on the rump to each, frightening them enough to send them all running in random directions. Their riders, in the meantime, tried to get up again and also began to run. They had enough discipline to run in the same direction, heading back across the bridge, the wizard hobbling along and the commander dragging his massive blade, leaving a groove in the ground. The two soldiers who had fallen in the river were desperately trying to pull themselves out and ran after their companions the moment they were back on their feet. Not one of them stopped to look back.

Sarin and Elis were also glancing back and forth between the stranger and the retreating force of soldiers. They seemed just as surprised and amazed as Carolyn was. Carolyn had something else on her mind, too. While it was obvious he was using magic, it was not obvious how. She remembered Treton mentioning that there were other forms of magic besides wizardry, but that most of them were shunned or forbidden because of their dangerous nature. It was very obvious that there was no gemstone or staff on the stranger's person, so what kind of magic was he using?

"Thank you for your assistance, stranger," Elis said, though he did not advance forward.

"It was my pleasure," the stranger said, his voice now at a normal volume, sounding kind and cheerful. "I couldn't stand by while they harassed you like that." He looked to be a young man, mid-twenties at best, with well-cropped, reddish-brown hair, and wearing dark green and brown leather clothes. He held his bow loosely in his right hand, his posture relaxed.

"Who are you?" Sarin asked bluntly, though from his expression he genuinely seemed more curious than suspicious. "What are you doing here?"

"My name is Goredian," he answered with a deep bow. "I'm a wanderer. I travel about, explore the land, meet new people. No one of much importance."

His face, his voice, and his eyes all spoke of a kind, gentle person, yet Carolyn could not shake her suspicions. After watching the way he had casually dispatched the ambushing soldiers and his powerful display of magic, it was obvious there was much more to this character than what he let on. He hadn't stepped any closer to them, maintaining a respectful distance, but Carolyn was watching carefully in case he made a move.

"How did you do that?" Carolyn asked, a bit more aggressively than she meant.

"Magic," Goredian answered simply. Carolyn waited for further clarification, but it quickly became evident that none was coming.

"What kind of magic?" she pressed on. Out of the corner of her eye she could see Elis' expression harden, and both he and Sarin held their spears at the ready.

"There are ways to use magic other than with staves and gems. I happen to use one of them," he answered elusively, his smile not wavering.

"I think we should head back now," Carolyn said firmly, keeping her gaze locked on the stranger; he continued to look her in the eye, as though searching for something. "Thank you for your assistance, Goredian," Carolyn continued, not wanting to offend him. If he did turn hostile, they would be helpless to stop him.

"Of course," Goredian seemed pleased to part ways, "I don't want to keep you here, I'm sure you're busy. It was a pleasure to meet you." He bowed deeply again as he said these words.

Carolyn turned Mirandi back north, Sarin and Elis following suit while remaining silent, and the three of them started off at a quick pace. The mist they had encountered was gone completely now; evidently it was just a cover for the ambush. When Carolyn finally glanced back a minute later, the stranger was nowhere to be seen.

"What in Aderil's name just happened?!" Sarin shouted as they continued, pushing their horses into a faster galop.

"I don't know exactly," Carolyn responded, "but something about him wasn't right."

"What do you mean?" Sarin was nearly yelling to be heard over the sound of the horses. "He just saved our lives!"

"Carolyn's right," Elis said, looking at his friend, "I didn't like him. His magic wasn't normal."

"So what?" Sarin pulled up alongside Carolyn, shouting to his fellow knight on her other side. "What do you not understand about 'he just saved our lives'? Shouldn't we be a bit more grateful? So his magic is a bit strange. Isn't all magic strange? What's your problem?"

Though he was looking at Elis when he said this, Carolyn felt Sarin intended the question more for her. She started to feel embarrassed, worried that she had made a mistake and overreacted. What did she really understand about magic? Was there anything wrong with what he did? Treton did say some of the other forms of magic, like alchemy, were considered acceptable; maybe she should've just assumed this magic was ok too?

"I don't know." Carolyn was barely audible over the clanking of armor and pounding of hooves, her voice as low as how she was feeling. "Maybe I was wrong."

"No, I don't think you were," Elis told her, his tone

reassuring. "Carolyn made the call, now we have to trust her," he retorted to Sarin. "If you disagree with her, we'll go to one of the master mages and see what they think."

"All right, fine," Sarin looked frustrated, but ready to drop it. "Just forget about it."

None of them said another word until they returned to the palace where Isana was again there to meet them. When she saw their faces, her expression turned grave.

"Report!" she demanded even before they had had a chance to dismount.

"We were ambushed, Madam," Sarin said immediately.

"Well I'm glad to see you all in one piece, then," she responded, though she looked both surprised and skeptical about this statement, "Come to the war room to give a full report. You three," she added, looking to the next patrol waiting to ride out, "wait here until I return." With that she turned to head inside.

Sarin, Elis, and Carolyn led their horses to the stables and left them to the stable hands before heading to the war room in the barracks. They found the General was already there with Isana, as well as Garinald. There was also another wizard Carolyn didn't recognize, an older woman with a ruby in her staff. She looked concerned.

Everyone in the room stood when Carolyn entered, a gesture she still wasn't accustomed to. She sat down in an available chair as quickly as possible. Everyone sat then, with Sarin and Elis taking seats beside her.

"I'm pleased to see you have returned safely, Milady," the General began, though a twitch in his mouth and his tone of voice seemed to indicate that he was inwardly gloating. "I'm anxious to hear your report of events, if you please."

"Sure," Carolyn answered quickly, looking away from him. Unfortunately, most other eyes were on her as well, and there was little else of interest in the room to catch her attention, other than the tapestry on the opposite wall. She took a deep breath to calm her nerves before diving right into her account.

With everyone's eyes on her, Carolyn described how they arrived by the bridge and encountered the strange mist. She explained how they were very careful to look all around for any sign of a trap or an enemy somewhere but found nothing. She kept glancing at Sarin and Elis for help supplementing the story, but neither spoke up. It was probably out of propriety, though Carolyn couldn't care less about that at the moment. She skipped the part of Elis' vow, instead explaining the soldiers appeared from the mist while they took a brief respite.

"What do you mean they appeared from the mist?" the ruby wizard asked, speaking up for the first time; her voice was kind but firm. "As in, they walked through it?"

"No, they *were* the mist," Carolyn explained, "The mist gathered together and formed into a bunch of people on horses. By the time we noticed, it wasn't mist anymore, it was *actually* a bunch of people on horses."

"A Mist Form spell," the wizard explained. "Difficult to use, but provides excellent camouflage. It takes a little while to return to normal form, that's probably why they waited until you were not paying attention to drop the spell."

"I see," the General seemed displeased; Garinald said nothing but looked like his usual grumpy self, "Why didn't you turn around the moment you saw something was wrong?" He referred this question to Sarin and Elis, not Carolyn.

"Sir, a knight does not retreat just because something is slightly off," Sarin boldly defended himself, "We investigated and found nothing threatening, as protocol dictates."

"Protocol says that when escorting a royal, you *do* retreat when something is 'slightly off', soldier," the General retorted, his face grim.

"I was *not* being escorted," Carolyn blurted out before she could stop herself. She instantly regretted it, but so long as everyone's attention was on her, she continued on. "I'm capable of helping in a fight. Remember that you'd still be sitting in the dungeon if not for me."

Silence fell. The ruby wizard looked appalled, Isana impressed. Garinald was raising his eyebrows as his frown deepened, and the General's mouth was a thin line as he silently fumed at her.

"My apologies, Milady," the General said finally, knowing the onus was on him to appease her, "I did not mean to indicate that you were helpless."

"Whatever, just let me go on," Carolyn said dismissively, trying to make it sound like no big deal, though she realized it was probably a mistake to dismiss his apology. "So, as I was saying, there were a bunch of soldiers on horses—eight, I think?—and one wizard with a ruby. One of the soldiers had a really big sword—I saw him the day I came through the portal—he seemed to be in charge. He recognized me, too, and wanted to take me prisoner, so Sarin and Elis were ready to fight, even though we didn't stand a chance."

"Excuse me, Milady," the General interrupted politely. "Did you make no attempt to flee at this point?"

"Oh right," Carolyn remembered; she always forgot something when retelling stories. "We tried, but the wizard hit us with lightning, so we didn't get very far."

"I see," the General nodded. "Please continue."

"Right, so here's where it gets interesting," Carolyn went on, causing everyone in the room to look more concerned, "So Elis got zapped again for talking back, then this big fight was going to start, and all of a sudden these strange arrows come out of nowhere and send the soldiers and the wizard flying off their horses!"

"Arrows?" the ruby wizard and Isana said in unison, confused.

"Yes, arrows," Carolyn repeated, "One arrow per rider. Then there's this voice shouting like he's talking through a loudspeaker—oh, you probably don't have loudspeakers here, so I wonder how that will translate. Anyway, this voice is shouting and I see someone standing not so far off holding a bow. Then he shoots again to knock everyone away again, and two of them even fell in the river. So they're all scrambling to their feet while he's shouting at them, then he fires another barrage of arrows that sends all the horses running, so the soldiers all have to run off on foot."

"You're saying a single archer fired a barrage of arrows that hit everyone at once?" Garinald interrupted, the only one that would not hesitate to interrupt a royal. "Did he have a staff?"

"Right, so that's what was weird about it. He fired one arrow and it split into a whole bunch, and each one hit perfectly! But he didn't have a staff on him or a gem anywhere that I could see."

"That's bad," Garinald stated bluntly. The ruby wizard nodded in agreement.

"I know, right?" Carolyn agreed, relieved that her apprehensions were warranted, though admittedly, she didn't realize *why* it was so bad, "I mean, I know that non-wizard types of magic are bad, right?"

"Yes," Garinald nodded slowly, "depending on what type. Some drive the mage insane."

"He didn't seem insane," Carolyn said thoughtfully. "Right, so he scared away the enemy soldiers, then he talked to us all pleasantly, like he just shooed away a fly for us. He wouldn't tell us how he used magic and I was wary of him, so we kept our distance. Then the three of us left."

"I don't know if it's relevant," Sarin put in, drawing attention away from Carolyn, to her relief, "but he said his name was Goredian."

Carolyn expected some kind of stunned silence or a roomful of gasps, but it seems the name didn't ring any bells.

"This report needs to be delivered to the King and Queen immediately," the General concluded, "and I think they will order you to return to Cansition, Milady, despite your competence in battle."

Carolyn sighed loudly. At least returning to Cansition would mean she could continue her magic lessons, hopefully even learn to do cool things like Jacim and Garinald.

"Agreed," Garinald nodded. "I'll take her after dark. Flying at night is the quickest and safest route."

"I accept your argument, archmage," the General agreed, "but would feel more comfortable if you took a couple of my knights with you as well, just in case."

"Sarin and Elis," Carolyn said quickly before anyone could respond. Everyone in the room looked at her with stares of surprise or—in the general's case—annoyance. "That's a royal order," she added, then quickly looked away from everyone while biting her lower lip.

"As you wish, milady," the General said, sounding like he was trying hard not to speak through gritted teeth. "Get ready to leave tonight. Dismissed," he added, looking to the two young knights. They both saluted with a "Yes, sir!" and immediately stood and left the room.

"I'll get ready to go, too," Carolyn said, hoping that was sufficient excuse to leave. No one said anything to stop her, so she left the room, shut the door, and leaned against the wall as she tried to wrap her head around everything that had happened. Less than a minute later, the door opened again, making her jump. She felt a brief stab of fear that the General would walk out and she'd be forced to confront him again, but to her relief it was Isana. She quickly closed the door behind her and turned to Carolyn.

"Are you all right?" she asked, her tone concerned now that the debriefing was over.

"Yeah," she nodded, "It's just been... quite a day."

"I understand," Isana smiled, then turned serious, "Carolyn, is there anything you're not telling us?"

"What?" Carolyn looked confused.

"You're not the best liar," Isana admitted, "and I can't help but feel there's something you're hiding."

"No," she answered quickly, then remembered she had left out the part of Elis' oath, "Oh, well, nothing important."

"Oh?" Isana looked curious.

"It was... kind of personal," she said. "Just a conversation we were having. I'd rather not talk about it."

"Fair enough," Isana seemed satisfied by this answer. "You should try and get some sleep now. It looks like you'll be travelling overnight again."

"Fun," Carolyn answered with a sigh.

CHAPTER 10

The Hidden Treasure of Herin

Carolyn tried to take Isana's advice, but she couldn't seem to fall asleep; there was too much on her mind. From the fight just a few days ago, to the sudden ambush and equally sudden salvation, a lot had happened to her recently. It was about this same time less than a week ago that she was resting to prepare for her ride here. Now she would be going back, again at night, but this time she'd be flying.

Why did I ever let myself get mixed up in this? she wondered, not for the first time. Sure, magic and flying were dreams come true, but Carolyn had faced her mortality one too many times ever since she'd arrived, and it seemed evident she would be doing it again before she got to go home.

Why did *grandmother choose me?* she continued to ask herself. If Jessica had been entrusted with the Ruby, there's no way she would have come to Herin and would have avoided getting involved in all this mess. Could grandmother see that about them? What exactly did she see in Carolyn that she didn't see in Jessica? It probably wasn't bravery - Carolyn didn't feel very brave - it was more likely stupidity and recklessness. Maybe staying home would have been the smart thing to do. Maybe Jessica was smarter than her after all.

Yet she couldn't completely regret it. She *had* learned magic, she *had* learned to defend herself, at least somewhat, and she *had* met new friends. Sure, not everything was easy, but life rarely was, and the greater the reward the greater the effort—and risks—that come with it. In this case, the reward was an unforgettable adventure. The risk was death. Did that make it worth it?

She found herself fiddling with the Ruby through her shirt, as she often did when she was lost in thought. It was easy to forget that was the whole reason she had come here in the first place. After all, Treton had hardly said a word about it since the first time she tried to use it. Considering the King's reaction at the time, it seemed unlikely they still wanted her to try, but surely they couldn't have forgotten about it entirely. Carolyn's presence was a constant reminder that it was around, so someone must still view it as an option.

As she considered all this, she had pulled the Ruby out and studied it. It was finely crafted and quite lovely, belying the immense power that lay within. Was it actually possible to control it once she had learned enough? Was it possible for her to control it now?

It was too dangerous to try and use it, not without Treton there to help her like last time, and yet she wanted to see what she could do. Curiosity overcame her judgment; she sat up and focused on the Derishz Ruby in her hand. *If I do this, I have to do it right,* she admonished herself, *I can't rush it.*

Focusing her magic, she let the smallest bit enter into the Ruby, then quickly severed her connection to it as it entered. The ruby lit up dimly for a brief moment and Carolyn felt the slightest surge of power for the blink of an eye, and then it was gone. Steeling herself with a couple of deep breaths, she focused her magic again and created a weak, easily broken magical tether to the ruby.

The effect was instantaneous. Carolyn gasped as a surge of immense power flowed into her. The last time she touched the ruby, she felt like an insect, tiny and insignificant as it pondered the complexity and vastness of the universe. Now she felt even smaller, but that smallness stemmed from understanding rather than a lack of it. Even with her limited magical knowledge she was able to grasp better the kind of power she felt, like she had some inkling about where to focus to try and extract the power she wanted. Yet that understanding made her awe even greater, because now she could see more accurately just how immeasurable it was.

Then there was the desire again. The intense desire to grasp the power fully and unleash its might on every human she could find, tearing them apart. The desire was expanding her vision outward again, searching for every living human nearby. This time she was expecting it and tried to immediately sever her connection. She hesitated as the burning desire for death washed over her, but she strengthened her resolve and cut the connection.

She was back on her bed, no longer looking through a tiny window into a world of cosmic powers beyond her understanding. Breathing heavily and unnerved by the experience she silently admonished herself for her recklessness. It could have turned out a lot worse, but she was pleased at how she had broken away with relative ease. It seemed her training had helped. With more, perhaps she could come to understand even more about magic and, eventually, overpower that burning desire for death with her own desire to help and protect.

After finally getting in a couple hours of sleep, Carolyn drowsily roused herself from bed. She was to leave almost immediately after dinner, traveling as an owl with Garinald, Sarin, and Elis. The rest of the knights would remain in Dor until they received new orders from the King and Queen, while Carolyn was to stay in Cansition... again. She got her hair more or less in a presentable manner with the brush provided her, then groggily stumbled down the hall to dinner.

Everyone was already at their seats when she entered, but it seemed no one had started eating yet, despite Duke Thordic already being there. Had they been waiting for her? Everyone stood, including the Duke, as she rushed to get to her seat, blushing. She quickly sat down and waited for the servants to bring her food, avoiding eye contact with the Lord of Dor.

"Did you enjoy your rest, Lady Carolyn?" the duke asked, giving her a sideways glance. Carolyn wasn't sure if he was still trying to flirt with her.

"Not really, no," Carolyn admitted. She offered no further comment as food was presented and she began to eat.

"What a shame," the Duke sighed. "I went to so much effort to make the palace fit for royalty again. I've been working hard every day, you know, to get things back in order since those ruffians tore it apart. It has been difficult work, but I am not a man of laziness and do not shy away from such efforts."

"That's nice," she said shortly, remembering their previous conversation, where she had implied that he did nothing of use. She was in no mood to entertain him or try to insult him again, she just wanted to eat in peace and leave.

"Of course, you probably understand little of these matters," the Duke went on. "I had time for a proper briefing on your origins, and I understand you've not experienced royalty but for a few months. You probably know nothing of the effort it takes to keep a palace running, let alone the province I am charged with."

He was trying to get to her now, and she had no patience for him. The temptation to magically launch a slab of sauce-covered beef at his face or make his fork fly out of his hand was very great.

"Of course, that's perfectly all right," he went on, starting to smile again. "All you need is a good teacher, someone to help you learn the royal ways, and to care for you. You need a real taste of what it means to be royal."

Carolyn put her fork down. He was still trying his luck with her, and she was disgusted. How could such a demeaning, arrogant, superficial jerk expect her to want to be with him? She couldn't even stand to sit with him at a meal, much less live with him. She turned to look him squarely in the eye. His broad smile inviting, but his eyes, cold and calculating, danced with excitement as he anticipated obtaining the object of his desire.

Thoughts of all the amazing, spectacular, and humiliating things she could do to him at that moment with her magic flashed through her mind. *No, she told herself, I need to be responsible; it's like a martial art, I can't just beat up everyone who annoys me.* She was, however, not going to stand this treatment anymore.

"I have two words for you," Carolyn tried to say calmly, but she was shaking with fury. "Shut. Up."

"I don't under—"

"No," Carolyn cut him off, waving a finger at him. "No, you don't get to talk anymore. I don't want to hear another word out of your mouth unless you can say something intelligent for a change. For now, leave me alone to eat in peace so I can leave and never have to see you again."

Carolyn did not yell, but she was speaking loudly enough that people at the nearby tables stopped and stared. Even some of the servants stopped briefly. Duke Thordic, red faced and teeth clenched, looked ready to retort, but he was cowed by Carolyn's glare and remained silent, returning to his dinner. Carolyn did as well, though the rest of the meal was not enjoyable for her. She finished quickly and left to wander the halls, trying to calm down.

Was that really necessary? she wondered. Thordic admitted he hadn't known she had come through the portal until today—yet he was still trying to flirt with her? That meant he was only interested in her superficially. Either he thought she was pretty or he wanted to marry a royal to improve his political standing.

Either way, his interest in her was motivated purely by selfish reasons. And then there was the possessive way he had grabbed her arm. She did *not* have to take that lying down. He deserved to be embarrassed for treating her that way and she would not apologize, nor would she refrain from doing it again if she had to.

Her confidence restored, Carolyn found her way back to her room. The only belongings she had brought with her were the supplies for the trip that Treton had packed, and her staff. She grabbed these and headed for the war room, where she was to meet Garinald, Sarin, and Elis. Garinald quickly reviewed their travel path before the four of them went out onto the ramparts. Garinald turned them all into owls, and then they were off, soaring through the darkening skies.

Flying the first time was an exhilarating experience, but Carolyn had been too focused on the battle going on at the time to fully enjoy it. This time she took it all in, the ground below stretching out for miles in every direction. It was especially amazing considering that the sun was setting as they flew, yet everything remained perfectly clear, if in shades of grey, thanks to her owl vision.

They rested briefly amongst the Dragontooth Crags, and then off they flew again, heading straight for the forest. They stopped to rest a couple more times in the forest, each time being careful to look around to make sure no one saw them first, before they continued on. Finally, as the sun was starting to rise and Carolyn thought she would fall asleep mid-fight, they came across the clearing with the hidden entrance to Cansition. Returning to human form as they landed, the four of them headed down the ramp to the hidden palace.

"Halt!" a voice shouted through the gate's peephole, "Who goes there?"

"Archmage Garinald and Lady Carolyn," Garinald

answered tersely, "and a couple knights."

There was a brief pause and a bit of commotion before the gate started to swing open. They marched in, not providing much of an explanation to the guards on duty, before entering the main gates of the palace.

"Their majesties are probably waking now," Garinald said once they were inside, "You three wait in your rooms. I'll find Rissin."

None of them complained. Sarin and Elis headed for the barracks with a brief wave while Carolyn plodded back to her room to get some rest. She fell asleep almost as soon as her head hit the pillow.

Other than a short meeting and some brief meals, Carolyn spent most of the day resting and taking it easy. The next morning, after getting a full night's sleep and feeling refreshed, she reported once more to Treton to continue her magic lessons.

"I must say I am quite impressed with your performance against Jiselda, Carolyn," he said with a beaming smile as he invited Carolyn into his office. "Perhaps now you will see my confidence is well placed?"

"I think it was more luck than skill," Carolyn shrugged, trying to brush off the compliment.

"Luck only goes so far against such a strong opponent," Treton countered, looking serious. "If such a thing even exists. No, I think it was more your ingenuity that won the day."

"So why are we staying in here?" Carolyn changed the subject. It had not escaped her that Treton was now sitting behind the desk rather than leading her out to their usual training room.

"Well, a lot has happened, so perhaps you don't remember," Treton began as he pulled out a small, leather pouch from the desk, "but just before you left, I was ready to start you on your next stage of training."

"Oh," Carolyn remembered the brief glimpse of a ruby

she had gotten just before the frightened knights started piling into the room. It seemed so long ago at this point, though really it had been barely a week.

"I can see you're excited," Treton noted dryly, "but this is a very important step for any wizard. You must now choose your mastery. You will receive a gem for your mastery and a staff to place it in as you begin to learn advanced magic."

"Nice," Carolyn was smiling now. "I finally get a nice-looking staff, then."

"Let's focus on one thing at a time." Treton pulled out a ruby from his pouch. "The first is the Elementalist, sometimes known as a combat mage. They are able to use all the elements in the same way you use fire. Imagine the implications when you can not only throw fireballs, but freeze your enemies in place, drown them in a deluge, or bury them underground, to name but a few uses. Of course, there's more to it than simply fighting, as you yourself know. The wizard that attacked you was an Elementalist wizard using a spell to turn himself and his companions into mist. Quite useful."

"Yes," Carolyn was nodding, thinking of the power she felt from the lightning strike she suffered; it would be nice to wield that kind of power. "That's definitely an option."

"Next," Treton now pulled out an emerald, which gave Carolyn a brief shudder, "I believe you're well aware of what this is for. Enchantment is the ability to enhance, detract, or otherwise modify the properties of an object or person. It can be used for many things: animating suits of armor, increasing the weight of an object, changing the temperature of an object, causing a person to freeze in place, etc. I don't think I need to explain to you how potent it can be in combat."

"No, I'm good," Carolyn shuddered again, remembering the scene of absolute terror she was plagued with temporarily, "I think I'd rather skip that one."

"Fair enough," Treton pulled out a sapphire, "Next we

have sorcery. Sorcery is hard to describe as there are a variety of spells that can be cast with it. In general, it is used for creating magical objects: platforms, barriers, or even weapons. It's other primary use is teleportation."

"That one sounds good," Carolyn nodded approvingly, "Let's keep that one on the table."

"I wasn't planning on throwing one away; they're all on the table," Treton said seriously, clearly not understanding the colloquialism. He pulled out the next one, an opal. "This is my mastery, as you know. It's called restoration and can do anything from repairing a tear in a piece of cloth to mending even fatal wounds on a person. It's also quite useful for restoring an emotional or mental state of mind to someone, as you saw when I cured those knights suffering from the fear spell."

"Right, that was cool," Carolyn remembered how Treton worked his magic... literally. She wasn't too interested, but she didn't want to admit it to Treton, in case he would be offended.

"Indeed." Treton pulled out a golden topaz. "This one is for an Illusionist. Unlike Sorcerers, an Illusionist can create a very complex and subtle three-dimensional image of anything they can imagine, but it's completely incorporeal. Any contact with it will reveal it to be a fake. Still, there are a variety of uses for it, for a clever wizard. It's not uncommon for an Illusionist to disguise their own appearance so that you never know what they truly look like, or to hide a trap in the ground so you don't see it until you've already fallen in. Illusions are only limited by your imagination."

"I have a pretty good imagination." Carolyn couldn't help herself from smiling widely as she imagined a giant, illusionary dragon flying into Mrs. Oak's class. That would be *so* worth it.

"Last but not least is one you know as well," Treton now pulled out an amethyst, "This is for a Morpher. A Morpher can turn themself into any beast and, with enough experience, can morph others as well. It takes a long time to master as you must be familiar with the animal you wish to morph into, but it's well worth it."

"That was certainly a fun experience," Carolyn said. She thought of the amazing, albeit colorless, view she had as an owl as they flew to Cansition.

"I should note one more, though it's not really an option," Treton went on, pulling a diamond out of the pouch. "The last branch of wizardry is temporal magic."

"As in time travel?" Carolyn asked excitedly.

"Yes, but," he held up a finger to stave off Carolyn's excitement, "only one temporal spell has ever been successfully cast—and by successful I mean the caster survived the effort—and that was the ability to slow time for the caster for a very brief window of time. So brief that ten seconds will pass for the caster while one second passes for the rest of the world. While this may sound impressive, it takes years and years of practice just to cast this one spell and even then, it drains a wizard of a large amount of their magic. Therefore, it's not really worthwhile for you to pursue."

"Too bad," Carolyn sighed. For a moment she thought she might be able to bend time to get all her homework done more easily and still hang out with her friends.

"Now, I understand that this is not an easy choice," Treton said, "Normally students are presented with the options at the beginning of their training so they have about a year to consider before they have to make a choice. I rushed your training and you skipped much of the disciplinary and physical fitness lessons, so your choice came much sooner. I won't force you to make a decision now. I suggest you take a day or two or even a week if you need it, but consider your options carefully before making your choice."

"Ok," Carolyn nodded. "So I guess that means no magic lessons until then?"

"We can cover some of the disciplinary lessons that we

skipped rather than let the time go to waste," Treton explained, "but we will not be learning more spells until you choose."

"All right," Carolyn sighed, "I guess I'll have to make a choice quickly." *Too bad I'm so indecisive,* she thought.

"Don't worry," Treton smiled. "There's no need to rush. It's important that you are certain when you make your decision. Once you've bound yourself to a gem, you can never bind yourself to another. That's all for now," he added as he stood from his chair. "We'll have another class tomorrow, whether or not you've come to a decision."

Over the next few days, Carolyn began to learn focusing techniques. Treton explained it was important for a wizard to keep focus while casting a spell lest they make a mistake and create an effect they don't intend to, or they could be so distracted they wouldn't manage to cast anything at all. This was not just important for battle, but for many uses of magic, he said, since it was not uncommon to have to cast spells in delicate or urgent situations. These lessons were considerably more boring and more difficult than the practical lessons, but Carolyn tried anyway. "Try" being the operative word. Her habit of daydreaming was starting to catch up with her.

At the same time, news of the war was coming in. It seemed the blitz strategy had worked. After remaining on the defensive for so long, Ferdri's troops had been lulled into a false sense of security and were ill-prepared to defend themselves against an assault. Many enemy troops had been killed or captured at Dor, but the bulk of their forces survived and were fleeing to the capital. Based on intelligence reports, it seemed Ferdri was planning on giving up and wanted his army to escort him out of the kingdom safely, but most of the ministers, including the Queen, were skeptical about that report. Even the intelligence minister indicated his source on this was not one he trusted implicitly.

Regardless, things were looking up. The knights were going to return from Dor in a couple days once other troops arrived to reinforce the palace, and the general mood in Cansition was one of triumph. The King would not allow himself any celebration, however, until he was certain the throne was back in his possession. He would not take any more chances with Ferdri.

The only one who was not feeling any of the elation was Carolyn. She was stuck in Cansition without even her normal magic lessons to keep things interesting, and she still had a decision looming over her head. She hated making choices, especially really important, life-changing choices, but she had to soon. Wandering the empty halls of the palace or lying on her bed were not helping her think, only making her feel more trapped. At least Sarin and Elis were around and she was not feeling lonely, but they didn't know enough about magic to give her any advice.

"I have a surprise for you," Sarin said to her one afternoon as she entered the barracks. She had taken to spending her afternoons with him and Elis again, though she was so distracted lately the tension was palpable.

"What is it?" Carolyn asked excitedly. She loved surprises. At least the good kind.

"Well, I can't give you magic advice," Sarin admitted; this was no news to Carolyn. "But I can tell you need an opportunity to clear your head."

"What are you getting at?" Carolyn looked at him suspiciously.

"I requested an audience with His Majesty asking to be allowed out for a stroll in the forest. With you," he explained.

"Nice!" Carolyn felt a surge of excitement. An opportunity to take a walk through the forest, clear her head, and spend time with a friend? It was almost everything she could ever want. "When do we go?"

"Right now," Sarin said with a big smile, "Six other knights will be coming with us as an honor guard, including

Elis."

"Yes," Elis said with a bit of a smirk. "Sarin had to talk me into it."

"Great, let's go then!" Carolyn didn't wait another second and nearly ran off to the stables. Sarin and Elis moved quickly to catch up.

"Yes, Milady," Sarin said with mock deference, "but Elis and I need our gear first. The rest of the honor guard is waiting in the palace entry for us with horses. You can wait there with them; I don't think donning armor is a very interesting process to watch."

"Ok, sure, see you soon," Carolyn gave a brief wave and walked off, only half listening. In the cavernous entrance were five knights, all in full armor, and eight horses, also armored. The knights saw her coming and all bowed deeply with a "Milady" spoken almost as one.

"Which one is my horse?" she asked as they straightened. Mirandi had been left behind since she flew back with Garinald and she would need a different one. One of the knights showed her to a beautiful, white stallion with a large blue feather protruding from its helm. It looked like a horse intended for royalty.

After a brief but impatient wait, Sarin and Elis came out from the barracks and took to their horses. Soon the lot of them were ready, the massive front gate was opened, and they trotted forth. They were in no hurry this time. No need to gallop at full pace and charge about like there was a nest of angry hornets following them.

Carolyn took a deep breath of fresh air. The smell of pine trees was strong, she heard birds chirping in the trees, and the afternoon sun streaming onto her face was warm and comforting. It was nice to get outside, finally, at a time when she could just relax. The six knights forming the honor guard took up positions all around them as they started trotting east, out of the clearing and amongst the trees.

"We are still at war," Sarin leaned over and explained,

"so we can't just gallivant about in the forest wherever we wish. The knights will guide us some distance east before turning back, but you're welcome to change direction any time you want. They'll make sure we don't wander too far in any direction."

"Sounds good," Carolyn said, staring up at the towering trees closing above her as they exited the clearing, "This place is beautiful."

"Yeah," Sarin smiled. Carolyn noticed out of the corner of her eye that he was looking at her, though he quickly turned away when she turned to face him. Before she could comment, some movement in the trees above caught her attention and she stiffened, alert.

"What was that?" she asked with concern, scanning the trees. Sarin looked up, undisturbed.

"It was probably a goon," he said casually, then pointed upward, "There, you see it? The forest is full of 'em."

Carolyn followed his gaze and saw a strange, furry creature in the tree. It had a zig-zag brown-and-green fur coat, strong legs, and a bushy tail. It was standing on a branch that was shaking slightly as it stuffed something in its mouth.

"What is that thing?" Carolyn asked with a combination of shock and curiosity.

"It's a goon," Sarin answered like it was obvious, "Don't you know what a goon is?"

"They don't have those where I come from," Carolyn answered.

"Oh, really?" Sarin seemed surprised, "They're a kind of large rodent. They hide in the trees, wait until a bird lands on a nearby branch, and pounce on them. The horncrest is it's favorite."

"Horncrest?"

"Oh boy," Sarin rubbed the back of his neck, "Things really are different where you come from."

They spent the next couple hours wandering among the trees, with Sarin pointing out all the animals to Carolyn.

Other than the goons, of which there were many, Carolyn saw a horncrest, a small bird with a red breast and a couple small feathers growing from the top of its head swept back, looking like backward facing horns. Then there was the longtail, some kind of predatory cat with a prehensile tail that let it move through the trees not unlike a monkey. The most interesting of them all was the sendar, tall creatures that somewhat resembled deer, but they had curved horns like a ram and a longer neck.

"Thank you for taking me out," Carolyn said with a smile, as the group made their way back in the direction of Cansition. Then she blushed as she thought maybe it sounded awkward and amended, "I mean, out into the forest... Not out, as in—what are you looking at?"

"There's something over there," Sarin said casually, glancing past her to the right. He gave a signal to the knights around them and they formed up tight, four on the right and two on the left, as they watched the forest closely.

"What is..." Carolyn started, searching through the trees herself. Then she saw it, a brief glimpse of movement between the thick trunks. At first, she thought it was another sendar, bounding among the underbrush, but then she saw the glint of steel. "Oh no," she concluded.

"There!" one of the knights shouted. "Protect the Princess!" he added as an order to the others. He gave a signal and four of them charged forward after the figure, now darting between the trees as fast as he could, realizing he had been caught.

"Forget being protected," Carolyn muttered. She urged her horse forward and, before Sarin or the other knights could stop her, she was charging forward just behind the other four. The remainder of her guard moved quickly to follow.

"Milady!" one of them said urgently as he rode up alongside her, "It may not be safe! We should stay back."

"I'll be fine," she said dismissively. She was focusing on the figure, trying to keep sight on him long enough as he moved between the trees. Despite her heart suddenly pumping faster, and the sound of horses running as fast as they can between the trees and through the underbrush, Carolyn was doing her best to steady her breathing and remain calm as Treton had been teaching her. She held out her hand, having no staff to direct her magic, waited until the right moment, and...

The fleeing figure lurched forward onto his face suddenly as Carolyn Pulled his legs out from under him. She heard a shout of dismay from up ahead as the four knights closed in and surrounded the figure. One of them got off his horse and pinned him to the ground while another, whom Carolyn realized was Elis, got down to disarm him. She came up as this was going on.

"Thank you for your help, Milady," one of the knights said, "though we would have stopped him. Your safety was more important."

"Yeah, sure," Carolyn nodded, not really listening, "Who is he?"

"He appears to be one of Ferdri's men," one of the other knights said as he came up from behind, "A scout, most likely."

"Does that mean Ferdri knows..." Carolyn stopped herself before she said another word. Does this mean Ferdri knows about Cansition? At the very least, it means he knows to look in the forest. How many other scouts were there? There could be some nearby now, listening.

"What are we going to do?" Carolyn asked, her voice higher-pitched than she intended. If Ferdri found Cansition, his soldiers would definitely be able to break in; there weren't enough knights to hold the palace forever, even with the chokepoint entryway.

"Please, Milady." Sarin said, standing beside her, "Let us do our job now. We'll take care of this."

Carolyn backed away as the knights were questioning the scout and giving him a thorough pat-down. A wave of dread and suspicion washed over her. All the animals they saw, and any of them could have been a Morpher spying on them. Did Ferdri have any Morphers in his army that the King didn't know about? They could be in grave danger. She began to look all about her, suddenly paranoid, searching for more enemy soldiers or even wilderness beasts. As she turned around her eyes locked on something and she stopped dead in her tracks, mouth agape.

Just a few feet away from her, walking slowly and carefully between the trees, watching Carolyn with an intense stare, was a unicorn.

It looked like a horse at first, but with a silvery-white coat, a pure white mane and tail, and a long, sharp horn on its forehead. Carolyn gaped at it, unable to tear her eyes away. Was this an illusion? A trick of some kind?

The unicorn walked up to her, treading slowly and carefully, keeping its gaze locked on her, before finally coming to a stop just a couple feet away. It was so close Carolyn could touch it. Something told her she should touch it. Tentatively, she held out a hand, reaching... slowly...

She felt the snout of the unicorn under her fingers. It was real, it was very real. As she touched it, an odd sensation came over her. It was like wind chimes were ringing in her mind, a sweet, pleasant sound that put her at ease. She felt that something was there with her, sharing the space of her consciousness, but it was so beautiful and kind that Carolyn didn't fight against it, instead she welcomed it. The presence seemed to move in, spreading warmth and comfort as it did.

The euphoric feeling lasted but a moment, then it was gone. Carolyn's hand was still resting on the snout of the unicorn, but whatever it had done to enter her mind, it was over now. Partially. There was still something she could feel, some kind of intrinsic link that seemed to have formed between them. Carolyn suddenly knew, without really knowing how, that unicorns were not simple beasts, but intelligent creatures with names, personalities, and families. This unicorn, for whatever reason, came to stay with Carolyn and to care for her. She was Carolyn's, and Carolyn was hers.

"Milady..." came a voice from behind her. Carolyn suddenly remembered there were seven knights in the forest with her. She had temporarily forgotten them in the surprise and enrapturing experience of meeting the unicorn. She turned around, removing her hand, reluctantly, from the unicorn's snout. They looked tense and many of them had their hands on the hilts of their swords. Sarin especially had an expression that seemed to be halfway between shock and fear. One of the knights was holding the scout they had captured, now bound up, who was staring with eyes wide.

"It's all right," Carolyn told them reassuringly, feeling an unusual amount of confidence. "She's not going to hurt you. Also, her name is Silvermist."

CHAPTER 11
Silvermist

"Silver... mist?" one of the knights repeated. "How do you know?"

"I just... know," Carolyn answered cryptically, glancing back at the unicorn. She had large, beautiful, golden eyes that spoke of hidden and ancient wisdom. Somehow, staring into them made Carolyn feel safe and confident, even invincible.

"Is she going to follow us?" Sarin asked tentatively. He eyed the unicorn, specifically its horn. His hand had already left his sword, but it looked tense, ready to grab it again.

"Of course," Carolyn chuckled, "She's mine now. Come, we have to get our prisoner back." Carolyn casually strode beside Silvermist and vaulted herself up onto her bare back. She hardly knew how to ride a horse, but she knew that with Silvermist it would be easy. She sat ready, watching the other knights as they continued to eye her warily.

"Are you coming?" she asked.

"Yes, of course, milady!" one of the knights answered swiftly. He shouted some orders and in moments the knights returned to formation around her. The prisoner, tied and blindfolded, was held on the saddle with one of the knights and a different knight took the reins of Carolyn's now rider-less horse to guide it along. In this way they started traveling back west, returning to Cansition palace. Silvermist seemed to know exactly where they were going, easily keeping pace with the heavily armored horses. Carolyn could feel the unicorn's powerful muscles moving beneath her. She felt they could go fast, very fast, if they wanted to, but now was the time for patience.

"Why don't you put the prisoner on my horse?" Carolyn wondered aloud. "That would probably be easier."

"We would, milady," Elis answered, "were it any other horse, but Randis is the Queen's mare; none is to ride her without Her Majesty's explicit permission."

"Oh," Carolyn nodded. That made sense, that's why it had the fancier armor than the others. Carolyn might have been embarrassed by the honor the Queen had accorded her had she not been more impressed by the fact that she was currently riding on a unicorn. Even without the majesty of decoration, Silvermist carried herself with more regality than even the Queen's personal mount.

The trip to Cansition Palace was a silent one. Between the prisoner they were escorting and the appearance of Silvermist, everyone was either too shocked or too confused to know what to say. Soon enough they found themselves back at the entrance to Cansition.

"Halt! Who—oh my word…" gasped the gate keeper, staring at them through the peephole.

"Open the gate," Carolyn called out, "By command of Princess Carolyn."

"Yes, milady!" the gate keeper called. Almost immediately the gate opened and Carolyn strode forward atop Silvermist—bold, confident, regal—to a chorus of silent stares. The other knights entered behind her and dismounted as they started giving orders to the guards on duty. Some of them responded, jumping to work, others continued to stare in disbelief. Finally, Carolyn turned to the nearest one.

"You," she commanded, "Fetch the King and Queen."

"Yes, milady!" the guard shouted enthusiastically before running off into the palace.

Carolyn waited patiently atop Silvermist's back. It felt strange to be sitting up there, out in the open in front of so many people, and yet not cringe in embarrassment at the attention. Usually she hated having so many eyes on her, yet now she was indifferent to it. Was this what confidence felt like?

"Milady," Sarin's voice came from beside her and she turned to face him. His brow was creased, his expression the opposite of how Carolyn herself felt at that moment. "Is everything all right?" he added in a whisper, just loud enough for Carolyn to hear, "You're not acting like yourself."

"I don't feel quite like myself," Carolyn whispered back, "I feel... better. It's hard to explain."

"Is the unicorn—"

"Silvermist," Carolyn interrupted.

"Is *Silvermist*," he corrected himself, "dangerous?"

"Of course not," Carolyn chuckled slightly. "She's here to help me."

"How do you know that?" Sarin pressed. "Did you talk to her? What did she say?"

"Well, not exactly," Carolyn answered, "I just... know it." Even now she could still feel Silvermist's connection to her. She wasn't reading her thoughts or controlling her mind—nothing creepy like that—it was just a presence that remained to provide comfort. Kind of like a hug, but in her mind.

"I see," Sarin didn't look convinced. "And can I ask how this kind of magic is any different from the kind Goredian was using?"

Carolyn hadn't thought about that. Goredian hadn't done anything to make them suspect him other than the unidentified form of magic he was using. On the contrary, he saved their lives and they should be grateful to him.

Silvermist, on the other hand, had done nothing for them. Not only that, but she seemed to have taken over Carolyn's mind and infected it with ideas that she didn't know where they came from. Isn't this also a suspicious form of magic? The King had said that no one understood what unicorns could do. With so little known about them, it was possible their intentions were malicious. They do have those sharp horns for a reason. *Maybe I should try to fight this influence?* she asked herself.

As the thought came to mind, she immediately dismissed it. There was something about the presence in her mind that rang of truth and purity. She was not possessed, nor were her thoughts being controlled. She was coming to her own conclusions based on the feelings she got.

"Because Silvermist is good," she answered finally. Sarin seemed to wait for further explanation, but Carolyn left it at that.

Before he could continue their conversation, the main gate opened again, and the King and Queen came through. Both stopped wide-eyed for a moment, but quickly recovered their composure, though they did grip hands as they walked slowly and reverently into the room.

"King Ketra, Queen Rorina," Carolyn started formally, "Allow me to introduce Silvermist. I thought you would like to meet her immediately."

"Silvermist," the King repeated as he approached, "Do they understand us?"

"Yes," Carolyn answered after a brief pause.

"Silvermist, welcome to Cansition Palace," the King welcomed her formally. When he said 'Cansition', Carolyn felt a sudden surge of warmth and happiness from the unicorn. "Might I ask what pleasure we owe to this meeting?"

There was another pause as Carolyn tried to interpret the feelings from Silvermist. "She says that she's here to protect me," Carolyn explained, "and will stay with me as long as I need."

"Does she speak with you?" the Queen asked, sounding both amazed and curious.

"Not exactly," Carolyn replied. "I just get these feelings and I put them into words as best I can. It's hard to explain."

"Fascinating," the Queen said, nodding. "Silvermist, might I ask what made you choose to become Lady Carolyn's protector?"

Another pause. Carolyn furrowed her brow as she thought. "Something about an ancient pact or mission or something. It's very important to her."

"Well, I'm afraid we don't have suitable housing available for a unicorn," the King said, sounding very serious, "Would it be acceptable to you, Silvermist, to remain in the stables with the horses?"

"Yes," Carolyn replied, "That is acceptable." She then felt a new feeling, one of being comforted. It seemed to indicate that something would change in a moment, though Carolyn didn't quite understand what, and that Silvermist was trying to reassure her that everything would be all right. Carolyn dismounted, keeping a hand resting on her side for a moment as she began to walk away.

As soon as she broke contact with Silvermist, the warm feeling diminished greatly. A wave of panic washed over Carolyn as a cold emptiness seemed to fill the void. She realized this is what she was being warned about, so she took a deep breath, steadied her breathing, and reminded herself that she was alright. There was still the slightest hint of their connection, but she could no longer feel Silvermist actively in her mind. She also seemed to have lost the temporary confidence she had gained and was now left with all her worries and fear of attention as before. She turned and watched as Silvermist disappeared into the stables, the door closing behind her.

"Come, Lady Carolyn," the Queen beckoned to her after Silvermist was gone. "We'd like to hear exactly what happened, and I believe Treton would as well."

"Right, sure," Carolyn came quickly, her cheeks growing

warm. She walked along behind the King and Queen, keeping her head down and trying to ignore all the people staring at her. She could still feel Silvermist's presence in her mind - just barely - trying to provide comfort and confidence, but none of it was getting through. All she could feel was shame and worry.

"Your majesties," Treton said respectfully, standing up as they entered the meeting room. "Lady Carolyn!" he added with more candor, "What happened? Are you all right? Where is it?"

"She," Carolyn sheepishly corrected him, "is in the stables. And yes, I'm fine." She quickly took a seat at the table and tried to shrink into it.

"Thankfully," the King remarked as he sat. "Others who have met unicorns have not fared as well as you."

"Would you care to tell us what happened?" the Queen asked politely. Though Carolyn knew she couldn't refuse, she appreciated the Queen speaking gently with her, considering how she was feeling.

"Sure," she answered, not really making eye contact with anyone. "We were out in the forest and saw someone. We chased him down and caught him. I don't know what the knights did with him, but they said he was one of Ferdri's scouts."

"A scout?!" the King nearly shouted in surprise, leaning forward in his chair. "Is he still alive? Did you bring the body back?"

"No," Carolyn was taken aback. "I mean, no he's not dead. We brought him back as a prisoner."

"I will question the knights afterward," the King said, settling back into his seat, though still with an anxious look on his face. "Please continue."

"So, we caught him," Carolyn went on quickly, "and the knights were tying him up and stuff. I was behind them and turned around, and then there she was. Silvermist."

"Silvermist?" Treton asked, "How do you know her name?"

"I just know, all right!" Carolyn nearly shouted, tired of hearing that question. Everyone at the table looked as shocked as she felt at herself for having lost her temper. "Sorry," she said, feeling her cheeks grow hot. "I just know. She touched my mind somehow. I can still feel her there, a little bit, but not like when we were touching." Carolyn went silent, brooding.

"Then you rode her back?" the King asked finally, breaking the silence. "And she let you?"

"Yeah," Carolyn nodded. "I just felt like it was the right thing to do."

"I see," the King stroked his beard thoughtfully. The Queen had a curious expression like she didn't know what to make of all this. Treton looked lost in thought.

"I have studied the topic of unicorns a bit, your majesty," Treton spoke up finally, "There are very ancient records of people meeting unicorns in the forest who would come and touch them, then run off. Many of them reported feeling the unicorn enter their mind and a generally positive feeling. That sounds not unlike what Carolyn has experienced."

"But the unicorn never went home with them in those reports, right?" the King asked.

"That is correct," Treton nodded. "The person would return home and never see the unicorn again. Some did report that, at a later time, they still felt the presence of the unicorn, if only slightly, but it was not like when they first touched."

"The last time that happened must've been hundreds of years ago," the Queen said, "Surely if such occurrences were common now, people would know about it."

"That's correct, your majesty," Treton responded, "The last known case was at least six centuries ago."

"Then what does it all mean?" the King wondered. "And does it have anything to do with Ferdri?"

"I don't think so," Treton shook his head, "except perhaps that the unicorns want to help us in our fight and Silvermist was sent as their representative. Like a champion."

"But why me?" Carolyn voiced her thoughts aloud. It was something she had been asking herself a lot lately.

"I don't know," Treton sighed. "There's very little we know about unicorns. Do you think Silvermist might be willing to allow me to run some tests on her? Nothing harmful or humiliating, of course," he added quickly when he saw Carolyn's shocked expression.

"I can ask," Carolyn shrugged.

"We can adjourn this meeting for now, I think," the King said, "I must speak to the knights regarding the prisoner. Treton, please dig up any information we have available on unicorns to study. See if we can't figure out why Silvermist decided to join us now. Lady Carolyn," the King's tone softened, "why don't you go and rest for a bit. It's almost dinner time."

"All right," Carolyn nodded.

The King and Queen left the table, followed by Carolyn, and out the door. As she left, she thought she saw Treton beckoning her to stay, but she didn't much feel like talking anymore, so she took the King's advice and returned to her room. There she lay down to rest and try to wrap her brain around her latest adventure.

The next couple days were among the most interesting so far. The whole palace was abuzz with conversation about Silvermist. Many of the servants tried to find excuses to head down to the stables to see her, and the knights still in the palace were spending most of their time tending to their horses. The King and Queen, as well as their advisors, also took a few trips to the stables to visit her, though no one else was brazen enough to try and watch that meeting.

Silvermist wouldn't let anyone touch her, however. A couple servants were stupid enough to try, resulting in some serious injuries that certainly got the point across. She also didn't seem to connect with anyone else the way she did with Carolyn. Somehow, that was a special connection that only they shared and Silvermist indicated she couldn't have one with another person now. Carolyn didn't really understand it, but it was a source of comfort to her.

The only one that got close to her was Treton. Silvermist allowed him to perform some magical examinations of her, on condition that he not touch her, to try and learn more about her nature. None of the tests bore fruit. Treton insisted that he did not have the proper equipment available to him in Cansition, but Carolyn felt there was more to it than that. Silvermist was able to conceal her abilities somehow, similar to how the unicorns could remain hidden from sight in the forest when they wanted to.

Carolyn had also come no closer to making a decision on which mastery she had to choose. The excitement surrounding Silvermist gave her an opportunity to push it off a little while longer, but it was always on her mind. The few opportunities she had to be alone with Silvermist was the best time to think about it. Leaning against her soft neck, feeling her warmth and comfort, was the only time she felt she could really think clearly.

Then the knights returned. When they arrived, they were surprised to find a unicorn in the stables, to say the least, and all the excitement seemed to stir up anew. Garinald—who returned to Dor after bringing Carolyn to Cansition—and Jacim returned with them, as well as the elemental wizard that Carolyn finally found out was named Sevina, and all of them went to see Silvermist right away. It was the most amount of emotion Carolyn had ever seen from Garinald when his eyes went wide in wonder at seeing the unicorn. Carolyn couldn't help but feel he was considering turning into one, now that he had seen a unicorn in person.

The next day, Carolyn went in the morning to spend some time with Silvermist only to discover that Jacim was already there. She had hardly seen him in Dor after the battle and hadn't spoken to him at all since then. She started backing off, thinking Jacim probably wanted to be alone, but as she reached for the door handle, she paused. *Am I really leaving just to give Jacim privacy?* she asked herself. No, she had to be honest, this was her running from a conversation she assumed would end up being awkward.

This was her normal response. It was always to run and hide, avoid having to deal with people, stay away from conversations she assumed would be unpleasant. Somehow, charging into battle against a powerful enchantress was easy compared to turning around and speaking with someone she didn't really know.

Carolyn's fist clenched tight, but not around the door handle. Steeling herself, she turned around and marched over to the far end of the stables where Silvermist was staying. As she walked up, seeing Jacim there, she felt her anxiety getting the best of her, yelling at her to turn back. *Why am I so scared?* she chided herself, feeling her hands shaking. Jacim wouldn't hurt her, he probably wouldn't even intend to embarrass her. *I* have to *stop this,* Carolyn told herself, *I need to control myself.*

"Milady!" Jacim gave a brief yelp of surprise and quickly bowed low as he noticed her presence finally. "My apologies, I didn't know you were coming." As Carolyn watched him straighten himself up, she couldn't help but think, *why me? Why did grandmother choose me?*

"It's all right," Carolyn said dismissively, trying to act nonchalant and probably failing. "And please just call me Carolyn."

"I'm sorry, milady," Jacim's eyes went wide as he bowed again, keeping his eyes downcast as he straightened. "I can't speak to you in such a casual tone. I have been trained my whole life to treat royalty with respect, and I can't so easily ignore that."

"All right," Carolyn sighed. "At least stop bowing so much."

"Yes, milady," Jacim's form began to bend, as if to bow again, but he stopped himself and gave an awkward smile. *Maybe I'm not the only one who feels awkward talking to people,* Carolyn wondered.

"Were you talking to Silvermist?" Carolyn asked, trying to strike up a conversation.

"Trying to, at least," Jacim answered, looking at the unicorn. His posture relaxed a bit. "She doesn't really talk back, though."

"No, she doesn't," Carolyn stepped forward, reaching out a hand to stroke Silvermist's mane. She was staring at her with her bright, golden eyes, so full of warmth and wisdom. As soon as she touched her, their minds linked again. Carolyn felt that rush of comfort, love, and confidence fill her once again, by now a familiar feeling. She sensed from Silvermist that she found Jacim pleasant and more honest than most of the people that came to visit her. He also showed enough respect to not even attempt to come close and touch her.

"May I speak freely, milady?" Jacim asked suddenly, breaking into Carolyn's thoughts.

"Sure, what is it?" she asked curiously, surprised that Jacim, of all people, would ask that.

"I have to admit, milady," he answered sheepishly, "And I mean no disrespect—although it will probably sound disrespectful—and you said I could speak freely, though..."

"Just say it," Carolyn interrupted with a hint of impatience.

"When I first saw you on the ride to Dor, I didn't expect much of you," he admitted. "I thought you were just another noble who thought themselves the best. I expected you would only get in the way. I wanted to apologize for that. I misjudged you, milady. You are indeed quite capable, and it was an honor to fight alongside you."

"Oh. Thank you" she replied quietly, taken aback. Leaning against Silvermist, feeling her warmth and confidence, Carolyn certainly felt capable. On the battlefield outside Dor, however, she definitely had not.

Yet where both Garinald and Jacim had failed, Carolyn had, in fact, succeeded. She kept telling herself it was just luck, that Jiselda had underestimated her, or had been weakened from fighting with the others, but she knew those were just contributing factors, not the real reason. The truth was, she *had* done it, but it scared her to acknowledge that she was capable of such an accomplishment. Now, with Silvermist, somehow that didn't scare her anymore. She was capable, and she was not alone. Feeling a burst of confidence, she felt suddenly that Jacim was exactly the person to speak with about her dilemma.

"Jacim," she turned back to him; he had been watching her and Silvermist's reunion with fascination. "I could use some advice."

"Advice, milady?" he asked in wonder, "What could *I* advise *you* with?"

"Magic," Carolyn answered plainly. Jacim's brow furrowed in confusion. "I need to pick a mastery," she explained, "and I'm having a hard time choosing which one."

"Ah," Jacim smiled and relaxed a bit, "I think I can help with that, milady. Have you narrowed down the options at all?"

"Yes—well, not much. I definitely don't want to learn enchantment; it brings back too many bad memories. No offense," she added quickly, remembering that Jacim himself was an enchanter.

"None was taken, milady," Jacim replied with a hint of a smile.

"I'm also not interested in restoration," she went on. "I didn't want to offend Treton, but it just seems boring to me."

"Yeah, I thought that, too, milady," Jacim admitted, "when I was first reviewing my options. Restorers are quite important, though."

"So someone else important can do it," Carolyn replied. "Those are the only two I've chopped off my list. That leaves elemental, morphing, sorcery, and illusions."

"How do you feel about each of those?" Jacim inquired.

"I love the sound of elemental magic," Carolyn said

eagerly. "Then I'd *really* be able to help out in a fight. That one wizard we met was able to completely shut us down with his lightning. I wish I could do the same."

"You already have an affinity for fire, don't you, milady?" Jacim asked.

"Yeah, so what?" Carolyn looked confused.

"I meant no offense, milady," Jacim said quickly. "I was just thinking that fire is one of the most useful elements to use in a battle, and *that* you already have control of. If battle is all that matters, then I think you only need to practice your fire spells more."

"That's a good point," Carolyn nodded. "Ok, well next is morphing. Garinald turning us into birds was the most amazing experience! I've always wanted to fly. I mean, I never expected to do it by actually turning into a bird, but man was it cool!"

"I don't think you can fly with any other branch of wizardry, milady," Jacim stroked his chin. "Anything else that appeals to you about morphing?"

"Morphing others," Carolyn answered immediately. "I'd love to be able to take my friends with me."

"Well, I do know that morphing others is extremely difficult," Jacim pointed out. "Master Garinald has decades of experience, so he's able to do it with ease. It would be a long time until you could do the same, milady."

"Ok," Carolyn shrugged. "It's still something I could do eventually, so it's cool. Then there's sorcery. I like teleportation, that sounds neat. I don't know what kind of magical stuff I would create with it. Treton was kind of vague on what else I could do, so I don't know about that one. Is the teleportation difficult?"

"Some of it is," Jacim replied, closing his eyes for a moment, thinking hard. "There are some simple, short-range teleportation spells that I think are easy. With time and practice, though, you could teleport others, even up to a hundred people, but it would take years to reach that level."

"Ok," Carolyn sighed. "I'll still consider that one, then. Last we have illusions. Treton said it's mostly limited by imagination, and I have a pretty wild imagination, so I could probably use it effectively. But it sounds more fun than practical."

"That all depends on what you want to do with it, milady," Jacim replied, smiling slightly. "Illusions are often used for deceiving people and learning information they couldn't otherwise. Disguising yourself as a town guard, for example, could allow you to interrogate someone for information. Or disguising yourself as an important merchant could get you into private parties. It's excellent for espionage."

"I'm not much of a spy," Carolyn shook her head. "I can hardly lie and keep a straight face. Maybe I'll forget about that one for now."

"I thought you might, milady," Jacim nodded, "It sounds to me like you mostly want something with immediate, obvious use. Illusions don't seem like your style."

"Okay..." Carolyn answered, "So of the three left, which do you think is my 'style'?"

Jacim stopped and thought about it for a moment, leaning against the stable wall and rubbing his chin, then glancing over at Carolyn. Finally, he nodded his head and said, "Elementalist, I think. You seem to care about fighting most, so go for that one. There's a reason people call them combat mages."

"Yeah," Carolyn tried to imagine herself shooting bolts of lightning and making the wind whip her enemies about. The image was amazing, but it was also extremely violent. Somehow, picturing it now, it didn't feel like it was something she wanted to be doing.

"I don't know, actually," Carolyn admitted finally, "Now that I think about it, I don't think that's what I want to do."

"Really?" Jacim sounded a little surprised at first, then he nodded slowly and seemed to agree. "In that case, I think I know what would really suit you."

Carolyn took the rest of the day to think over her decision, not even mentioning that she had made up her mind yet to Treton during her lesson. She decided she would wait one more day before making her decision final.

At breakfast the next morning, conversation was on the latest turns the war had taken, troop movements, and so on, but she only caught snippets of it, still thinking about her mastery choice. From what she heard, Ferdri's forces were gathering in the capital to set up defensive positions, expecting a protracted siege. Discussions about how to break in abounded, but the real arguments happened only in private meetings, not at the breakfast table. The war effort was very important to her considering the only way for her to get home—a topic which she tried not to dwell on too much—depended on Herin's victory.

Shortly after the meal had ended, Carolyn marched to Treton's office prior to her lesson, her mind was finally made up. She entered his office with a quick knock, walked up to his desk, and pronounced, "I want to..." she paused momentarily, "make a decision," she concluded anti-climatically.

"Excellent," Treton smiled, looking excited. "What is your decision then?"

"Sorceress. I want to be a sorceress," she blurted out before her mind could try and change itself again.

"A wonderful choice," Treton nodded, a look of understanding on his face. "I think that would suit you nicely."

"So now what?" Carolyn wondered, finally taking a seat. "How do we do this?"

"There is a process involved," Treton said, standing from his desk, "where you place your magic inside the gem you chose. It's not a difficult process, not unlike when you attempted to use the Derishz Ruby."

"I didn't bond with *that*, did I?" Carolyn felt a stab of fear as that thought occurred to her. What if her reckless little experiment had gotten her into trouble after all?

"No, not to worry," Treton chuckled, "some more intent is involved." The archmage opened a cabinet in the corner of the room and pulled out a master's staff of dark wood, almost as tall as Carolyn herself. The head of it was squared with the very top rounded with four, curved lines that formed a partial dome, clearly meant as the setting of the gem. Just under the squared head were carvings of thorny vines wrapped all around and on the head itself was a relief of a unicorn on each side. The whole thing together was a beautiful piece of art, one fit for royalty.

"I had this commissioned after we started our training," Treton said, laying it on the desk. "Admittedly, I didn't think we'd need it for a while yet, but here we are."

"It's beautiful," Carolyn said, mesmerized by the skill with which it was crafted, especially now that she had a closer look at it.

"Indeed," Treton agreed with a nod, "It was made for a princess."

Carolyn almost felt guilty at taking something so amazing for herself, especially since she still didn't feel like a princess. Regardless, she reached out to grip the haft. It was strong and smooth, dense and a bit heavy. She stood and hefted it experimentally, testing the weight, standing it up, and even giving it a couple swings. Now this would *definitely* give someone a headache. It was only missing one thing.

"Where's the sapphire?" Carolyn wondered, studying the head where it should have gone. In the base of the dome, under the setting, were carved some abstract patterns. The more Carolyn looked at them, the more she felt like they had purpose.

"When I commissioned the staff," Treton began as he opened a wooden case that had just been placed on the desk, "of course I didn't know which mastery you'd choose, so I had to get one of each."

Carolyn saw inside of the box were six gems, each in an

elongated, diamond shape, resting in velvet-lined grooves of the box shaped to fit them. There was one of each, like Treton said: ruby, sapphire, emerald, topaz, opal, and amethyst. They looked quite beautiful lined up together like that. Treton pulled out the sapphire and closed the box again gently.

"This will be your gem, Carolyn," Treton said formally, holding it up for her to study. It was beautifully cut, shining in the source-less light that lit the room. "Sit back down, and we'll begin the process of binding your magic to this gem."

"All right." Carolyn sat back down slowly, mesmerized by the beautiful gem, still gripping the staff tightly in her hand.

Treton gently placed the sapphire on the desk in front of her. "Focus on the sapphire," he began, speaking softly but clearly, "and reach out to it with your magic."

Carolyn did so, much as she had with the Derishz Ruby not long ago. She had much better control of her magic now than she had back then and very easily released some, sending tendrils of magical energy to grasp the gem. She felt the gem, in that odd, magical sense, and wrapped her magic around it tightly.

"Enter into it," Treton continued. "Let your magic flow through it."

Carolyn allowed her magic to seep inside the sapphire. She could feel it swirling about, becoming one with the gem. She also felt a strange, foreign power within the sapphire. It scared her at first, but she realized this was the innate power of the gem that allowed for sorcery to be used. She welcomed the feeling.

"Feel the inherent power of the sapphire," Treton said, watching the process intently, "Invite it into you. Bond with it."

She entered more of her magic into the sapphire, and as she did, she began to feel some of that innate power of the sapphire flowing back to her. She invited it in, longed to feel it within her. It entered her, though the sensation was not one she could put into words. She felt a new strength growing within her, fortifying her magical powers, adding new dimensions to them, honing them. Carolyn could now feel the power of the sapphire inside of her as well as in the gem, while at the same time feeling a constantly flowing bridge of magic between her and the gem. They were one, and their power was one.

"Now cut off the connection," Treton said. Carolyn obeyed, releasing the magic that was holding them together. She expected to feel a complete severance of connection. Instead she felt the sapphire's energies within her, absorbed into her magic, while the magic she had left behind within the gem was present but distant from her.

"It is done," Treton concluded with a smile. He gingerly picked up the sapphire, now shimmering with an innate glow, and placed it into the top of Carolyn's staff. Once it had slipped in, the carvings around the base of the setting flashed briefly and went dull. Carolyn could feel some enchantment of the staff locking the sapphire in place, preventing it from ever being removed.

"You are now," Treton said slowly, with a flair of drama, "a sorceress."

Carolyn stood up, holding her staff tightly and regarding her sapphire. She was a sorceress. Carolyn the sorceress. It had a nice ring to it. She felt like someone important now. Not because of her title—that she still didn't feel that she deserved—but because of her accomplishment. She had worked hard to practice her magic, something she hadn't even known existed just a few short months ago, and reached the first major milestone in that pursuit. She had done it. And she was speechless.

"Now I think you should make use of your new powers," Treton said excitedly, walking toward the door. "Come with me and we'll see what we can practice."

Carolyn followed him out the door, her staff gently thumping against the carpeted floors in much the same way Treton's did as she walked. It was an amazing feeling. Just carrying this staff made her feel more powerful, more competent. She was now a force to be reckoned with, no longer a simple apprentice to be disregarded and stepped over.

The two of them arrived in the training room. There were a few knights sparring with each or practicing their spear thrusts. Since Carolyn had been doing disciplinary exercises, they hadn't had need of the training room for a few days, so the knights went back to using it. Now they stood and watched as the two wizards entered the room, one a master and the other a freshly appointed sorceress. Carolyn could feel their stares as she walked in, but she did not shrink from them. She kept her head held high and proud.

"We will be needing the training room again," Treton announced. "I apologize for the interruption. Stay if you wish, but keep out of the way." He led Carolyn to an unoccupied corner of the room as he spoke. A few of the knights left, but most of them didn't, keen to stay and watch.

"It will be difficult for me to teach you sorcery," Treton started as he turned to face Carolyn, "as I myself am not a sorcerer. I can, however, teach you the most basic concept of sorcery: creating objects. Up until now, any spell you cast created a temporary effect which lasted as long as the spell did. A push spell involves magic thrust outward in a direction and then vanishing, for example. Never did the magic persist, and its ability to interact with the physical was limited. Now with your powers bound to your sapphire, that is no longer the case. To demonstrate—attempt to create a simple sphere in the air with your magic and release it from your control."

Carolyn nodded. This was not unlike her first lesson, though this time she had significantly more control. She easily created a sphere in the air no larger than a coconut. She was surprised at first to see that her magic was no longer appearing as a red glow, but as a deep blue one. Once her sphere had taken shape, she released the magic. The sphere hovered in the air for a moment after being released, but it didn't entirely keep its shape. It began to deform and slowly float down, then suddenly burst and dissipated.

"Excellent first try," Treton nodded his approval. "Try again. This time focus on the shape first and foremost."

"All right," Carolyn took a breath and tried again. This time she took her time to form as perfectly round a sphere as she could, willing it into existence before her. The small blue ball hovered perfectly still in the air, glowing brightly, as Carolyn focused on it. As soon as she released the spell, however, the shape deformed slightly – but only slightly – as it again began to sink slowly to the ground.

"Better," Treton nodded, "Keep trying."

It took a few more attempts until Carolyn achieved a perfect, spherical shape. It still slowly fell through the air, but it remained round the whole way. Curious what it would do when it hit the ground, Carolyn watched carefully, disappointed to see it merely sat there doing nothing before she dismissed it.

"Why does it do that?" Carolyn wondered. "Fall, I mean."

"The main advantage of sorcery," Treton explained, "is the ability to create magical objects that interact with the physical world. That means that they interact with the normal laws of physics, such as gravity, weight, force, etc."

"Didn't you say I could create platforms?" Carolyn eyed him suspiciously. "What good is a platform that falls to the ground?"

"You can," Treton answered immediately, "we'll be getting to that soon. Before that, though, is controlling the density of the object. This step is less straightforward. From what I understand, it's done mostly by feel and it's something that many sorcerers take a long time to master."

"What do you mean, exactly?" Carolyn asked.

"The density," he repeated, "In this case, how heavy your object is in relation to the air. If you make it heavier than air, it will fall. If it's lighter than air, it will float. If you find the perfect balance between them, it will remain in place, but can still be moved."

"So a platform that falls only when you jump on it?" Carolyn felt disappointed, "Like in a game?"

"Patience," Treton said firmly. "First density. Create a sphere again, but this time try to intentionally make it heavier. See what happens."

With a sigh, Carolyn began to focus on her magic again. This time, as she formed the ball, she tried to will it to be heavier. Unlike with the shape, where it was obvious how to form her magic, it was difficult to determine if her intentions of density were working. She tried forcing a little extra magic into it without expanding the size of the orb to see if that would work. When the spell released, the ball fell to the ground rather rapidly. It hit the ground with a faint *bzzt* sound and began to roll slowly.

"That worked," Carolyn nodded, impressed with herself. Without waiting for further instruction, she attempted to make a second one, this one even heavier. It fell to the ground with a loud *bzzt* and a slight *crack*. In dismay she saw the faintest of cracks in the stone floor under her sphere. "Oops," she said, looking back up at Treton. "I made that one too heavy."

"Quite," Treton agreed with a nod, "but you do seem to have picked up on this rather quickly."

"What can I say, I'm a natural." Carolyn tried to sound confident. She dismissed the two balls on the ground and attempted to create a new one, this one significantly lighter. She watched as the sphere began to float slowly upward the moment the spell released. She created a second one after it, this one even lighter, and watched as it zoomed up to the ceiling and hit it first. She was feeling pretty satisfied that she'd got the hang of the density rather quickly.

"I can see I had no cause for concern," Treton smiled slightly. "Would you like to continue, or should we end for today?"

"Can I learn how to teleport now?" Carolyn asked

excitedly. That's something she was *really* looking forward to.

"Ah, I'm afraid I'm not able to teach you that," Treton admitted, "Teleportation is a very difficult topic and can only really be taught by an actual sorcerer. I can only guide you in the creation of magical objects."

"Ok," Carolyn sighed, "At least tell me how to make a floating platform."

"I'll tell you how to make a floating sphere," Treton said, "you can figure out the shape later. You can create objects that ignore certain laws of physics, with some difficulty. Specifically, these shapes can ignore gravity and remain stationary even when force is exerted against it. This has the benefit of allowing you to create a floating platform that is guaranteed to remain in place as you walk along it. This is also useful for creating protective barriers. The only thing to know, then, is that these objects can be destroyed if sufficient physical force is used. For example, a platform might be shattered if something too heavy drops on it, or a barrier might break from a relentless attacker. Still, both functions are incredibly useful, once you've learned to use them properly."

"Ok, great," Carolyn nodded, "But what do I actually do?"

"Excellent question," Treton admitted. "You just have to will it to remain stationary. It's probably more complicated than that, but I should repeat that at best all I can do is guide you in the theory. I know no more than that."

"All right, I'll try," Carolyn answered. She took a deep breath as she tried to focus, slowly forming another ball in the air, this time willing it to remain in place. She focused on it for a good minute, hoping the extra effort would help, and released the spell. When she looked at it, she was amazed to see it holding perfectly still.

"I did it!" she cried, not believing it was so easy.

"Not quite," Treton informed her. He reached out a

finger and flicked the sphere, sending it hurling away. "You balanced its weight, but did not make it stationary. You'll need to practice that some more, but I think for now we should call it a day."

"Yeah, all right," Carolyn nodded. Though she hated to stop, she had used up a fair amount of magic with her practicing and wouldn't be able to go much longer. She realized that utilizing her sorceress magic expended more magic than the spells she had learned before. With time and practice, she could probably learn to cast more efficiently, but for now she was very limited in what she could accomplish.

Carolyn left the training room, staff in hand, still thumping rhythmically on the carpet as she walked. It might take more time until she could really put her powers to use, but she left the lesson feeling confident. She was now, and forever would be, a sorceress.

CHAPTER 12
The Wrath of Derishz

Over the next week, reports continued to come in about the continuing war effort. The resurgence of the Herin army was giving hope to the people, which in turn demoralized the enemy troops. Some of the mercenary bands Ferdi had bought out took this opportunity to flee from his army, weakening and further crippling his forces.

Almost all of Ferdri's troops were back in the capital now, setting up fortified positions to defend against a siege. That, unfortunately, made it more difficult to get information in and out of the city, but some was still making it through. The rest of his troops had positioned themselves in some of the towns further north, setting up a blockade against Herin troops heading for the capital. Any day now those forces would clash.

There was still no clear picture of what Ferdri was planning. The scout they had captured and interrogated revealed little useful information. It seems he was one of about twenty scouts sent into the forest that morning. The only instructions they were provided was to look for anything unusual, so they all assumed they were out looking for unicorns. If Ferdri did know about Cansition, he didn't let anyone else in his army know it.

At the same time, Carolyn continued to practice her sorcery. She was slowly getting better at controlling shape and had finally managed to create an object that hovered in the air and remained there. Trying to stand on it, however, was less successful.

"Try it again," Treton said patiently.

"Sure," Carolyn nodded. She created a small square in the air, no more than three feet in either direction, hovering just a couple inches off the ground. This time she poured a little more magic into it to make it a bit denser. The last attempt had been too weak and the square had shattered the moment she got her second foot on it. She experimentally placed one foot onto the new one, pressing down with her weight a bit. It didn't budge. That was a good sign; she didn't accidentally give it weight by using too much magic this time. It also didn't show any signs of giving. Tentatively she lifted her second foot off the ground. The platform held. Treton watched apprehensively as she placed her second foot on the platform. It held. Carolyn sighed a breath of relief.

"Excellent," Treton exclaimed. He seemed almost as excited about Carolyn's studies of sorcery as she was. "You will still need to practice this more until you can do it at a whim, but this is definitely a step in the right direction."

"Looks good so far," Carolyn nodded, impressed as she looked down at her glowing blue platform. Out of curiosity, she did a little jump and landed on the platform. It immediately shattered. Her feet fell the extra couple inches and hit the hard, stone floor.

"Like I said," Treton sighed, "you will still need more practice."

"Right, yeah, I'll work on that."

"I think that's enough of sorcery for today," Treton said, but he left the phrase hanging.

"But not of the lesson?" Carolyn reasoned, looking

confused.

"It's time we... We have to spend some time..." Treton stammered, looking uncomfortable. "The King still expects you to attempt to use the Derishz Ruby."

"Oh right." Carolyn looked down at the chain around her neck, pulling the necklace out from under her robes. There it was, the Derishz Ruby, what she had once called her lucky necklace.

"Try and connect with it," Treton said quietly, "like you did the first time. I'll be here to protect you again."

"All right," Carolyn replied, hiding her nerves. She'd never told Treton about her private attempt to use the Ruby, and that incident had both grown her confidence and frightened her even more. Facing it a third time was not a happy prospect

Regardless, she took a deep breath and focused on the Ruby. Not unlike how she'd bonded with her sapphire, she reached out tendrils of magic, just tiny ones, and touched the Ruby. As they connected, she could feel its power thrumming, filling her mind with its vastness. Such a great power, unfathomable, too great to be controlled or directed. She felt herself swallowed up in it.

The latent desire she had come to expect slammed against her mind, attempting to force itself on Carolyn, to drive her to unleash its destructive potential. She refused, but her refusal felt so inadequate against the intense pressure it brought to bear against her.

She attempted to ignore it and explore the endless depths of power it contained, to try and understand it. As she explored, reaching out with her mind, she felt there was much more to this artifact than just destruction and death. There was also the potential for healing and building, for life and creation. Its power seemed able to perform any task, if one was only strong enough to control it. But the desire kept pressing against her, threatening to consume her. She felt it wearing down her willpower, trying to break through.

With a brief scream of defiance, Carolyn broke her

connection to the Ruby. While they were connected, it had been glowing and hovering in the air in front of her. Now it plopped down against her chest; lifeless, innocent. Carolyn took a few deep breaths to steady her nerves, hearing Treton speaking to her but unable to make out the words.

"I'm all right," she said finally as her breathing returned to normal. She wanted to sit but there were no chairs in the room. At a whim, she made a small platform just behind her and sat on it tentatively. It held, so she let herself relax.

"What happened?" Treton asked nervously.

"Not much different than last time," Carolyn shook her head, "but I was able to resist it better. The desire to be used for death is *very* powerful. It feels... suffocating at first, but if I get past the initial shock it becomes easier to tune out."

"So you think you can control it, then?" Treton asked, apprehensive.

"No," Carolyn looked up at him. "No one can control this. Do you have any idea what this is?"

"Of course, it's the Derishz Ruby," Treton said, but he was avoiding her eyes.

"Where did this come from again?" Carolyn pressed him, feeling like she was missing something important. "The Queen said it came from a powerful mage, right? What kind of mage?"

"I don't see why that's relevant," Treton dodged the question. "He was a madman, bent on destruction. The Derishz Ruby was his weapon of destruction. We can control it just like he did."

"But this isn't a weapon of destruction," Carolyn stood up now, facing the older wizard, though she was nearly a foot shorter, "There's much more to it than that. The power is vast. Limitless." She remembered the endless expanse of possibility that opened to her as she tapped the Ruby's power. "It doesn't just destroy," Carolyn added. "It can create as well."

"So what?" Treton grew agitated, and he still avoided looking straight at her. "So this mage's greatest tool of destruction was also a tool for creation. I don't understand what this has to do with the ability to use it or why it's important for you to know."

"It's important," Carolyn retorted, "because I'm the one using it, and I want to understand it before I use it.'

"That's not something I can help you with, Carolyn," Treton countered, his shoulder slumping. "Nobody understands it. You, who have touched it yourself, probably understand it better than anyone."

"Fine," Carolyn finally turned away, frustrated at not getting answers. "I think we're done here." She turned and left without another word.

There was something Treton was hiding about the Ruby, and she guessed there was more about the previous owner than he was letting on. Maybe it wasn't some mysterious mage, maybe it was actually her ancestor Naritha herself. Was it possible *she* was the crazed mage? No, then she would've used it to dominate Carolyn's dimension after going through the portal. That also didn't explain the vastness of the power. It seemed like something far beyond human ability to create. Or control.

Someone had to know the truth about this, but Treton was not willing to talk. The only other person Carolyn could think of was the Queen. Thinking back to her first meeting with the King and Queen, she remembered how Queen Rorina had cut off King Ketra when he was talking about the origin of the Ruby. She *had* to know something about it and wanted it kept secret from Carolyn. She was the one Carolyn would have to talk to if she wanted to get the truth.

Since her return to Cansition with Elis and Sarin, Carolyn had continued her sword lessons. They had a lot more free time at Cansition and Carolyn wanted to make the most of it. That evening, however, she was distracted as she practiced her swings in the same room where she had attempted to use the Ruby earlier that day. Elis could sense she was troubled and called an early halt to the lesson.

"What's bothering you today, Carolyn?" Elis asked, genuine concern in his tone.

Carolyn sighed, uncertain if or how she wanted to respond. She was accustomed to keeping her thoughts and concerns to herself, though she knew it was unhealthy. After some consideration, she finally patted the necklace hidden under her robe and stated simply, "This."

Elis visibly shuddered and he looked away. "What about it?" he asked, his tone troubled.

"I tried to use it today," she explained, fiddling with it idly, "Treton said it was time I gave it a shot."

"What's it like?" Elis wondered aloud, staring off into space, clearly scared to hear the answer. Carolyn did not disappoint.

"Frightening," she gave a shudder as she remembered, "So much power, and this overwhelming desire for death. I feel lost in it every time I use it. I'm afraid... I'm afraid I won't ever be able to control it."

Elis just gave a slight nod, trying to express understanding but his whole body radiated fear. The two stood in silence for a while, neither one certain what to say.

"Do you know who created it?" Carolyn asked suddenly. Elis was pretty well schooled, it seemed likely he'd know something about it. That, and she was hoping he'd be willing to tell her whatever it was that Treton was hiding.

"What?" Elis looked at her now, "Oh, w-well not really, no," he stuttered uncharacteristically, but quickly regained his composure, "I mean, very little is known about it in the first place. It's named after Derishz, it's last owner, but who knows if he made it? I've heard of other ancient relics that exerted their own will over the user, this could be the same."

"Hmm," Carolyn studied him closely. *He's hiding something, too.* She hated when secrets were kept from her, but she trusted Elis. If he wasn't telling her something, she knew he had to have a good reason.

"Oh well," she sighed, "I guess it's not important."

The next day, Carolyn went to meet with Treton for her lesson. As she entered, he looked like he had not forgotten their previous confrontation and hesitated to make eye contact.

"I'm sorry for getting angry at you yesterday," Carolyn said without preamble.

"Oh," said Treton, looking surprised. "I'm not accustomed to a royal apologizing to me."

"I'm not accustomed to being royal," Carolyn replied with a smirk.

"Yes, I suppose that's true," Treton nodded. "I accept your apology, and would like to also request forgiveness for my tone. It was inappropriate for me to speak with you in such a fashion."

"I forgive you," Carolyn replied, "Though I would appreciate at least a reason for why you won't tell me the *real* identity of the Derishz Ruby's previous owner. "

"I..." Treton began, but stopped himself with a sigh, "I'm not at liberty to speak about it."

"Is it classified or something?"

"Yes, that's right," Treton agreed eagerly, as though glad for an excuse to be offered.

"Well, you could've said that," Carolyn said. "Forget about it for now. Let's get on with it."

That lesson, Carolyn worked on learning to move the permanent, floating objects that she created. By focusing on them, she could glide them around slowly. Sometimes she didn't make the platform strong enough and attempting to move it caused it to crumble. Other times she had a hard time controlling its movement, or it moved slowly. By the end of the lesson, she was able to move them a bit and fairly consistently, but not very quickly. Still, she was making progress. Her platforms were also getting sturdier and more reliable, able to take weight or act as barriers.

"We should try the Ruby again," Treton said tentatively near the end of the lesson.

"We?" Carolyn replied. "I'm pretty sure it's only me

who's trying it."

"All right," Treton conceded. "Then it's time for *you* to try again. Perhaps you should sit down first this time."

"Yeah," Carolyn nodded, casually creating another small platform to sit on. She was getting the hang of that.

"I hope you're ready," Carolyn said. Before waiting for a response, she connected herself to the Ruby.

Ignoring the usual press of the Ruby's desire for death, she focused on her field of vision, which was totally filled with an undulating expanse of red and black splotches as far as the eye could see. As she focused, different sections of it coalesced to form clusters. When she approached each one, she could sense the attributes of the power of that cluster, like pain, death, or healing.

She explored further, veering away from the power of death, finding instead powers of enhancement. She began to reach out for it, wondering what it would do and how she could use it, but she stopped herself. She might lose herself in this power; she needed to be able to feel it and use it without losing her own senses.

Carolyn attempted to pull herself out of the Ruby's depths of power without breaking the magical connection, trying to see with her own eyes. It took an incredible amount of effort, but slowly the redness faded and Treton come into view, his brow creased. She could still feel the power, still reach through it with her mind, but now she could do so without losing her ability to see.

The moment her eyes came fully into focus, however, the desire for death redoubled. Somehow upon seeing Treton right in front of her, the intense desire of the Ruby wanted to kill him even more, pressing against her to utilize it for his destruction. Without a second thought, Carolyn broke her connection to the Ruby completely. As she did, she noticed for the first time that the Ruby, which had been floating just in front of her, had also been wreathed in fire. As the connection faded, the flames went out and the Ruby fell harmlessly against her.

"That was different," Carolyn said, staring at the multi-faceted face of the Ruby.

"You probably don't realize this," Treton said, "but every time you do that, you seem to go into a trance, but other than the Ruby floating and glowing, I have no idea what's going on."

"I thought you could sense how I was feeling, or something like that?" Carolyn asked. "The first time I did this, you saved me from it."

"I can sense your resolve," Treton explained. "More or less. It's more complicated than that, and it's a very imprecise art."

"Gotcha," Carolyn nodded. "So usually when I try to use this thing, I can't see or hear anything around me. This time I tried to force myself to use my senses normally while connected with it."

"And were you successful?"

"Yeah, but then it wanted to kill you even more."

"Ah," Treton sighed. "I'm glad it didn't."

"It can't," Carolyn shook her head, "I still don't really get why, but all it can do is *want* to kill people; it can't *actually* do it. That's why it tries to convince me to."

"Well, I think that's enough for today, then," Treton said, looking thoughtful, "We can—I mean, *you* can try again tomorrow."

"No, I want to try one more time," Carolyn protested.

"You do?" Treton asked, raising an eyebrow.

"Yeah," Carolyn said, "I feel like I'm getting better at resisting it and close to actually using it. Let me just try-"

Carolyn was cut off as the door to the training room suddenly slammed open. She stood up suddenly, holding her staff tightly in an anxious grip, as she turned to face whoever was coming. To her surprise, it was Merilda, rushing over to them and looking quite flustered.

"Milady!" Merilda cried as she came closer, doing a sort of rushed bow, "Master Treton! The King asked for you both to come immediately!"

"What happened, Merilda?" Carolyn's brow furrowed, seeing the fear in her eyes.

"We're under attack!" she nearly shouted in reply.

"Attack!" Treton shouted in response, rushing to the door. Carolyn and Merilda quickly moved after him.

"What do you mean by attack?" Carolyn asked urgently.

"I don't know, milady," Merilda shook her head, eyes still wide, "I wasn't told, all I know is that Ferdri's soldiers are on the way here."

"Oh, no," was all Carolyn could think to say, reeling with worries. How did they find out they were in the forest? Ferdri's army was much bigger than the number of knights here. How long could they hold out against an invading army? Were there any other exits, or were they stuck in here? What if the soldiers just camped outside and laid siege to them? They would all starve - a slow, painful death.

Treton moved aside to allow Carolyn to enter the meeting room first. She entered quickly and sat down on the King's right. A few of the other ministers, including the General, were already there. Treton came in and took his seat at the table and Merilda closed the door behind them, leaving them in the tension-ridden room.

"Let's get right to it," the King started the meeting off, "Ferdri's troops are heading here right now. They'll arrive in this region of the forest within an hour."

"How did they get so close before we heard of it?" Treton asked, sounding nervous.

"Norostar has been locked down recently," the intelligence minister explained, "ostensibly to fortify the city against attack. It seems Ferdri gathering his troops for defense was a ruse; really he was gathering them to attack us here. One of my spies snuck out of the city while the army was marching, but he had to take a round-about route to get to us without being seen."

"How many troops?" the General asked, looking thoughtful.

"Around two thousand," the minister responded, "Not

huge, as far as armies go, but well beyond our ability to handle here."

"So what are our options?" the King asked, though his tone portrayed his lack of confidence that there were any.

"I think you will have to evacuate, your majesty," Treton said, "You should start preparing for that immediately."

"How?" Carolyn blurted out before she could stop herself, "Won't they see you leaving?"

"There's a secret exit," the King said quickly, "for just such a situation. Do they know exactly where we are, or will they have to search first?"

"Unknown," the intelligence minister shook his head, "For now, I think we should assume they know where we are and prepare our defense. We can hold the gate for a while. It should give you the opportunity to retreat."

"We can't hold it for long," General Drakson shook his head, still looking thoughtfully at the table. "But we will hold them off as long as we can."

"We need to send a message to our forces immediately," the King said, "Treton, can Garinald be sent to them? We need them to march here post-haste."

"Yes, your majesty," Treton nodded. "There's one other thing which may tip the scales in our favor." All eyes in the room focused on Treton.

"I'm listening," the King said, looking curious.

"Lady Carolyn has begun trying to use the Derishz Ruby," Treton said, drawing some gasps and mutters from the ministers, "She seems confident that she's improving. It's possible she could use it already in any upcoming battle to even the odds."

"Lady Carolyn," the King said, turning to face her, "What say you?"

"Uh," Carolyn stuttered, uncomfortable with the attention. "Well, I might be able to."

"That's not very reassuring," the King commented, "I think it might be better to hold off on that."

"No," Carolyn replied, trying to sound confident. "I can

do it. I've been getting better at understanding it." This is what they had brought her here for, after all; she would find a way to control the Ruby. Somehow.

"All right, we'll keep that as a last resort," the King nodded. "You'll be at the gate, ready to help defend. If things take a turn for the worse, you'll be escorted to the secret exit and taken out of the palace."

"Okay," Carolyn nodded.

"Let's get to it," the King concluded. "Garinald will send for our forces right away. The knights will hold the gate for as long as they can, hopefully long enough for our forces to arrive. The Derishz Ruby will be held as a backup in case all else fails, otherwise Lady Carolyn will be evacuated as well. The Queen and I will prepare to evacuate, but will not leave until we hear word of how the siege is going. Dismissed."

Am I really ready to use the Ruby? Carolyn thought as she walked from the meeting room to the main gate. Despite the confidence Treton saw in her, Carolyn felt she needed more time to practice before she could effectively use the Ruby in battle. She could barely use her new sorcery powers in a lesson, much less in combat; so how was she going to control something as complex as the Ruby?

Carolyn stopped by the barracks where there was already a flurry of activity. She wasn't sure if they knew what they supposed to be doing yet, but the knights had to have their armor on and gear at the ready no matter what they were asked to do. Would they be this enthusiastic if they knew they were essentially being left to die while the King and Queen escaped?

That's really what the plan came down to. The King didn't seem confident Carolyn could use the Ruby, so he was assuming the knights would be overrun. They would stay and hold off the enemy as long as they could while the people in charge could run away. Carolyn found herself disgusted by the thought of it.

She couldn't really disagree with the decision, though. If the King and Queen stayed, they would be slaughtered as well, or captured and tortured. Either way, the people would be demoralized, and the struggle would be lost, with Ferdri coming out the victor. It was important they save themselves to keep up the war effort. Their responsibility was for the kingdom as a whole, not just one small troop of knights. Still, she couldn't feel comfortable with it. She had friends among the knights—Sarin, Elis, Isana. How could she just leave them to die? They had all fought so hard to just lose now.

No, Carolyn couldn't just let them go. The army couldn't get there in time to help, she was the only one who had a chance at saving them, and for that she had to use the Derishz Ruby. She strengthened her resolve, determined to succeed for the sake of her friends, to protect them from the certain death they would otherwise meet.

Carolyn made her way to Sarin and Elis among the other knights. Both were pulling on their gauntlets and strapping on their swords as she stepped up.

"How you guys doing?" she tried to ask casually, though there was tension in her voice. There was also palpable tension in the room. There was a lot of tension, actually.

"All right," Sarin shrugged, "We were afraid this might happen as soon as we captured the scout."

"Now we just have to do our jobs," Elis said, sounding more relaxed than she expected. No, not relaxed, it was more like acceptance. He knew what was probably going to happen and he was facing it with determined calm. "How about you? What are you doing?"

"I..." Carolyn trailed off. The confidence she had sought left her quickly as she struggled to find the words.

"You're leaving with the King and Queen, right?" Sarin asked, not looking at her. His tone was strange, sounding uncharacteristically sad. It struck her that he was expecting this would be the last time he would see her.

"No," Carolyn said firmly, "I'm coming to help defend."

"Really?" Sarin looked surprised.

"Yeah," Carolyn nodded. "I'm going to be using—" she

lowered her voice to a whisper—"the Ruby."

Sarin's eyes went wide and Elis stopped what he was doing to study her, as if in disbelief.

"Are you ready for that?" Sarin asked quietly, sounding concerned.

"No... Maybe... I don't know," she stammered. "I think so, but it's not like I have much of a choice."

"Of course you do," Sarin looked at her, his expression grave. "You can go with the King and Queen. You always have a choice."

"No," Carolyn shook her head. "Sometimes the choice is so obvious, it's not really a choice. I won't just leave you to die when I can do something to help."

"That's our job," Elis said, also speaking in grave tones. "We fight, and we die, for a greater cause."

"That doesn't make it any easier," Carolyn retorted, tears prickling her eyes.

"We want to keep you safe," Sarin said, "as much as you want to keep us safe. That's what makes us friends."

"Yeah," Carolyn nodded. He sounded unusually wise at that moment. "I'm coming with you," she said firmly. "I'll fight alongside you. I'm not afraid to die, if I have to."

"Carolyn," Sarin began, looking at her with admiration. He seemed to be looking for the right words to say, but instead he suddenly wrapped his arms around her and gripped her in a tight embrace. She in turn tried to reach her arms around his bulky, metal-clad form. "Thank you," he whispered in her ear.

They held each other for only a brief moment. She was still royalty and Sarin could get in trouble if he was seen treating her so in public. They broke apart and then couldn't quite look one another in the eye. An awkward silence started to grow between them before Elis spoke up.

"Thank you, Carolyn," he said, placing a hand on her shoulder. "You have a noble heart." Carolyn just nodded, not sure what else to say.

She exited the barracks into the training room, which

was empty at the moment. She had been there hardly a half hour ago with Treton when Merilda came barging in. She leaned against a wall by the door, sliding down into a sitting position, and rested her face in her hands.

Why did she ever have to come through the portal with Sarin? Sure her life had been boring, but at least she'd never had to wonder if her friends would be ordered to die for her. She never had to worry about facing death, or evil gems of destruction, or hopeless wars. The worst issues she had to deal with was what to wear and whether or not her shoes clashed with her outfit.

The tears were streaming freely now. When she finally looked up, she almost expected to be back in her room at home, but she wasn't. She was still in the training room, leaning against the wall, and all alone. After taking a deep breath she pulled herself to her feet and left the room for the entry cave.

None of this would have happened if grandmother hadn't *chosen me,* she told herself, mulling over the same question that had bothered her for weeks. *Maybe she knew this would happen and wanted to torture me.* That answer was not very satisfying, nor did it seem very likely. If grandmother had even known what the Derishz Ruby was, she certainly couldn't have known what was going to happen. *Why did she give it to me in the first place?* Carolyn asked herself in frustration, *why didn't she give it to Jessica?*

Elis had told her just now that she had a noble heart. What did he mean by that? Maybe that was what grandmother had seen in her: nobility. What about her was noble, and how did everyone else see it but her?

At the entry cave, the guards on duty were extra alert and looking uptight. Soon the knights started to come in, one troop at a time, setting up their formation. She saw Sarin and Elis, led by Isana, marching out as well. Carolyn's fears got worse, seeing them standing there, knowing what was coming. Soon after, Treton came out of the palace along with Jacim, Sevina, and a couple lower ranking elemental mages she didn't recognize. Treton spotted Carolyn standing on her own off to the side and walked over to her.

"How are you feeling, Carolyn?" Treton asked gently.

"I'm fine," she lied. How she was really feeling was more complicated and she didn't feel like getting into it.

"You should know," Treton said, "despite all these measures we're taking, there's a good chance Ferdri's troops won't even find the secret entrance to the palace."

"But you don't believe that," Carolyn pointed out.

"No," he admitted. "There are too many tracks in the forest. It seems likely that once they're searching thoroughly, they'll find us quickly enough. Remember," he added, "the Ruby is only to be used as a last resort, and only if you think you can control it."

"Yeah," Carolyn nodded, absently, "I know." *But I'm going to use it no matter what,* she told herself.

Treton remained nearby with Sevina. The other three mages spread out amongst the troops. Then came the waiting. Everyone in the room was very tense, and more than one of the knights seemed to jump at the smallest sound. Not that Carolyn was any better, constantly glancing around and thinking the shadows were turning into enemy soldiers.

They continued to wait for a little over an hour before the first sounds came from the ramp. Carolyn tensed up, expecting this was it, but the gate was opened ever so slightly as a single soldier stepped inside. The gate was shut and a heavy bar set in place to secure it after him. Based on the whispering of the knights, this was a scout left at the top of the ramp. The officers moved amongst their knights a bit as the news quickly spread: they were coming.

All was quiet for nearly another hour before the sound of clinking armor could just barely be heard from outside the gate. It was soft at first, hardly audible but for the total silence inside the gate, but it got more frantic as the sound receded. *Someone came down to look quietly,* Carolyn told herself, *then ran back up.*

Then, finally, came the rhythmic stomp of marching soldiers descending the ramp outside the gate. It was the sound of death approaching. Now the tension really rose as the anticipation of imminent battle set in. This was it, no more waiting, no more uncertainty: battle was upon them.

The gate was tall enough that there were arrow slits high up where arrows could be fired down at approaching troops. All the arrow slits were occupied and very soon Carolyn heard the *twang* of multiple arrows being loosed at once. The archers quickly reloaded, took aim, and fired again. Hopefully they were thinning out the enemy ranks, but it wouldn't be much.

The marching sounds abated, leaving in their wake an eerie silence broken only by faint shouts. Before Carolyn had time to consider it, there was a *crack* of sudden thunder as bolts of lightning reached through the arrow slits and struck the archers. One of them locked up from the electricity and plummeted down while the others tried to shake it off and fire again. That lightning meant there was a wizard on the other side, and who knew what they could do to the gate.

It wasn't long before the answer came. Just a moment later the whole gate shook as a loud *slam* could be heard from it. Sevina lifted her staff, the ruby glowing bright, creating two pillars of stone that shot up out of the ground right behind the gate, helping to hold it in place. The gate shuddered again from another impact, but this time less; the pillars were holding it for now. Another impact, but the gate still held.

There was a brief respite before something else impacted the gate, though it seemed not to hit it too hard. Carolyn watched closely, trying to figure out what had been thrown, when there was a second, weak impact. At first she thought Sevina had done something else to reinforce the gate, but then she began to see the flames. It may have been a sturdy gate, but it was still wooden, and now it was on fire. Sevina acted quickly, dousing the gate with water, but some damage had been done.

The fire and other, stronger objects continued to impact the gate a couple more times, then it stopped briefly. Worried about what they would attempt next, Carolyn kept a close eye on the gate. It seemed to be whole, but dust was coming from somewhere and the gate didn't look as tall as it used to. Carolyn gasped when she realized the gate was beginning to splinter as the roof caved down on top of it. Sevina noticed as well, and shifted her focus to the roof, her ruby now glowing incessantly. The roof stopped collapsing, but Sevina's focus was now held, actively working to prevent it.

The pounding on the gate continued for a while, along with the flames slowly burning through, though Sevina and the other combat mages did what they could to stop it. With each impact, rhythmic like the beating of a heart, the gate shuddered more furiously, no longer contained by the myriad spires of rock conjured to keep it in place. With every impact, a chill went down Carolyn's spine, expecting to see the hordes of enemy soldiers pouring through any second.

One final *crack* resounded as the reinforced beam that locked the gate in place cracked and splintered, the whole gate shuddering on its hinges. With the next *boom*, the doors were thrown open, hanging loose on their hinges. The massive boulder that had cracked through them came hurtling into the knights. Many of them jumped out of the way in time, but others were not so lucky.

Beyond the boulder and through the now ruined gate Carolyn could see them finally: the enemy soldiers, a mass of armored bodies, all with weapons poised to attack. Among them were two combat wizards, the rubies on their staves glowing bright, as well as a restoration wizard, keeping further back. The enemies rushed through the gate as the knights moved forward to defend, holding their formation to prevent their enemy from gaining any ground. The space was packed so tightly there was barely even room to fit the knights, let alone maneuver, but the knights kept their formation regardless.

Sevina and the other elemental wizards moved forward among the knights, blasting out powerful bolts of electricity at the oncoming foes, or spraying them with spears of ice. Jacim had moved forward and was near the front of the crowd, fighting with his sword and enhanced strength. Treton began to cast his own spells to restore strength to fallen knights at the front of the line. With him around, they would be able to survive otherwise fatal wounds and continue the fight.

Then there was Carolyn. Being all the way at the back, she felt so removed from the battle. Even if she were closer, she didn't know what she would do. Her fire magic tended to be a bit wild and was liable to injure her friends as much as her allies. She wasn't practiced enough with her sorcery to accomplish anything meaningful. Out of the corner of her vision she saw someone moving quickly into the main gates of the palace, presumably a messenger to inform the King and Queen that it was time to flee. Flee. That's where she was supposed to be, running away and hiding while others did the work.

I can't do it, she shook her head, *I can't run. I* need *to do this.* Carolyn's whole body was shuddering, looking into the mayhem playing itself out before her. She would not—could not—leave others to die for her, not when she could still help them. With her sorceress' staff gripped tightly in her hand, she focused on the troops on the ramp outside the gate, beyond the line where any friendly knights could be injured, and shot off a massive ball of flame.

The great ball of fire, burning with her determination, soared over the heads of the knights and smashed into a group of enemy troops. Some of the soldiers broke formation and went running, others dropped to the ground to put out the flames, while yet others held their ground. Undaunted, Carolyn fired again.

This time, the fireball never met its target. As it came

close, a sudden gust of wind blew it off course, causing it to smash harmlessly into the ceiling. One of the enemy wizards, his ruby shining bright, had deflected her missile. He and his companion then followed up with their own attacks, sending fire and boulders flying into the groups of knights. They took a similar tactic to Carolyn, aiming beyond the front line to prevent injury to their own troops. Now Sevina and her companions had to go on the defensive, using wind to deflect the flames and an earthen hand—grown out of the ceiling—to grab the boulders out of the air.

The battle dragged on with the mages on both sides continuing to exchange blows in this way. Carolyn did her best to help, but it all seemed to be of no avail. In the end, the mages seemed to cancel one another out, making it a fight between the soldiers and the knights, and there were a lot more soldiers than knights. The gate made a convenient chokepoint to fight in, which meant the enemy couldn't overwhelm the knights with their superior numbers, but slowly the knights were being forced back, with no more knights to come and help.

The Herin troops would not get here on time; they were on their own, and they were going to lose. Breathing heavily, partially from effort and partially from trepidation at what she was about to do, Carolyn reached for the Derishz Ruby.

"Carolyn!" Treton appeared at her elbow, shouting over the noise. "I think it's time for you to flee. Come with me—"

"No!" Carolyn shouted back, her conviction unshakable. "It's time for something else." She pulled the Ruby out from under her robe.

"Are you certain you can control it?" Treton asked desperately. "Are you certain?" He sounded like he wanted to convince Carolyn she couldn't, like she needed to stop this mad decision. For a brief moment, she thought maybe he was right. But no, this was the only chance, so she *had* to succeed. *I* will *control it,* she told herself. *This is why grandmother chose me.*

"Yes," she said emphatically, "I have to."

Before Treton could protest again, Carolyn reached out with her magic and connected with the Ruby. This time she did it without hesitation, gripping the Ruby with a powerful burst of magical energy, forming a firm connection between them that would not break easily.

Immediately she felt its power, the incredible, world-breaking power of the Derishz Ruby that had caused it to be banished for over a century. She delved into it headfirst, ready to use it for herself.

Carolyn immediately tried to repress its burning desire for death, instead trying to see what was going on in front of her instead of becoming fully enveloped in the power. Her eyes came into focus and what she saw before her was a cacophony of death and chaos. So much violence, so much death, so much discordance. The desire came back, that intense desire to destroy and to kill, reveling in the sight before it. And this time, Carolyn didn't fully reject it.

Yes, she told herself, nodding, *that's what I need right now.* She moved herself toward that part of the Ruby's power she had avoided. *I need the power to fight.* She felt the desire getting stronger, starting to envelop her as the powers of destruction started to flow into her, becoming a part of her very being. *I need the power to kill.* She reached for it, absorbing it, inviting it into her. *To destroy my enemies. I want to destroy.*

Something snapped at that moment within her. Carolyn had never felt so *alive* before! She felt so strong, her limbs moving so quickly; her senses were sharpened far beyond what she had ever experienced. Suddenly everything was moving so *slowly.* She watched the people swing their swords as though moving through water, and their movements were sluggish and awkward. They couldn't move, but she could.

She pushed herself off the ground and leaped, nearly flying, through the air. She was able to watch the silly people with their sticks of metal and their sluggish limbs as she soared over their heads. As she neared the ground just behind the enemy lines, she casually thrust out her arms and sleek blades of red energy tore out in either direction. Three enemy soldiers were sliced clean through, killed instantly where they stood, as Carolyn landed between them majestically. As she rose dramatically to her feet, their bodies fell, and the sounds of surprise and horror began.

She turned around swiftly. She was surrounded by people dressed the same as the ones she had killed, and they were her enemy. She lifted her hands in the air and all the silly little people with the armor style of her enemy went flying up, hovering some eight feet above the ground. Then she clapped her hands and all the little people slammed together in a massive ball of squirming limbs as they were crushed to death, falling lifeless to the ground in a bloody heap.

She turned again, accompanied by the screams of her enemies, and saw a massive boulder hurtling toward her. She casually walked into it, allowing it to impact against her and splinter into mere gravel as she continued forward unscathed. In front of her were many more people, and all of them were her enemies. There was no need to be careful here, she was free to do as she wished.

For starters, she waved a hand and searing flames roared outward, traveling up and out the ramp, so hot they burnt to a crisp every person they touched. Now she got hit by a bolt of lightning, but other than blinking, she hardly noticed. She saw the wizard that had done it, an older one standing nearby. Casually she flicked her wrist toward him and he flew through the air, landing sprawled on the ground in front of her. He looked familiar, like she had fought him once before, but she gave it little thought as she tread over him, crushing his throat.

With another wave of her hand, searing flames burned through all the people to her right, then another wave consumed the people to the left. Pretty soon there was nobody left for her to kill, so she ran forward, heading up the ramp. As she ran, she came across more people that looked scared and confused. More red blades of energy took care of all of these on the ramp.

Open air surrounded her, the light of the midafternoon sun on her skin. Around her were many more people waiting and even some horses. Many of them looked like they were getting ready to retreat. Carolyn couldn't let that happen. More red blades came out, slicing through the people in front of her, through some of the people on horses, only the horses themselves were spared. There were more, still, those were her next…

No.

The voice came unbidden into Carolyn's mind. What was that voice? Was that her voice?

No, it said again, *this is wrong.*

What…? What was wrong? These were her enemies, she had to kill them. She had to kill the people… All the people.

No, the voice came again, *you need to protect people.*

Carolyn stopped. The people in front of her took this as a sign they should leave while they still could. Not one hesitated to mount a horse and flee as fast as they could, glancing back at her as they did. Carolyn watched them go in confusion, thinking she should be killing them, but holding herself back.

I should be killing them, Carolyn told herself, *Why shouldn't I?*

Because you only kill if you have to, the voice said, *when you have no other choice.*

A feeling started to creep up on her, invading her mind. She felt a familiar presence, one she'd felt for the first time hardly two weeks ago, out in the forest. Carolyn turned around and there was Silvermist, standing among the bodies of the slain, her eyes staring intently into Carolyn's. Carolyn's self, swallowed by the Ruby, began forcing its way back to the surface from where it was repressed, thanks to the unicorn's presence. Carolyn looked about her, seeing the bodies of the dead, brutally murdered.

"Did I...?" she began, looking in disbelief. She looked down at her hands and saw the Ruby there, still attached to its chain, hovering in the air in front of her and glowing with immense power. She looked down at herself and saw she was surrounded by a red aura. It was as if she and the Ruby had become one.

It was the Ruby's desire, she realized, *but it was* my *will.* She had wanted to use it for the first time for exactly what it had wanted this entire time: to kill. Its desire had become her own, and so she willed herself to follow its desires and allowed it to control her. She felt the connection with it and suddenly wanted to break it desperately. For a moment, it felt like the Ruby was holding on, refusing to let go, but then Silvermist pressed her snout up against Carolyn and she gained the resolve she needed. The connection between her and the Ruby shattered.

The world returned to normal speed. Carolyn gasped for breath as though she had just broken the surface of a pool. The red aura faded and the Derishz Ruby fell gently against her chest as her whole body shook violently. Glancing around one more time at the mutilated bodies and ashen piles of empty armor, she threw her arms around Silvermist's neck and began to cry.

"What have I done?"

CHAPTER 13

The Sorceress

The next half-hour was a blur. Carolyn hardly noticed as Silvermist crouched down, pulled Carolyn onto her back and proceeded to carry her back into the palace and to her room. Carolyn kept her arms wrapped tight around the unicorn's neck, her face buried in her flowing mane, crying uncontrollably. The unicorn slid Carolyn off her back and onto the bed, where she immediately curled up into a ball, hugging her legs and continuing to cry. Silvermist lay her head beside her for comfort.

I'm a monster, was Carolyn's only coherent thought. *I'm disgusting. How could I do this? All those people...*

At some point, Treton entered the room bearing Carolyn's staff. She hadn't even noticed dropping it after activating the Ruby. He leaned it against her bedside table, and looked like he wanted to say something, but after a long moment he left the room. Others came by, but after opening the door to look, they turned and left.

No one wants to be with me now, Carolyn told herself. *I'm a horrible person.*

Once the initial shock wore off, she tried to convince

herself that it wasn't her fault, that it was the Ruby that made her do it. But the images of marching through enemy soldiers and slaughtering them without hesitation caused her to throw away any excuses she could conjure up. I *did it. I murdered them all.* I'm *a monster. The desire needed* my *will to guide it, and I gave it exactly what it wanted.*

Eventually, the tears ran out, but even with Silvermist's encouraging presence, Carolyn couldn't forgive herself. She'd had some idea of what the Derishz Ruby was capable of and she hadn't been careful enough. While trying to be confident and reliable for her friends, instead she'd lost control and gone on a rampage. She knew she hadn't attacked any knights, fortunately, but she also remembered how she was thinking. Once the enemy soldiers were gone, what guarantee was there she wouldn't have turned on the knights as well? She very well could've wiped out the entire palace if not for Silvermist's intervention.

Carolyn was uncertain how long she was lying in bed when someone entered the room, closing the door behind them. She waited for them to leave like all the others, but they persisted, so she finally consented to look up and saw Sarin standing next to her bed, looking at her with a soft expression. *Why doesn't he look scared? Isn't he horrified by the things I've done?*

He came over to the bed and sat down beside her, not saying a word. He opened his mouth a couple times to speak, but seemed to think better of it. He was still wearing his armor, battered and scratched from the battle. Why hadn't he taken it off?

"I'm sorry," was the first thing he said, though he sounded uncertain about it.

"What are *you* sorry for?" Carolyn asked more harshly than she intended.

"I don't know," Sarin admitted, sighing, "I guess for bringing you through the portal? I know I'm sorry you—that during the battle..." He looked away from her as he spoke, his expression downcast, but Carolyn saw the flash of fear in his eyes.

"You mean when I slaughtered everyone? Thanks, I feel much better now,' she added sarcastically, rolling over to put her back to him.

"I—" he started, but he stopped himself, "I don't know what to say," he added in a whisper.

Carolyn didn't respond. She felt like retorting somehow, but this wasn't his fault. She didn't really know what to say either.

"We're moving out," Sarin said after a brief silence. "We're going to take Norostar back."

"What?" Carolyn turned to him in surprise.

"The army is on the way," Sarin said, nodding, "and the bulk of Ferdri's forces were..." he trailed off, glancing at Carolyn briefly. "The King says this is the best time to attack, before Ferdri has a chance to rally his forces."

"So you're saying it's a good thing I murdered people," Carolyn stated coldly.

"No!" Sarin said quickly, then hesitated, "I don't know. People die in war, and armies fight, and sometimes a lot of soldiers die. I don't know what to think, I don't know what to say, I'm just...!" He left off with a growl of frustration.

Silence fell again and Sarin walked back to the door. "I hope you feel better," he said haltingly. There was something else on the tip of his tongue, but whatever else he had to say, he kept to himself. The young knight turned and left without another word.

It was a long time before there was another knock on the door and Queen Rorina herself entered the room. Surprisingly, she wasn't dressed in one of her regal dresses; instead she was wearing a set of polished, chain mail armor with the Herin emblem emblazoned on the left breast. At her side was a long sword in a gem-studded scabbard, and under her left arm was a helmet with a royal crown topping it. She looked equal parts beautiful and deadly

"I came to see how you were doing," the Queen stepped forward, walking with grace even while decked out for war, "before I left." She placed her helm on the bedside table and sat down on the edge of the bed.

"What? Where are you going?" Carolyn wondered. She felt like the answer should be obvious, but her thinking was muddled.

"To Norostar," the Queen replied, "The King in I will be leading the charge."

"Really?" Carolyn sat up to look at her. The royalty here didn't make any sense. "Isn't that dangerous?"

"Of course," the Queen replied with the hint of a smirk, "but it wouldn't be right for us to sit back and relax while our soldiers did all the work."

"That's what you've been doing until now," Carolyn stated simply. It probably came across as incredibly rude, but she didn't care.

"So long as the war was dragging on, it was important to remain safe," the Queen explained, unperturbed. "The people need their leaders to guide them through difficult times. Now that the war is drawing to a close, it is equally important for the people to see their leaders fighting with them, rather than sitting back while they are asked to die."

"The people need their leaders *after* the war also," Carolyn pointed out.

"True," the Queen nodded, "I suppose that's just the philosophy in Herin. That's what works for us."

Carolyn didn't have anything to say to that, but she did have a bone to pick with the Queen.

"You knew," she said quietly. "You knew there was more to the Ruby than what you told me, didn't you?"

The Queen raised her eyebrows, but nodded knowingly. "I knew there was more to the Ruby, yes," she answered guardedly, "but I didn't have any idea of its full scope. I've only heard stories and I thought half of them were exaggerations."

"Then what was it you were hiding from me?" Carolyn pressed her, feeling frustrated, "When we first met, you stopped the King from telling me the what the Ruby really is. Even Treton wouldn't tell me when I tried asking him! What's going on?" she asked angrily.

"It was important to hide it from you," the Queen explained, her expression hard. "If you knew the true origin of the Ruby, you may well have been too afraid to use it, and that's not something we could afford. We sent for you out of desperation; we could not have that plan fail simply because you were too afraid. That's why I ordered Treton never to reveal the true nature of it to you."

"So that's why he was so dodgy about it," Carolyn said, her voice cold fury. "Your lie caused this mess, led me to think I could control this thing. You used me!"

"I know you're upset," the Queen replied, her tone level, "but it worked in the end. You used the Ruby when we needed it most and gave us the window we needed to win this war."

"Well you'll have to win it without me" Carolyn yelled, "because I'm not using that stupid thing again!"

"That's all right with me," Queen Rorina answered smoothly. "It's done its job; we don't need it anymore."

Carolyn seethed. There was so much more she wanted to yell at the Queen, but nothing seemed sufficient. Instead she just growled in anger and turned away, wrapping her arms around Silvermist's neck once more.

"I'm sorry, Carolyn" the Queen said, her tone soft, "but we were desperate. I hope you'll come to forgive me."

The Queen got up and lifted her helmet. Carolyn looked up briefly as she was about to exit the room.

"What is it?" Carolyn asked, her tone still harsh, but softer than it had been, "Now that I'm not using it anyway, where did it come from?"

The Queen hesitated, her hand on the door handle, as she turned back to regard Carolyn. She looked uncertain for a moment.

"Derishz," the Queen said slowly, "was the lord of the demons." She left, the door closing with an ominous *click*.

Carolyn continued staring at the door in shock. The lord

of demons? She looked down at the Ruby, hanging from its chain around her neck. Suddenly its multi-faceted face looked sinister and malicious. This jewel was the weapon of some demon lord, undoubtedly used to wreak death and havoc. And now Carolyn had used it to do the same.

She took the necklace off and stared at the multi-faceted face of the Ruby, expecting to see a demonic face grinning back at her. With disgust she threw the Ruby against the door. It hit the wood with a satisfying *thwack* before falling softly to the carpeted ground. It was not her lucky necklace anymore, it was a disgusting, cursed thing and she wanted nothing to do with it.

The silence of the emptied palace deepened as she sat brooding in her bed. Everyone she knew in Herin—other than Merilda—was on the way to Norostar to throw themselves against the enemy. Some of them might even die. Would she ever see Sarin again? Or Elis? Or Isana, or Jacim? Even Treton and the King and Queen were not guaranteed safety. They were all off to fight while she lay around and moped for herself.

I've done my part, she told herself. *They only wanted me for the Ruby anyway.*

And yet, despite her anger, despite feeling betrayed, she found she could not give up. Perhaps it was her noble heart, as Elis had put it, or the power of fire to keep going even when all hope seemed lost, as Treton had said. Was that why she kept succeeding when she tried to convince herself she would fail? The more she thought about her time in Herin, of everything she had learned and everyone she had grown to know—she knew she could not abandon them now.

Carolyn stood and, with great reluctance, picked up the Ruby from the floor and brought it back to the bed. In the last battle, she'd been forced into the decision to try and control it without knowing its true origins. Now that she knew what it was, could she bring herself to try and properly control it?

But why even bother?, she thought, staring at the Ruby with distaste. *The Queen said it's not needed anymore.* But the reason they'd brought her to Herin in the first place wasn't to turn the tide of a battle; they had wanted to use the Ruby against Ferdri's super-soldier, the one too powerful to beat. Didn't they still have to deal with him? He was probably in the castle, guarding—

In the castle! The Derishz Ruby was demonic. The memory of Carolyn's first attempt at accessing the Ruby's powers came to mind. It had gone out searching, looking all around for more people to kill. Her vision had expanded outward, eventually including the castle, where it found one being that it had no desire to kill. The super-soldier. A demon.

"Oh no!" Carolyn put a hand to her mouth. Ferdri had been searching for something, but no one knew what. The theory that he was searching for the Ruby had been dismissed because no one knew the Ruby hadn't been destroyed. But if Ferdri had found a demon, perhaps the demon was controlling him, using him to find the Ruby! And in their desperation to defeat Ferdri, the King and Queen had brought the Ruby into Herin for the demon to find!

Was the demon Derishz himself? Maybe it was another demon lord, just as powerful, or even more so? Either way, the knights wouldn't stand a chance, they would be decimated. They were marching straight into a death trap. The only thing powerful enough to kill him was the Ruby.

This thing is evil, she reminded herself, staring at the necklace in her hand. *I can't rush into this like I did last time.* Elis had said that she always had a choice. If she felt forced into it, was rushed, stressed, and unable to focus properly, it would all go to pieces again.

I do have a choice, she told herself, *and I choose to be in control this time.* Taking a deep breath, her fingers closed around the cold metal of the necklace, and pulled it around her neck once again.

"Silvermist," she said, turning to her unicorn. Silvermist

was standing beside the bed, studying Carolyn closely; she already knew what she was thinking. "We have to help," Carolyn concluded.

Silvermist's eyes flashed with anticipation as Carolyn felt an affirmative feeling in her mind. She leapt onto Silvermist's back, held out her hand to Pull her staff into it, and shouted, "Let's go!"

Carolyn Pulled the door open, allowing Silvermist burst through, her powerful legs carrying them quickly down the halls. Speeding through the grand entrance of the palace she saw a couple servants staring at her in wonder. The main gate was still in pieces, allowing them to easily charge through, maneuvering around the guards and servants working on repairing it. Silvermist jumped over the makeshift barricade that was set up and charged out up the ramp and into the forest.

They easily wove among the trees, Silvermist's grace and familiarity with the woods allowing them to navigate it without pause. The sounds of the woodland creatures stopped as they went by, entranced by the unicorn.

It wasn't long before they were out of the forest and in the open air. Silvermist moved faster than any horse Carolyn had seen. They made it to a river, too wide for a normal horse to leap, but Silvermist cleared it without hesitation. Carolyn could sense the excitement emanating from her, the thrill of having left the forest for the first time, and the anticipation of helping to fight.

The open fields around them passed by in a rush as Silvermist sped toward the outer walls of the capital city. Carolyn had only been in the city once, and then as a helpless bystander, liable to be killed with ease. That was months ago. Now she was an apprentice of magic, a student of the top wizard in Herin. Now she was a sorceress.

They reached the outer wall where the nearest gate was open wide with clear evidence of a battle having recently taken place around it. There were bodies of fallen soldiers on both sides and even a few horses. Carolyn looked away from the carnage, which stirred up memories of her own carnage from earlier. She couldn't think of that right now, she had to focus.

They sped through the gate, following the signs of battle raging among the city streets. There were more soldiers felled in battle, dropped weapons, helmets, scratch marks on the buildings, and even some burn marks from the wizards. It looked like the knights had moved through quickly and the troops had made little or insufficient effort to stop them. Remembering back to their escape, the Herin knights had magical "keys" to open the gates with ease, so the defenders must've realized the outer gates were a poor place to set up a defense. The main battle was more likely to be taking place in and around the palace.

Silvermist navigated the streets and the mess left in them with ease, bringing them eventually to a main boulevard. This road led straight from the northern gate and to the palace at the opposite end of the city, which was situated on a small hill. Up ahead, crowded around the main gates to the palace wall, was a cluster of soldiers and knights, all trying to force their way forward. From her vantage point she couldn't see much, but there was definitely a large presence of enemy soldiers on the hillside beyond the gate. Silvermist charged toward it, faster than she had yet gone, shooting like a bullet down the road. Carolyn saw arrows flying in both directions as the sounds of combat grew louder.

As she and Silvermist approached, Carolyn wondered how she was supposed to help when she was all the way at the back like this. The streets were too crowded for the knights to effectively let her pass even if she wanted to. An idea occurred to her, but it was so crazy it couldn't possibly work. *No,* she told herself, refusing to feel defeated. *No, it can work. I can do this.*

Clutching her staff tightly in her hand, she recalled her recent lessons on sorcery. *Reinforce it, make it strong enough to hold weight, a lot of weight. Make sure it doesn't obey gravity, don't let it be moveable. I can do this!* As soon as she was close enough, she took a deep breath, steadied her nerves, and loosed her spell.

Silvermist began to rise into the air. Her hooves were no longer clacking on the hard cobblestones of the city; instead, they were pounding with a slight buzzing as they impacted against the magical surface of Carolyn's ramp. Carolyn felt a jolt of fear that the platform would not be able to bear the weight and crack beneath them, but it held. It was a long but steady ramp and soon they found themselves reaching the end of it just as they were reaching the back of the line of knights.

Her confidence restored by her success, Carolyn quickly created a second one, this one longer, going right over the heads of the knights. Silvermist continued to charge forward straight across the magical bridge. She could sense Carolyn's plans when they were linked, and she was as confident as Carolyn in its success.

Rushing forward at breakneck speed, Carolyn could hear the shouts of surprise from the soldiers below as a unicorn rode over their heads. Every few seconds she would have to cast again, creating a new platform so they could keep going, fast approaching the front of the line. As they got closer, another volley of arrows came straight at them.

Carolyn fashioned a platform in the air above, meant to block the arrows. Many of the arrows caught in it, but this one was rushed and she didn't get the strength right. The barrier shattered, leaving the arrows to shower onto the knights below, but they had slowed enough from the impact that they were no longer lethal. A few of them showered around Carolyn as they sped on, but she ignored them.

They reached the gate where the main battle was raging. The King and Queen were there along with Treton, fighting alongside the other knights, leading the charge. As Silvermist approached, everything seemed to stop momentarily. Friend and enemy alike stopped to stare in wonder—and some in horror—at the sight of the unicorn charging through the air. Carolyn laid out one more platform to get them over the gate. When Silvermist reached the end of it, she leapt off, a blur of sleek white fur topped by a scarlet rider as they rushed to the ground.

Silvermist landed gracefully amidst the enemy soldiers. Before they had a chance to react, she gored the nearest one on her horn, then kicked him off. Carolyn turned in the opposite direction and shot off some fire to scare the soldiers away. Silvermist reared up on her hind legs and let out a piercing whinny that sounded like a battle cry. All the soldiers around flinched and cowered at the sound.

A cheer was heard from the gate as the Herin forces were bolstered and pushed through. With the disruption to the enemy lines, they were finally able to break past the defense and began swarming into the palace grounds, striking down any soldiers in their path. Silvermist continued butting her horn at enemy soldiers, impaling them when they got too close and scaring off the rest, while Carolyn used fire to keep them back. As they did this, they suddenly found themselves surrounded by Herin knights and soldiers.

"Carolyn!" a voice shouted. "What are you doing here?"

Carolyn turned and saw the Queen riding up beside her, dressed in her regal armor, now spattered with blood, and with a spear in her hand. The King rode up behind her, also looking to Carolyn for answers. Their honor guard, including Treton, moved to surround the three of them.

"It's a demon!" Carolyn blurted out, as she tried to organize her thoughts.

"Yes, I know Derishz is a demon," the Queen's expression hardened. "I'm the one that told you that. Did you come all the way to continue that discussion?"

"No, no," Carolyn shook her head emphatically, "I mean the super-soldier. It's a demon, too!"

The King snapped to attention at this information. "Are you sure?" he pressed her urgently. "How do you know?"

"When I first used the Ruby," Carolyn explained, "it seemed to be searching all around for people to kill." She had to pause for a moment as she tried to rid some disturbing images of her mind, images of the Ruby succeeding. "But there was one person in the palace it found that it *didn't* want to kill."

"The super-soldier," the Queen concluded. "The Ruby found the super-soldier, and didn't want to kill him because he was a demon."

"We could be walking into a trap," said the King. "We're not equipped to face a demon. We have to call a retreat."

"No," the Queen said firmly. "This demon has been seen and he's no larger than a tall man. He can't be one of the powerful demon lords, but he's still a demon. We'll have to be careful when we face him."

"That's why I came," Carolyn said, "Not just to tell you, but to help you. I know I messed up once, but I know I can control the Ruby's power, and you need it if you have to face a demon."

The King and Queen regarded Carolyn carefully for what seemed a long time. She felt uncomfortable under their scrutiny, but she did not back down. Carolyn held her head high and looked each of them in the eye.

"All right," the King nodded. "We'll have to see the situation inside the palace first. Then we'll take an elite squad to find the demon and kill it, along with Carolyn's help. Stay near for now," he added with a nod to Carolyn. He and the Queen then charged back into the fray of combat, their honor guard moving with them.

Carolyn could sense Silvermist's excitement, so they also rode forward into the front lines. The sight of the unicorn was both beautiful and frightening. Sleek white fur with a cream-colored horn, both streaked with blood as the creature gored her enemies with movements both graceful and precise. Carolyn allowed Silvermist her freedom while using her fire conservatively, worried it would run out long before she reached the demon.

There were still a lot of soldiers and arrows were raining down on them from the parapets, but the tide of battle had certainly turned with the appearance of a unicorn. Many soldiers were fleeing in terror the moment they realized they had drawn Silvermist's ire. Watching the way she charged with such fury and struck with incredible power, yet feeling the gentle presence in her mind at the same time, Carolyn was reminded of Isana. It was amazing how someone could both be strong and fierce on the one hand, yet kind and sweet on the other. It was all a matter of knowing when to apply each trait.

Herin troops pushed forward up the hill, trying to get inside the main gate of the palace. Carolyn took the opportunity to practice her sorcery as a combat tool. Soldiers brave enough to face the unicorn tried flanking her, only to find themselves slamming into a shimmering blue wall that had not been there a moment before. It was almost comical, if not for the horrible reality of battle around them.

Soon they had made their way through to the main palace gate, which opened willingly thanks to the same magic that had allowed them to escape in the first place. Knights poured in, led by Queen Rorina and King Ketra along with Treton and Sevina. Carolyn followed just behind on Silvermist, charging past the twin courtyards toward the double doors into the entrance hall.

Enemy soldiers were crowded around the entrance, trying desperately to keep the knights out. Behind them was the grand staircase, now lined with soldiers and all holding shields at the ready. Above them was a balcony running around three walls of the room, and it was all lined with soldiers. At the top of the stairs was the grand entrance to what must've been the throne room, flanked by silver statues of unicorns reared back. The proud seal of Herin was emblazoned on the door, beckoning them to reclaim its halls.

A crack of thunder nearly deafened Carolyn as a flash of lightning shot from Sevina's staff behind her. Two soldiers locked up as they fell to the ground, but others moved up to take their place. The King and Queen were near the front, trying to press through the door, but there were too many soldiers blocking the path. Twin fireballs were launched as Carolyn and Sevina attacked in unison, trying to clear the blockage. Silvermist refused to stand still for the exchange, eager to get back into battle. She squeezed between the horses of the other knights, so close Carolyn's legs were scraping against the horses' barding, but soon they were past the King and Queen and making their way to the front.

Arrows rained down, but Carolyn casually Pushed them away. Silvermist whinnied a battle cry, lunging for the nearest soldier, tossing him neatly back. The courage of the enemy soldiers broke along with their formation on seeing the angry unicorn barge into their midst. Carolyn was beginning to think that Silvermist was accomplishing more than anyone else in this battle.

More soldiers fell and scattered before the unicorn's fierce onslaught, allowing the Herin knights to stream in behind them. Carolyn kept her focus on the archers, shooting fireballs at them as she kept an eye out for another volley, ready to Push it away. Scanning the enemy troops, she caught a glance of one mounted enemy commander. Upon seeing him, Carolyn felt a burst of anger. It was the knight-commander with the sword too big to be held who had been blocking the entry arch when she had last been in this castle. He shouted a few more orders before spurring his horse forward, coming to meet her.

The entry room of the palace was quickly filling up with soldiers and knights moving all about, but there was still plenty of space as the two of them paused briefly to stare each other down. Silvermist sensed the tension and calmed herself enough to focus, ready to work together with Carolyn. It felt like this was the time for some overly dramatic, pre-battle banter, but instead she simply decided to shoot him.

Blazing fire shot from her staff, aimed right for the enemy commander as he began to charge. He didn't even flinch as he rode straight into the flames, lifting his gauntleted left hand like a shield to block it. There was a brief, yellow flash and the flames were sucked up into an opal on the back of the gauntlet and vanished.

What the...? Carolyn stared in surprise but had little time to consider. Her opponent didn't have enough open space to reach full speed in his charge, but the short distance meant he was on top of her very quickly. She ducked as Silvermist dodged to the right, just missing the massive blade swinging over their heads. She turned and tried to fire again, but again it was absorbed into his gauntlet.

The commander turned again, trying to cleave her in two with an overhead chop. Silvermist quickly stepped back, getting out of range in time. Luckily, despite his inhuman ability to wield it, the sword was still big and slow. Dodging wasn't an issue, but if they got hit by it... Carolyn tried not to think about it. *We have to keep on our toes,* she told herself, *...and hooves.*

After one more attempted fireball was absorbed, she abandoned the fire plan and began attempting to Push him off his horse. With every spell she tried, however, the gauntlet came up and absorbed her magic. Nothing she did seemed to get through to him.

"I'm... finally... going... to... kill... you..." she heard her opponent growling angrily as he swung. His eyes, visible through his helmet, were blazing with hatred and anger. He was dead set on ending her here and now, and with her magic being blocked, it seemed he would succeed.

Desperate for a moment to think, she threw down a pillar of fire between the two of them. The knight's horse reared back in fear and surprise. Carolyn used the pause to catch her breath and study her opponent, trying to find an opening she could exploit.

The gauntlet is obviously enchanted, Carolyn told herself. As the knight turned his horse so he could use the gauntlet to remove the pillar of fire, she saw even his right gauntlet had a gem set in the back, this one an emerald. *Maybe they're both enchanted,* she realized, *one for protection, the other lets him lift that sword. But how can I use this?*

Ideas came to mind, but she wasn't given time to formulate a plan as her opponent charged once again. She was forced back in the face of his sweeping blow, but now—Carolyn realized with dismay—they were almost backed up against a wall. Whatever she was going to do, she had to do it soon.

The sword came swinging down again in an overhead slash, and here she saw an opportunity. Silvermist sensed Carolyn's feelings and moved to assist her plan. They dodged out of the way of that attack, but next came another horizontal swing. This time they stepped into it as a small but potent, shimmering blue barrier appeared in the air just in front of the knight's hand.

The power of the swing is in the blade, not the wrist, Carolyn told herself, *that's the point to stop it.* His hand hit the barrier, causing the swing to rebound, leaving him wide open. Silvermist's body surged forward in a smooth motion, getting Carolyn close enough to grab the knight's wrist with one hand and bash him in the face with the staff in her other.

"Ahh!" he shouted in surprise in pain. Carolyn felt his hand start to tug away from her so she had to move quickly; she would never be able to keep a grip on him. With her hand on him for that brief moment, she was able to cast a spell that was too close for the gauntlet to absorb. Another small barrier appeared, this one a circle around his wrist, below the gauntlet. He tried to pull his hand free but found it stuck in place, caught in a shimmering blue ring. Before he could try to absorb it, she let loose another pillar of fire just by his horse's snout, frightening it enough to pull away suddenly.

"No!" the commander shouted. He was yanked away, but the gauntlet caught on the glowing blue ring as his hand slipped out. The gauntlet hung in the air, stuck to the blue ring, while the massive blade dropped to the floor with a heavy clatter.

For a brief moment, the commander looked at Carolyn

in shock, confusion, and fury. Blood was pouring out of his nose from where Carolyn had whacked him, but he didn't seem to care. He quickly went to pull a sword from a scabbard on his side, but Carolyn turned her attention on the glove now stuck in the air beside her. She switched her staff to her left hand to shove her right into the gauntlet. Instantly she could feel the surge of power in it, like she could lift anything.

The glove itself was too large for her to wear it comfortably, but it would work for now. She dismissed her blue ring barrier. Pulled the giant broadsword from the ground into her waiting gloved hand, and held it point outward toward her opponent's now drawn short sword. Any confidence the knight may have had fled him as he stared down the length of his own blade. He stared at it for a good thirty seconds before turning his horse around running off into the fray to take his chances with the other knights.

"Off with you," Carolyn said, and breathed a sigh of relief. Her plan had been reckless, and if it had failed, she certainly would be dead. *But it worked,* she told herself, *I did it.* She had used more magic than she would've liked, but there was nothing to do about that now, she would have to make do. Dropping the sword and gauntlet, she rode toward the staircase.

There were already a few other knights fighting at the base of the stairs, but they were unable to overcome the uphill advantage of the defenders. Carolyn shuddered as one knight was pierced by an arrow and fell to the ground, unmoving.

Silvermist sensed Carolyn's intent, quickly building up speed as they crossed the distance to the stairs. Once again she let out a frightening battle cry-like whinny, quickly drawing attention to them. A volley of arrows flew just over their heads as Silvermist's horn found the first of the defenders. The enemy soldiers shouted in fear, but held their ground against the unicorn. They knew that they still had the uphill advantage and they were going to use it.

Up close with the enemy soldiers on the stairs above her, Carolyn suddenly realized the necessity of armor in combat. While Silvermist was stabbing with her horn and Carolyn flung fire in all directions, the enemy soldiers tried to press against her, swinging their swords with deadly precision. Her staff—enchanted to be nigh unbreakable, or so Treton had told her—was good for deflecting attacks, and she did her best to dodge out of the way as necessary—with Silvermist's help—but a few blows did land. She screamed in pain as a long gash was sliced down her thigh. She shoved the butt of her staff in the face of her attacker in retribution. Another attacker hit her in the ribs and there was a disturbing *crack*, followed by a fresh bout of pain. Silvermist backed off, carrying Carolyn out of the fray as she clutched her side

"Let me see it," came a voice from behind. Treton rode up alongside her, looking at her side. He placed his hand over the wound as the opal on his staff began to glow.

"AAHHH!" Carolyn shouted in pain as she felt something shift in her side. There was a disturbing grinding sound and a strange clacking, then the pain was gone. She felt her side to find that, other than a mild soreness, the wound was gone.

"That's much better," Carolyn sighed in relief. Treton wasn't paying attention, however. He had moved on to check the leg wound, examining her thigh closely as he prepared for another spell. Carolyn felt uncomfortable having him look at her like that, but she reminded herself he was just a doctor treating her and nothing more.

"You shouldn't be so reckless," he began to say as he healed up her leg. "You should be—"

"In the back, I know," Carolyn nodded, watching as he also did her the favor of quickly repairing enough of her robe that her thigh was covered again, "I won't make that mistake again."

"Good," Treton nodded, "Now we need to break their

defense. How confident are you with your sorcery in battle?"

"Sorcery?" Carolyn wondered, "I've done a couple things and it's worked out so far. What do you have in mind?"

"Create a giant ball," Treton explained, looking toward the stairs, "At the top of the stairs, in the air."

"A ball?" Carolyn looked at him in confusion.

"Yes, but not one that floats, the kind that falls, preferably hard."

"Oh," Carolyn nodded in understanding, then she smiled. "I think I can do that."

"I'll protect you while you do it," Treton offered, turning his attention back to the battle around them.

Carolyn tried to focus. Her magic reserves were running low at this point, which did not bode well for battling a demon after all of this. She thought back to her lessons regarding gravity and density as it pertains to magical objects. After working on creating immobile platforms and barriers, intentionally creating a moveable object now took extra concentration. She chose a point in the air just above the top of the staircase crowded with archers.

The shape of the spell began to formulate in her mind, but she held it back until she was ready. She didn't want a slowly forming ball of shimmering blue light to suddenly appear and give the soldiers a chance to react. Once she felt she had gotten the balance correct, she unleashed her spell.

Carolyn felt a void within her as the large amount of magic left her. All at once a glowing blue light appeared in the air at the point she chose, rapidly expanding in the blink of an eye to the size of a small boulder. The moment it was large enough, the ball released, falling to the stairs below.

"Aaah!" came the shouts from the stairs above as the ball fell on the soldiers underneath it.

"What is that?!" came other shouts.

"Look out!" came the warning too late.

The boulder ploughed into the soldiers like a marble hitting a chain of dominoes, knocking soldiers into one another as it cascaded down the stairs. When it was about halfway down the stairs, soldiers ran up from the base and braced against it to prevent it from going further, but the damage had already been done; the Herin warhorses immediately leaped into the new opening, trampling their fallen foes and forcing their way up the stairs.

"Excellent work," Treton said, "Now come with me. We're going into the throne room with the King and Queen. Oh, remember to dismiss your spell," Treton added as they set off up the stairs.

Carolyn looked up the stairs and saw the soldiers that had caught the boulder were now preparing to release it to hit the oncoming horses. With a dismissive wave of her hand, the boulder vanished just as they were letting it go, leaving them dumbfounded and frustrated.

As knights cleared the way in front of them, kicking the defending soldiers over the railings, Treton and Carolyn stormed up the stairs just behind the King and Queen. Soon they had reached the top of the stairs and stood before the mighty, double doors, already being forced open by the knights ahead of her. The defenders were cleared away from the entrance as the King and Queen charged through with Sevina, following by Treton, Carolyn, and a few other knights to see what was waiting for them.

CHAPTER 14
Ferdri's Servant

They entered into a high-ceilinged room carpeted in deep blue with gold and crimson trimming along the edges. Surrounding them were stairs, wrapping around the entrance and leading to the main floor. At the top of the stairs before them were the grand thrones themselves, with massive backs that reached almost to the ceiling. Sitting on one was a skinny, gangly man dressed in deep purple robes with a fur-lined collar and a jeweled crown on his head: Ferdri. He held himself with a regal air, surveying their approach with keen eyes.

Standing next to him was a giant of a man, at least eight feet tall, dressed head-to-toe in heavy plate armor. In his hand was a wicked looking battle axe, its head resting on his shoulder. He was the reason Carolyn was there: the super-soldier. The demon.

Lining the path from the top of the stairs to the thrones themselves were more soldiers, at least another dozen. On either side at the top of the stairs were crossbowmen, their sights trained on the intruders but holding fire. Carolyn knew their little raiding party was outnumbered two-to-one, but they had more mages than Ferdri did and that gave them an edge, the demon notwithstanding.

The King and Queen halted at the bottom of the stairs and dismounted, the knights and mages following suit. Carolyn dismounted Silvermist hesitantly, thinking it would be a waste for her to just sit here doing nothing. The unicorn sent a mental nod of agreement and turned around to rejoin the fray. Carolyn gave her only a brief glance of longing as she followed the others up the stairs. All of the knights—which included Isana—were keeping an eye on the crossbowmen, holding swords and shields at the ready.

Carolyn could see that Ferdri's impassive confidence was actual a mix of disdain and fear. Perhaps he was less than confident in his demon's ability to protect him after all? Maybe they had a better chance than they thought.

"You've lost, Ferdri," the King declared, the first to break the silence. "Surrender now, before any more innocent lives are lost."

Ferdri shifted uncomfortably on the throne. "I still have him," he retorted, though his voice quivered noticeably. He pointed his thumb at the soldier by this side. "You haven't won yet."

"Do you really think that's enough?" the King said, "We have the Derishz Ruby, or did you forget about how we decimated your army in the forest?" He indicated Carolyn, who was looking away, trying to erase those memories from her mind. "Please stop this madness now!" There was a pleading note in his voice, but anger as well.

"Yes, the Derishz Ruby," Ferdri nodded, looking directly at Carolyn. She tried to glare at him, but hated looking into those eyes and turned away. "You don't look much like you want to use it again," Ferdri observed dryly. "Hand it over and I'll call off my forces," he demanded tersely.

"So be it," the king nodded, shifting into an offensive stance.

Several things happened at once. The twang of firing crossbows sounded from behind them and Carolyn felt a gust of wind blow past her as Sevina swiftly turned to repel the bolts. The two rows of enemy soldiers formed into ranks to defend their liege, while the knights of Herin encircled the King and Queen. Treton cast a spell that infused the Herin group with a faint glow and a warm feeling. Carolyn could feel minor cuts and bruises on her swiftly closing up as the warmth surged through her.

Battle began in earnest. Carolyn turned back with Sevina, setting her sights on the crossbowmen behind. All the bolts that were fired clattered harmlessly to the ground from Sevina's powerful blasts of wind, which even toppled a couple of the crossbowmen. Together they bombarded them with fire and lightning, not giving them a chance to reload. The sounds of battle—metal clanging against metal, shouts of fury and pain—reverberated around the room. When Carolyn chanced a backward glance, she noticed that the only one that had not joined the battle yet was the demon himself. He stood in front of Ferdri as though shielding him, but despite his inaction, the excitement emanating off of him was nearly palpable.

Once the last of the crossbowmen were down—Carolyn secretly hoped she hadn't actually killed someone—the two wizards turned to join the main battle. The King and Queen were in the center of the fray, taking the brunt of the enemy attacks. Some enemy soldiers had already fallen on the ground, but the knights still stood. As Carolyn watched, Isana took a hit to her arm, slashing through her chain mail, but the wound left behind rapidly healed itself up thanks to Treton's preemptive measures.

Sevina's ruby began to glow in preparation for a spell, but before she could release it, there was a dark blur of movement and Sevina was sent skidding back, crying out in pain as she clutched at a deep gash in her stomach. Standing where Sevina had been a moment before was the demon, his battle axe clutched firmly in his hands, dripping with blood.

"Sevina!" Carolyn cried, trying to make her way over

toward her. She shot some fire at the demon, not really expecting it to do anything, as she moved closer. The fire impacted on his armor, but he showed no sign of having even noticed it. He began to charge again as Sevina readied another spell, the wound on her stomach closing, but not fast enough. His axe came down in an overhead swing, biting deeply into her chest.

"No!" Carolyn shouted, horrified. Sevina's limp body fell to the ground, her wounds continuing to close, but too slowly. Carolyn stopped dead in her tracks, breathing heavily as she saw the demon turning its attention to the knights.

Two knights broke off from the group and moved to face the demon. Carolyn tried to support them with her fire, but to no effect. One knight tried to catch his opponent's blow on his shield while his companion flanked him, but there was a strange warping of the air around the demon as he struck. His axe cleaved straight through the shield, the knight's plate armor, and almost all the way through his torso. The knight gasped, his eyes wide, and fell unmoving as the demon pushed him off his blade. The other knight landed a blow, but the demon remained unfazed, lashing out with his axe and cutting the second knight down as well.

By now, most of the enemy soldiers had been felled. A few Herin knights were lying on the ground, but there were still six on their feet as well as the King and Queen. Two of them continued the fight against the last couple of soldiers while the others turned their attention on the demon. Treton attempted to move around behind the knights, staying away from the demon and inching closer to Sevina.

The line of knights pressing up against him only made the demon notice the older wizard moving about. He began to swing his axe wildly, forcing the knights to remain in a defensive position, and then moved in another blur. Like with Sevina, the demon appeared right in front of Treton, slashing through his stomach. Isana was right beside him when it happened and turned to retaliate, scoring a strike to the demon's head. He turned to her with a hiss and cut her down, his axe biting deep into her shoulder.

"No, no, no!" Carolyn felt so helpless. Her best option for offense was fire and it was useless in this situation. She watched in horror as both Treton and Isana were struck again before the rest of the knights reached the demon.

Three more knights fell, one of them with his shield cloven in two. *What was I thinking?* Carolyn wondered, watching the King himself fall to the demon's blade, *Why did I think my place was on the battlefield?* Another knight dropped, but the demon had taken a few hits at this point. The Queen was focusing on his head, seemingly trying to bash his skull in or at least disorient him. *Everyone's going to die.* Carolyn felt tears begin to well up, too shocked to move. *There's nothing...I have to use it.*

The last knight was felled, and it was just the Queen and the demon left. A glance toward the throne showed Ferdri was looking a lot more smug than when they had first entered. The Queen scored one more good hit on the demon's head, this one dislodging his helmet. As it went flying away they saw for the first time the demon's face.

Its head was rounded, with a small bump like a snout under its small, black, lizard-like eyes. Its face and head were completely covered in black scales. On the sides of its head, close to the neck, were things resembling normal human ears, but thicker. At the end of its snout were two slits opening and closing as his chest puffed in and out, and just below that, a wide opening for his mouth. It was lined with rows and rows of sharp teeth, and beyond those, a forked tongue. The tongue rolled out as he hissed in anger at the Queen.

For all her skill, even Queen Rorina was horrified enough by the sight before her to pause momentarily. That was just enough for the demon to attack with another of his swift, armor-cleaving strikes and fell her as well. Finally, he stood alone, with only Carolyn and Ferdri still in the room. Carolyn was now clutching at her necklace, looking for the will to use it, but unable to find it. As much as she knew it was necessary, the images of slaughter from the morning still haunted her. *I can't control it*, she told herself, *I'll only make things worse. It's hopeless.*

"Well then," Ferdri's voice was rich with power, surveying the scene and settling in his chair. "Give us the Derishz Ruby and we'll spare your life. Otherwise Lishrezan here," he waved a hand toward the demon, "will cut you down as he did your companions."

"I will cut you down regardless" said the demon in a hoarse, rasping voice.

Before Carolyn could react, there was a blur. In that brief heartbeat that the demon vanished, she knew what would happen next. Instinctively a small, blue barrier appeared in the air right in front of her stomach just as Lishrezan's axe swung toward her. The barrier shattered and the axe struck home, but the barrier removed enough of the force from the blow that the wound was shallow. Carolyn grunted and skidded backward from the force of the blow. If she wanted to fight back, she had to start quickly.

Carolyn jumped back as he swung again, narrowly avoiding the attack. It was slower this time, not like the first strike that was so fast she couldn't see. She continued to dodge backward, deflecting blows with her staff, or conjuring another little barrier to get in his way. Reflex was taking over as she moved to protect herself without stopping to think about it.

She wasn't attacking, though, too focused on defense. He struck so quickly with his battle axe and with such ferocity, Carolyn didn't have time for anything but to desperately cling to life. The wound on her stomach slowly healed up as she moved, the lingering effects of Treton's spell, as she attempted to find an opportunity to turn things around.

Then another blow came like the first, so fast Carolyn couldn't even see him move. Before she realized what had happened she felt the blade of the axe slice into her right shoulder with an audible *crack*.

"AAAAHHHHHHH!" Carolyn screamed in agony, her head swimming, the pain bringing tears to her eyes. She heard a clatter as her staff hit the ground, all feeling gone from her right arm. She stumbled back, looking back at her opponent with fear in her eyes. *Is this the end?* she wondered. She watched as if in slow motion as the deadly blade was raised again, readying for the final strike. Lishrezan's face was unreadable, a blank expression as he casually prepared to slaughter his foe. The blade came swinging horizontally, aiming for her neck.

No, she told herself, biting back the pain, *I will* not *die here.* She raised her left hand swiftly, as if to ward him off, Pulling her staff off the ground. She held it in a tight grip just before the axe connected. There was a burst of magical energy as the magically-enhanced attack, the one he had used to cleave through the armor of the knights like tissue paper, fizzled against the protective magic of the staff. It still hit so hard she nearly lost her grip, but she held firm, stepping back quickly once he was off-guard. Feeling started to return to her right hand as she felt her shoulder slowly stitching itself back together, though she could feel that the magic was wearing off.

"Impressive," Lishrezan looked surprised, for the first time, as he steadied the axe in his hands, readying himself for the next round.

His super speed must be difficult to maintain, Carolyn realized, taking the brief pause to analyze her opponent, *that's why he can only use it on occasion. If I can block it, that's my opportunity to strike back.*

"That's not all I can do," Carolyn said, trying to sound intimidating though she knew her voice quivered. She tried to think of something more to say, but her mind was drawing a blank. Based on the last attack, she was pretty sure she could estimate how long he had to wait between his super-speed attacks, but she needed him to attack with it one more time so she could try and predict the next one. All she needed to do now was stall until he did it again and do her best to avoid it.

Lishrezan, however, was not interested in any manner of banter. His deep, red eyes focused on her, his muscles tightened up as he gripped his axe at the ready.

Now! Carolyn said to herself, raising her staff just as she noticed him tensing. Her timing was nearly perfect. She raised her staff; Lishrezan vanished and reappeared right in front of her, his axe impacting against her staff. The edge of it nicked her in the ribs, but she evaded a lethal blow.

The demon was unperturbed by this, however, and renewed his furious assault against her. Once again Carolyn let reflex take over, using her gymnast's dexterity to duck, weave, and dodge out of the way, parrying blows with her staff on occasion. All the while, she carefully tried to count seconds, trying to time when the next attack would come. She watched her opponents face, looking for any manner of indication of when it would come and knowing that by the time it did it might be too late. Her right shoulder was still aching, the restorative magic used up before it could heal completely. There was no way she could risk getting hit again, so her timing couldn't be off.

And... she said to herself, feeling her pulse increase and the sweat bead her brow, *now!*

Carolyn stopped her dodging and stood her ground against the next attack. The moment she felt the axe bounce off her staff, a thick, powerful, blue barrier materialized in the air above her. Almost the same instant it appeared, Lishrezan struck with his lightning-fast speed, only to have his axe get stuck in the barrier.

My turn, Carolyn thought. The barrier had been high, predicting another downward slash, so she was able to duck under it easily and ram her staff into Lishrezan's gut. The demon grunted, but otherwise didn't seem bothered by the blow. Carolyn hadn't really expect it to do much, but she had little else at her disposal at the moment. Right now, she just had to keep him on the defensive.

Lishrezan pulled his axe free as Carolyn materialized a basketball-sized sphere of energy behind her and flung it forward, catching Lishrezan on the side of the head as he tried to regain his posture. Another one came, this one a bit smaller, from behind as Carolyn again whacked him with her staff, doing whatever she could to keep him guessing. He batted away at that one, ignoring the jab of the staff, but as he turned his attention back to his opponent a barrage of blue ping-pong balls came at him from all directions, bouncing against his head, arms, and back. Amid the chaos of flying spheres of energy, Carolyn attempted to bash the demon's fingers to loosen his grip on his axe, but to no avail. He had a tight grip and would not lose his weapon easily.

Carolyn stepped back for a moment, trying to catch her breath as Lishrezan batted away the ping pong balls angrily. She was very low on magic and wouldn't be able to last much longer if she had to rely on that. She could see Ferdri still sitting on the throne some distance away in the massive throne room, looking annoyed, impatient, and perhaps a bit nervous. Not far from him were the bodies of her fallen companions, whether dead or unconscious she didn't yet know. She had watched this creature tear through experienced mages and knights with ease, and yet here she was, standing her ground against him. What did she have that they didn't?

The ability to continue on, even when all hope seems lost. Treton's words to her from so long ago echoed through her head at that moment. Carolyn was finally starting to realize how true it was. Despite every reason for her to have stayed behind, here she was fighting for her life against a terrible menace.

For the first time she realized that she had the will to press forward as well as the ability to succeed. She was powerful. She was competent. She was going to win.

There was only one thing left to do. Lishrezan batted away the last of the spheres of irritation and turned to her in time to see her pull out the Derishz Ruby. Lishrezan paused, eyeing her in surprise and fear.

I can do this, she told herself. *I can control it!*

She bonded with the Ruby just as she had that very morning. She felt the wave of incredible power surge into her. The desire to kill and destroy flooded through her, picking up the presence of a human sitting nearby, and many lying on the ground, barely clinging to life. It sensed one presence in the room that it had no desire to kill. On the contrary, it seemed oddly comforted by the presence of Lishrezan. It didn't matter, though, because Carolyn was going to bend it to *her* will.

She reached for the powers of destruction once again, but she didn't grab at it hungrily like she had last time, instead gripping it in a firm and confident hold. *You* will *do what I want*, she said to it, not certain if it could even understand her, *your power is mine now.*

Power flooded through her entire being, saturating her body with immeasurable strength. She saw Lishrezan charging her, utilizing his inhuman speed, and yet it was sluggish to her. She reached out a hand and casually batted him away, sending him sprawling.

Inside her she could feel the burning desire for death within the Derishz Ruby trying to overwhelm her, to turn her attention away from the demon and toward the humans. It seemed almost desperate, trying to distract her. She paid it no heed and ran forward, reaching Lishrezan and kicking him across the ground. She heard a crack as he went flying away. She jumped to reach him, landing with a savage punch into his gut, sounding another crack.

The desire of the Derishz Ruby was growing stronger, and more urgent as well. She was closer now to the humans, the weak, pathetic humans that were foolishly clinging to life on the ground. It would be so easy to go and finish them off. This demon should be left alone...

No, Carolyn shook her head, firmly dismissing the notion, *no, we're going to save them.* She backhanded Lishrezan, sending him flying toward the thrones, skidding to a halt just in front of Ferdri. He had dropped his battle axe at some point while getting smacked around and his armor was cracked and dented all over from the impacts. She walked toward him as fire began to form around her hand. It had done nothing to him before, but now it had the might of Derishz behind it.

Flames shot out from her arm and completely engulfed the demon. He screamed a harsh, guttural cry as the fire assaulted him from all around. Carolyn could feel pity well up inside of her, but she shoved that feeling away. She could not feel pity for an unrepentant murderer. If she didn't stop him now, he would just kill again and again. She would not let that happen.

Finally, the screams dulled to low moans of agony. Carolyn dismissed the flames to see what was left. There on the ground where once was a demon, powerful and tall, there was now a burning husk, curled up in a fetal position and whimpering faintly. Carolyn could see, though how she couldn't fully explain, that his life force was rapidly diminishing He was not long for this world. Pity welled up inside her again and this time she welcomed it. She could not bring herself to finish him off, but she wouldn't help him either.

Oddly enough, the intense desire to kill had shifted its focus now. Upon seeing its apparent ally suffering on the ground, it now tried to push on her the desire to help him. Without the fear of harming her friends, she was inclined to give in to the desire to help. Her willpower began to slip as the desire began to merge with her own, allowing the power to overtake her fully.

I have to keep control, she told herself, shaking her head again, trying to drive away the Ruby's desire, *no matter what it wants, I can't give in.* Still, she could feel her willpower wavering. She wouldn't be able to resist it much longer, she would have to break her connection to the Ruby, and fast. She shook off the Ruby's control, taking command of its powers again.

As she had discovered, the Ruby could do much more

than kill and destroy; it could heal as well. The powers of restoration, brought to the forefront when the Ruby was trying to convince her to heal Lishrezan, flowed into her. The power of the Ruby now became angry as she turned her attention to the fallen knights. Its assault on her mind was almost too much to handle.

Healing magic began to pour out of her like a river flowing over the bodies of the fallen. With her mind being assaulted, she was too rushed to avoid healing the enemy soldiers. Soon she could sense the life force of all the fallen begin to swell and become strong once again. Some that she hadn't sensed before winked into existence once again. For a moment she thought that she had actually brought some of them back to life, but she had no time to consider that. Once she was confident that they were on their path to recovery, she cut her connection to the Ruby.

Carolyn felt like she had the wind knocked out of her. The world seemed so mundane again, so sluggish. Her limbs suddenly felt heavy and weak, exhausted from the endeavor. Her shoulder throbbed with dull pain where she had been struck. All around her were moans of pain as the knights and soldiers began to stir, slowly blinking their eyes and trying to make sense of the situation. Carolyn nodded with satisfaction as she looked over them, breathing heavily. Her staff was still held in her hand and she used it now to hold her exhausted body upright.

She turned her attention back to Lishrezan and felt a stab of fear. He had pulled himself up onto his knees, still breathing heavily and looking quite charred, but she thought his strength was coming back. Ferdri sat right behind him in the throne, looking at the demon with fear and uncertainty. The demon was holding onto the throne for support, but he made no move to pull himself onto his feet. Instead he pulled off one gauntlet, revealing a black, scaled hand with vicious looking claws, and turned his attention to Ferdri.

"You," the demon said in a hoarse whisper, "must never

tell." With a last burst of speed the hand was swiftly around Ferdri's throat. Before he could so much as gurgle in fear, a strange aura of dark energy surrounded them both. Ferdri's face contorted into a horrifying visage of pain as his skin withered and all signs of life faded from his eyes. Lishrezan's hand fell as his body collapsed limp on the ground, its remaining life force gone, now just an empty husk. Carolyn looked away in disgust.

"So it's over," a voice spoke up from nearby. Carolyn was shocked to see the Queen pulling herself up into a sitting position. All around her knights, soldiers, and the King were starting to stand up as well. "What happened?" she added, her voice strained.

"We, uh, won,' Carolyn stammered. She wasn't positive what Lishrezan meant with his final words, but they disturbed her. "I think we need to stop the fighting now."

"Whas' going on?" came another voice as one of the enemy soldiers sat up and looked around. He saw Ferdri sitting dead and withered in his chair, then turned and saw Carolyn standing above him, and the fallen knights lifting themselves to their feet once more. The soldier's face turned quickly from confusion to terror. "Please spare me!" he shouted quickly, throwing himself into a prostrate position on the ground.

As others began to rise, the remainder of the soldiers that Carolyn had accidentally healed were also quick to surrender. Carolyn ignored them and walked over to Treton and Sevina to check on them. They hadn't stirred yet and she worried they were too far gone, or that she had missed them with her last burst of healing. Luckily, both were alive, though their breathing was shallow.

"Lady Carolyn," the King said, standing tall and proud despite the pain he obviously still felt. "Thank you. We are in your debt."

Carolyn nodded. Despite all her doubts, she had done it. The war was over.

CHAPTER 15
The Ride Home

After the battle in the throne room was over, Carolyn was almost surprised that there was still fighting going on in the entry hall. Most of the knights who were guarding the door to the throne room had paid the ultimate price for their stalwart defense, but still no one had been able to get close enough to interfere with the throne room battle thanks to Silvermist. The angry unicorn had frightened the soldiers into keeping their distance and thus the door remained safe.

Once the door opened and the soldiers realized that Lishrezan was dead, most were quick to surrender. Knowing the strength of the demon, even if they didn't know his identity, they were not keen on facing whoever defeated him. There were still a few stragglers who preferred to fight to the death rather than deal with the consequences of surrender. A handful of them escaped, but most were eventually hunted down and killed. The rest who surrendered were carted off to the dungeons to await judgment.

After that came the reclamation. The throne was reestablished by King Ketra and Queen Rorina as the news was spread throughout the kingdom that Ferdri had been overthrown. There was still some fighting from the remnants of Ferdri's forces in the outer regions, but there were few casualties at that point and most simply fled. When these reports came in, Carolyn anxiously listened for any news of Jiselda, but none came. If she was still alive, which still seemed doubtful, she was nowhere to be found.

Some of the smaller towns and outer regions were beset by bandits due to the lack of proper law enforcement and it was taking some time to get things back in order. The worst was in the capital, however, where many businesses and shops had been abused by Ferdri's soldiers and had suffered a lot of damage over the past few weeks. The King granted generous funds to these and others who were harmed during the takeover in order to help get them back on their feet.

During this whole process, Carolyn stayed in the palace and helped with the restoration efforts. The main hall was not in the most pristine condition considering two battles had now taken place in it, one of them quite extensive. Like with Dor, it took a lot of work to get things into normal working order again, but after a few days it was looking much better.

Once the important steps in restoration were put into motion, the King focused on the next major task: celebrating their victory. With the atmosphere turning from distress to joy, a mounting excitement could be felt throughout the city. The King and Queen planned to hold a gala on the castle grounds and invited the entire city to join. Bakers, butchers, florists, entertainers, and wizards were all contracted to help make this celebration one to be remembered.

Throughout the preparations, however, Carolyn found herself having a hard time feeling excitement. Now that the castle had been reclaimed, the one thing that Carolyn wanted most was to just go home.

When she first got involved in the daily routine at

Cansition, the time seemed to fly by, filled with magic lessons and meeting interesting new people, but Carolyn knew it had been a few months since she had left. She hated to think what her parents were going through, or how they would react when she suddenly showed up again. In the excitement of the preparations for the festivities, however, nobody seemed to be thinking about getting Carolyn home, and it was hard for her to find a chance to talk about it. Finally, the afternoon before the big event, Carolyn was strolling through the castle grounds when she came across the King and Queen walking together.

"Excuse me, your majesties," Carolyn tried to sound polite even though she was going to rudely interrupt their conversation regardless of their response, "I need to talk to you."

"Certainly, Lady Carolyn," the King smiled welcomingly, inviting Carolyn to walk with them.

"To get straight to the point," Carolyn said bluntly, moving to step in time with them, "I want to go home."

"Hmm," the King sighed, "Yes, I expected you did."

"So why am I still here?" Carolyn pressed him.

"We haven't forgotten your desire to return home, Lady Carolyn," the Queen said sharply, an implicit rebuke for Carolyn's disrespectful tone, "and we have every intention of accommodating you. We were hoping you would stay with us for the celebration, at least. It was *your* victory more than anyone else's."

"Yeah, but..." Carolyn hesitated. She *did* want to join the party, and maybe another day wouldn't hurt, but it pained her just to think of the worry she had put her parents through. "My parents are waiting for me," she said finally, shaking her head, "I can't wait any longer."

"I see," the King nodded. "Well, that's not really an issue, then."

"What?" Carolyn said in confusion, "Why not?"

"Oh, well because—"

"—Your majesty!" a page came running up, his tone

urgent. "I'm sorry to interrupt, your majesties," he said with a bow, "but I have a response from King Thedoric."

"Excellent, come with me," the King nodded, turning to leave. Then he turned back to Carolyn and added, "I'm sorry, we'll pick this up later. If it is your wish, we will return you home tonight."

"Oh... Ok," Carolyn answered dumbly, watching as the King and Queen walked off with the messenger.

She sighed and wandered off to examine the stands being set up for the celebration the next day. This was going to be a very grand event, indeed. Farmers, merchants, artists, and craftsmen from all over the kingdom were gathering for the celebration.

There were stalls for selling wares, showing off prize produce, carnival games, puppet shows, tents for plays and circus performers, and even a combat arena for duels. Most everything was set up by this point with the owners of the various stalls camped out among them, there to keep an eye on their property, with a plethora of guards posted all around. At this point in the day, any work being done was dying off as sounds of labor were replaced with sounds of fires being started for dinner and people talking jovially among one another. Carolyn loved to see how people came together in the wake of disaster and helped one another, building relationships even with complete strangers.

As she wandered, looking around at the peaceful scene, one she knew she had a part in creating, she came across a lone knight in dress uniform leaning back on one of the stands. As she passed, the knight glanced toward her.

"Carolyn!" the knight exclaimed, turning toward her.

"Oh, hi, Sarin," she responded, recognizing his face in the failing light of sundown. He had been seriously wounded in the battle and Carolyn had gone to visit him often. He was released after a few days, as Treton and the other healers had worked overtime to get everyone fit as quickly as possible. The King had said something about needing to reinforce borders and appear strong before the neighboring kingdoms.

While in recovery, Sarin had been acting strange. The elation of victory seemed short lived and was quickly replaced with despondency. Carolyn had chalked it up to the pain he was suffering through and had hardly seen him since he was released.

"How's it going?" he asked, trying to sound casual, but there was something off about his tone. His eyes were downcast and no smile—not even the hint of a smirk—graced his countenance. *Maybe he's upset because he failed in the last battle?* Carolyn reasoned.

"I'm all right," Carolyn sighed, but then shook her head and added, "No, I'm not, I'm just used to saying that." She walked over next to him and leaned forward against the stand, staring into the sun on the horizon.

"What's the matter?" Sarin asked, though the way he said it sounded more like a statement, as though he knew the answer.

"I want to go home," Carolyn admitted, not looking at him. "It's been a lot of fun being here, and I can't say I regret it, but I miss my family—even my older sister—and my friends. I want to see them again and let them know that I'm not dead. They're probably worried sick about me."

"Yeah," Sarin nodded. "I..." he started, but stopped himself.

"And what's the matter with you?" Carolyn said, turning to face him.

"I..." he stopped himself short again. His normal cool was completely shattered, replaced instead with an anxiety Carolyn had never witnessed in the brave, young knight before. He stared off at the darkening horizon, unable to formulate his thoughts.

"Sarin," Carolyn said softly, putting a hand on his arm, "What's wrong?" Her voice was filled with concern for her friend and she realized that whatever troubled him, it troubled her, too.

"Carolyn," he sighed, looking down, "I... I'm..." His voice

faltered, but this time steeled himself and finally spoke up, "I'm going to miss you."

"Oh," Carolyn felt taken aback, removing her hand from his arm and looking away.

"I knew you wanted to go home," Sarin went on, talking slowly, his eyes downcast, "but I had been hoping you'd want to stay a little longer first."

Carolyn didn't know what to say. She could feel a tension in the air between them that she hadn't felt before. It seemed pretty obvious that she would return home at the first opportunity, why was this suddenly a cause for regret? Was the regret just Sarin's, or was it hers as well?

"I can't stay here," she said finally, "I don't belong here. I feel so out of place."

"You could belong here," Sarin suggested, "You have friends here, and you're a hero. What are you missing?"

"There's more than that," Carolyn shook her head, feeling frustrated at her inability to translate her feelings into words, "I just... don't fit. This isn't my home. I need to get back to where I belong." She felt a sort of frustration, almost anger, but whether at herself or at Sarin she couldn't know.

Sarin sighed and fell silent. The two of them continued to stand there for a few minutes, neither one speaking, neither one able to look at the other. There seemed to be an unspoken understanding between them what was causing the tension, but neither one was willing to say it out loud.

"At least you'll be here for the celebration tomorrow," Sarin said, finally breaking the silence again. "We can have one more day to enjoy together."

Carolyn could feel her body tensing up and her fist clenched. She had just told the King she wanted to leave immediately. She hadn't considered at the time how anyone else would react. She had been focused on her needs and her concern for her family and friends at home, but she forgot about her family and friends here.

"You are coming, aren't you?" Sarin asked, sensing her discomfort. Now he turned to face her finally and placed a hand gently on hers. Out of the corner of her eye, she could see the pleading look in his face, accompanied by a blush as he gently wrapped his fingers around her hand. Carolyn turned to look him in the eyes, for the first time feeling sadness that she was going to be leaving. Despite all the fun she had had here, her main concern was always returning home. Staying here had never been a consideration. Now she found herself reconsidering.

"Yes," she said firmly, though her hand was trembling under the knight's gentle touch.

"Thank you," Sarin said, a smile slowly returning to his face. He released Carolyn's hand and turned toward the castle. "I'll see you tomorrow then," he said, walking off without a second glance.

Carolyn watched him go. Her mind was a muddled mess as she tried to make sense of their conversation, and of things left unsaid, staying outside among the stalls until long after the sun had set. Finally, she returned to the palace to turn in for the night. As she walked through the halls, one of the servants suddenly approached her.

"Lady Carolyn," the servant said with a deep bow, "His majesty asked me to wait for you. He wishes to know if you still desire to return home tonight."

"Oh," Carolyn felt taken aback briefly, shaken from her train of thought. "No, I don't," she said with a shake of her head as she walked off, sinking back into her own muddled thoughts.

The next morning was the dawn of the big day. Carolyn had shirked her fancy dresses the moment she received her first robe, preferring the comfort and convenience over getting dressed up. She looked at the two dresses she had received, the original purple one she had selected and a crimson one that had been made after. The dress was a status symbol of sorts, a sign of her royalty, while the wizard's robe was a testament to all she had worked for since arriving. It seemed to fit her much better than a dress ever would.

Whether the King and Queen were surprised when she came to breakfast in her robe, neither of them showed it. The knights were all wearing their dress uniforms and all the nobles of the palace were decked out in their finest. Carolyn provided a stark contrast to their bright jewels and flashy outfits, but she didn't care. Once she might have felt embarrassed by being different, but that didn't bother her as much anymore. She was proud to be who she was, even if that was different than the norm.

"I'm glad you decided to stay with us an extra day, Carolyn," the King said to her as they ate, "It would have been a pity for you to miss the ceremony at the end of the festival."

"Ceremony?" Carolyn wondered, giving him a quizzical look.

"Of course," the King nodded in response, "To show honor to everyone that helped bring about our victory."

"Oh," Carolyn answered simply, turning back to her meal. After a moment's consideration, she turned back to the King and asked, "Does that include me?"

"Of course," the King smiled, "It would've been hard to honor you if you were gone."

Carolyn's natural response was to shrink from the attention. Would she have to stand up in front of people? Would she be expected to give a speech? Would they be talking about her in public? But she shook herself out of it. *I'm fine with that,* she told herself, *I do deserve it, after all, don't I?*

"You will then be welcome to leave," the King continued. "We're going to have the Portal Device prepared tonight."

"Thank you," Carolyn answered quietly. She still wanted to return home, but since the previous afternoon, it didn't seem like such an obvious choice anymore.

"Though we'll miss you, Carolyn," the Queen added. "Hopefully you'll be able to return sometime."

"I'd like that," Carolyn smiled.

After breakfast, Carolyn found Sarin and Elis waiting outside the dining hall. As soon as they noticed her, they turned to greet her with a bow each.

"Hi," she said awkwardly, looking more at Elis. Sarin seemed to be avoiding eye contact with her.

"We know you're leaving tonight," Elis responded, taking a step forward, "and we wanted to help you enjoy your last day in Herin."

"Wow," Carolyn said, "I guess news spreads fast, huh?"

"Yes," Elis nodded, "but don't worry about that now, let's go have some fun."

For the rest of the day the three of them wandered through the castle grounds among the crowds, seeing the sights and enjoying the food. Carolyn participated in many of the games, such as tossing wheat kernels into glass bottles, running a short obstacle course, and attempting to hit a gong loud enough that the enchantment on it would flash. She failed a lot, but she had a lot of fun, especially since she had friends to do it with her. She and Sarin did speak over the course of the day, but very casually and with little eye contact. Despite the discomfort in their interactions, Carolyn was happy just to be with him.

Toward evening, the crowds started to gather by the main stage set up in the center of the grounds. There the King was going to address the people, followed by the reward ceremony. The King ascended the stage, the Queen at his side, with the setting sun behind him, bathing him in the light of its fading glow.

"Welcome to all the people of Herin who have joined us today," he started, his voice amplified magically to carry over the crowds of people. "We have come together today to celebrate a momentous occasion. As you all know, the usurper Ferdri stormed our peaceful kingdom and took the throne for himself. While we were forced into hiding, our eyes were ever watchful for opportunities to take back the throne and remove the usurper. One of my kinswomen from a distant land traveled here to help us, and with her aid and formidable powers, we have overthrown the usurper and restored peace to the kingdom!"

A cheer went up from the crowd in answer to this proclamation, but not from Carolyn. She had been positioned along with a few other important officials to the side of the stage. She knew the King was referring to her, and it was not lost on her that her true identity—and the source of her power—were kept secret. Carolyn understood that it was important for governments to keep their secrets, so she would have to keep her mouth shut about it as well.

The King continued on with some flowery speech and epic tales of the battles, pointing out the specific contributions of certain individuals, though he kept names out for now. The sun was getting lower on the horizon when he stepped aside and allowed the Queen to take center stage.

"While we may celebrate today," she started as the cheering crowd quieted down, "we must remember the sacrifices of those who fought to attain this victory. Many brave knights, soldiers, and wizards have lain down their lives in order to protect us, and we can't forget their heroism in the face of the enemy. Their names are to be engraved on a monument here in the castle courtyard so they may never be forgotten."

The crowd was quiet at this response, though many seemed to be mumbling under their breath. Carolyn heard many of the officials around her doing the same, but she could only catch a couple words. It sounded like a prayer for the dead.

"Nor can we forget the importance of those heroes who are still with us today," the Queen went on after a moment, "whose heroism is no less for the fact that they survived. Many decisive battles were hard won by these knights, soldiers, and wizards who were willing to make the ultimate sacrifice, if they had to, but survived to defend Herin for another day. Today we will do them honor that befits their feats."

Rissin, who had been sitting near Carolyn, now rushed onto the stage with a small box in hand. He gave a quick bow to the King and Queen, and then stood by the Queen's side. Queen Rorina began to call out names, one at a time, of individuals who distinguished themselves enough to deserve personal recognition by the King and Queen themselves. Many of them were people Carolyn didn't know, but she recognized a few as some of the knights that joined the fight in the throne room.

"Lieutenant Isana Polyer," the Queen called out. The knight stood from her seat and marched humbly onto the stage, standing before the Queen.

"For your deeds of heroism in defense of the kingdom, you are to be granted the Crest of Herin," the Queen pronounced, taking a pin bearing the emblem of Herin in pure gold and pinning it to Isana's uniform. This honor had been, so far, granted to everyone who had been called up.

"In addition," the Queen continued, "You are henceforth promoted to Captain Isana Polyer." The Queen then produced what looked like a patch—similar to the rank symbol on the sleeve of Isana's shirt—and placed it gently into place on each side. The patches must've been enchanted because they automatically stuck on and melded with the uniform. Carolyn had a perfect view of Isana's face from where she was and could tell the officer was ecstatic, though she was trying hard to contain it. She bowed respectfully and left the stage before the Queen called the next name.

Carolyn watched with a growing sense of anticipation and anxiety as the Queen went through the list. Carolyn had to be coming up soon and she couldn't help but feel nervous about it. And that crowd watching ruby was so big. *I can't think about that,* Carolyn shook herself. *I can do this; if I can fight a demon and win, I can certainly stand in front of a crowd and survive.*

"Archmage Treton Zavider," the Queen called. The older wizard walked humbly up to his Queen and bowed before her. "For your deeds of heroism in defense of the kingdom, you are to be granted the Crest of Herin," she pronounced, taking the pin and attaching it to his robes. "As you have already been recognized as a High Mage of Herin," the Queen went on, 'we instead award you the Medallion of Excellence for your service to the Crown." The Queen took out a medal that looked to be made of gold with some overlaid silver forming a pattern Carolyn couldn't recognize from where she was. The Queen placed the medal around Treton's neck before he bowed again and left the stage.

Now the Queen rolled up the scroll she had been reading names from and handed it to Rissin. For a moment, Carolyn thought she wasn't going to receive any recognition at all, that she had been presumptuous to think she would. She felt a mix of relief and frustration. She got out of having to walk out onto stage, but it was frustrating to have all her efforts so easily dismissed, something she had experienced too often. Before she could dwell on it too long, the Queen spoke up again.

"We have one more hero to show our appreciation for," she started, the hushed crowd listening intently. "A distant kinswoman of the throne, long living far from home, has returned to us in our hour of need to grant her formidable powers to our cause. It is no exaggeration to say that without her, this victory would not have been possible. We cannot conclude the ceremony today without showing our heartfelt gratitude for all of her successes."

Carolyn felt her cheeks grow warm from blushing as her anxiety began twisting her stomach in knots.

"The last of our great heroes for this war is the one to whom we owe the most," the Queen continued, "Her ladyship Carolyn Jones, Princess of Herin, Master Sorceress, and companion to the Unicorn Silvermist!"

All was dead silent. The crowd and even many of the nobles around her were glancing about, waiting with bated breath, looking for the first glimpse of this spectacular individual. Carolyn was amazed at how impressive her title sounded, much better than what she thought she deserved. Her legs felt like lead when she pulled herself to her feet, staff in hand, feeling every eye within the courtyard and every sentry on the palace wall turn to look at her.

There was no doubt that every face was turned in her direction as she strode onto the stage and up to the Queen. It reminded her of her last day at school, before this whole adventure started, where she was forced to walk out in front of her gymnastics class, hanging her head in shame. This time she stood erect and proud, focused on the Queen. "For your deeds of heroism in defense of the kingdom and answering our call for help at our time of dire need, you are to be granted the Crest of Herin," she pronounced, giving Carolyn a reassuring smile. Carolyn watched as the pure gold emblem was pinned onto her robes, a proud reminder of her accomplishments.

"For your skill and mastery of sorcery in service of the Crown," the Queen went on, "you are hereby recognized as a High Mage of Herin." The Queen produced a gold ring with an engraved obsidian stone set in it depicting some manner of runic design. Carolyn studied it closely as she offered a hand for the Queen the slip it on. Somehow, more than the pin, it felt like a real sign of power. Just wearing it made Carolyn feel stronger.

"Finally, for your unwavering dedication to serve in this time of need and your deeds of valor," the Queen continued, "we award you the Medal of Excellence." Like with Treton, a medal was pulled out of the box before it was finally closed, the last honor taken from it. Carolyn could see now that it had a thick, gold border with three lines of gold protruding into the center and silver in the space in between. It was quite beautiful.

She leaned her head forward for the Queen to place it around her neck. She felt the weight of it press the Derishz Ruby, still hidden under her robe, into her chest. For a brief moment, she thought all this respect she was given wasn't hers to receive. Really it was the Ruby that saved the day, not her. Then she reminded herself that she had done more than just that. She had fought hard even before trying to use the Ruby, and when she did wield it, it was her control of it that saved the day, not the Ruby itself. She was, indeed, a hero.

Carolyn looked up at the Queen who quietly mouthed the word *bow*. Carolyn bowed deeply, and as she did, a cheer went up from the crowd. When she stood up erect again, she looked out for the first time at the myriad faces staring up at her as they cheered for her, clapping, waving their hands in a signal of triumph, and even shouting "Lady Carolyn!"

She felt so humbled by the honor they were giving her when they probably had no idea what she had even done. Swept up by the emotion of the scene, she didn't stop to think what she was doing and bowed toward the crowd. The cheering intensified as she turned and walked back to her seat.

After a closing speech by the King as the last rays of sun disappeared over the horizon, the ceremony was brought to a close. Braziers had been lit all over the grounds and the festivities continued into the night. Carolyn attended the final, celebratory banquet reserved for the nobles, though she didn't talk much there.

She had been quite overwhelmed by the honor she had been bestowed and found herself constantly fiddling with the ring on her finger. Now that the day was coming to a close, her thoughts were returning to the topic that had been plaguing her since the battle was won; it was time to go home. When she had eaten her fill and felt she needed some time alone, she excused herself from the table and went to lay down in her room. It wasn't long before there was a knock at the door.

"Who is it?" Carolyn called out sleepily. Merilda was not back in the room yet; Carolyn had excused her for the day to enjoy the festivities. There was a response, but Carolyn couldn't make it out, so she dragged herself to her feet to open the door.

"I'm sorry to disturb you, Milady," said the page at the door, "The King has requested your presence in the main hall. He asks you to bring all your belongings with you."

"Oh, ok," Carolyn blinked at him, "I'll be there shortly."

The day had been exhausting and she was too tired to think. She grabbed the few articles of clothing, all of which had been washed, that she wore when she first came through the portal, as well as her staff and two dresses. She had silk covers to protect the dresses and a simple, leather bag to hold the other clothes. Thus laden, she opened the door to find Merilda just arriving.

"I've come to help you carry your things, milady," she said with a small bow.

"Thanks," Carolyn nodded, handing her the dresses.

"Also, I wanted to say… Well, that it's been an honor to serve you, milady" Merilda said nervously.

"Oh," was all Carolyn could think to answer. They walked on in silence for a few minutes before realization dawned on her. "Oh!" she repeated, "I've been happy to have you as an assistant. I hope we meet again."

"Thank you," Merilda said quietly with a slight blush.

Carolyn's sleepy mind hadn't quite processed what was going on, but now it was obvious. The time had come, and she was going home. Why did they have to do it so late at night, though?

In the main entry hall of the castle, where not so long ago Carolyn had been fighting for her life, she found the King and Queen waiting for her, along with Rissin, Treton, Jacim, and a few knights, including Sarin, Elis, and Isana. Carolyn smiled at seeing all the people she had gotten close to come to see her off.

"Are you ready to go, Lady Carolyn?" the Queen asked as they approached.

"Yes, just a bit tired," Carolyn responded with a smile.

"As you should be," the Queen answered with a wry

smile. She and the King turned, leading the group down one of the wide hallways on either side of the grand staircase.

"Why's that?" Carolyn couldn't help but be wary at the Queen's elusiveness. After all, the last secret she held from her was the demonic nature of her amulet.

"You left at night, it only makes sense you should return at night," she answered, though Carolyn felt like that was only half the truth. When the Queen saw her look, she added, "You'll understand when you get back."

"Lady Carolyn, you should know that it has been an absolute pleasure having you with us," the King put in, smiling at her.

"It's been a pleasure to meet you both," Carolyn responded, "and everyone else."

They arrived at some large, double doors to their left. When they were opened, Carolyn recognized the room they entered. There on the right was, sure enough, the portal device. Without any threat to her life, she could get a better look at it now. It consisted of two parts: a tall, bronze cylinder and a large, half-circle, one end reaching the ground and the other opposite it in the air. On the cylinder was a small panel jutting out with various colored jewels, buttons, and levers, like a control panel, and just above it were a couple drawers.

The strange, magical contraption that had brought her here was not alone, though. A couple wizards who Carolyn didn't recognize were working on it. As they approached, the two wizards turned and addressed the King.

"Everything has been set properly," one of them, a sorcerer, declared.

"To whom am I to give the Portal Stone?" the other one said, this one not carrying a staff but wearing a pin that Carolyn had been taught was the sign of an alchemist. He presented a dark blue stone that was round, a couple centimeters thick, and perfectly smooth on either side. Carolyn recognized it as the same stone Sarin had used to open the portal on that fateful night.

"To Sir Sarin," the King nodded to the young knight. "Thank you for your efforts." Turning back to Carolyn he added, "Now is the time for your final goodbyes. I am certain we will meet again, though when I could not say."

"Thank you for everything," Carolyn said to him, feeling a desire to hug him but knowing it probably would not be appropriate. Instead she smiled at both him and the Queen and added, "Thank you to both of you."

"Thank you, Treton," she turned first to the archmage, "for everything you taught me, and for believing in me, even when I didn't believe in myself."

"You are full of potential, Lady Carolyn," Treton smiled in response, "Even without magic, I expect you to accomplish great things. It has been my honor to be your teacher."

Carolyn felt tears starting to form. She was never good at goodbyes and always felt that what she said wasn't sufficient.

"Jacim," she turned to the younger wizard, who was very stiff and formal, but clearly honored by being brought to this final farewell, "Thank you for being there when I needed advice. You're a good friend."

"I-i-it was my honor, milady," he said with a deep bow, his cheeks turning beet red.

"Isana," Carolyn turned to the recently promoted knight. "Thank you for your support when I needed it most." Tears were starting to run down her cheeks now. She tried blinking them away, but to no avail.

"Of course, milady," Isana said with a bow of her head, "I'm always available if you need someone to talk to."

"Elis," she turned now to the younger knights, "You've been a great friend. Thank you for always being there."

"It has been my pleasure to serve, milady," he said with a bow. Despite how steady his tone was, she could see the tears on his cheeks as well.

Finally, with a heavy heart, Carolyn turned to Sarin. As she opened her mouth to speak, she found herself at a loss for words. She began to wipe away the tears as she tried to find her voice.

"You can wait on your final farewell," the King put in, "Sir Sarin is escorting you through the portal."

"Oh," Carolyn managed to say as she dried her cheeks, looking gratefully at Sarin, "All right then."

Merilda handed the dresses to Sarin to hold, his other hand clutching the Portal Stone, as he walked side by side with Carolyn up to the Portal Device. The mages pressed some buttons on the control panel, causing a shimmering blue portal to appear in front of them.

They stood mesmerized by it for a moment, Carolyn's heart beating quickly She was finally going home. She still didn't know how she was going to explain all this to her parents, but those thoughts were driven away by thoughts of bidding Sarin farewell privately on the other side.

The idea of staying crossed her mind for a brief moment, but it passed and she stepped forward into the portal. Remembering the freakish experience of travelling through the portal the first time, Carolyn shut her eyes the moment her hand touched the edge of the shimmering, blue light.

Carolyn opened her eyes suddenly. She had heard something that roused her from her sleep. Picking herself up out of her bed, she grabbed her phone from the desk to check the time. It was about half past midnight, March 10th. It was the same day she left.

Was it all just a dream? she wondered. It had seemed so vivid, so real. How could it all have been a dream? A deep disappointment welled up inside her, but before she could dwell on it much, there was a flash of blue light from the window.

She glanced outside just as the last traces of a shimmering, blue light vanished from the middle of the street. She smiled as her whole body relaxed, watching those traces of blue light vanish.

She turned back to her bed, seeing two dresses wrapped

in silk coverings draped across the back of her desk chair. She sat down to remove her leather boots, placing them next to the sapphire-topped staff beside her bed. She removed the medallion around her neck, placing it on her bedside table. She lay down, exhausted from her long day, wrapping the folds of her red robe around her. As she felt sleep returning to her, she thought back to her adventures, fiddling with the obsidian-topped ring on her finger and smiling.

Someday, she told herself, *I'll go back.*

ABOUT THE AUTHOR

Meir Anolick is a religious Jew who grew up in America and now resides in Israel. Storytelling and writing have always been a passion of his and has always dreamed of being a published author. In his free time, he enjoys playing D&D with friends and family, gaming, and spending time with his wife and four children.